THOSE MARTIN GIRLS

Wayne slipped his hands under his head as he lay with his face turned to the stars in the dark prairie sky.

Try to remember the girls now as they stood in a row and see if you can name them.

Sabina. Tom Bostwick is in love with her.

Emily. Sang lustily off-key.

Jeanie. One of the jolliest.

Phoebe Lou. Something of a tease.

Melinda. Kind of a tomboy.

Celia. Maybe the prettiest.

Suzanne. The youngest, with reddish-brown hair and big gray-blue eyes that shone ... like the stars ... on the lonely prairie.

Oh, yes, I remember....

Great Reading from SIGNET VISTA

SONG OF YEARS

BY

BESS STREETER ALDRICH

A SIGNET VISTA BOOK

NEW AMERICAN LIBRARY

NAL BOOKS ARE AVAILABLE AT QUANTITY DISCOUNTS
WHEN USED TO PROMOTE PRODUCTS OR SERVICES.
FOR INFORMATION PLEASE WRITE TO PREMIUM MARKETING DIVISION.
NEW AMERICAN LIBRARY. 1633 BROADWAY.
NEW YORK. NEW YORK 10019.

RL 7/IL 6+

SIGNET VISTA TRADEMARK REG. U.S. PAT. OFF. AND FOREIGN COUNTRIES
REGISTERED TRADEMARK—MARCA REGISTRADA
HECHO EN CHICAGO, U.S.A.

SIGNET, SIGNET CLASSIC, MENTOR, PLUME, MERIDIAN AND NAL BOOKS
are published by New American Library,
1633 Broadway, New York, New York 10019

First Signet Vista Printing, November, 1985

1   2   3   4   5   6   7   8   9

PRINTED IN THE UNITED STATES OF AMERICA

CHAPTER 1

THE Valley of the Red Cedar is in eastern Iowa—a long strip of fertile land sprawling out beside the river whose name it bears. The Red Cedar River itself is not much more than a sturdy creek until joined by the waters of the Shell Rock and West Fork where it suddenly becomes of importance, a thing of width and depth with the right to boast of having mothered many a sawmill, grist-mill, and factory before a wheel on its banks was turned by electricity.

Just below the junction of these waters—which come together in the shape of a wild turkey's foot—two towns lie very close to each other. Originally the tiny settlements from which they have grown were named Sturgis Falls and Prairie Rapids, and although it has been nearly a century since they were so called, the old names shall serve them here. Those who live in the Valley—or have lived there—will recognize them at once. Others will not care what they are called.

They are modern little cities, the one leaning to industry, the other proud of its fine college. Like sisters they lie there together by the Red Cedar which saw their beginnings nearly a hundred years ago. And like sisters they quarrel and argue on occasion, but stand up for each other indignantly if any outsider ventures criticism.

Between the two towns on the north and east side of the curving river is a strip of fertile farming land which was preëmpted by some of the first settlers in the Valley.

If you follow a paved highway a few miles to the north and west of it, turning at a certain point onto a side road, you will come to a wide iron gate set in a fence surrounding farm fields. Open the gate and follow the grassy trail which hugs the wire fence, and you will arrive in time at a second gate far up the sloping hillside. If it be early summer and the green corn young, you can catch a glimpse of that which lies at the end of the trail. But if the corn is high you must come to the second gate before you can see the tall white tombstones, the close-clipped grass of the plots, and the graveled paths that lie between.

Here rest those first settlers.

It is a place of utter peace. There are times when no sound penetrates but the rustling of the corn or the dropping of a pine-cone. Sometimes, though, one will hear a combine at work near these sleeping men who cut their grain with a cradle, or, perchance, a plane zoom over the heads of these quiet ones who followed the grassy trail with oxen.

But though there is a deep peace about them now, almost can you hear their loud laughter that this is so. They would tell you that peace may be here at the end of the trail, but there was very little at the end of that other one which led westward from Dubuque.

Because they who lie here are all connected by blood or marriage or neighborhood ties, the life of one in its bare outlines is the life of all. But what of those other things—the loving, hating, feuding, fending—all of the emotions that were stilled when the last old settler was brought here? For the life of one can never be the life of all.

The tall old stones with their drooping angel-wings and clasped hands cover long-forgotten interests as intertwined in that period as these vines on the marble shafts—the ashes of emotions as burned out now as the old camp-fires beside the trail. You will note a monument to *Sabina*, to *Emily*, to *Ceila*, one to *Melinda*, to *Phoebe Lou*, to *Jeanie*. Almost at the end of the central path where it curves you will see a shorter heavy stone which reads:

SUZANNE
BELOVED WIFE
OF

But what else it says you cannot know because a thick growth of old clinging woodbine and a clump of sweet-william cover the secret of whose beloved she was.

Reading the inscription chiseled long ago, it seems of such small consequence whose name is hidden under the vines. But, oh, to Suzanne it mattered so very, very much.

This is the love story of the Suzanne who lies here by the side of the curving graveled path. And because the years of her youth were the years of the settling of the Cedar Valley, the telling must include, perforce, the story of these others who lie beside her at the end of the trail.

It begins, perhaps, on a June day in 1854 with a young man walking steadily to the west in the light-footed rhythmic way of the prairie-wolf. His body bent a scarcely perceptible degree into the warm west wind, arms hanging loosely free from any encumbering luggage, he swung on.

All day he had walked to the west in those same evenly paced strides. All that day through the rank prairie grass, and part of the two moonlit June nights before, and all of two previous sunlit days! For those three days and part of two nights he had swung along in that easy way, every sinewy muscle rippling in accord with every other one, the whole mechanism of his perfect body in tune. Six feet one and broad of shoulder he was, but he walked as light-footed as the antelope he had sighted near the Wapsipinicon. A perspiring Adonis in buckskin breeches and open-necked flannel shirt there on the unsettled Iowa prairie in 1854!

The lush green of the prairie grass, tall enough now to bend before the breeze, stretched as far as eye could see. The world to-day was a thing of green and blue, white and gold. Green of the prairie! Blue of the sky! Gold of the sunlight! White of the clouds that appeared to be floating only a little too high for mortal to touch—white sails above on the blue, their shadows gray sails below on the green!

There were other colors which the young man's far-seeing eyes did not quite note—the blue of lupines, the pink of wild roses, the delicate mauve of wind-flowers, the magenta of wild sweet-williams, the harsh red of the prairie lilies. Even though he did not see these in detail, still he was sensing vaguely their presence in the colorful whole. Though his mind was on very practical things, he was feeling unconsciously the beauty of Nature's tapestry rolled out there under his agile feet.

All morning the prairie flowers had turned to the east. Now, obedient to that unseen force which gave them life, they, too, like the young man, looked toward the west and the sinking sun. Only the compass-plants, those flat-leaved little flowers which guided the Indians, refused to follow the sun's urge but stuck loyally to their north and south directions.

The trail was none too distinct in the distance. Far ahead it appeared always to end suddenly but never really came to that point, for the ruts made by wagon wheels were always visible for a little way. Only when one looked too far in the distance did the hope of finding the trail in an ocean of grass fade. Something about that phenomenon might apply to life, the lad was thinking—perhaps that was a good way to look at the future, not too far ahead, else one might grow discouraged. Ten years from now, for instance—would he have wealth and satisfaction with living as he planned? Or failure and discouragement as he decidedly did now anticipate?

Swiftly he decided that was no conundrum, for he could make the answer whatever he chose. It was as easy as—as this journey. Make every decision with the same care you used when fording streams and avoiding swamps, and life would be whatever you made it. No riddle to that. Just plain horsesense.

He shrugged his shoulders lightly at his brief moralizing and broke into song:

> *"The wee birds sing and the wild flowers spring*
> *And in sunshine the waters are sleeping. . . ."*

His voice rose so clear and full-throated it is a pity there was no one there to hear.

> *"But the broken heart it kens*
> *Nae second spring again. . . ."*

Even so, had there been some one to hear, that person must have laughed heartily at the incongruity of this blithe young traveler singing of broken hearts.

All afternoon to the west he walked as though he, too, like the prairie blossoms, the moon, and the stars, must follow some vagrant urge.

Sometimes he sang again, not too loudly to consume precious breath, but low disconnected snatches of melody.

Sometimes he thought of his long trip from the east: the ride on the steam-cars to Chicago, a big place of nearly thirty-five thousand now; the change to the train which took him to Warren, Illinois, the end of the railroad; then the stage ride to Dubuque where he ferried across the Mississippi. He recalled the site of that town of three thousand perched there on the river's bluff, and the interview with the government officials.

Once or twice he reached in his pocket to make sure that the paper they had given him was still there—the list of unpatented and unsold lands out here in the far-off Valley of the Red Cedar. And for the hundredth time he touched the ridge at his waist-line which was the quilted belt containing money for a portion of that land.

Sometimes his thought dwelt on the folks at home, his father, mother, brother, and sister he had left behind two weeks before in the New England town. Queer they had made so much howdydo about his leaving, mother and sister crying over him, even his father, formerly sympathetic with the plan, growing regretful at the last that he had consented to the venture out beyond the Mississippi. It had seemed the end of the world to them all—almost so to himself. And yet here he was at the end of the world.

For himself he held no regrets. For the first time in his life he felt entirely free, completely his own boss. For the first time he would own property—rich land out here in this new raw state. A great many people thought it would never be settled. It was true there were no railroads, no big towns, only a few settlements clinging to rivers.

"Even if you *do* raise something," his mother had said in her argument against his coming, "how can you ever expect to sell it? Who is there to sell it *to?* You can't ship it. . . ."

Once his mind dwelt on another memory—a girl. She had come down the village street; meeting him, stopping to speak about his leaving, she had suddenly broken down, grown tearful and foolish. He was ashamed for her. Nice girls didn't throw themselves at you like that. He had no hankering for a sweetheart, would have none for many years. When he did . . . if he ever did . . . His mind formed a very indistinct picture of some beautiful unknown creature in a nebulous mist of white, a sort of blurred outline of a wingless angel floating in clouds. Anyway, if the time ever came he would know her when he saw her—of that part only was he certain!

Then quickly he tossed this sketchy and imaginative picture aside as lightly as crumpled paper. No time to think about girls out here. He desired nothing so much as land and crops and stock, freedom to come and go as he wished, to get rich and perhaps parade his success a bit back home.

The trail still stretched ahead over the prairie, the bent and broken stems of wiry grasses, crushed flowers and indistinct wagon ruts pointing the way to the two little settlements there so close together in the Valley of the Red Cedar.

Ever since he had come from the log tavern back there at a point called Independence, the trail had presented no cabin or sign of humans. Only the knowledge that two settlements,

Prairie Rapids and Sturgis Falls, lay at the end of the wagon ruts, six miles apart, gave him the assurance that the journey would end in anything but that great green sea. On the crude map in his pocket were penciled the two settlements, and the locations and numbers of the few patented sections surrounding them. All besides these were government owned and from these he was to choose that which would be his. It must be near one of the settlements, it must have water and timber.

He broke into singing again, low, deep-throated, a song with no meaning but its sheer exuberance of feeling.

And now there were black dots in the distance at the left, a half dozen spotted about on the open prairie and another straggling group on the opposite bank of the river that came down from the northwest. The Red Cedar! Sparkling in the afternoon sunlight, with blue joint grass to the water's edge, and timber in the distance. Prairie Rapids! The larger settlement, Sturgis Falls, would be six miles beyond.

He stopped now to reconnoiter and plan. To-night he would stay in the log house over there in Prairie Rapids which he had been told passed for a tavern, or at one of the three in Sturgis Falls beyond. Just now he would walk on the six miles to the other settlement, keeping his eyes open and appraising the lands that lay at his right between the two.

As he walked he saw that the timber along the river's bank to his left became heavier but open prairie still lay to the north.

He had gone perhaps three miles when he came to another stream, a mere rippling creek with no great depth. But something in the clear little stream, a song of its own in the ripples, the whiteness of its sandy banks, the clean gravel along its waters, gave him pause and after he had slaked his thirst, guzzling like any other prairie animal, nose and mouth in the cool water, he sat down on the bank to ponder a bit.

From his pocket he drew the penciled plan given him in Dubuque by the government official. Here it was. This land, this part of the trail where he now sat, was taken. In fact a few log cabins along the trail were visible from this point. Farther to the northwest a section away, the plan showed unpatented acres: a scribbled notation across the sections said, "rich land, water, timber, sand, gravel."

Abruptly he turned off the trail and followed the creek bed to the northwest. Hickory and hazelnut scrub lined the banks so that he must keep close to the creek bed for the trail, or stay outside of the green border. Squirrels scolded about this intrusion. Wild ducks flew up from the water with a whir of beating wings. A startled heron took to the sky like a graceful blue-gray boat sailing into limpid gray-blue waters.

This, too, was preëmpted land; only that which lay still farther was unentered. He swung along the creek bed for a few rods, estimated with practised eye that he had come a mile from the trail, consulted the paper again.

This now . . . about here . . . ended the preëmpted claims. That which extended beyond was all government land. The lush grass bent before the wind. A spring bubbled from the sand of the creek bed. The thin wooded border of the winding creek merged into a small grove of maples, elm, oak, and ash.

The young man drew a quick excited breath. Wood . . . creek . . . gravel . . . sand . . . flowing spring . . . rich loam . . . only a mile to the north of the beaten track, about five from Prairie Rapids . . . only about three, probably, from Sturgis Falls. *This was it.* For this he had come the long miles by steam-cars, stage, and foot.

"God!" he said aloud. Some of it was mere careless ejaculation. But some of it was genuine thanks to the addressee.

All this had been surveyed. Two years before a group of surveyors had completed their work in this part of the new state, so the official there in Dubuque had told him. Somewhere there in the grass, then, covered by an inverted piece of prairie sod lay the corner stake of the section. *His* farm!

Long he stood gazing on the picture of the green grass and blue sky, running creek water and white sandy bank, and the trees beyond. It was possible that no man but the surveyors had stood in this spot before, for it was north of the beaten trail. No one had done so at least with proprietary eye, for the surveyors had but done their work and gone on.

"This is it." He spoke aloud as though the saying so before these grasses gave the choice definiteness and solemnity. "Yes, this is it."

His voice trembled a bit with the emotion of the moment. To have come all this distance to claim that which was his own, not knowing just where it would lie or what contours it would have. And now at last to see it before him with satisfying clarity.

It was something like the sudden meeting with a person of whom you had long heard but whose face you had never seen. It was almost like keeping a tryst with . . . Why, it came pretty near to being like the first meeting with that girl he'd sometimes imagined.

He took off his cap and the sun brought out the glints in his yellow hair.

"Wayne Lockwood," he grinned widely, "do you take this land to be your lawfully wedded own, to have and to hold in sickness and in health?"

Jocularly he made his answer in a feminine voice: "I do."

"Section . . ." He consulted his papers, naming aloud the numbered notations there. "Do you take Wayne Lockwood to be your lawfully wedded. . . ?"

"Caw, caw, caw!" The grackles wheeled and dipped in noisy inquisitiveness. All the solemnity was gone. Wayne Lockwood threw back his head and laughed at Nature's raucous answer to the impromptu wedding.

"Well, anyway," he said boyishly, "I pronounce you mine . . ."

The gay words died in the utterance for not a half-dozen rods away to the east, a top-buggy with glistening body, pulled by a sleek pair of prancing bag horses was coming directly toward him through the prairie grass.

He stood there and stared. It was rather unbelievable. All afternoon he had seen no living thing on the beaten trail. And now to the north of the trail, off that one path between Dubuque and the twin settlements of Prairie Rapids and Sturgis Falls, came a buggy containing two men.

When they drew close, the bays stepping in perfect unison as though on some city boulevard, Wayne saw that the men were well dressed, that one was older than the other, and that they were more surprised to see him, if such a thing were possible, than he was to see them.

The team stopped with a few prancing didoes and the driver leaned forward toward Wayne as though expecting him to come to the buggy. It was characteristic of Wayne Lockwood, perhaps, that, tall and straight under the maple at the creek's edge, he should stand unmoving.

Apparently seeing that Wayne was not making any move to come to them, the younger of the two men got out. He was a personable young fellow not much older than Wayne himself, dark, with dapper mustache, and he was now saying: "How do you do?"

" 'Do, sir."

"Little off the trail, aren't you?" He spoke affably.

"Quite a peace."

"Looking for land?"

"Yes, sir."

"Good land up this way. We've located several fine sections. You will probably find something you like."

"Yes . . . I've found it."

The young man was not quite so cordial now. "Not this section?"

"This *quarter*-section."

"Oh, no . . . this one is mine . . . this *half*."

Wayne looked down at the paper still in his hand, traced the penciled line of the creek to the numbered section. "I made this out from a government map . . . and it's not filed on yet, according to this," he said quietly.

"No." The young chap admitted it readily enough. "We're driving back to Dubuque, though, to-morrow to attend to that matter."

He smiled with such oily condescension that Wayne took an immediate dislike to him. And when he asked: "Did you walk out from Dubuque?" it seemed to take on the tone of a superior addressing an inferior.

"Yes."

"I thought I didn't see any conveyance about."

That was perilously close to a sneering comment. When Wayne remained silent, the stranger volunteered affably enough: "Well . . . we'll go on. We're staying at a tavern in Sturgis Falls but will be driving back to Dubuque to-morrow."

Not particularly versed in the nuances of the human voice, still Wayne thought he detected the semblance of a threat in the statement.

The stranger could well afford to be pleasant, though, with those prancing bays stamping the praire grass, ready to take him back to the land-office one hundred miles away. So he was saying cheerfully: "Better luck in your next choice."

He had walked back to the carriage now where his silent companion awaited him. One foot on the buggy step, he turned. His eyes narrowed and his voice held distinct arrogance and insult. "And don't you try anything foolish around here to make trouble."

They were gone, driving away to the southwest, presumably to join the trail again and go on to Sturgis Falls for the night.

Wayne walked over and threw himself down on the creek's bank. He was disappointed and chagrined. To be sure there were countless other unclaimed sections. Almost was there all of Iowa from which to choose. It was foolish to be so upset because he could not have the one he had picked so enthusiastically. He was no child to be angry because he could not have his way. But this particular section had everything for which he could wish. Over in his mind he called the roll of those characteristics: rich loam . . . water . . . white sand . . . gravel . . . timber . . . only a few miles from the twin settlements of Prairie Rapids and Sturgis Falls.

If that smart Aleck had really owned it now, he would have walked on with no thought of covetousness. But that was the hardest thing to swallow in the whole business, that, after all, it was not yet the other fellow's any more than his. Only by virtue of owning that swift team would the stranger be able to claim it.

And now he could see his folly in failing to purchase his own team at the sale there in Dubuque. Because he wanted to be sure of this venture, satisfy himself first that the lands were good, worth their dollar and a quarter an acre, he had held off from buying horses, using his own two good legs for the journey.

Yes, his legs were good but scarcely could be expected to compete with those prancing bays. The dapper stranger had said they were going to stay all night at a Sturgis Falls tavern and then start back to Dubuque to file on this.

"Gosh all hemlock!" He sat up suddenly as a wild idea took possession of his mind. "If only . . ."

He leaped to his feet and stood looking to the east where even now the late afternoon shadows were beginning to cluster. Pools of pale yellow light lay on the prairie like gold breastpins on a woman's green dress. Dubuque! One hundred miles! It might as well have been half a world away. He thought of the three long days and half-nights on the trail, sleeping a few hours in a log house at Delhi, another time at the log tavern in Independence.

But added to the certainty that the men were going to Sturgis Falls for the night were a few possibilities. It might be late in the morning when they would get started. There was just a chance he himself might be overtaken by some one with whom he could ride part of the way.

He looked down at his strong young limbs incased in calfskin boots as though there he might find the answer to his questioning. If only they were the seven-league boots of his childhood tales.

Suddenly he sat down again on the creek's bank, unloosed

the straps, removed the boots and stockings, and bathed his feet in the cool water. Drying them on the heavy socks, he took a fresh pair from a coat pocket, put on these and his boots. Then he rinsed out the first pair and hung them on a scrub oak.

"To hold my property down for me," he grinned.

Now he let his glance once more sweep the coveted section, seeing it under the slanting rays of the sinking sun. Already shadows were crowding into the thick undergrowth of hickory, hazelnut, and burr oak there on the creek's bank.

The land, slightly higher than that nearer the trail, rolled into faintly discernible swales like solidified waves of a green sea.

A deep longing for the real ownership of that which had already taken on familiar lines and an obstinacy within him, as well as an intuitive dislike of the young stranger's condescending tones—all of these feelings, which could not take the decision calmly, spurred him on.

Suddenly he turned and in that light Indian-footed way of his strode back toward the east.

CHAPTER 2

THE moon came up, yellow as a prairie cowslip, Dew settled clammily on the course grass so that an odor of crushed moist herbage penetrated Wayne Lockwood's nostrils and walking was more difficult for the wetness. Sometimes in his long steady strides he flushed out a bevy of startled prairie-chickens. Wolves howled in the distance. And once he sighted a long, lean, pointed-nosed figure silhouetted against the night sky.

The moon slipped to his back, paled in the gray dawn. Ribbons of pink and mauve and gold shot up over the earth's rim. Prairie larks sprang from the diamond-tipped grass and flew singing into the sun. At a tiny stream he threw himself down on its bank, buried his face in its clear depths, and went on refreshed by the coldness of the water.

The Wapsipinicon was too high for crossing anywhere except at a safe ford, so he headed straight for the little settlement of Independence. And now other travelers were on their way for the day. From the east came a covered wagon drawn by three yoke of oxen, the driver walking at their side, occasionally snapping his black-snake high over their broad backs and swaying heads with horns brass-tipped and shining in the morning sun. The man's stentorian tones "Hey . . . Hey" came across to him.

For unlike the usual stopping and exchanging of information on the sparsely traveled prairies, Wayne kept straight to his self-chosen path a quarter of a mile north of the trail, scarcely glancing toward the travelers.

In the early afternoon he had crossed the "Wapsie" and eaten at the log tavern. Miles beyond, his young limbs sent up their first protesting so that he threw himself down on the open prairie, face on his arm for a moment of relief. Lying so

16

close to the grasses magnified them, distorted the slim stalks so that he appeared to be looking into a forest under which twined a great undergrowth of giant wild morning-glories, lupines, and prairie roses. Lying there, the scarcely perceptible swaying of the miniature tree trunks close to his arm caught his eye and he sprang to his feet as a long, loathsome thing slipped, belly-flat, through the grass. Suddenly he had no stomach for staying, and went on at once.

On to the east, then, all the afternoon. And all night again through the wet clinging grass under that huge cowslip of a moon, with the prairie-chickens flushed from their coverts and a lone owl hooting and another lean gray form silhouetted against the night sky. Skirting swamps, fording streams, putting miles of that moon-drenched sea of grass behind him!

Day again! And not yet had the bay team appeared on the trail to overtake him. And not yet had a traveler with whom he might ride come by his way to the east. Like the sun and the moon themselves, the few travelers were moving always to the west.

It was late afternoon now with shadows lying lightly on the prairie like phantom boats on a mystic sea. By his calculations and a landmark of remembered swales, Dubuque must be not very far away. Glancing over his shoulder in that constant watch for travelers, he saw movement on the trail. Every faculty alert, he watched the oncoming speck until that moment when he could make out whether it was to be some one with whom he might ride or the men whom he wished to avoid. His tired eyes deceived him for a time, made out that it was a lone horseman, suddenly could no longer keep the truth from him. For over there to the right, on the trail going eastward, trotted the pair of bays with the shining buggy.

And now disappointment and despair struck him like a spell of illness. All of his spirit and courage dropped away as gas from the balloon he had seen at the fair. This wild-goose chase seemed the height of stupidity. Why had he done it? Why had he let an obstinacy and dislike of that young stranger's manner lead him into this foolish procedure? With practically all of Iowa from which to choose, he had clung with silly tenacity to the one section. Disgust was enveloping him as he stood and watched the dark speck disappear into the east.

Fatigue was conquering him. Augmented by that feeling of despair and disappointment, his mind could scarcely make those young limbs of his obey. But some dogged determination kept it the master. From now on it was as though there were conflict between the two—the driving brain and lagging body—as though the one lashed the black-snake, and the other, oxen-like, could do naught but sluggishly obey. The mind and the body fought for supremacy, but it was as though he himself were only the physical, some other person the mental.

"No . . . I can't go farther."

"Go on, you coward."

"But it's too late."

"It's never too late to try."

"They'll get there long before I do."

"They might get there after the office is closed, and stay all night at a tavern. Then you would have equal chances."

All through the night, with his body protesting and his mind scourging, he plodded on. Through the rolling timbered hills, now, he trudged in the paling moonlight and the last mile of the trail into Dubuque.

His eyeballs were as hot as though sands from the Deer Run Creek bed were in them. When he stopped walking his flesh quivered and every muscle of his body twitched spasmodically, like a thin sawblade vibrating for a moment after the woodcutter has finished using it.

And now he was passing down a street of the town perched there on the cliffs above the Mississippi, named for Julien Dubuque, the French-Canadian who had been the first white man to settle permanently on Iowa soil.

He was too weary to give much thought to the town, and its founding, scarcely remembered his excitement on arriving here beyond the Mississippi a week ago and his interest in the story of Julien Dubuque's adventurous career, how by flattery and wiles and perhaps an understanding of the Indian character, Dubuque had obtained from them the lead mines hereabout. Well, one need not waste any sympathy over the affair. Julien Dubuque had been dead forty years—buried by the Indians here near Little Fox Village. And only the year before, the long-drawn-out trial over the ownership of the mines had been decided—they had reverted to the Indians.

Only a few people were astir: some making ready to pull out in the gray dawn in their wagons, a shopkeeper opening a little store, the ferryman starting the day's first crossing to the eastern side of the Mississippi.

There it was—the government land-office where he had obtained all his information only a week before. It was too

early for it to be open. But how long had it stayed open the
night before? Had the high-stepping bays arrived before the
hour of its closing?

With one long exhalation of breath he dropped on the
wooden step, pillowed his head in his arm, and slipped into
the oblivion of sleep.

From somewhere, in time, came the blurred consciousness
of activity around him, and a vague realization that his body
was being shaken vigorously. Even then he could scarcely
reassemble his scattered faculties. The sun was in his eyes. A
man was bending over him saying something that sounded
like a half-angry, half-amused: "If you want this office open
to-day . . ."

He was fully awake now, and jumped lithely to his feet. A
line of a dozen land-seekers stretched behind him, all laughing good-naturedly at the blond young giant who had filled
the step and threshold of the building with his bulk.

"You must have been here all night."

"Just getting ready to all take hold and heave you into the
Mississippi."

"Found a gold mine or somethin' you're afraid'll get away?"

There was more rough banter and then Wayne Lockwood
was in the building and the first of the line in front of the
wooden railing and desk.

"Name?"

"Wayne Lockwood."

A few other questions and then: "Number of your claim?"

"Black Hawk . . ." He named the three sets of figures.

The agent ran a none-too-clean forefinger across the map
and down the column of a large book."

"All right. It's yours."

Wayne opened his shirt and from the quilted band around
his strong young body got out his gold and paid it over—a
dollar and a quarter per acre—and signed the necessary papers, placing his government deed in the quilted belt. Then he
sauntered over to the high iron stove in which no fire was
burning this June morning and sat down on a wooden bench
behind it, concealed from the vision of any one in the line.

He did not have long to wait. Two men in fresh linen, one
younger than the other, came through the door, and in the
course of time worked by degrees to the agent's desk.

"Well, well, Mr. Bedson." For the first time the agent
jumped up and shook hands with an applicant. Evidently Mr.

Bedson was a personage here. "Back again. Did you find what you wanted?"

"Yes . . . several. First and best to my mind . . . Black Hawk . . ." He, too, named the three sets of figures.

The numbers must have seemed vaguely familiar to the agent for he frowned and ran a finger, a little more soiled by now, down the map and consulted also the large book for verification.

"Sorry, Mr. Bedson. That's filed on."

"Oh, no, it couldn't be. There's some mistake."

"No, there's no mistake. Young fellow by the name of Lockwood. Was here first thing this morning. Found him asleep in the doorway."

From behind the stove, his cap pushed back on his light wavy hair, a smudge of dirt across his face, eyes bloodshot, his boots caked with swamp mud, stepped Wayne Lockwood, grinning. That widespread grin had in it something of the mature malevolence of Mephistopheles and something of the boyish impudence of Puck.

For this hour had he lived. For this one exalted moment had he walked, sleepless and hungry, the long way from the Valley of the Red Cedar, forded the streams, pushed through swamps, and trampled down a hundred miles of prairie grass.

It was worth it—worth all the torturing strain he had put upon his strong young body to be able to step from behind the high iron stove there in the government land-office and say to the stranger:

"Yes, it's mine. And see that you don't try anything foolish around there to make trouble."

CHAPTER 3

ONE week later found Wayne Lockwood nearing the end of his second journey to the Valley of the Red Cedar, nearly back to the quarter-section he had chosen with such swiftness of decision, and tramped a hundred weary miles to obtain. This time, however, he had his newly purchased team and wagon, a plow and a few other tools, a buffalo robe, a hidebound chest with brass bands which his grandfather had once carried to sea, and a box of bedding from his parents' home there in the New England hills, these last two having been left in Dubuque until his entry was made.

All these days he had been on the westbound trail again, from Dubuque to Delhi, with its one-roomed log house for travelers, from Delhi to Independence and its slightly larger log tavern, from Independence to Prairie Rapids with not a single cabin ever in sight between these points.

The previous night he had stayed at Prairie Rapids and now he was on the last lap of the long journey, driving the five miles across the prairie to his land. His land! It gave him a queer feeling in which pride and a sense of responsibility were the leading emotions, but running through both, like a scarlet thread in a gray coat, was the boyish jubilation over winning out in the entry of it. All he needed to cheer him in any moment of homesickness or fear for his ultimate success in the new country was to recall that look of amazement and chagrin which had come over the face of the dapper young fellow whom he had beaten out of it. Even now as the new wagon jolted over the trail he laughed aloud at the remembrance.

Yes, it was his right, thanks to a quick decision and two good legs, and no finer land lay anywhere in the new state, he would wager. A little nearer to Sturgis Falls than to the

Prairie Rapids settlement, and a mile north of the beaten trail which paralleled the river, it was ideally placed. Just which one of the two settlements he would like better, which he would honor with his patronage—he grinned at that—remained to be seen.

Because his mind was his only companion, he passed the time of his journeying with thoughts of the previous day's happenings, pictures of it slipping through his head in changing sequence; the Prairie Rapids settlement as he had seen it the day before, a little handful of log cabins scattered over the prairie on both sides of the river, a few split-rail fences, a tent, two or three families still living by the side of their wagons.

He had fully expected to drive to his own land the evening before and sleep in the wagon, but reaching the settlement late, with threatening clouds rolling up from the west, he had decided to stay at the log tavern. Here he grinned to himself again at the memory of the evening spent at the Sherman House.

After he had made his team comfortable under the straw-thatched shed he had gone inside the tavern, had been talking to Mr. Sherman, with pen in hand ready to sign the register, when his rival for the land came in. He had relished that moment, that handing of the pen over to the dapper young fellow with a flourish in exaggerated politeness, as though the name of Mr. Bedson must necessarily precede that of Wayne Lockwood.

The chap had signed it with a cool nod of acknowledgment, and then, with his own underneath, the two names had stood there together on the book even as the two men were side by side.

Cady Bedson.   *Wayne Lockwood.*

It was a queer episode and it made him wonder just how often they were going to run into each other out here. But it was the next move that had given him the best laugh. Mr. Sherman had said to a young boy standing near: "Show Mr. Bedson up to Room 12 and Mr. Lockwood to Room 16."

"Room 12?" Cady Bedson had said in surprise. "Why, is that a *single* room?"

"Certainly," the proprietor had answered seriously enough. And the two had gone up to the loft, not high enough in the center to allow a six-footer to stand straight, sloping to a mere three feet on the sides, an opening in each gable-end for ventilation, and eighteen bunks on the floor through which there was just room to walk, but very truly a "single room." The boy had broken into loud guffawing and said proudly: "He cracks that joke every time."

A calico curtain inclosed one bunk at each end which, a young blade on the pallet next to Wayne informed him with accompanying smirks, contained some brides and grooms.

Before the night was over the beds apparently were all occupied. They were hard and damp from a recent shower which had seeped in between the logs. The pillows were small and might have been stuffed with goose-quills. One fellow called down the loft stairs: "Hey, Sherman! I'm afraid to go to sleep . . . afraid a pillow will work into my ear," which brought forth loud laughter.

All night there had been more or less commotion. A woman sobbed. A shower caused some one to find and put up an umbrella. Some of the roomers called out to keep quiet and let them sleep, others snored, oblivious to the thunder rattling around the log roof. This Bedson was not up yet when he left. Oh, well, he might never see the fellow again. There was no certainty he belonged permanently in these parts.

And now he was almost home. *Home!* That was a queer word to apply to the prairie grass and the creek and the clump of timber lying off there to the north. But in no time at all he would have a good snug cabin. He would break out the sod, raise fine crops, stock his farm, bring in sheep, buy more land. Ten years from now he would have a transplanted New England home, but larger and finer. It was a pleasant picture. He broke into singing, true and resonant:

> *"Oh, ye'll tak' the high road an' I'll tak' the low road,*
> *An' I'll be in Scotland before ye;*
> *But I and my true love will never meet again—"*

He broke off suddenly. There were the four cabins plainly visible now, scattered over the prairie, and a high spiral of smoke in a grove to the left gave mute evidence that another one nestled there in its shelter. Five cabins! There lived his neighbors. Who might they be and from whence had they come?

It gave him a queer sensation of excitement and curiosity not to know the answers, for his life in the next few years, no doubt, would be more or less intertwined with those of the unknown persons in the five prairie shelters.

On his own land at last he made camp in the little grove at the creek's bend, grinning to himself at the welcome sight of his socks on a bush. His horses, having snatched greedily at the lush grass when first unharnessed, had settled down to a contented browsing as though discovering there was ample food to last forever.

The afternoon was spent in assembling wood for fires, choosing the site for his cabin, setting stakes to show its dimensions, clearing the brush, marking the trees to be cut. These were to-day's small tasks. Not until the first tree was felled on the morrow would he feel that he was accomplishing anything.

He worked until dark, made a fire, and cooked corn-meal mush and slices of smoked meat which he ate with the hearty relish of a healthy young animal. Then he put green branches across the fire and went to see that the horses were comfortable, patting them, rubbing their noses, speaking to them as one would to humans, "Good night, Belle! Good night, Blackbird." They responded with friendly little sounds and a nuzzling of their long lips.

All day at his work he had been busy and contented. Now he felt lonely here in the great expanse of prairie under the wide sky. Now he knew a mental and emotional let-down, experienced the flat feeling of an anticlimax after some great adventure. This was dull reality. To-night, home seemed very far away. All those days in which he had been traveling westward, hurrying to make true the dream of land that would be his own, home had been something from which he was released, something shaken off with boyish abandon so that he might be free to use the money given him by his seafaring grandfather as he wished. Now that the feverish activity of getting the claim was over, the decision made, a large share of his money spent, his severance from "the folks" complete, he was in a bit of a mental slump. Physical fear he had never known. But to-night the vastness of the prairie, the stillness of it, the lack of friendly voice, of human companion, was almost overwhelming. It was scarcely understandable when he had been alone and uncomplaining on the prairie during so many nights before.

He climbed into the wagon-box, pulled a blanket and the buffalo robe over him, for the night had taken on the chill dampness of falling dew. The silence of the prairie was almost as loud as ever noise could be. Then, suddenly, a wolf howled from some point along the creek bed. Another answered faintly from a distance. An owl hooted in the timber. Some little night creature started a tick-tacking in the grove near-by. All the silence of the prairie became pregnant with the sound of living things—things that crept and moved, hooted and howled, tapped and tiptoed, swayed the grass and stole forth from tree trunks.

More than he had ever wanted human companionship, he wished for it now. That girl—that schoolmate of his sister's who had cried over him—probably she would have come out here with him if he . . . Lord, no, he hadn't even *liked* her.

His mother had said: "Wayne, when the time comes for you to marry, come back here for a wife."

He had laughed at that, telling her there was no one he would want, keeping it to himself that he could half-way visualize a girl—oh, maybe not her features, but she was there all right, dainty and demure, in a kind of a haze that framed her face like a white cloud.

He slipped his hands under his head and looked up at the long streaming white veils of film slipping between him and a million stars—long white veils—that framed a face—

And slept.

Thus did Wayne Lockwood, in the year 1854, in the young raw state of Iowa, sleep the first long night away under the prairie sky. And thus did the curtain go up on the little play which was to contain all the elements of every life's drama: work, play, joy, sorrow, disappointment, achievement, love, hate.

CHAPTER 4

THE beginning of this day took upon itself the beginning of his real pioneering—so Wayne Lockwood thought as he struck ax into the first stalwart hickory.

If only rain would hold off until he had his house completed! But that was too much to hope for, as a single pair of hands would make protracted work of putting up a cabin. Oh, well, he had his wagon-box and its heavy canvas. He had been too many days and nights on the prairie to worry about that.

It was far into the forenoon, with the first tree lying prostrate and denuded of part of its branches, when from the southeast he saw two horses galloping toward him. As they approached he made out that one was ridden by a man, but that skirts were billowing out, balloon-like, at the side of the other.

When they rode close and reined in, the man proved to be middle-aged, black-whiskered, shaggy-browed and dark-skinned, with that tinge of complexion which Wayne was to find later came from the taking of much quinine. He sat his horse with ease, the trunk of his body as erect as the tree Wayne had just marked for the next cutting, but his head drooped forward as though he must be forever urging his mount on.

As the new-comer swung his long legs off, he stood level-eyed across from Wayne so that he, too, must have been fully six feet one.

The billowing skirt (collapsed now into a long gray calico one) belonged to a young girl who might have been any age from twelve to sixteen; it was difficult to tell it, clothed as she was in the full-skirted, tight-waisted garment of the prairie female person.

She had been wearing a gray sunbonnet as stiff as a reed-basket, but it now straddled her neck where it rattled starchily in the brisk wind. Her hair was reddish-brown, vaguely wavy, he could see, for it had partially tumbled out from a black net in the swift riding over the prairie. Her gray-blue eyes looked too large for the slim oval of her face and too mature for a certain childishness.

"Well . . . what's goin' on here?" was the man's bluff and hearty greeting as soon as he had dismounted.

Wayne met him pleasantly enough with: "Oh, I'm sort of setting up housekeeping." He could see now that under the bushy, black eyebrows peered blue eyes so sharp and bright that they looked like bits of sparkling ice in dark timberland pools.

"Taken over some land?"

"Yes, sir . . ." Wayne threw out his hand at the surrounding scene. "My front yard."

"Well, now, that's just about the best news I've heard for a spell."

"I take it you're one of my neighbors."

"You took it right. Jeremiah Martin's my name. I'm an old-time settler now, come two years ago this month. Live over there at the edge of that grove on the trail. You can't rightly see the house from here but she's there all right with eleven folks in her when they're all to home."

"My name is Wayne Lockwood."

"Glad to make your acquaintance, Mr. Lockwood, and welcome you to the Red Cedar Valley."

They shook hands, and when Wayne unconsciously glanced at the young girl, high on her tall horse, Jeremiah Martin said: "That's one of my girls. Let's see now, slips my mind at this time just which one she is." His little blue eyes were twinkling behind their black bushes, the only apparent evidence that he spoke facetiously. "Turn around here 'n' let's see if I can make out." And when the young girl smiled complacently down at the two as though this sort of joking were an old and common custom, he spoke in the manner of one who suddenly remembered. "Oh, yes, now I recollect . . . this one's Suzanne."

Wayne Lockwood, raised in the atmosphere of his parents' genteel New England home, took off his cap and held it at his breast while he stepped to her mount's side and shook the girl's hard little hand.

"I'm pleased to make your acquaintance, Suzanne."

"Howdydo." She was neither forward nor shy, merely matter-of-fact, as though strangers were an everyday occurrence.

There was conversation between the two men about the land, the number of sections taken, prospects of other land-seekers coming in and, surprisingly to Wayne, the offer from Mr. Martin in behalf of himself and the other settlers, to help build the cabin. When Wayne protested that he had expected to do everything himself, wouldn't want to take them from their own work, Jeremiah Martin broke in with: "We'll all be ready to help cut to-morrow morning'."

He mounted his mare, turned her preparatory to riding back toward his home, and then said as casually as though he had spoken of it before: "We'll look for you to supper to-night."

"Oh, but . . . I've got supplies."

"Just as important to break bread together out here as to break sod."

"I just meant . . . it wasn't necessary."

"Friendship is one of the most necessary things in this world anywhere, my lad, but you'll need it out here more than you ever have back home."

"Well, I thank you . . . of course . . ."

They were starting away. The girl looked back over her shoulder and spoke for the first time since her brief salutation.

"We eat about sundown," she called back. And as casual as it was, Wayne rather liked the fact that she had added her voice to the invitation. It gave a feminine slant to it, as though she represented the women of the household who had the cooking to do.

The two were gone now—Jeremiah Martin, tall and dark-skinned, black of beard and eyebrows, looking as sturdy as any hickory tree, and little Suzanne Martin, her gray print dress blowing into a huge puffball as her horse galloped across the prairie.

All afternoon the sounds of Wayne's ax rang out where ax had never been before. When the sun was near the horizon he brought water from the creek and washed. Uncertain whether or not to get out his best suit with stock and vest, he finally decided against it, merely brushing his breeches and putting on a clean dark shirt.

Then he combed his thick light hair in front of the little diamond-shaped mirror set in the cover of his hidebound chest. He mounted Blackbird and, leading Belle, set out across the prairie toward the smoke column there at the edge of the grove. Indians were camping by the river and while he had been told in Prairie Rapids that no one feared them greatly, a horse grazing by itself would be a temptation to any chance redskin passer-by.

All the way over toward the cabin he was wondering about the approach of these strangers. He had no great liking to meet new people under any condition, and if, by any chance, Jeremiah Martin himself or the young girl were not around, he had an idea he would be feeling rather foolish to present himself to any of the others with a "here-I-am, feed-me" air.

Mr. Martin had spoken of other girls. That meant at least two others. Girls! He hoped he wouldn't have to see very much of them. This was a man's world out here.

The sun had started slipping over the rim of the world now. As he rode, the scene spread out before his eyes challenged him again, as so often it had done in these days he had known the Iowa prairies. He turned in his saddle to get the picture in all its phases. To the west and north, wind rippled the tall grass so that it dipped in long swirling waves of dark-green foam on a light green sea. To the northeast only the thin fringe of timber that clung to the creek bed broke the green sea line. To the south of the trail over which all settlers came stood a large patch of timber land, open prairie beyond, and in the far distance the thick woods along the Cedar. A fine enough sight for any one's eyes.

And now at the edge of the patch of timberland was a log structure he was to find out later was the school-house, and just beyond it the log cabin of the Martins sat behind the only stake-and-rider fence he had seen in the country. Surprisingly, it was a large log house, much larger than the little tavern at Independence, and equally surprising was the fact that it was whitewashed. To be sure the whitewashing could not cover all that irregularity of logs—stretches of black alternated frequently with the fresh white—but the effect gave him a momentary thought of the good farm-houses back home.

On closer view, its appearance was strangely like two log houses which some giant had pushed together, the end of one flush against the side of the other to form a letter T, and both parts showing small glass windows on the lower floor, solid wooden openings in their lofts.

Because of its two parts it seemed to sit among the native trees like a big speckled brown and white bird in its green nest with one wing outspread, for branches of the oaks and maples, cottonwoods and walnuts nearly touched its roof at the back and sides. The prairie fell away from it at the north so that the front yard would have had only the horizon for its boundaries if the fence had not put limitations upon it, giving the whole place more of a settled appearance than that of any of the other cabins which dotted the trail. A wide opening in the fence denoted the wagon drive, but in direct line with the door of the cabin a small split-rail gate, hung on leather hinges, was evidently a concession to old eastern ways.

And now Wayne was turning into the wide opening in the stake-and-rider fence.

Yes, his fears were to be realized, for although the cabin door stood open there was not a soul in sight. Only from the rear of the house came a high clear voice singing that it had been washed in the blood of the Lamb.

He would have to go through that embarrassing moment then of knocking and saying his little speech of "Here I am, ready to be fed." He was wishing heartily that he was back at the wagon by the side of his own camp-fire, when two shaggy dogs bounded forth from somewhere, noisy with prospects of attack, but deciding he was not an enemy, went into a mild form of hysterical welcome as he dismounted and tied the horses to the rail fence.

At the noise of the dogs, immediately there were two comely young women appearing in the front doorway. Another with a pan in her hand peered around the corner of the house. From the loft at the left the solid wooden shutter opened outward and two feminine heads appeared. Wayne was vaguely conscious that there were others behind them. It gave him a feeling of embarrassment and indecision, brought a sudden memory of arriving home one afternoon back in New England when his mother was holding a meeting of the ladies of the church. This could hardly be anything of that sort, could it?

Of one thing he was certain—there was no necessity to make himself known in any way, what with girls looking out of windows and tumbling out of doors, and the dogs yelping their excited welcome. Girls! Gosh all hemlock—he didn't even *like* girls.

The two young women in the doorway came on down to the log stoop. The young girl with the pan emerged in her entirety from around the corner. Heads were hurriedly withdrawn from the loft windows so that he had a definite intuition the group of femininity in front of him was about to be enlarged.

In that he was quite right. For one fleeting moment he was under the impression that a couple of dozen girls had descended upon him. In reality seven had arrived around the log stoop with much laughter and swishing of full calico dresses. One of the number was holding onto something dangling at the bottom of her skirt. The last two comers were laughing themselves sick over this just recently ripped braid, so that the first of the group, although not knowing what it was all about, joined in merrily, apparently from sheer sympathy of infectious risibilities. There was almost wild commotion, with the great dogs leaping and barking and seven girls emitting laughter in various keys and degrees of volume.

Wayne faced them, unflinching, as he would have done any other brave thing, meeting wolves on the trail, unfriendly Indians, a striking rattler. He had his cap off and the rays of the sinking sun touched his light hair with flecks of bronze. He looked very stalwart and manly standing there in his woodsman's clothes, his arms folded across his cap. Unconsciously he had his eyes on the young Suzanne, grinning cheerfully at him, who, in all this hubbub of strangers, seemed like a tried and true friend of long standing.

They were closing in on him and at least three of the girls were saying: "You're the new neighbor?"

"Yes."

"We knew it," from four. And he had thought girls out on the raw prairie like this would be shy, backward.

"Pa said . . ."

"He told us you'd bought land and . . ."

"We're glad to see you and we hope . . ."

One after another they shook hands with him, still talking, not one listening to another. Only Suzanne remained quietly at one side. Having extended her hand to him in the morning, she evidently considered that act enough of the civilities for the day.

"Now we'll tell you our names and all about us."

"Yes, tell him."

"You, Jeanie."

Wayne bowed to the one designated. "Miss Eugenie," he said politely, thinking it was the first introduction.

They all shouted with laughter.

"Not Eugenie, just *Jeanie*."

"She meant '*you*, Jeanie.' "

Wayne laughed, too. One couldn't help it—their laughter was contagious.

"Yes, I'm Jeanie. I'm third from the oldest—that is, of the

girls. Henry and Phineas, our brothers, are the oldest of all. They'll be here in a few minutes. Now pay good attention. *I'm* Jeanie.''

"Go on . . . *go* on," they all were saying.

"You've told him that."

"All right then." She pushed them all into line, apparently according to age, so the seven made a long row of laughing girls. She kept her own place, third from the end, leaning foward to introduce each one.

"Now, this first one with the black hair, like a crow, and the beautiful wild-roses complexion and the snapping black eyes—but look out for her ornery bossy disposition—is Sabina, the oldest.''

They all laughed immoderately, Sabina with the others, her black eyes crinkling merrily.

"This second one with the red hair is Emily. She's got more freckles than a wild turkey's egg but she can cook a good meal out of water and sawdust, and make a nice dress out of flour sacks.''

Emily was picking off her freckles in pantomime, pretending to scatter them as one would scatter seed.

"*I* come next. My name is Jeanie. I have a better disposition than Sabina and I . . .''

Her voice was drowned out: "Oh, she does not," and "She talks about her beaus in her sleep," and "That's enough about *you*."

"All right, I'll tell you the rest some other time when these jealous cats ain't here. This is Phoebe Lou. You can remember her by her molasses-colored hair and her green eyes and the hole here in her cheek. She thinks it's a dimple and pokes it in with her finger . . .''

It set them off, so she did not try to finish.

"This is Melinda. She looks a little bit like Sabina, you can see. We can tell them apart though because she's taller and her mouth is bigger and she always tears her clothes." This was the one with the dangling braid. "She's the gadabout, too . . .''

"Oh, I am not."

"Yes, she is," they chorused. "She always goes out and sits in the wagon, and Pa finds her there waiting.''

When the hubbub subsided Jeanie went on: "This one is Celia. She says her hair is golden, but we all think it's more like a pale frozen punkin. She thinks she's grown up, too, and no one could make her believe she ain't the prettiest. She ain't though, is she, girls?"

"No," they hooted in one voice.

"This one is Suzanne, the baby. She's Pa's pet. She's a queer sort . . . you'd think she lived in a hollow tree . . . she can sing, too, like a meadow-lark . . ."

"You mean a tree-toad," another put in, and they all laughed.

Suddenly, some one started it, and as though it were a part of the introductions they began singing a doggerel with no melody, merely on the ascending notes of the scale.

"Sabina and Melinda, Emilee and Phoebe Lou,
Suzanne, Celia, Jeanie. We have told them all to you.
We are a band of sisters, and you see we're not a few.
We are a band of sisters, may we faithful be and true."

It ended in breathless laughter as though at the expense of their own silliness.

Wayne was speechless, not from embarrassment or bashfulness now. He merely could not have talked if he tried. But he was no longer fearful of meeting the Martin family. He had never known anybody just like them but decidedly he was not bereft of his ease with them. It was as though they were not *girls* at all—just people.

And now the men folks, evidently through washing after work in field and barn, came around the house, one by one. Jeremiah, himself, the father of these gay magpies, tall and black-bearded and jovial, shook hands with Wayne again and welcomed him to his home. Then Henry came—their oldest brother, several volunteered—black-bearded like his father, but either naturally retiring in disposition or merely quiet because he could not get a word in edgewise. And then Phineas, sandy-haired, with sideburns and a roving eye.

In the midst of all this commotion, the mother, Sarah Martin, came out to the log stoop and shook hands with Wayne. She was so small and wiry-looking that he had a moment of wonderment over her giving birth to all these offspring. She, too, was sandy-haired so that it was easily seen where the red-haired children got their coloring. In fact, the crow-black hair and bright blue eyes of the father, the reddish hair and snappy dark eyes of the mother had been handed down to the nine children in all sorts of combinations and modifications so that no single description could cover the physical make-up of the family as a whole.

Supper was all ready to take up, Sarah Martin, the mother, was saying, and they must come right in before it got as cold as spring water. Talking and laughing, they all trooped up the great tree-trunk step and into the main room of the queer log house.

CHAPTER 5

THE Martin cabin was something of an architectural triad. Not only was it built in three parts, but each part represented one of the summers in which the newly settled Valley had known the family.

The large room into which one entered through the thick battened door was the original cabin of 1852. To the left, but at right angles to it and so forming the clumsy T, stood that portion which had been erected in 1853. Back of the original cabin, in this year of 1854, had been erected a large one-story lean-to, also of timber cut from the neary-by woods but made into lumber at the Overman sawmill in Sturgis Falls. So the Martin establishment, with two large cabin rooms topped by sleeping lofts, and the new lean-to, in comparison with most of the settlers' cabins, was a castle of a house there in the Red Cedar Valley.

At the right of the main room a huge open fireplace, through which stars were visible in the daytime, held a four-foot backlog and a wide swinging crane with iron pot. Iron shovel and tongs leaned against the wall. Wild-turkey wings, tallow candles, and snuffers were on a mantelshelf topped by crossed firearms, while another gun hung above the lintel of the lean-to door.

In the middle of the shelf stood the clock, a big Seth Thomas timepiece, on whose glass door the great American eagle encircled by thirteen stars spread his wings, held pointed darts in his claws and an *E Pluribus Unum* banner in his beak. Iron weights on heavy cord descended to the clock's depths throughout the night and day, only to be wound back into place each evening by an iron key held in Jeremiah's steady hand, at the end of which ceremony he invariably remarked: "There, now. Day's over. Everybody gets a fresh start tomorrow."

A walnut cupboard with plump knobs and wooden buttons for fastening its four doors was against one wall, a walnut bureau flanked another. Built-in shelves with calico curtains across them were in two of the corners, a walnut what-not filled a third, and large braided rag rugs lay on the puncheon floor.

Several chairs stood about, made from sturdy flour barrels out of which part of the staves had been sawed, the round heads inserted for seats and the whole covered with red calico. A large arm-chair held a place of honor near the fireplace while a small calico-covered rocker sat opposite it—the specific property of Jeremiah and Sarah, no one else ever sitting in them if the parents were present. A barrel-stand was near the front door, this, too, covered with bright calico, and with a removable top which formed a receptacle to hold the current pieces of sewing, while on it reposed the Bible, representing the religious life of the family, and a spy-glass, representing the earthly or non-spiritual side of existence as exemplified by the girls in trying to "make out what the neighbors were up to." There were a few books in a corner shelf, among them an atlas, Fox's *Book of Martyrs,* a volume of poems called *Footprints,* a New York Agricultural Report, *The Indian Lover, the 1847 Parlor Annual,* and *The Mother's Recompense.*

On the clay-plastered whitewashed wall hung a walnut-framed steel engraving of a tomb beneath a willow, with a drooping figure in black weeping copiously with the willow but evidently sustained by the verse:

Wherefore weep o'er those who sleep?
Their precious dust the Lord will keep
Till he appear in glory here,
The harvest of the world to reap.

There were other pictures—two of former Presidents Taylor and Fillmore, good Whigs, and a third of General Winfield Scott, recently defeated Whig candidate, this political art gallery showing a fine disregard for the present democratic President Pierce. There were colored pictures of two infants, sex undetermined, one with daisies around its head labeled *Day* and the other with poppies titled *Night,* both the sleeper and its less lethargic mate surrounded by pine-cones glued to a home-made frame. Waxed autumn leaves were fastened to the walls, and several crude if colorful paintings of sprays of wild flowers were framed in shells gathered along the Red Cedar's bank.

The room to the left contained in one end a walnut bedstead with calico valance around it and a tester of the same flowered material. In the othered a dark calico curtain concealed artfully the bed that any chance company might wish to use, while another calico curtain formed a clothes-closet. In truth, calico was a prominent furnishing, almost human in its predominance of the scene.

A walnut chest of drawers stood at the east wall, a reed-basket on top held balls of carpet rags in various sizes, and in the center of the room was an unfinished rug whose connection with the colored balls was apparent.

Back in York State and later in Illinois there had been a trundle-bed in use, and although it had been years since even Suzanne's youthful legs could curl up in the wooden boxlike affair, Sarah had insisted on bringing it out to the new home where it now reposed under the walnut bedstead (upon which she and Jeremiah nightly slept), waiting for company's children or a potential grandchild. Unlike some of the settlers who had moved to the Valley in a single wagon, the Martins had formed a cavalcade—three big linch-pin wagons and a buckboard, drawn by three teams of horses and two yoke of oxen. It was the only way in which Sarah Martin could be budged from her obstinacy against the move, by allowing her to bring some of her cherished belongings.

Strong ladders made from hickory saplings mounted upward like open stairs into lofts above both of these log rooms. Henry and Phineas slept over the main room, sharing it with any male overnight guest. Ordinarily Celia and Suzanne slept in the bed behind the calico curtain in their parents' room, but when company came, which was often, for never would Jeremiah Martin's hospitality turn any one away, the two youngest of the girls climbed the ladder of saplings also and disappeared somewhere into the region above with the other five sisters. Up in these lofts the snows sometimes sifted through the log chinks onto the comforts, or little streams of water trickled in. Sometimes the night grew so cold that a few of the girls shiveringly descended the ladder, stirred the logs in the fireplace, and rolled themselves in their quilts in front of it. Sometimes the night stayed so hot under the low roof, with mosquitoes buzzing and moths flying through the open

windows, that they brought their pillows down to the doorway of the main room or lean-to where it was less stifling if
no less buggy.

The large lean-to, made of real sawed lumber, was the
general eating and cooking part of the house now. No longer
were Sarah and her daughters compelled to cook over the
fireplace of the main room or in an outdoor oven. There was
a four-legged stove with an elevated oven and a short hearth
which protruded like a black lip forever pouting at some
unknown insult. Sarah's planning and industry had been the
means of purchasing it. After the men folks had tapped the
maples this year she and the girls had boiled down enough
sap to make and send two tubs of maple sugar to Dubuque for
it. A few things they admitted could still be cooked well over
the old open flame—the big black kettle on the crane continued to hold prairie-chicken stew and dumplings or a slowly
roasting venison rump.

The solidly packed clay hearth was always brushed neatly,
a constant cause for work, as the swallows habitually flew
about the chimney and sent fluttering feathery contributions
into the room. Indeed, life to Sarah Martin was one long
warfare with dirt, dust, sand, manure, grime, mud, and fly-
specks. She hated flies with an inborn deadly hate. From
across the room she could see a moth flit behind a calico
curtain. She kept her milk pans and butter jars scalded and
shining. She pounced upon a bit of mud as a bird on a worm,
slipped slyly up on a fleck of dust like a creeping Indian.
From early dawn until night fell she waved an energetic but
futile war against dirt, teaching her daughters to fight it with
her, and if she accompanied her quick energetic movements
with much nagging, vehement complaints, and pessimistic
prophecies as to the good it was all doing, the family looked
upon her sputtering as it looked upon the wind in the maples,
a sound to be heard afar off, but unheeded.

Besides the new stove in the lean-to, iron utensils hung on
the walls and more braided rugs were on the floor. There
were built-in shelves, flour barrels, the long table, a wooden
waterpail and dipper, pegs for hanging wraps and a huge
woodbox, above which hung a bootjack and the usual harness
always in a state of being oiled. Eight straight-backed heavy
wooden chairs surrounded the table, and three sawed-off
tree-trunks, so that part of the tri-daily commotion in getting
to the table consisted in seeing which three members of the
family were left out and had to use the backless seats. Except

for the understood ruling that the parents had good chairs, the effect of a general call of "Dinner's ready" took upon itself the semblance of a game of "going to Jerusalem."

Fly-roosts hung from the ceiling, long streamers of paper with spots of molasses on them upon which one hoped optimistically the flies would stick, but which they had a happy faculty of evading. Before every meal in summer the room was darkened by pinning aprons over the small windows and driving the pests out through the open door into the sunlight.

As it was always Celia's and Suzanne's duty to brush out those insensitive ones that returned unwelcome to the feast, each girl, with her sawed-off stick upon which strips of stiff paper had been bound, would rustle her long-handled brush over the big table so vigorously that, if one could have counted them, probably not fifty flies remained in the room.

To-night, in the excitement of the new young man's arrival, Celia and Suzanne had forgotten their warlike duties and were now being hustled in ahead of the others by their mother's, "I declare, you're as bad as the flies themselves. Let up on you a minute and you've settled down. Shoo!"

So the two were vigorously swaying brushes when Wayne Lockwood arrived in the lean-to, ushered there by a half dozen hospitable and talkative Martins.

The long table had been set with a nice white cloth, one of the good ones which Sarah Martin had owned back in York State. Against it the sand-polished steel knives and forks with their black handles looked very fine. In the center of the table was a mass of wild bouncing-Bets in an old tureen, their shaggy pale-pink blossoms lovely against the delft blue of the bowl.

"Oh, that Suzanne! She always drags flowers into the house," one of the girls was saying, so that Suzanne whacked her brush vigorously to hide her red face, and her father said, "Any of you make sport of Suzanne and her flowers I'll thump you."

They shouted with laughter and Sabina explained to Wayne: "Ever since I was a little girl he's said that . . . 'I'll *thump* you' . . . and he's never touched one of us yet."

"But Ma has," Jeanie said, and they all laughed again.

"Don't you go to makin' sport of Ma, either, or . . ."

" 'I'll thump you,' " they mimicked in chorus.

The most unusual family he had ever known, Wayne thought, saying bold, mean-sounding things to each other, but seemingly having bonds of affection underneath.

When Henry had brought out a barrel-chair from the main room to complete the seating accommodations, the lean-to was quite filled, with twelve people in it milling around to their place but taking pains to-night to see that the company had a chair and suppressing their usual scramble to avoid the sawed-off tree-trunks. Phineas even went so far as to take one voluntarily. Black iron kettles on the stove were steaming. The two shepherd-dogs sat on their haunches just outside the south door looking wistfully into the room, as though afraid of Sarah's sharp tongue, and licked their jaws hungrily at the smell and sight of the eatables.

Emily and her mother were taking up food.

"Melinda," the mother was saying, "put water in this kettle to soak, and watch out, it's hot."

"What'll I do if it sizzles?" Melinda called.

"You just sizzle right back," Sarah retorted, and the whole family laughed.

"You can't get ahead of Ma," Phoebe Lou was telling Wayne. "She's quick with her tongue."

Jeremiah, the father, sat at one end of the table and Sarah, the mother, at the other. On one side were Henry, Phoebe Lou, Wayne Lockwood, Melinda, and Emily; on the other, Phineas, Sabina, Celia, Jeanie, and Suzanne. At both ends of the table were platters of steaming stewed prairie-chicken. Several large bowls held white-flour saleratus biscuits in prairie-chicken gravy. Wayne knew just how those shepherd-dogs felt licking their chops outside the door. He felt like doing it himself after eating so much corn-meal and smoked ham these last weeks. There was a pyramid of the dry biscuits also, and a glass container with wild-grape jelly.

"Save room for crab-apple dumplings with maple sugar and cream," Celia was saying to Phineas even before they were quite seated.

And now Jeremiah's head was bowed and there was a slow trickling off of that constant feminine chatter as though it were as hard to stop as vinegar dripping from a barrel's bung-hole.

"Thank Thee for this food and bless it," Jeremiah's voice rumbled into his big black beard. He did not call the Lord by name, merely addressed himself humbly to some great Unseen Power who was the woods, the prairies, the moon, the sun, the winds, the rains. "And bless the stranger within our gates as he now becomes our friend. Amen."

Chatter broke forth immediately like the cider that must

flow again from the barrel after being held back a moment by a wooden plug. The plates which had been upside down were turned over with an artillery-like sound of clattering crockery. The great platters and bowls went around.

Constantly Wayne was on the alert to get this family straight in his mind. It was going to be something of a task, but whenever any one of that raft of girls was addressed by another he darted his eyes toward her to place the face and name together.

The talk flew about from one thing to another like the sound of wild grackles in the maples—chatter, chatter, chatter. Here was no group of femininity, uncertain and bashful, too shy to take part in masculine affairs, too genteel to dip into rough subjects. They were noisily fun-loving, opinionated, argumentative, could not be backed down when taking sides. He had not known any one just like them, could see plainly that although he might admire them as friends and neighbors, there was not the slightest chance of ever feeling anything else toward any one of them. There was no lovely creature floating in a white veil of cloud here among these healthy and hearty girls. It gave him a pleasant feeling of security that he could treat them friendly and on equal ground with their brothers, Henry and Phineas.

He was learning much about this new locality that he had not yet known. Sometimes he wished he might get the facts straight from some one of them without all the others chipping in to tell the same thing. Of them all, Henry and the young Suzanne said the least. Apparently Henry lived in his own thoughts more than the others for he ate methodically without taking much part in the talk. On those rare occasions when he ventured an opinion it had the effect of a stone dropping into a well, so that genuine attention was given him. Suzanne was quiet, too. But when she raised her big gray-blue eyes from her plate, Wayne could see how her emotions were mirrored in their depths, embarrassment, pleasure, distress, wonderment. It rather fascinated him to see how the light came and went in them like candles burning or blown out.

From the tumult of volunteered information in answer to his questions, he evolved some semblance of knowledge.

There had never been a white man stepped foot in the Valley until seventeen years before. He had been Gervais Paul Somaneux, a Frenchman, who had built a cabin on the bank of the Red Cedar. He had hunted and fished a few months and gone on. Then a white trapper by the name of Dorwit had lived around the streams for a time. For eight years afterward this part of the Valley had not seen any one but red men. But nine years ago a white settler by the name of Sturgis had come in from Michigan and built a cabin on the Red Cedar; a few months later a relative by the name of Adams built one near the springs over on Dry Run. Three other families named Hanna, Mullen, and Virden had located down the river. The Hanna family had been the nucleus around which the little Prairie Rapids settlement was beginning. The Sturgis and Adams families had moved on now, but before they left, seven years ago, the Overmans had come and bought the Sturgis claim and water-power, built a saw-mill and a grist-mill. They were the big people over at the Sturgis Falls settlement, having started a ferry, platted a town last year, and given a block of it for a court-house to be built some day.

At Wayne's question concerning which of the two settlements the Martins looked upon as their own for trading, Sturgis Falls or Prairie Rapids, Jeremiah said at once: "Sturgis Falls. We're closer for one thing. It's older and bigger. It's a platted town now which Prairie Rapids ain't. It had the first post office . . . mail brought on horseback. . . ."

Sarah, his wife, sniffed. "Demsey Overman carried the letters in his stovepipe hat. Never went out of his way none. When he happened to meet anybody who had a letter, he'd take off his hat and pull it out."

"Now, Ma"—Jeremiah spoke in conciliating fashion—"I'd just as soon get a letter out of Demsey Overman's hat as out of a big post-office building."

Wayne decided that Jeremiah Martin liked to promote good feeling, enlarge a little upon events, make them seem progressive and panning out well, that Sarah, his wife, enjoyed pricking the bubbles of his enthusiasm by minimizing events and their good effects. Probably she had not wanted to come out here to the new state with its few settlers, still carried the grievance with her.

"And another thing," Jeremiah went on, "Sturgis Falls is the county-seat . . . has all the court records . . ."

Sarah gave her preliminary sniff. " 'All the court records,' " she mimicked. "A little black book bought at Dubuque. Has two items in it, they say—and one of *them's* the seventy cents they paid for the book. Court-house is a little two-by-four room in the loft over Mullarky's store where you couldn't stand up straight if you tried . . .''

''Now, Ma,'' Jeremiah said dryly, ''some of 'em that comes to do business couldn't stand up straight if they had all the room in the world,'' which had the effect of setting every one off into laughter again.

Wayne liked them, warmed to their gay merriment over nothing, their simultaneous chatter as though one never listened to another. Such trivialities set them off, such inconsequential happenings gave them pleasure. Here were girls who seemed unconscious of their femininity, who would never cry over a man with their hearts on their sleeves.

Jeremiah was inclined to sit on when the meal was over, telling Wayne tales of the Valley: of Mrs. Hanna, the first settler down near Prairie Rapids, saying when she saw the sparkling river and green grass, ''I never knew there was such a place this side of Heaven. Boys, here's where we'll have a town''; of the Indians, the Musquakies, camped above the bluffs beyond Sturgis Falls, getting maple sap from a grove claimed by a white settler and how the settler took an ax and destroyed all their butternut troughs, so that only the diplomatic intervention of Mr. Virden prevented a massacre; how the Overman girls baked corn-meal pancakes one morning for an Injun who went away and told all the others and they kept coming until the girls had fed the whole tribe.

But Sarah said to come now, the dishes wouldn't do themselves, and started every one to her work.

It amused Wayne to see the diminutive, wiry woman order all these grown girls about. ''Phoebe Lou, you and Suzanne red up the table and take care of the dogs and the vittles. Sabina, you wash. Melinda, wipe. Jeanie, put away. Emily, set buck-wheat for breakfast. Celia, tend to the candle-lightin' and take the chairs in the other room.''

There was some dissension from Melinda. ''Candle-lighting, Ma. That's too easy for Celia with me wiping all these dishes.''

''That'll do for *you*,'' little bustling Sarah said. ''Scoot, now.''

And Melinda scooted.

By the time the last girl was through with her appointed task, a good-looking man with black side-whiskers arrived on horseback and was introduced as Mr. Tom Bostwick. He was dressed in a nice suit with fashionable stock, so that Wayne wished for the first time he had dressed likewise, thinking of

his own best suit and stock up there in the brass-bound chest
on the prairie.

Tom Bostwick was from Sturgis Falls where he had recently located to buy and sell grain and to dip into various
enterprises in the little settlement. He was an interesting
talker, having been to California in '49, relating to Wayne
how he had gone from Dubuque down the Mississippi to
Point Isabel, across the Gulf of Mexico and the Mexican
Republic to Masatland, up the coast to San Francisco, all in
three months, stayed there a year and then, coming back by
way of Panama and New Orleans, had located in Sturgis Falls
which he thought now was to be his permanent home.

He had come visiting at the Martins' on account of one of
the girls, Wayne was quite sure, but which one? It was like a
conundrum that must soon reveal its answer. He found himself looking them all over again, wondering which would be
his choice, if *he* were Tom Bostwick: Sabina? Emily? Jeanie?
Phoebe Lou? Melinda? Celia? No, Melinda, Celia, and Suzanne were too young for Mr. Bostwick. Before he had
decided which of the other four it could be, Jeremiah got a
jew's-harp off the fireplace mantel and settling it against his
full-lipped mouth, after much pushing aside of heavy beard
and mustache, twanged out a lively air. Then Phineas took a
gray calico bag from the side of the cupboard and removed a
fiddle which he told Wayne had been left to him by a German
hired man back in York State.   ·

And now the evening's "sing" began. Hymns—folk-songs—
romance. All the voices rolled out lustily, with Phineas turning out a lively if uncertain accompaniment.

Wayne was enjoying himself, letting his voice out to its
full volume in order to hold his own with this energetic tidal
wave of feminine voices. One, he noticed, was rasping and
off-key and he located it soon as Emily's. The others knew it,
too, and made no bones about joking her.

"I hear it inside me all right," the unabashed Emily explained, "but when it comes out it's not just the way I meant
it to be." And laughed at herself with the others.

Tom Bostwick was singing, too, peculiarly, in a thin
high voice which should have come from a small person,
and sounded somewhat ludicrous emanating from his large
frame.

The answer to the riddle was apparent. It was Sabina, there
was no mistaking.

> "... one cold winter's night
> And the wind blew across the wild moor ..."

Tom Bostwick's eyes were on the crow-wing hair, the rosy cheeks, and the snapping dark eyes of Sabina, his high thin voice almost cracking in its fervor:

> "When Mary came wandering home with her babe
> Till she came to her own father's door ..."

That was to be the last song, for it was late and all were to get up early to help Wayne. The voices rose in a perfect orgy of volume and emotion:

> "The villagers point out the spot
> Where the willows droop over the door
> Saying 'There Mary died once a gay village bride
> By the winds that bled 'cross the wild m-o-o-o-r.' "

With Emily holding onto the last note longest, loudest and off-key, so that the song broke up with laughter.

The evening was over, but Tom Bostwick lingered protectingly in the corner a moment with the object of his regard as though the winds blowing over the wild moor might have had their effect on the rosy cheeks and crow-wing hair of Sabina.

Jeremiah told Wayne he might as well stay all night— plenty of room up there in the loft with Phineas and Henry. But Wayne said he would go back to his wagon-box, be there to get a good early start in the morning.

"Any time you see a storm comin' up, though, get right over here to be under shelter. Now, you mind." This from Sarah, the mother, who was evidently not altogether the exasperated nagger she appeared to be.

When he left they all trooped out to see him off. Suzanne ran ahead to the small gate in the stake-and-rider fence with a lighted candle, cupping her hand over the little flame to protect it.

"Look," she called from her perch on the topmost rail, and pointed to the bright north star, "somebody else is holding up a light for you to see by."

The glamour of the friendly evening and the musical outpouring still hung over Wayne when he rode Blackbird home across the prairie, Belle trotting along by his side, and somebody holding up the bright north star to guide him.

All the way his voice rolled out in mellow cadence through the silence of the summer night.

> "... *That my vows were false and my old love cold.*
> *That my truant heart held another dear*
> *Forgetting the vows that were whispered here ...*"

He cared for the horses, took off his boots, crawled into the wagon, and pulled the robe over him. The warmth of the Martin friendliness enveloped him like the warmth of the buffalo blanket.

What a raft of girls! He wondered if he could ever get them all straightened in his mind. This would be a good time to try. He slipped his hands under his head as he lay with his face turned to the stars in the dark prairie sky.

Remember them now as they stood in a row and see if you can name them.

Sabina. The black-haired rosy-cheeked one with the snapping dark eyes who stood at the head of the line, so she's the oldest. Mr. Tom Bostwick is in love with her.

Emily. The carrot red-haired one, freckled, blue-eyed, taller and slimmer than Sabina. Sang lustily off-key. Helped her mother most with the dinner. Made lots of droll remarks.

Jeanie. Honey-colored hair with dark eyes that made an attractive contrast. Her nose turned up a bit. Made her look sort of saucy. One of the jolliest.

Phoebe Lou. Molasses-colored hair with greenish-blue eyes. A kind of a dimple by her mouth when she laughs. Something of a tease.

Melinda. Jet-black hair like Sabina, but taller and thinner. A wide red mouth. Kind of a tomboy.

Celia. The yellow-haired one with the fairest complexion and finest features. Maybe the prettiest.

Suzanne. The youngest, with reddish-brown hair and big gray-blue eyes that shone ...

There, I did better than I expected ... I'm dropping off to sleep ... under the stars ... on the lonely prairie ... where was I? Oh, yes, I remember ...

Suzanne, with gray-blue eyes that shone ... like the stars ... on the lonely prairie. ...

CHAPTER 6

THE Martins were up at daybreak. There was much work to be done before Jeremiah and the boys could leave to assist the new Wayne Lockwood with his cabin. Phineas had ridden Queen to the neighbors' on the river road the afternoon before—to the Burrills', the two Akin families' and the Mansons'—to tell them about helping Wayne. This early summer morning Sarah was giving her orders with all the snap and brevity of an army general. Some of the girls were helping with the outdoor chores and some with the housework. Later one was to take lunch to the men up on the north prairie.

"Celia will get to, you see." Melinda was darkly foreboding in her prediction to Suzanne.

"I can ride lots better than she can and carry the things at the same time," Suzanna admitted modestly.

"Melinda always works it some way to get off the place," Celia in turn confided to Suzanne—those two, Celia and Melinda, counting that day lost whose low descending sun found either one of them had failed to "get ahead" of the other.

Breakfast was the inevitable noisy meal. Hot corn cakes and side pork dipped in egg batter and dropped into deep fat constituted the bill of fare. Sarah, the mother, fried the pork and Emily constantly and deftly flopped the cakes on their great iron griddle that extended the width of the stove.

"Why don't you let one of the girls do that meat, Ma?" Jeremiah was in one of his rare moods of polite solicitude over his wife's welfare as she stood, red-faced and perspiring, over the hot stove.

But Sarah enjoyed her martyrdom. "It takes watching. You can't be gabbing and then get a good do on it."

There was, indeed, plenty of "gabbing." Because Wayne Lockwood had been there the night before, he was the general topic of conversation this morning.

Phineas began it as, a late arrival, he straddled one of the sawed-off hickory logs. Traces of his recent washing at the tin basin outside the kitchen door lingered on his sandy hair and side-whiskers. "Well, which one of you is going to set your cap for him?"

"Yes, girls." Their father was not averse to teasing his comely daughters, either—"plaguing them," they called it. "Sabina might's well count herself out of the general contest, with Mr. Tom Bostwick comin' out from the Falls every excuse he gets."

Sabina tossed her crow-wing head. "Mr. Tom Bostwick! Why, I wouldn't marry him if he was the last man in the county." This speech was not unexpected, girls being all of a pattern in that particular. Neither Sabina Martin out here in the newly settled Red Cedar Valley nor her cousins back in that growing city of thirty thousand souls, Chicago, would admit she could so much as tolerate the sight of a man until her wedding invitations were practically on their way to potential guests.

"Emily, you better cabbage onto him quick. You're second in line after Sabina and it looks like she's taken."

"Pooh! I'm older'n him," Emily emitted from the region of the hot griddle.

"That don't hurt. Mrs. Burrill is older than Mr. Burrill."

There were ceaseless remarks on all sides, containing no noticeable lack of frankness.

"Jeanie will want to add his scalp to her belt alongside of George Wormsby and Sam Phillips."

"Celia's begun eyes at him a'ready. I could see her shake her hair and look up admiring at him." Melinda's day for getting ahead of Celia was well on the way.

"Hush that!" from Sarah, the mother. "Celia's too young for that."

"But with big-lady notions."

Celia tossed her yellow head. "I'd rather have big lady notions than tomboy ones."

"If you'd mind your own business . . ."

"Come now . . . I'll thump you girls," Jeremiah threatened.

"Phoebe Lou and Jeanie will probably catch him together and then draw straws for him."

Talk! Talk! Talk! It flew back and forth over countless corn cakes and fried side pork, like that sound of the grackles outside in the trees at the edge of the timber, as unchecked and as pointless.

In an unusual cessation of this flow of light words bandied back and forth, Suzanne raised her gray-blue eyes from their serious attention to her plate.

"I saw him first," she said quietly.

They all shouted with typical Martin hilarity, for long moments could not get over the joke of it—that Suzanne had said this funny thing. All the rest of the meal, one had only to look at Suzanne or to say in mimicking tone, "I saw him first," to start the whole table off into gales of laughter, with Jeremiah threatening to thump them even while he roared with them.

Sarah was provoked, hushed them and scolded about teasing such a young girl, but the laughter swept up and around her like prairie wind which there was no stopping. Life was real and life was earnest to Sarah Martin; most decidedly fun was not its goal, and all the years of her living she could never account for that gay foolish laughter of her offspring.

Breakfast was over and the long day of work under way. After all, it was Suzanne who was sent up on the prairie. It never occurred to any one to question Ma's decision when she said Suzanne was to go and carry the big basket in front of her and mind her business when she rode along or there'd be pork sausage and corn-bread a-plenty a-feedin' of the gophers.

So Suzanne in her gray print dress that ballooned out, sometimes showing her calico pantalets, mounted Jupiter, took the covered basket gingerly in front of her, and galloped away up north on the prairie where there was a faint trail marked in the grass by broken blossoms of blue lupine or wild mustard from her father's wide-rimmed wagon wheels and the hoof prints of Wayne Lockwood's horses.

Arrived there she found eight men at work—her father and her own two brothers, those other brothers, Mr. Horace Akin and Mr. Wallace Akin, Mr. Mel Manson, Mr. Burrill, and Wayne Lockwood himself—so the cabin would be going up in short order. It was to be good-sized, too, sixteen by twenty-four, Phineas said. Some of the cabins in the Valley were only ten by twelve, or twelve by sixteen. When Suzanne was setting out the lunch on a grassy place near the little grove, she heard Mr. Burrill joking Wayne Lockwood about going back to get a bride from the east to live in the good-sized cabin.

Suzanne cocked her ears, barely stirring, so she might hear the answer and have news a-plenty to tell at home. It would be big fun to be able to tell the girls all about the eastern bride coming out here after their silly joking this morning. It would serve them right, too, for laughing so at her. Probably some of them were already setting their caps for him, and this would just knock their caps over on their ears.

But Wayne only laughed at Mr. Burrill's insinuations. "Ho-ho!" he said at once. "I've no betrothed back home, no woman on my conscience, and I'm of no mind to marry. I'm going to get a lot of land ahead and bring in some sheep before I think of that, and make money, too, I hope. No, I've no girl awaiting me at all, *any*where." He made it so emphatic that if Mr. Burrill had been versed in the plays of one William Shakespeare, he might have thought that his informant, like a certain person did protest too much. But Mr. Burrill was no Shakespearian addict, and Wayne Lockwood was merely stating his convictions as he felt he should. For how could a practical and hardworking young settler be saying that foolish thing which was in his heart, that somewhere there waited for him a beautiful lady?

Suzanne looked at him shyly out of the corners of her big eyes. She thought she had never seen so good-looking a young man. Something made you like just everything about him, the way his wavy light hair went back from his forehead, his direct-looking blue eyes, the way he held his head, the way his mouth pulled up at the corners when he smiled, that light-footed way of his walking. Even his strong brown hands pleased her. Well, if he didn't have a betrothed back east, maybe after all one of the girls *could* get him. She would think it all out on the way home.

That was a play Suzanne had of her very own which no one of the family knew anything about. She had a secret gift whereby she could live in either one of two worlds, just as she chose, and she scarcely knew which one she liked better. It was no trouble at all to change from one to the other, as easy, almost, as opening the wooden door between the main room and the lean-to. There was the real world in which you worked, played games with Celia, built a store by the log stable, ate fried prairie-chicken and wild strawberries, went to school in the new log school-house, made corn-cob dolls, rode Jupiter over the prairies, went down the trail to meet Pa or Henry when they came from Dubuque with a load of merchandise—oh, a hundred nice things which you could see and touch and really do. But the other—that was a lovely world, too, and no one knew about that one and no one could enter it but herself. She went into it whenever she chose. All you had to do was to open the door . . . and there you were. She had tried once to tell Celia about it, would have liked to have Celia live in it sometimes with her. Celia was only a year older than she was, but even though they were so close in age and slept together, Celia could not seem to understand. "What do you mean that you know people who don't really live? Ghosts?" she had asked. "Ma says lots of folks think ghosts come back to earth . . . and she herself has had lots of premernitions . . ."

"No . . . oh, no, Celia. They just *seem* alive. They're handsome people and they move around in my mind. I can see them as plain as day and can make them do anything I want to."

"You need sassafras. I'm going to tell Ma."

"Oh, don't, Celia. Ma wouldn't understand either." Yes, of all people she knew Ma would be the least likely to understand. Ma's world was so definitely one of corn-bread, soap, and carpet rags.

On the way back home, relieved of her basket, she walked Jupiter and gave herself the pleasure of changing worlds. Besides, there was no use getting home too soon with candles being dipped.

Now she had a new person to inhabit this country which no one entered but herself—Wayne Lockwood. This was the first time a real person had ever been admitted, the only time that any one of flesh and blood was nice enough and handsome enough to mingle with all those other people who lived in her fancy.

It was going to be almost impossible to take any of her sisters into that imaginary place, not one being beautiful or good enough to fit into it, but she would do her best to try them out, stand each one up by the side of Wayne Lockwood and see how she fared, giving them all the benefit of the doubt, as it were.

Wayne and Sabina? No, Sabina was too bossy and older than Wayne. There wasn't much use bothering with her, anyway, because Mr. Tom Bostwick was always casting sheep's eyes at her and no matter what she said now, Sabina would probably marry him.

Wayne and Emily? Emily was lots of fun and Ma always

said she was her right-hand man, but she wasn't the one at all with her red hair and freckles.

Wayne and Jeanie? Jeanie was prettier than Emily and men and boys liked her when she rolled her eyes around as though she knew something they didn't know. She had two beaus now and she admired to have them fight over her. But whoever liked Wayne Lockwood must never like any one else.

Wayne and Phoebe Lou? No. Phoebe Lou teased people too much and made jokes about every one. And a girl who liked Wayne must like him more seriously than Phoebe Lou could ever like any one.

Wayne and Melinda? Ma wouldn't let Melinda go yet with a beau. Besides she acted just like a boy dressed up in girls' clothes and whoever mated with Wayne Lockwood must not be tomboyish.

Wayne and Celia? Celia wouldn't be ready for a beau for a while either. Folks over at the settlement said Celia was pretty. But for some unexplainable reason she felt especially strong against Celia having him.

Oh, well, it looked as though there could be no match with any of the Martin girls after all. It would just have to be some strange lady like those that moved around in her play—a pretty lady with a silk dress and a carriage parasol. She could see her now looking something like the beautiful Miss Tyndal in the *1847 Parlor Annual*, sort of bursting out of the top of her tight basque and holding a lace handkerchief and a nose-gay. Or maybe the Grecian Exile with her hands tucked under her chin and her eyes as big as saucers. She could see her sitting in a carriage, and Wayne Lockwood, so tall and handsome, coming up to talk to her. He would reach out to take the parasol and . . .

"Su—*zanne!*" Phoebe Lou's voice hallooed lustily across the intervening space of the prairie with emphatic syllables. "We've found . . . the first . . . ripe straw . . . ber . . . *rees* . . . You . . . have . . . to . . . pick."

As easily and as speedily as one slams a door, Suzanne abandoned her magic country and its people, left Wayne Lockwood suspended in mid-air reaching for a parasol he was never to possess, slapped the reins on the surprised and indignant Jupiter, and flew along over the trail of broken grasses into the world of candle-dipping and berry-picking.

CHAPTER 7

THE cabin was finished, thanks to the practical neighborliness of the settlers, and for the first full day this eighth of July, 1854, young Wayne Lockwood was alone on his place. With youthful energy he put in every moment of his time. So much was there to be done that he could scarcely hold himself steadily at one task for wanting to break off and start another. There was wood enough for countless fires from the trimming of the house logs so that was one piece of work which need not take his time. But a hundred other things should be done, one almost as important as the next. Paramount among them was to be the breaking of the land. Then, too, he must prepare shelter for the sheep he was going to bring in soon. This one day, however, he devoted to getting his cabin livable.

For his bed he set up a single maple-tree trunk, slender and strong, fastened straight branches from this supporting post to the cabin wall, and laced an intricate crisscrossing of rope from one side to the other. Then he brought from the wagon the bedtick his mother had made for him. Something in the blue and white cloth, the familiarity of the striped pattern, and the neatness of its small stitches, gave him a momentary twinge of homesickness so that he must work the harder to lose the memory of the look on his mother's face as she said good-by to him. He must write to her. This very night after it was too dark to work longer.

With his scythe he mowed some prairie grass, letting it lie in the sun to dry so that he might fill the bedtick, thinking that when he harvested his first oats he would refill it with good oat straw.

All day he worked at his homely tasks, eagerly, almost gaily, because this was his own land and his own house. On the first rainy day he would start making chairs, a table, and cupboard. But for the time being, sawed-off logs would constitute his furniture. At night-time he brought water from the spring, washed the mark of the day's labor from his strong young body, and ate his supper of corn-meal mush and smoked side meat. Then near the light of a tallow dip that flickered in the night breeze which came through a half-opened window he started the letter.

MY DEAR MOTHER:

It seems very lonely here to-night and so I shall use this occasion to take my pen in hand and tell you all that I have so far accomplished . . .

He broke off, head up, to listen. From across the prairie he could hear the sound of thudding hoofs, wagon wheels, tinkling laughter, so that his heart bounded in swift response to the fact that humans were coming near.

He was standing in the doorway when they drove up singing at the top of girlish voices: "The Martins are coming, oh, ho, oh, ho!"

Appropriating the song of the Campbell clan they had substituted the words of their own:

"The great Jeremiah, he goes before.
He makes his singing loudly roar
Wi' sound of trumpet, pipe, and drum,
The Martins are coming, oh, ho! oh, ho!

"The Martins are bringing their supper so,
Their loyal faith and truth to show
Wi' bonnets a' rattlin' in the wind
The Martins are coming, oh, ho! oh, ho!"

They broke into hilarious laughter on the last shouted note, so that Wayne was laughing excitedly with them, thinking that to be young on the Iowa prairie in this year of 1854 made life zestful.

Yes, the Martins were coming, were already here in full force. On the seat of the lumber wagon sat Henry driving, with one of the girls beside him. That would be—Wayne peered into the darkening prairie twilight—Phoebe Lou? No, Melinda.

Suddenly he remembered, and smiled at recalling that it

was Melinda who always wanted to gad about, whom the others had accused of sitting in the wagon when any of the men folks were going away. Back of the spring seat was a makeshift one of a wide board with three girls on it, and still farther back were two girls in chairs, one swaying back and forth energetically in a rocker. All had light shawls around their shoulders and bonnets tied under their chins. Six girls. One then was missing, but which one?

And then Phineas and Suzanne rode up on horses, Suzanne's bonnet back on her shoulders, her hair escaping from its net.

Behind the cavalcade came Jeremiah and Sarah in the buckboard, Sarah in a black dress, black shawl, and black bonnet with Phineas' fiddle in its gray calico bag across her lap. She was forty-eight years old and had worn black outside her home for fifteen years. There had been room in the wagon for the two but it was wiser to bring all the horses. The Indians were not dangerous, no one was afraid of them; the Musquakies, Pottawatomies and Winnebagoes, the tribes which came along the river here or camped up at Turkey Foot Forks were peaceful. Only the Sioux farther up in the northern counties were the bad ones. But there were always some who would annoy the settlers with their peeking, prying, and stealing. A horse or two left at home could be the biggest sort of temptation, but, as Jeremiah said, "By granny, not even an Injun would try to steal a dumb ox."

As Wayne stood in the doorway, a little excited over his first company and no longer lonely, he could hear other wagons trekking across the prairie. The Burrills proved to be in one and the Horace Akin and Wallace Akin families in others, the Mel Mansons and Mrs. Manson's young brother, Ed Armitage, in another. Wayne was to find out that all of these people like himself were of sturdy old American stock, from New England, York State, or Pennsylvania. A few years later the Danish and German people were to come, thrifty folk who helped to make the Valley a thriving center of agriculture and industry, but for the most part these first comers were of such as the Martins whose families had been in this country long before the Revolution.

This was the first Wayne had seen of the women folks of the river road, other than the Martins. He saw now that the short dumpy Mrs. Wallace Akin bore a resemblance to the pictures of Victoria, the thirty-five-year-old queen, with her round face and thick-lidded eyes. She had three children, and

Mrs. Horace Akin, younger and delicate-looking, had a small lisping boy and a baby. Mrs. Burrill was tall, long-boned, with a slim red neck and prominent Adam's apple, so that she gave the appearance of a turkey gobbler lacking only the wattles. Her daughter, Evangeline, appeared to be cut from the same pattern, holding her small head high on its slender neck. If dressed in trousers both of their spare figures would have passed for men's. Mrs. Manson, Ed Armitage's sister, was the youngest of the wives, a bride of a few months, with round black button eyes and a little buttonhole mouth.

All these crowded now into the new cabin with their baskets containing the party refreshments and donations toward Wayne's housekeeping. The Martins had brought some butter and lard and a stone crock of fresh strawberry jam. The two families of Akins had two live hens and a rooster for him, and a sack of new potatoes. The Mansons had only some corn-meal which they offered with apologies but which Wayne sensed had been a generous gift. The Burrills had brought freshly made hard soap of a pale yellow shade. Phoebe Lou whispered to Emily that Mrs. Burrill's soap was so much better than her cooking that she'd rather eat it any day than her cakes and pies, which remark passed on down through the group of girls, so that they were all suppressing runaway laughter as they put their bonnets on Wayne's bed.

The little cabin was filled with them—twenty-six adults and children besides the Akin baby at the back side of the bed with a rolled quilt in front to keep him from sliding off, getting mixed with the head-gear, or being unceremoniously sat upon. Tom Bostwick, and two other young men, Sam Phillips and George Wormsby, all arriving on horseback at various times, added to the crowd packed into the sixteen by twenty-four space.

"You will be lonely and friendless out there," Wayne's mother had argued.

The eating came first, Wayne being the only one who had partaken of supper, but now that there were others here and better things to eat, his appetite appeared to be as good as that of the famished company.

They brought in wagon seats and chairs, piecing out with sawed-off logs, while the children sat on the floor.

After supper there were games, "King William was King James's son," "Clap Hands," and "Miller Boy." Then there were some dances, with Jeremiah at the jews'-harp, Phineas doing the heavy work with the fiddle on "Old Dan Tucker" and Horace Akin calling, "Salute your pardners . . . join hands and circle to the left . . . first lady swir out and second lady in . . . then join hands and circle ag'in . . ." And when there was the short lull of a quiet moment, Phoebe Lou, grinning mischievously, said, "I know . . . let's play the game 'I saw him first' and Suzanne can be '*It*.' " Which set the Martin girls off into gales of laughter, so that Suzanne's face turned crimson, Sarah said to stop their foolishness, and Jeremiah threatened to thump the next one who plagued Suzanne.

Emily, to tide over Suzanne's discomfiture and the intermittent laughter at it, suggested settling down to a good sing, and began it herself by starting off a tuneless version of "Bonnie Charlie's now awa' " pitched impossibly high, so that it ended in laughter and a fresh start with a more reasonable attack.

> *"Bonnie Charlie's now awa'*
> *Safely o'er the friendly main . . ."*

Their voices rose lustily, Sabina's true and strong, Suzanne's sweet and clear, Tom Bostwick's thin and high, Wayne's rolling out with resonant melody, Emily's off-key, Jeanie's a little indifferent because she was turning her brown eyes first toward Sam Phillips and then George Wormsby, getting a good deal of fun out of their surreptitious glaring at each other.

> *"Mony a heart will break in twa . . ."*

The candles on the shelf above the fireplace flamed up wildly in the wind, for in the deep interest of the singing, no one had heard the horseman coming or noticed the first creaking of the door which was flung open so suddenly as to knock Celia against the wall.

A man stood on the threshold, wild-eyed, breathing hoarsely. He flung it at them like a ball of burning pitch. "The Indians are coming!"

The song broke off as suddenly and definitely as a brittle plum branch snapping in the wind. Every one stared at the messenger.

It was not believable that such an evil thing could tear its way into the midst of all this friendliness. No one moved for part of a split second. The news hung there in stillness like the silence of the prairie after a crashing report of thunder has ceased.

It was Jeremiah who spoke and the steadiness of his voice brought back their reassurance. "Aw, hell," he said scornfully, "we've heard that yarn before."

"It's true this time." The messenger's voice rose in a frightened crescendo. "A man run his horse all the way down from the Big Woods. They're on the rampage above there . . . startin' with Clear Lake . . . down through Clarksville . . . they killed all the Clear Lake settlers . . . They're pretty near to Janesville . . . hundreds of 'em . . . war-paint on . . . killin' and burnin' everything as they come. All the whites are comin' down the Cedar."

He was gone on into the night to spread the alarm. They could hear the thud of his horse's hoofs on the prairie to the east.

Wayne felt his heart beating wildly in that moment of awed silence which followed, realized he was standing motionless and numb when he should have been doing something. Queerly the thought went through him that the folks at home had warned him against this very danger. "A peaceful prairie country," he had called it. "I was wrong and they were right," he thought, staring at the assemblage, only a moment before noisy with song and laughter. There was no song now and no laughter. Bonnie Charlie was never to get across the friendly main.

Not a half minute had gone by, but it was like an hour with that silence, concentrated, frozen, in which they were all mummified figures dug from some ancient tomb.

The younger Mrs. Akin had snatched up her baby, pressing it tightly to her breast. The men were standing frowning, incredulous-looking, the women and girls white-faced, all merriment gone and joking forgot. The candles back of the gray-blue of Suzanne's eyes had been snuffed out, leaving nothing but darkness.

For just that moment the silence and fear were merged and timeless as though some gigantic force held them all in its relentless grasp.

And then Sarah Martin, reaching for her black bonnet, broke the spell. "Let's get on home," she said dryly. "No old Injun is goin' to stick his dirty thumb into my fresh strawberry jam."

CHAPTER 8

WAYNE, hitching his horses hurriedly to the new wagon, experienced a definite feeling of anxiety over his move out here, the first uneasy questioning of its wisdom. Everything had appeared so auspicious, and now this. What would the night bring forth? An attack by the redskins? A firing of the cabins? Death to any of this group?

Boyishly he thought of the unwritten letter to his mother. If anything happened to him. . . ! He wished it had been finished and sent. He looked toward his newly completed cabin and, thinking of all the work he and these new friends had put on it in the last few days, lost his fright in a sudden anger and felt he could kill a dozen Indians single-handed.

The attitude of Jeremiah Martin and his sons steadied his jumping nerves. If they were frightened they were concealing it admirably as they loaded the pails and baskets into the wagon-boxes.

"By granny, I don't believe it, yet. Somebody's always hollerin' about 'em," Jeremiah was saying. "For two years now we've heard of hairbreadth escapes from bloodthirsty Injuns; homes burned north and west of here, stock drove off and I don't know what all. It always turns out to be some Sioux kicked a Winnebago in the seat of his britches, and yet by the time it gets to us it's another Injun raid."

Yet Wayne noticed that he made Suzanne get into the wagon with the other girls and had Emily drive the team, while Henry, Phineas, and Tom Bostwick rode their horses at the wagon's side. They made quite a cavalcade—all the Martins, the Burrills, the two families of Akins, the Mansons, Ed Armitage, Sam Phillips, George Wormsby, Tom Bostwick, and Wayne.

Some of the women were "taking on" about supplies and

keepsakes left at home, but there was no talk of any one going out of his way to retrieve them. By common consent all were sticking together and bound for the Martin house, the largest and strongest of all those belonging to settlers. Mrs. Burrill, in particular, was moaning, wringing her hands, and cursing the day she had ever let Burrill talk her into coming out to this God-forsaken country. Ed Armitage, riding furiously up and down the length of the cavalcade, was not adding anything to the pleasure of the evening's situation by intimating to each wagonload that out of all the ways to die, to be killed by a damn Injun was the worst. But the Martin girls were quiet, and Wayne, driving just ahead of them, knew now that for a Martin girl to be speechless was either to be asleep or laboring under a very strong emotion. Only once had they broken the silence. Melinda had said, "Oh, I'm not going to worry. If they come, Pa'll thump 'em." And they had all given way to low nervous laughter.

There was something ominous about that long snaky caravan wending its way across the prairie there toward the river trail. The silence of the people who had been so filled with song and jokes and laughter a short time before was louder and more affecting than ever noise had been. The creak of wagon wheels, the faint clank of harness, the swish of horses' hoofs through the deep prairie growth, the odor of the crushed grasses under the night dew, the clammy mist rising from the bottom of swales, the little new moon caught by a dark rift of cloud—it was like a steel engraving etched on the mind with such strong strokes of fear that one knew it could never be erased in a lifetime.

If the Indians came at all it would be from the north or west, down the Cedar or Shell Rock, so more than one pair of eyes were constantly straining in that direction. When at last the wagons turned into the Martin inclosure behind the stake-and-rider fence, the sturdy log house loomed up as a haven.

Sarah and Emily hurried ahead at once into the main room, lighting a candle or two until the others could see to pick their way in. Already the thirty there made something of a crowd. But in two hours' time twenty-one others from the north prairie had arrived by wagon and on horseback, turning instinctively to Jeremiah Martin, partly on account of the size of his cabin and partly because he was a natural leader and counselor.

They filled the three downstairs rooms, men, women, children, and their belongings. Those who had come straight from their own houses brought freshly baked loaves of bread, their best shawls, sacks of herbs, hens, feather-beds, Bibles, scrap-books, dishes of jam, wall pictures, knives and forks, bags of dried corn, precious keepsakes from ''back home.'' Almost all had live stock tied to the ends of the wagons. Children clutched treasured corn-cob dolls or spool carts. A few men said they had buried some of their possessions; one had hurriedly dug a trench for his grindstone.

There was a strange quietness about so large a crowd gathered in such close quarters. The men talked together in knots, planning what would be best to do under given circumstances, keeping their voices low as they discussed plans, not to put too much fear into the minds of the women folks. They looked over the guns and hurriedly made wooden bolts for the lean-to doors which had never possessed any.

All this time, Jeremiah and the others of steady nature belittled the danger, scoffed at any Injuns around there having the guts to harm them. ''Any I've ever met up with hadn't no aim to molest.'' He and Henry and Phineas, Wayne Lockwood, Mr. Burrill, the Akin men, and Ed Armitage stayed out around the log stables for a time and in angles of the stake-and-rider fence, listening to the prairie sounds, watching for any potential sign of trouble. Among other emergency plans, they adopted a password so that any man riding off the premises and coming back in the dark might make himself known to the others.

About one o'clock Ed Armitage, excitable and impulsive, hearing a noise near the timber, shakingly challenged the marauder, and when he thought the answer was the guttural grunting of an Indian, blazed away at him. He reported it excitedly to the other men who looked over the ground cautiously but saw nothing more suspicious.

Sarah made Mrs. Horace Akin lie down with her babies on Celia's and Suzanne's bed behind the calico curtain. A few other women with their small children lay down on the floor of the main room on various makeshift pallets. By two o'clock Sarah told Celia and Suzanne to go on up the ladder to a bed there, but at their protest that they would be more afraid up in the loft than down here where folks were, she told them to get into her own bed then, but with their clothes on. Suzanne on the outside lay there tense with fright, knowing she could never shut an eye, but turning to whisper to Celia she found her sound asleep with her regular nightly layer of sweet cream on her face as though not even an Injun could come between her and her good complexion.

Suzanne kept thinking, I'll never go away from the house again as long as I live. No one can ever get me to go down near the slough. When I think of the times I've been off down there by the prairie-chicken circle, I don't see how I ever went. I never will again.

It was queer to be here in her mother's bed, bigger and softer than her own. She hadn't been in it since the last time she had the ague. There was a joke about that. People were always saying, "Trust the Martin girls to see the funny side of it." Well, this had a funny side, too. Both times she had slept in her mother's big tester bed she had been shaking, once with the ague, and this time with fright about the Injuns.

The calico tester was drawn tight and people were stirring around right outside. Somebody was so close to her she could have touched him through the curtains.

The voices were low, almost whispering—and in a moment she knew they belonged to Sabina and Mr. Tom Bostwick. She could hear a murmured questioning sound and then Sabina must have parted the tester cautiously and looked in. She only sensed it for she had shut her eyes and was breathing heavily, so that immediately she heard Sabina say, "Yes, they're asleep." And Tom Bostwick's voice said: "And so to-night has made me know I couldn't bear to have you away from me. When I think if I was over at the Falls and you out here . . . not knowing if there's anything to this scare or not. . . . You have my whole affection, Sabina . . . my whole heart. If we both get through this night all right . . . will you . . . will you do me the honor to be my wife?"

Suzanne was trembling now with more than fright. Emotion and the fear of moving were added to her discomfiture. Her eyes stared into the darkness of the calico curtains and she felt little prickles go up and down her back. The Indians were coming and she was hearing a real love proposal, not an imagined one, right by her ear. The combination of the two exciting things made her feel dizzy and a little sick to her stomach. And now Sabina was saying, "Oh, Mr. Bostwick . . . well, Tom, then . . . I admire you, too. . . . No . . . you mustn't . . . with all these people."

Quite suddenly, with Suzanne's face hot from the excitement and secrecy of it, as plain as day she saw Tom Bostwick and Sabina step over the threshold into her magic world. When they were driving home from Wayne Lockwood's she would not have believed that she could ever think of that other world again for the fear of the Injuns coming. But here in Ma's bed she was remembering it. Nor would she have believed that plump Sabina and tall black-whiskered Tom Bostwick could ever get over into that secret country of hers. But now there they were. It was very strange and very exciting. She lay unmoving thinking it all out, not quite so fearful of the Injuns now. No matter what the Injuns did, they could never follow you into a magic country.

The next thing she knew, she could smell sausage frying and the strong odor of coffee. The Injuns hadn't come yet. She looked over at Celia still sleeping, with the cream dried on her cheeks in wrinkled patches like a map of the colonies in the atlas. She sat up and swung her legs off the high bed and peeked out between the calico curtains. The rooms were still full of people, but they were no longer scared. They were laughing and talking, and agreeing that if the Indians hadn't come by now, it was all a false alarm. Horace Akin was saying that this scare was just like the others they'd had, all just started from somebody's idle talk and that bad news always went like a prairie fire. And Pa was roaring and slapping his knee and saying it was worth the loss of a pig to see Ed Armitage's face when he found he had shot an old sow instead of an Injun.

Breakfast for fifty people was a queer confused sort of meal collected from every one's supplies. Suzanne, eating her mother's sausage and corn cakes and trying politely ever and anon to bite into one of Mrs. Burrill's hard fried cakes, kept glancing out of the corner of her eyes at Tom Bostwick and Sabina around whose heads she had expected to see halos shining this morning but which were strangely missing. Only Wayne Lockwood, tall and handsome, was still a hero.

While the big crowd was eating, a Mr. Cady Bedson from Prairie Rapids rode into the yard on horseback on his way up the river road to see if there had been any depredations in the night. He told them a lot of queer things that had happened around Prairie Rapids. One man had thought some stray colts following his team were Indians and had taken his family off into the corn-field at a wild gallop and was still out there as far as anybody knew. A woman in her nightgown had wandered all night in the woods, which seemed to amuse him no end. Several families had really started for the more thickly populated country down around Cedar Rapids.

He took the center of the main room while he talked and

gave the impression of thinking that they should consider themselves honored because he was here. Suzanne, looking at him from the corners of her gray-blue eyes, saw that he was quite good-looking with his dark hair and dark mustache. But she had no desire to take him into that other world where she so easily took Wayne Lockwood. Every time she tried to put him into her imaginary country she could not make him stay there. He popped right out again. Some people belonged in that magic world and some did not, and nothing you could do about it would make them stay if they did not fit.

While he was talking and making fun of the people who had been so afraid, as though he were the only one who was not, Suzanne looked over at Wayne Lockwood. He was standing at the side of the fireplace listening to Mr. Cady Bedson's belittling of every one, and grinning as though to himself. It was a queer grin and just as sure as though he had told her in plain words, Suzanne knew that Wayne Lockwood did not like Mr. Cady Bedson.

As the days passed, more news filtered into the neighborhood about the Indian scare. The people of Janesville which lay up beyond Sturgis Falls had plowed ditches around the little settlement and made a rude stockade. Some young blades in Prairie Rapids had indulged in a noisy charivari for a newly married couple and the noise had so frightened one man who thought the Indians were massacring the people that he had thrown his most cherished possessions into his wagon, including his wife and children, and galloped away, giving the alarm as he rode. It had taken much explanation to get him to believe that he had heard a charivari instead of the noise of Indians at their scalping, and much persuasion to get him to return.

A company of volunteers had gone from Sturgis Falls clear up to where the Winnebagoes were camped and run down the source of the rumor—a white boy and an Indian had really exchanged shots, and while there was no need for all that excitement, the episode might have ended in more serious results. When the company came back they rode into town at breakneck speed, firing their guns and trying to make much of the affair, one man riding his steed into the Carter House and around the stove in high spirits, largely because of the "spirits" he had acquired on the trip.

Jeremiah Martin, sitting at the head of the long table, his knife and fork held perpendicularly from the bases of his two big fists, made much of the episode: "There'll always be hot-headed people in this country as long as she exists. And the level-headed folks might as well get used to havin' to clean up the messes that the fly-off-the-handles make. A hundred years from now there won't like as not be any Injun scares . . . maybe no Injuns even . . . a body can't tell. But they'll be somethin' else. Hot-heads will be kickin' up a lot of dust of some kind or other and level-heads'll be doin' their best to settle it. You can just mark my word and see if I ain't right."

"But how can we mark your word, Pa, and see if you're right that many years from now?" Suzanne asked.

"By granny!" He was thoughtful. "I *will* be deader'n a doornail, won't I? Funny, how you just can't believe that you won't live always and see how the new state and the country and everything pulls through. Biggest affirmative argument I know in favor of 'If a man die, shall he live again?' is just the way you feel inside you that nothin' can stop you from livin' on. Why, did you children ever stop to think you can't do away completely with anything? That fiddle of Phineas' was once a tree—wind makin' music in the top of it. Cut down that there maple tree outside the lean-to door, burn the trunk to ashes, and Ma'll up and leach the ashs for lye. Scatter the leaves and they'll make winter mulchin'. Seeds that have been shook off will come up. No, sir, if you can't kill that old maple you ain't goin' to be able to kill *me*. I'll be in somethin' a hundred years from now, even if it's just the prairie grass or the wind in the timber or the wild geese ridin' out the storm."

Because the Indian scare had gone into nothing, Suzanne's avowal never again to go down near the slough alone went into nothing, too. And as the rumors died down gradually her temporary fright over being far from the house by herself had left entirely by a later July Sunday, so that after dinner she slipped away to her favorite haunt.

It lay to the south and west of the house, this cut in the timber containing a large slough, perhaps forty or fifty acres of greenish water, with great patches of wild rice at its edge, making it a gay summer resort for animal life—swans, wild ducks, wild geese, mud hens, muskrats, and minks. There were various species of herons, too, the bittern which the Burrills called a "stake-driver" and the Martins called the "pump bird."

Occasionally on a clear day when Suzanne had heard hoarse throaty sounds above her, she had distinguished cranes up in the blue sky, and watched them circle in a queer flight as they rose higher and higher, making a gigantic hoop-skirt out of their flying.

It had given her a queer longing to do it, too—the impossible to which humans would never attain—to rise up in the air and look down on all the Red Cedar Valley. Sometimes these sandhill cranes with their long, lean necks and long, thin legs would land a little totteringly in the grassy clearing near-by like old men grown uncertain of their movements. Once Suzanne had seen one run all the way across the clearing, its outstretched head and slim body looking so funny on those thin legs, as though it were running stiffly on stilts, that she had rolled in the grass to laugh and think that no wonder Pa was always telling about some one running like a sandhill crane. And once in the springtime she had glimpsed a big flock of them stepping about foolishly, acting like the Indians at their dance up at Turkey Foot Forks and had told about it at the table. Everybody had laughed at her, but Pa had said to answer a little girl right, that the cranes were courting and mating, and he'd thump anybody making fun of her.

Close to the slough was a circular open patch of ground where the prairie-chickens assembled, leaving always a watcher or two at the outer edge of the sociable circle to give the alarm if the enemy approached. The booming notes of the cocks could be heard up at the house and far across the prairie.

All day long redwing black birds, kingfishers, snipes, kill-deer, bobolinks, chewinks, brown thrushes, grackles, and dickcissels came and went through the green undergrowth by the brackish water. Prairie larks flew out of the grass with gay abandon, and dragon-flies, the gauzy-winged snake-feeder, darted over the water on ceaseless hurrying errands. From the near-by timber phoebes and mourning-doves called, and wood-peckers knocked all day on maple and walnut doors through which they were never admitted. The ducks and geese would go away on some unknown foraging trip in the daytime but at sundown they would come flocking back to the slough to spend the night on the water, and a little later hawks would dip low with their hollow *boom*.

In the marshy grass a queer orange-colored tiger-lily bloomed, from whose stamens one could get a reddish-brown powder to color one's cheeks, and back from the marsh grass grew the bouncing-Bets and the wild sweet-williams, daisies and soap-wort. Down deep in the damp timber for long months one could find Dutchman's-breeches, violets, columbine, shooting-stars, anemones, wild crab-apple blossoms, the heavily scented waxen Mayflower, and the very loveliest flower of all, the blue-bells. The color of a bed of bluebells in an open patch in the timber was so beautiful it hurt you.

That was another thing Celia never could understand. "Of course, it's pretty," she would say, "but it doesn't *hurt* you. You're touched in the head."

But Suzanne knew better. It *was* true, no matter what Celia said—somewhere down in your throat their beauty hurt you.

This afternoon was hot. But, then, it had been that way all summer—Pa said the hottest of the three since they came. The folks were always talking about the weather, this was the hottest summer or the rainiest fall or the coldest winter or the worst snow-storm. The weather was like some one human, but neither a man nor a woman, just "it." "*It* may turn off cooler." "*It* will be better for threshing." This afternoon she was tired of the folks' talk, with the Mansons and the Akins all sitting around the tree-trunk steps and discussing the weather, making guesses as to what day Henry would get home from his trip to Dubuque, saying that Prairie Rapids was being platted and was already having the gall to want the court records over there, that the surveying for a railroad out of Davenport on the Mississippi was under way, that there was even talk of some day one west of Dubuque out here along the old trail, and Pa saying his everlasting: "A shame Ioway hasn't no railroads yet—pesky shame! Just you wait till she gets railroads." That was another funny thing—the weather was "it" but the state was "she."

Just as Pa had started on the Whigs . . . . that he hated to go back on his own party, "but by granny, our Whig leadership have showed they can't grapple with modern problems . . . now take this convention up at Jackson, Michigan . . ." she had run off down here by herself in the prairie-chicken circle near the slough.

There were no sounds now in the sleepy warmth of the day excepting a few plaintive mourning-doves' calls and the occasional plop of some water animal. A wild mother duck sailed lazily and noiselessly with her brood not far away. This would be a good time to call out Echo. She lived over there to the southeast, not far from the Indian council tree. If you stood in a certain open place back from the slough where the land dipped toward the river and called out "Ho-ho," she answered; and if you sang, she sang with you, but always a note behind you, never catching up. There was something pretty creepy about it, too, because of the Indian girl. Off there in that same direction, but back from the river a ways, a dead Indian girl was in a blanket up in a red cedar. She'd been there for four years, people said. It was almost as if it was the dead Indian girl who sang back. Maybe it *was*—how could you know for sure? The eeriness of the thought fascinated her so that, wanting to call out, she was yet half afraid to do so.

And then suddenly she heard movement in the bushes as of light-footed walking, and her heart stood still with fright. Her body turned cold and she shook a little in the summer heat, recalling her avowal never again to go away from the house alone. And yet here she was and twigs were crackling and bushes moving. "Give me one more chance," went through her mind. "If I get through it all right this time, I'll *never . . .*"

Then Wayne Lockwood, gun in hand, came through the underbrush and stood there, tall and stalwart and handsome.

"Well, hello, there," he was saying. "Where'd *you* come from? Are you lost?"

"Oh, no." Suzanne, relieved and happy, laughed aloud at that. "This place *belongs* to me."

She had never been one moment alone with him. The few times she had seen him the whole family had been around, as like as not plaguing her, too. For the first time she felt at ease in his presence.

"So this is your lake, is it? Then I must be trespassing. Well, Princ-*cess* Suzanne"—he swept off his cap, placed it across his breast, and bowed low in mock homage—"will you kindly allow me to cross your domain so that I can get to my castle on the other side of the Black Forest?"

Suzanne's eyes were wide with astonishment and she could not know how the playful words had lighted the candles that lay behind them. No one had ever said anything like that but her secret people. That was the way they talked. That was the way they acted. Her face grew pink with the excitement and embarrassment of it, and her voice trembled when she said shyly, "Yes, I guess I'll let you this once."

Long after he had gone on, turning around to laugh that he was walking here only by her permission, she remembered just how he looked and what he said.

It was going to be very, very easy after this to live in that magic world.

CHAPTER 9

THE general store over at Sturgis Falls had been opened by one Andrew Mullarky four years before, and for two years of that time the Martin men folks occasionally had made the long hundred-mile trip by ox team to Dubuque for the owner, taking grain to sell there and hauling back supplies, receiving credit at the store for their pay. From Dubuque the grain was hauled by other teams to Warren, Illinois, loaded on the cars for Chicago, that young city which surprisingly just now was beginning to pass Detroit in population.

Jeremiah liked to be the one to make the trip. Harder than the farm work, if by chance great storms came up while en route, still the journey was more interesting than being tied down to the fields. He was a garrulous soul and he liked an audience; he enjoyed the contacts with the merchants in Dubuque and the stopping on the way to talk with incoming settlers, the opportunity to puff up the valley of the Red Cedar in his conversation and influence new-comers to locate near Sturgis Falls. More than once his chance meeting with families on the trail, journeying westward to locate but not knowing just where, had ended in their making straight for the prairies north of the two settlements. A lone horseman usually meant some single man, who would soon marry and who was looking in the meantime for suitable holdings, or the head of a family coming on before his folks to choose and purchase their land. These Jeremiah always hailed in friendly fashion and if they sounded promising he steered them to localities near his own place. Sometimes he met men who apparently did not relish telling their prime objects in arriving in the Valley. These he always put down as the land speculators and proffered them little encouragement. Altogether, probably no one of the settlers gave so much advertising to the section by word of mouth as did talkative Jeremiah Martin.

It irked his wife, Sarah, so that she scolded a great deal about it to the girls. "You'd think Pa owned the Valley and was parcelin' it out to the rest of the world."

The girls usually stood up loyally for their father.

"Everybody likes Pa and they know his word is as good as gold, Ma," they would say. "Folks look up to him. He's kind of a big man in these parts. Even the men at the settlement know that."

"Well, you can have too much of this 'big man' notion."

But all Sarah's scolding about it was as the wind in the maples to Jeremiah. At the slightest provocation he rode Queen to Prairie Rapids or to Sturgis Falls, talked up improvements long hours in the taverns and on the wooden platform of the little store, took the tedious trips to Dubuque, returning with news of people he had met and more than likely influenced to come to this section of the Valley.

This particular time, though, it was Henry who had gone on the long journey, taking a load of wheat and expecting to bring back supplies for the Mullarky store. He had been gone nearly two weeks, and every day now the girls looked down the trail to see if they could catch sight of Red and Whitey, Baldy and Star. They had a wager about whichever one should first see them—that this girl might choose her work for the week among all the tasks, hoeing the sweet corn, baking, cooking, cleaning, berry-picking, carrying water in from the newly dug well by the east lean-to door, helping with the chores, mending, herding cattle on the prairie. Sarah had agreed to the foolishness reluctantly, scolding that it would mix things all up and her orders wouldn't be obeyed. But it made life exciting to see which one would win. They kept the spy-glass handily on the barrel-stand near the front door while Sarah complained that the work lagged from some one of them having an eye glued to it every minute of the day.

Even then it turned out that Celia and Suzanne saw them simultaneously without the aid of the glass, so there was no chance of a decision between the two. Far down the grassy trail they had seen the wagon, the huge heads of the oxen swaying and the brass knobs of their horns gleaming in the slanting afternoon sun.

"Henry's coming," they shouted, and the call was relayed from yard to house, to loft, to garden and field.

It was such a long time that the oxen's slow old legs were taking to get along the trail that the two girls ran a half-mile to meet the merchandise wagon. In fact, so slow were the clumsy old creatures that they did not even have to be stopped to allow the girls to clamber on the back of the wagon and hang there, laughing breathlessly, swinging their legs precariously above the lush grass.

Henry was, as Wayne Lockwood had noted, a silent serious fellow. Twenty-five years old this summer, he had never looked at a girl, just worked along steadily as though there were nothing in the world but the task in hand. All that he said now, plodding by the side of the oxen, was "Hello, young 'uns," and "Anything new at home?" He had been gone only thirteen days. With the best of time it took five or six days to go each way, and another one to unload the grain and collect the merchandise for Mullarky's store. Often it took many more. There were spongy swamplike places on the trail, a bad one near Delhi, creeks to cross with a great deal of creaking of the wagon wheels, the Wapsipinicon to ford, and if there chanced to be black Iowa mud, the oxen could not make more than ten or twelve miles a day. Often some unusually bad place would find a dozen outfits bunched together, pulling each other out.

Yes, there had been a lot of things happen. Both girls answered at once, in Martin fashion, Henry to gather from the chattered duet the remnants of news. Mr. Miller and Mr. Hosford were going to start a bank in Prairie Rapids in one corner of the general store. Pa said they were talking of platting the part of the settlement that was on the east side of the river, too, and that to save his neck he couldn't see why a town couldn't stay all on one side of the river or the other and folks not always have to wade, swim, or ferry between the two sides.

Then there was the joke about the drinking over at Sturgis Falls, each girl breaking in on the other to tell Henry this funny thing. One night ten days ago four men got drunk over in Sturgis Falls and when they sobered up the town official had set them to grubbing stumps out of Main Street. Now they say that if you get drunk and get out early in the morning and of your own accord go to work on the Main Street stumps, you don't even get hauled up before the town officer—and Tom Bostwick says you can hear axes going early most any morning. There was a joke on Mr. Mel Manson, too. That buckwheat he'd planted up on the prairie north of him, after he'd sent Ed Armitage to break the sod, would be the last up there he'd ever plant, for the land was bought a'ready and he'd once said it would never be sold, that he could always depend on it being public. Pa said last night that a'ready about a tenth of the land in the county was taken.

They gave their news a mannish slant, knowing that Henry cared nothing about their new bead rings or the finding of the biggest grape-vine swing they had ever run across down in the timber.

And then it was Henry's turn. He said in Dubuque they'd asked him all about the six thousand Injuns that had come rampaging down the Valley from Clear Lake way, killing and scalping all the settlers.

They all had a good old laugh at that, with Henry saying that bad news always got worse the farther away from home it got, and he guessed good news got belittled. After that he lapsed into silence until they noticed that his bearded lips were drawing down in the peculiar way they always did when he was pleased about something.

"What is it, Henry? Your nose is curling down, so we know you've got something else to tell us."

Yes, Henry admitted knowing two big pieces of news which he hadn't told, but for that matter didn't know when he could ever make up his mind which one to tell first, teasing them in that fashion. But by noisy pestering they got it out of him. One was that Aunt Harriet in Chicago had sent THE BOX. Her brother-in-law, the grain-buyer, had brought it to Dubuque so that whoever came with grain from the Valley was to haul it out to the girls. And here it was in the wagon. They had scarcely recovered from the excitement of that one before the next crowded right on its heels.

Henry said there in the wagon, all covered up with bolts of cloth and packed in barrels of crackers and sugar and molasses, was the bell for the tower of the new frame schoolhouse on the banks of Cat-tail Pond over at Sturgis Falls. And what did they think of that? It had been waiting in Dubuque for some one to get it for weeks—bought with that money raised by the ladies at a festivity back on Washington's Birthday and sent out from a Mr. Meneeley's at Watervliet, New York. It had been shipped by train to Buffalo, around the lakes to Chicago, by train to Warren, Illinois, by stage to Dubuque, by ferry across the Mississippi, and "the rest of the way by the old Martin oxen, by gum!" Which sent the girls into peals of laughter. Henry was as full of fun as anybody when he was away from the rest of the family.

"And you can remember to tell your grandchildren what they told me in Dubuque," he added. "You're riding along to-day with the first bell that was ever brought west of the Mississippi into the State of Iowa to be hung in a tower."

But foolishly, as young girls do, both Celia and Suzanne developed the giggles concerning the reference to the grand-children they might have, rather than thinking with awe upon any potential historical data.

They laughed long and hilariously, swinging their legs off the wagon, lying down on the merchandise to look up into the prairie sky in which puffy clouds sailed low, jumping off to pick wild ragged-robins or shaggy pink bouncing-Bets, running to catch a ride again behind the plodding oxen.

"Look, Celia . . . the clouds are big fat white geese with their wings flapping and their necks stretching out. What do they look like to you?"

"Oh, I don't know—just clouds, I guess. You and me having grandchildren!" Celia rolled, laughing, in the limited space between a molasses barrel and a plowshare.

"Imagine that time ever coming," Suzanne echoed her.

Time was such a slow old thing. The years were as slow as . . . as oxen. She half closed her eyes and looked up at the clouds again. Now they were puffy white roses quilted on a huge blue tester to cover a bed for the world; the low gray clouds against the horizon made the valance.

She felt very close to Celia to-day, and friendly. This was one of her real days. The Red Cedar Valley was the interesting world, not that imaginary country in which only beautiful people lived. In the outdoor oven Ma was baking loaves of bread from wheat cracklings Pa had had ground at the Overman mill. Indoors Emily was baking cookies with caraway seeds on top. Phoebe Lou was looking over and washing a bushel of wild plums. Pa and Phineas were getting pounds and pounds of wild honey from a hollow locust tree. Sabina, Jeanie, and Melinda had gone in to Sturgis Falls to take some of Ma's butter and see the lot Tom Bostwick was buying near the court-house square for sixty dollars. Sabina and Jeanie had planned to go together but when they went out to the buckboard they had found Melinda all fixed up in her other dress, sitting in it waiting to go, too, and saying that Ma had told her she could.

She, herself, and Celia had new bead rings. Aunt Harriet

from her nice home in Chicago had sent THE BOX. So many pleasant happenings! Suzanne knew she didn't care one bit to-day that her own folks were all plain and familiar-looking and unromantic. The magic world where only strange lovely people lived seemed very far away, and a little silly.

THE BOX sat in the middle of the lean-to table. To Suzanne it looked like a human being crouched there, biding its time until all should gather around. Last year it had been upright and fat and square. This one was low and long like an old man lying asleep just before he would waken and bestow gifts on a waiting world.

It was an interminable time before every one was ready. Sabina, Jeanie, and Melinda must put up the horses first and bring in the brown sugar, salt, and tea which Ma's butter had bought. Phoebe Lou had to finish putting the plums in their stone jars and covering them with spring water which would form a scum and preserve them for pies away into the winter. Emily and Ma, their faces red and sweaty from the baking, wanted to wash up a bit before presenting themselves at the shrine of THE BOX. Henry, man fashion, had driven on over to town, but even though Pa and Phineas pretended only a casual interest, they came in after the honey-gathering to attend the ceremony, with Pa taking charge of the opening in order to keep the nails in good shape for future use and the boards for shelves.

At the tearing, ripping sound of the wood, Suzanne wondered whether in all the world there was a noise so pleasant. It made her shiver with delicious chills of anticipation.

Over the top and crushed around the sides were newspapers which Pa lifted out carefully, smoothing them tenderly, so anxious was he to see what the Chicago paper had to say about that new policital convention in Jackson, Michigan, called for all those who were getting dissatisfied with the Whigs.

All right! Here come The Things now. Oh, my goodness, how could life hold anything anywhere more exciting. Suddenly Suzanne felt sorry for Evangeline Burrill who had no cousins in Chicago, sorry for every one who was not standing here in the lean-to this very moment to see *no-telling-what*.

Pa's contribution to the ceremony finished, there was some delay because of an unaccustomed politeness as to which one might have the honor of lifting out The Things, with "You,

Ma," and "No . . . let Sabina . . . she won't be here next year when it comes."

So Sabina, who was to trade this great annual excitement for matrimony, took out the things carefully amid rapt attention and contributory remarks from the side-lines. A gray-blue dress and a blue plaid cape to match, with Pa saying it was as big around as that traveling showman's tent down to Prairie Rapids. A great hank of red yarn, crinkled from having been raveled out of something, but pounced upon by Ma with satisfaction. New red flannel. Another voluminous dress, dark green, with a little soiled linen lace still at the neckline, and a dark red one with enough rows of black silk galloon braid around its wide skirt to trim several dresses under Emily's efficient planning. A pair of hoops! And every one was calling out, "They've got down to you, now, Phoebe Lou. These are yours."

There was a bolt of new unbleached muslin which by common consent was laid in Sabina's willing arms, and which she held lovingly like a baby, and a bolt of gray calico which Ma took charge of, saying she would parcel it out as needed.

And then, you could not believe your eyes. Suzanne's face turned pink in embarrassment as though some mental activity of her own had brought the thing to life—a parasol of dark green silk, small as a toadstool, on a long slim handle and with only a few little splits in the silk where a rib or two stuck through. It sounded almost wicked for Ma to be asking what in time would they send that out here for, and Phineas to be saying it would be good to fasten over old Star or Baldy in the heat instead of a wet sack when he was plowing.

When the box was emptied, Suzanne experienced a let-down feeling of there being nothing now to live for. Several times before supper she went into Ma's bedroom to pull out the trundle-bed and look at the lovely green parasol lying there, trying to bring back some of that delicious excitement she had known.

As though this day were like all others they were soon sitting down to supper with the usual confusion. Phineas and Celia had arrived simultaneously at the last unoccupied wooden chair, and Phineas, by virtue of his masculine strength was lifting Celia away from the coveted seat with much teasing laughter on his part and indignant shrieking on hers, so that it was not until Sarah had told them to hush and Jeremiah with bowed head had said mumblingly into his beard, "I'll-thump-you-both-bless-this-food-to-Thy-Glory,'' that there was enough silence to hear the queer foreign sound.

''Hark!'' Phoebe Lou and Jeanie said together. ''What's that?''

Others had heard it, too, so that several jumped up and ran outdoors, leaving the dishes of corn-meal mush steaming at each plate like so many miniature camp-fires sending up a white smoke. .

The sound was so faint and from so far away, that almost was it not heard at all. But because the wind was coming from the Sturgis Falls direction, it brought that distant eerie tinkle.

''Hush up your noise,'' Sarah said crossly to a rooster taking that particular moment to crow near her, so anxious was she to hear his unusual thing.

Every ear was strained to catch it, the sound of the new school-bell ringing from the tower of the little frame building over at the settlement among the trees and stumps.

''All listen to the first tower bell of the Mississippi,'' Jeremiah said. He held up his hand and spoke solemnly as though he were pronouncing a benediction. ''Eddication has come to Ioway.''

They all went back into the house where the flies had gathered near the corn-meal mush during their absence, so that Suzanne and Celia had to get the long-handled brushes again and whack awhile before they could clear them out.

Jeremiah talked about the bell all through the supper hour until every one grew a little tired of it. ''It's a sort of symbol. You'll see . . .'' He bragged as though he were going to be personally responsible. ''Ioway'll maybe stand at the very head of the Union some day in schools. Like Massachusetts . . . and Connecticut . . . and the others. I want to live to see it . . . free schools, too, common schools . . . no tuition . . . for rich and poor alike . . . all over the state. School funds ought to have better management . . .''

They all laughed at that. ''Well, Pa, you're school director here for our new district. What you been buying for yourself with the school funds?''

Well, he meant all over the Valley and other newly settled parts of the state. If all were run as honest as this one there wouldn't be need of much complaint. He hoped this Ambrose Willshire who'd walked clear up from Iowa City to see about getting the school would be all right. Here now they had this good log school-house right on the corner of their own land,

and even if it was small and not many scholars to attend, it ought to be just as good as a bigger one back east. That was the right way. A chain wasn't any stronger than its weakest link, and the Iowa school system couldn't ever expect to be what it should be unless every little log school-house did its share.

They grew impatient over the continuation of the same subject so that they tried to get Pa off on other topics but every little while he would return to it like a puppy shaking an old rag. For with very little schooling himself, Jeremiah Martin was still wanting education for those who would come after him.

Wayne Lockwood had heard the faint far-away sound, too, from his cabin across the prairie and now came riding Blackbird over to the Martins' to find out whether he was sane or had a ringing in his head.

The Akins heard it, and the Burrills and the Mansons, and all felt an unexplainable elation over the sound, knowing that something pleasant and substantial had happened to the new country. In truth, outside of every cabin within hearing distance of that ringing stood a group of people, bareheaded, silent, as though they had stopped work to worship at the sound of the Angelus.

All night the bell rang jubilantly. When one citizen grew tired pulling the rope, another took his place. It was as though they could not stop the celebration, as though now for the first time Iowa had something of Pennsylvania and Ohio, York State and New England—something which made it seem like "back home."

CHAPTER 10

THE fall term of school began now for Suzanne in that little log building on a corner of the land which her father had donated to the newly formed school district. Like his house, it sat at the edge of the timber which swept up from the south so that trees formed a background to its dark logs and the prairie fell away from its door. There was a tangle of underbrush at its windows—hazelnut and scrub oak and the wild sumac that appeared to be setting fire to the black logs, its scarlet branches licking at the little building like tongues of flame.

Inside, there were hand-hewn benches over which the children climbed to be seated with their backs to the center of the room, the boys with swaggering straddle, the girls carefully, with a clutching at wide skirts to keep the showing of pantalets at a minimum. The desks were fastened to the wall on two sides of the room, each one a long sloping box with a lidded compartment for every two children.

A water-pail with long-handled dipper stood on a built-in shelf so that this particular corner was always in a state of dripping moisture on warm days and of icicle formation in winter. That tin dipper constituted the sum total of the improvement of this year's equipment over last (which had been the school's first year of existence) inasmuch as all those gallons of drinks of the yesteryear had been consumed by way of a gourd dipper which was discarded now because of the jagged appearance of its rim caused by the sharp teeth of the consumers.

Melinda, Celia, and Suzanne were the only Martins to be in school this fall. Sabina and Emily had called their education finished before they came to Iowa. Jeanie and Phoebe Lou had both gone part of last winter at Pa's insistence but when Jeanie found she could spell, parse, and read better than the little old man who taught them, she had made a big fuss about it and stopped, too. And now Phoebe Lou would go no more for she was away helping Mrs. Manson who was expecting a baby.

A week before, Mrs. Manson's unmarried brother, Ed Armitage, had arrived in a two-wheeled cart, dashing madly up to the lean-to door as though finishing a race, to see if one of the girls could come over to help his sister. Jeremiah, fond of his little joke, had said: "Well, now, Ed, I can't let any of my girls go for to be hired girls, but if you want to marry one, take your choice—you got seven to pick from."

"Only six, Pa." Phineas had winked, teasingly. "You forget Sabina's spoken for."

"That's right, Ed . . . Sabina's the only one we can get off our hands."

Ed Armitage had turned red clear down into his buckskin coat collar, and the girls had all made an excuse of going into Ma's bedroom where they stifled their laughter at Ed's discomfiture in the feather-beds whose acoustic properties were negligible.

But Phoebe Lou had gone to help, riding away bouncingly in the two-wheeled cart with the perturbed Ed, and throwing a languishing look over her shoulder at the assembled family as she clasped her hands imploringly behind his broad back, so that the girls had run into the house and laughed themselves sick.

Neither Celia nor Suzanne liked the new Ambrose Willshire for a teacher, and Melinda frankly said she could cheerfully mop the floor with him, although no one could put her finger on just what was wrong. He was polite to a point of saturation, correct and stiff in his manner, but so mean about little things, holding up the oldest Akin boy to ridicule when the lad merely meant to be informative, making Celia write "I think I am pretty" fifty times for twisting a curl over her ear during class, so that Melinda and Suzanne who had often and unhesitatingly confronted her with the same accusation now escorted her home between them in deep clannish sympathy and high dudgeon.

As an embarrassing aftermath, that turned out to be the very night Ambrose Willshire moved in at home, bag and baggage, for he was boarding around and there was not going to be room for him and the stork both in the one-roomed cabin of the Mansons. The family had all talked noisily and naturally (which were synonymous terms) at that first meal, excepting the three school-girls who were still in a state of revolt.

Indeed, Ambrose Willshire's pedantic presence cast a shadow on them all through the sunny days of October—there was such an air of condemnation about him at their chatter and laughter. Sometimes he corrected them in their speech and often he spoke about attaining perfect goals in life.

But his four weeks were up and he had gone on to the Horace Akins' this Saturday. Every one felt relieved.

Jeanie said she was going to let out and sing at the top of her voice all day for she had been just like a bird fascinated by a snake when she was alone with him and he looked so long at her. Even Jeremiah said it was nice to have a good eddication but there wasn't no call to be long-faced about it, and he guessed having some schooling didn't need to prohibit you from cracking a joke once in a while.

This October Saturday, with the timber in the Valley burning red under the fire of bright maples and burnished oak leaves, with the smoke of the Indian camp-fires near the river drifting lazily into the fall sky, Henry and Phineas were breaking the last of their new prairie sod for the next spring's planting. Emily was baking. Jeanie and her mother were making soft soap in an outdoor kettle, for which task they had leached their own lye from wood ashes. Melinda was bringing out the pieced comforts to hang on a line stretched between two trees which had been topped to form clothes-line posts but which had broken out into foliage this year, as though the mere duty to which Sarah assigned them was too commonplace.

Sabina was drying the last of the sweet corn with Celia to help her. The sheets for her new home were bleaching on the coarse grass of the yard, the color of the muslin having already changed from a mulatto tan to a pale saffron under the warm prairie sun.

Suzanne's job was one which called for much locomotion, for she not only had to whack her fly brush of paper streamers over the drying sweet corn and the soap grease which were on opposite sides of the cabin, but ever and anon she had to dart hastily toward the sheets as she saw an inquisitive chicken ambling in that direction, and toward the clothes-line as a bird gave evidence of alighting.

Jeremiah was on his way up to Wayne Lockwood's on Jupiter this afternoon with weighty things on his mind and fire in his eye, deeply concerned about a serious political problem. Indeed, the whole newly organized county was excited.

There had been a real bounded county only since June. The court records over which Sarah had waxed sarcastic were in Sturgis Falls safely ensconced in the loft over Mr. Mullarky's combination house and store, a room twenty feet square and seven feet high for which the county office was paying eight dollars per month, the rental including a table and two stout wooden chairs. Thus Sturgis Falls, by virtue of being the older and larger of the two settlements and platted now for two years, was the county-seat.

More rumors had been coming out of Prairie Rapids via the mouth-to-mouth route that the little upstart settlement had its eye on the county-seat, claiming it should be the chosen site because centrally located.

All of Jeremiah's indignation was fomenting as he rode to where Wayne, with Ed Armitage to help him, was breaking sod.

For a long time the two stood by their plow while Jeremiah "talked turkey" to them, explaining, gesticulating, going into countless reasons why Sturgis Falls should retain the county-seat.

Wayne was neither agitated over the question nor conclusive in his choice of the two towns, as was Jeremiah, and he said so. "I can't think but maybe Prairie Rapids *is* the one to have a court-house. After all they're right in bringing up the fact that they're more central."

Jeremiah's black beard bristled like the hair of old Major over some wiggling thing in the grass. "Ain't you *nearer* to Sturgis Falls both in miles and your feelings for it?"

"A little in actual distance," Wayne admitted, "but not any closer in feelings, as you say."

He was sorry to rile his neighbor. Jeremiah Martin had been more than good to him, but after all he was his own boss and entitled to his own opinion.

It was fully an hour later that Jeremiah rode away with a parting: "Well, you sleep over this and you'll come to see it rightly. I'll warrant, come daylight, you'll see the light and throw in your weight with the Sturgis Falls folks and help hang onto the court records there."

He had been gone across the prairie only long enough to be a toy man on a toy horse when Wayne saw a pair of bays and a shining buggy coming across the open spaces.

Only a few times had he seen Cady Bedson and now here the fellow was, but for what purpose?

"Looks like we better get ready to serve afternoon tea . . . so many callers, Ed," Wayne said, as the two saw the team making for them.

Right after Jeremiah Martin's agitated visit, it was not taking Wayne five minutes to see the reason for this other call.

"Watch the sparks fly, Ed. I just don't have any extra liking for this lad."

"How are you, Lockwood?" Cady Bedson was affable enough.

"I can't complain."

"Nice farm you'll have some day."

"That's what I thought the day I picked it out," he answered dryly.

Cady laughed. Evidently he was in no mood to quarrel.

"Land settling up in fine shape through here. Some of these days all the land will be taken in the whole new county."

"I agree. But I doubt if I'm going to agree to do what you're out here to get me to promise."

"Why, what's that?"

"I guess you're here to get me to pull for a change in the county-seat all right."

"I hadn't mentioned that, had I?"

Wayne grinned. "No . . . and now you won't even need to."

Why did he dislike him so—his slick looks and his dapper little mustache and his oily affability? Just one of those things you could not understand. "I just don't like him and I'm of no mind to try," he said to Ed, after Cady was gone.

Ed Armitage laughed at Wayne and his complete about-face on the subject of the court-house site so that Wayne laughed too.

"Yes, I guess I'm committed to a decision now." Queer that the dislike of a personality was what had convinced him. That was what you would call being prejudiced for a certainty. How Jeremiah Martin and the girls would laugh when he told them what had decided him to stand by Sturgis Falls.

He would have a chance to tell them the next day, too, for there was to be preaching in the log school-house and Emily had asked him to dinner between sessions. Some Brother Osgood, an itinerant preacher, was to arrive at the Martins' and hold service both morning and afternoon.

Sunday turned out to be a rare jewel of a day set in the necklace which October was wearing. The little log schoolhouse was crowded. Saddle horses and those hitched to lumber wagons, buckboards and two-wheeled carts, were tied to trees at the rear, so that during the long sermon Jeremiah figuratively cut and set two dozen hitching-posts in front of the school grounds already worn bare in spots by hi-spy and ante-over games.

Brother Osgood, a shriveled brown gnome of a man, preached in droning flat tones from an Old Testament text, but also covered decisively, if sketchily, the subjects of baptism, conversion, punishment, redemption, prayer, and predestination, while mothers slipped sprigs of caraway to their offspring to smell in order to keep them awake, and surreptitiously took a whiff themselves betimes.

It was a most auspicious occasion for Suzanne to dream, lulled as she was by the monotonous tones of Brother Osgood. For time unending the voice mumbled through her consciousness like the bumbling of a far-off bee.

Jeremiah was nodding into his black beard, jerking up and looking about him indignantly. Sarah's thin sharp face under its black bonnet was upturned to the speaker, her heavy red hair sagging down from its pins, and her lips pursed as though she was trying to keep herself from a snapping retort to the little man's orthodoxy. Henry and Phineas were outside the door, half glad that their late arrival was keeping them there.

Sabina and Tom Bostwick were holding hands surreptitiously under the edge of Sabina's gray shawl. Emily was pleating her black mitts in nervous fingers, planning the dresses from Aunt Harriet's box. Jeanie rolled her dark eyes under her green bonnet from Sam Phillips to George Wormsby and even toward the pedantic Ambrose Willshire in impartial and regular sequence.

Phoebe Lou, sitting with the Mansons, looked a little self-conscious over the proximity of Ed Armitage. Melinda, gazing out of the window whose open wooden shutters revealed the vast stretches of prairie, was far afield on one of those journeys she was always sighing to take. Celia's head under her white straw bonnet was bent decorously low. To the casual observer Celia was in a state of pious worshiping, her pretty face carrying an expression which was dutifully reverential. But the casual observer could not have known that Miss Celia had a broken piece of mirror in her white cotton mitt and was gazing therein quite as fascinated by what she saw as Narcissus at the pool.

It is not to be wondered at that Suzanne, in her half-dreaming state, seeing all these familiar figures as through a veil, for one brief moment lost consciousness of where she was, so that when a late fall fly lighted on her hand, trained as she was to be fly-conscious, she started up suddenly from her bench, thinking to get the long-handled brush, only to drop back onto the seat in deepest mortification when she realized that this was "meeting," that every one was glaring at her, and that Wayne Lockwood from across the room was grinning at her discomfiture.

And now almost to every one's surprise, as though they were not quite sure it could ever end, the morning session was over. There remained only an announcement, a song, and the benediction. The announcement was that there would be a sermon again at two-thirty which would contain something of the lives of the major prophets at the close of which a collection would be the order of the day. The song was sung, pushed along by Sabina's and Wayne's strong voices and held back by a dozen unmusical ones. The benediction, which Mr. Noah Webster's *American Dictionary of the English Language* said was a short prayer with which public worship was closed, proved to be all that Mr. Webster had said of it excepting that it was not short. It was very long, indeed, so that it was going to hurry the women folks to get dinner and the dishes done in time to get back to the afternoon preaching.

Because of the lateness of the hour there was not the usual loitering to visit as on most occasions when the settlers got together. This time it was the women who tugged at men's sleeves, instead of the usual, "Come, come, you women never know when to stop talking." For most of the men wanted to talk to the old trapper, Rab Dorwit, who in regular frontier clothes and coonskin cap with tail down the back, had returned to the Valley to see what it looked like under modern conditions.

The man had roamed through this section fifteen years before, trapping and fishing, living with the Indians at first, later in a hastily constructed log hut by the river. He was not at all the Jeremiah Martin type of settler coming into Iowa to make a permanent home, belonging instead, to that other period, the era of the transient—an old man now who had been one with the beavers and the pike and the antelope, free as the prairie winds or any wild thing of the river or forest, finding these modern modes of living too settled.

Already Jeremiah was asking the old trapper to come over to dinner, so that Melinda said to her mother: "For goodness sakes, let's get Pa home before he asks the whole congregation."

Sarah had sent Celia and Suzanne ahead to get the table set and now added: "Melinda, get the fire going up under the chicken. I'll be along as fast as I can come. Now scoot!"

There was no need to give orders to Emily. Already Ma's stand-by was half-way to the house, scurrying along alone, with her skirts held as high as she dared to avoid the dusty October weeds. Phoebe Lou, working for the Mansons, was excused temporarily from orders. Sabina, strolling along slowly toward the house with Tom Bostwick, existing in a state of romanticism, also carried a certain insurance protection against her mother's curt orders.

Jeanie, although unbetrothed as yet because of a coquettish desire not to admit which scalp she desired to retain permanently, was walking home between two able protectors, Sam Phillips and George Wormsby, but when half-way there, overtaken by Ambrose Willshire, she thought it a good joke to leave the body-guard in the lurch and step back with Ambrose.

Celia and Suzanne arrived breathlessly at the cabin, for Ma would brook no fooling to-day, and tied aprons around their waists, beginning at once to piece out the table with wooden sawhorses and boards, for in addition to Brother Osgood, Tom Bostwick, and Wayne Lockwood, Pa was bringing the old trapper and as like as not a half-dozen other folks.

Happily, the usual fly-brushing task was over for the season as only a few stragglers remained. That first killing frost had done more than get rid of the black pests. It had wrinkled the great pumpkin vines, left the morning-glories a soft black mass of pulp clinging limply to the side of the cabin, and turned the timber into such ruddy colors that it appeared to have caught and held some particularly vivid prairie sunset in its tree-tops.

And now the girls could hear their father's voice shouting: "No necessity of your goin' 'way home to try to get back at half-past two," hospitality oozing from its every inflection.

"Yes, but he don't have to try and squeeze them around this table," Celia growled.

"Or be the one to wait if there's too many." Suzanne was laying the knives and forks the length of the pieced-out table, covered now with both long white cloths her mother had bought in York State years before, when either one had seemed of infinite capacity for any potential family.

She was wishing she knew where Wayne Lockwood was going to sit. Just what difference the knowledge would make was difficult to see, as the same black bone-handled knives and forks, the same heavy white plates with their English stamps on the back served for all. But she laid each one down with loving touch so that she might not miss the favored place.

The men sat around outside in the nice October weather waiting for dinner to be called, avoiding discussion of the courthouse feud to-day out of deference to Brother Osgood and his supposedly peaceful inclinations, dwelling rather on the differences between the old days when the trapper was monarch of all he surveyed and the way the lands of the Valley were now being gradually patented and settled.

When Suzanne saw that her mother and Emily were beginning to take up the huge platters of prairie-chicken and dumplings and the corn-bread which Sarah had hurriedly "whacked out" when she saw the crowd would "eat her out of house and home," she ran outdoors to see if there was something left with which to decorate the center of the table.

All the flowers were gone—even the hardy goldenrod was black and soft—but she could get a few short branches of shining oak leaves, copper-colored in the warm sun, and of maples as red as the blood of the Lamb. She could see Celia in the east door of the lean-to, one arm high on the casing, her yellow head bent in such fashion that Suzanne knew she was trying to stand elegantly for the benefit of the onlookers in the yard; she heard Melinda calling out, to take her off her high horse: "Celia, if you're trying to look like the Grecian Exile I can tell you it's not a very good imitation with a *smudge of dirt* across your nose!"

But Suzanne forgot Celia, Melinda's teasing, and the dinner, in the joy of looking into the red and yellow and bronze of the trees so soon to be weighted down with the snows of winter.

"Don't it seem sad," she called back to the two girls, her voice husky with emotion, "that these leaves will all be gone . . . and never again will we see the same crab-apple blossoms or wild sweet-williams or shaggy bouncing-Bets?"

"There'll be more next year, silly," Celia retorted.

And Melinda yelled cheerfully: "Ma will bouncing-Bet you if you don't get in here to help with the benches."

They gathered close on the chairs and long boards—eighteen people, with the Mansons' new baby asleep in a deep ravine of the mountain that was Sarah's high feather-bed.

Old Rab Dorwit in his coonskin cap with the tail at the back had sat down when he suddenly remembered he was to eat in the presence of others than birds and squirrels, removed his head-gear politely and, with accurate aim, shied it neatly across the room into the woodbox.

Jeremiah nodded to Brother Osgood who bowed his head and addressed the Deity promptly, fluently and, to the waiting diners, unendingly. "Oh, Lord, bless this Thy food for Thy servants. Bless this Thy friendly gathering. Bless these Thy people. Bless their neighbors. Bless this Thy community. Bless Thy church. Bless the head of this home and all the inmates herein. Bless the new state carved here out of the wilderness. Bless Governor Hempstead and all his acts. Bless President Pierce and give him wisdom to guide the nation. Bless the Congress . . . and all the cabinet members. Bless . . ."

Wayne Lockwood, wedged between Phoebe Lou and Jeanie, sensed rather than felt the first faint tremor of a girl's body on either side. He bit his lip and glowered at the "Made in England" stamp on the back of his plate. If a single girl so much as made a faint beginning of that dangerous Martin chuckle, he knew they were done for, and so was he. Never could he have the self-control to stand up against the concerted action of the Martin risibilities.

Although there were moments when it seemed that life never would be anything again but the sound of a droning ministerial voice and the consciousness of a painful effort to keep that uncontrollable Martin laughter from spreading, the prayer eventually came to an ecstatic Amen. As though released from some brush dam too slight to hold the flood waters longer, low laughter rippled up and down the long boards. So that there must be an excuse for it at once, Jeanie was saying: "My goodness, Suzanne! Bringing in old oak leaves for flowers! It makes me laugh."

The laughter exploded then into a noisy whirlpool of sound as the plates were turned over.

"It makes me laugh, too."

"Me, too."

"I never saw anything so funny."

With united cause they took it up as an excuse for the sudden gay outburst, so that Suzanne was embarrassed, and Wayne, looking across the table at her red face and the distress in her gray-blue eyes, was sorry for her. Poor girl, he thought, they ought not take it out on her.

He leaned across the red and bronze of the leaves with "*I* think they're pretty, Suzanne," noted how the brightness came back into her eyes as though candles had been lighted there. It was not an unpleasant sensation to have lighted those candles.

At half-past two, the eighteen, all the other river road people and a few from the north prairies were back at the schoolhouse. It was so crowded that a group of men stood outside the door, and each of the four windows open to the Indian summer weather contained the heads and shoulders of others, so that from the inside they looked like nothing so much as pieces of rustic statuary set along on the wooden sills.

By four o'clock Brother Osgood had left the major prophets behind and was about to bring forth the foibles of the minor ones, when the old trapper, who was squeezed in between Jeremiah and Ed Armitage, must have decided suddenly and conclusively that he had heard enough, for rising abruptly and stomping up to the desk, his coonskin cap pushed back off a perspiring forehead, he reached a hairy hand into his pocket, drew out a small coin and slapped it down on the printed account of the prophets, both major and minor, with a gruff "That's my share," and stalked majestically out of the school-house into the great open spaces.

For the second time that day Wayne Lockwood sensed the laughter of the Martin girls being held in check with superhuman efforts, its dangerous compression manifested by reddening faces and shaking shoulders. This time there was no outlet for it as there had been at noontime over poor Suzanne, and he was wondering how they would get through the ordeal without disgracing themselves, when the preacher asked Sabina to start a closing hymn.

Rosy-cheeked Sabina, whether by accident or design, he could not know, immediately pitched and started: "Come on, my partners in distress," so that the unmusical shouting of it by the congregation served its purpose in covering the mirth which was strangling them all.

So many things as there had been going on all day! Suzanne thought at night when it was all over that probably no one anywhere—the Chicago cousins or people in York State or New England—had had such a full day or so much excitement as she had just known. And when Pa wound the big weights of the clock with the iron key and said: "There now . . . another day's over. Start fresh to-morrow," it made her sad to see it go.

CHAPTER 11

THE year of 1854 was nearing its close now; it was well into November with every one on the river road as busy as the little fur-coated animals up at Beaver Dam. In truth the humans and the rodents had the same objectives in life—to be sheltered and fed. These were the paramount problems of the day.

Outside the cabins there were great piles of wood to be cut for the omnivorous appetites of the fireplaces and cook stoves, the stock and chickens must be made as comfortable as possible, fences built in spare time, water brought by rope and bucket from the newly dug wells, hogs butchered, corn hauled to the Overman mill to be ground into meal.

Inside there was the never-ending procession of daily tasks—baking, cooking, washing, ironing, sewing, scrubbing. But the settlers' interest in life did not cease with these. With the hard work went a capacity for enjoying their pleasures to the full, for sympathizing with a suffering neighbor, for grasping at knowledge of outside affairs hungrily, for soaring to exultant heights and groveling in miserable depths. Humanity remains much the same. Only the settling and the times change. "I love you" spoken in whatever tongue or generation springs from the same rapturous feeling. "He is dead" brings the same black despair.

At the Martins' now in addition to this regular fight for the family's subsistence were two big and exciting affairs to which the girls must apply their wits and energies—Christmas and Sabina's wedding on New Year's Day.

Added to the interest occasioned by these coming events was the constant talk about the Prairie Rapids people attempting to get the court-house records away from Sturgis Falls.

The feud had gathered momentum as the weeks passed.

Clearly Prairie Rapids meant business. The desire for the courthouse was no longer merely wishful thinking—it had come out in the open as a definitely expressed aim. Bitter words were passing up and down the prairie trails and to the ends of the county. Settlers who once would have divided their last piece of corn-bread with others were turning stiff backs on them when they passed.

Now that the issue had come to a state of almost open warfare, it was the subject of conversation at every gathering in town house and country cabin, at every general store and on the trail. Whenever two or more people came together there was wild discussion about it. If the group all chanced to be for Sturgis Falls or all for Prairie Rapids, the conversation was agreeably one-sided, if vehement. But if it happened to be of mixed sentiments, the debate was deadly.

Those living along the river road were divided in their allegiance to the two towns. The newer families in the eastern half were all for Prairie Rapids, those at the western end righteously indignant in the cause that Sturgis Falls should retain her own possession—the county-seat, named legitimately, as it had been, by commissioners appointed through the legislature the year before. But Prairie Rapids, ambitious little settlement, wanted to be, as the Akins expressed it, the shire-town. It was almost as though a line of demarcation ran through the river road at right angles to it half-way between the two settlements. Deer Run Creek became a figurative Great Divide like the top of a mountain range where the waters separate, one part flowing to the west and one to the east.

Thus the members of several families who drove to Prairie Rapids for their mail and their trading, talking up the change of the court records as they did, became practically estranged from the Martins and the Akins, the Burrills, the Mansons and Wayne Lockwood, all of whom pulled for Sturgis Falls.

Jeremiah Martin could not stay away from the fight and almost abandoned his farm work in the interest of Sturgis Falls. Sometimes he rode Queen or Jupiter over there to reconnoiter and plan with the town men, and sometimes he rode to Prairie Rapids into the enemy's camp, as it were, to see if he could "get wind" of their intentions.

Ed Armitage, impulsive and excitable, was always bringing him news of what this or that one in Prairie Rapids was threatening, riding into the Martin yard as wildly as though pursued, and stopping so suddenly that his horse would almost sit down on its haunches in its unplanned cessation of speed.

Wayne Lockwood, usually conservative, was wrought up, also, over the quarrel. That Prairie Rapids, the newer and smaller of the settlements, should have the gall to try to take the court records away and become the county-seat even after the Overmans had donated a fine centrally located acreage was too much to swallow. Revolutionary War blood in him had not yet run its course.

He was thinking these things as he went out to get a horse to ride into Sturgis Falls this Saturday night. He had worked hard all week building a shelter for the sheep he had brought in, as well as doing his regular tasks, and to-night his thoughts turned toward the little town of three hundred lying there to the southwest. The bright lights called him as they were calling young blades in eastern cities, only here the lights were but tallow candles stuck in bottles and jugs along the wooden counter at Mullarky's general store.

He had just mounted Blackbird when but a few feet from the log shelter he heard loud squawking, and looked up to see a big gray wolf making off with his rooster. Without a gun and with scarcely time to think of anything except that his property was being carted off ignominiously, Wayne took after the loping beast across the prairie, yelling to him to "drop that," which strangely enough the great lank animal did, bounding on up the creek as the half-stunned fowl shook itself and crowed lustily. He took the ruffled bird home, laughing at his own temerity in practically slapping a timberwolf's jowls, smoothing the insulted dignitary and saying: "Those two old-maid hens couldn't raise much of a family without you, could they?"

Riding Blackbird, he went in a straight line from his cabin down to the river road. Although it was unfenced prairie land, he knew he was making the permanent trail, that the way his horse went was the way of the road which one day would be traveled by others north of him. Already the Martin girls were speaking of it as "the lane road" although it was but a path in the frozen grasses this frosty November night.

Those Martin girls—they were certainly a lively crew. He almost laughed aloud, thinking of their latest antic, how, one night when the men folks were all gone, Jeanie and Melinda had dressed in their brothers' clothes and slipping unseen by the others out to the stables had swaggered around there with pretense of drinking and smoking, so that the girls in the house had been frightened, and Suzanne, afraid to go to the stable for a horse, had slipped out the front door and run all the way to the Horace Akins' to ask him to come over. Getting a joke on each other appeared to be their prime object in life.

He was on the river road now, riding to the west, the short distance into town. The road here was more clearly defined, the trail had become a thing of brown dirt packed solid by wagon rims, but with coarse grasses still running down the center.

Nearly to the settlement he passed the bayou road down which some of the men of the community rode only after dark. Already he knew about the woman down there, in a cabin, whose daughters were hospitable, too. No, thanks! He had no wish to become entangled there.

He passed the tavern and the clustered cabins of that part of the settlement which lay on the north side of the river, rode down the bank of the Red Cedar and into the water at a point where the fording was usually made. A man by the name of Cameron had run a ferry for part of the past summer but it was slow and tedious and there was talk of a bridge some day. The water was cold with an occasional scum of ice, and Blackbird, totally opposed to the trip, threshed about for a little time before she would go on. Soon the ice would form in solid covering and one could cross on it.

Emerged from the river bed with Blackbird shaking herself as though in disgust, Wayne rode along the trail a few rods, over the rough half-frozen clods, tied Blackbird to a hitching-post near the general store, and went into the little building which stood there on Main Street, called this by courtesy, although it was but a trail cut through the timber, with sawdust and shavings from the sawmill lying along one side in lieu of a walk. The Winslow House, the most pretentious of the few dozen buildings in the whole town, stood near the general store. Far up the trail winding among the trees with the stumps in its center stood another tavern called the American House.

There were a dozen men in the store, lounging about, with Phineas Martin and Ed Armitage looking on. It was always Phineas who was in a crowd of gossipers, never Henry, Wayne was thinking.

Besides the candles stuck in bottles and jugs, the wooden counter held some boxes of eggs and a few bolts of cloth. There were hogsheads of molasses and sugar, salt and beans, crackers (huge thick squares that could have been used for paving blocks), dried herring and codfish, strips of jerked buffalo meat, a sack of dried wild crab-apples which some settler's wife had exchanged for calico, tobacco in two or three forms. All but the crab-apples, buffalo meat, and eggs had been hauled the hundred miles from Dubuque.

Wayne was greeted by Phineas and Ed and other loungers in a thick tobacco atmosphere. He made his purchases, tied them together for his saddle-bags, and settled down to listen to the talk which ranged from gossip anent the girls down the bayou road to the court-house quarrel.

To this particular group around the stove, affairs outside the immediate community were not very well known. To be sure, every one knew there was a newly elected Whig governor, Governor Grimes, who was to take office next month in the old territorial capital over at Iowa City. He had been elected on a bold platform of the repeal of the Missouri Compromise with the slogan of "No more slave states." There was a bitter fight on, too, about moving the capital from Iowa City to a more centrally located point in the state. Iowa City in the eastern part was the center of population all right, but many contended that it should go into the geographical center on the supposition that the western part of the state also would be settled some day. But the whole fight was so far away it did not come very close to the interests of this lounging group. After all, Iowa City was seventy-five miles away as the crow flies, and no one could fly with the crow, so that it was several days distant in the best of weather, the other side of nowhere if there was mud or snow. But the county court-house now—that was a horse of another stripe, right under one's nose, as it were, and in danger too.

There were comments and lurid statements, wild surmises and a few definite threats around the wood-burning stove there in the log building which was house, general store, and courthouse. There was a checkers game with a few mild bets under a dim candle, a surreptitious drink or two, and then Wayne, Ed Armitage, and Phineas Martin were leaving for the river road.

They had just emerged from the dimly lighted store to get their horses when it happened. Under the pale November half-moon, they could see a dozen or more men on horseback coming from the south, riding quietly down the street picking their way among the stumps.

All three stopped in their tracks to watch, made no more

move to get their mounts, rather stepped back into the shadow of the store.

"What's up?"

"Damn if I know."

"Something on their minds, that's certain."

They pushed back quietly into the room, Wayne and Phineas watching from the half-opened door, Ed Armitage slipping over to the small window.

They could see about half of the men dismounting and without tying their steeds, pass the bridle-reins over to the others, then bunching together and starting to come toward the store.

"The court records!" Each of the three was saying it simultaneously to the others.

"Get the eggs," Wayne commanded.

Immediately, as though working in perfect unison, they dashed past the loungers, scattering some to the floor in sprawling posture, grabbed the boxes of eggs, and were back to meet the delegation at the door with a deadly barrage of the daily effort of Sturgis Falls hens.

"So you'd get the court records by just taking them, would you?" Wayne's jaws were set. Plop! A large gent received one in the underbrush of his whiskers.

Phineas hit a right eye with studied precision. Ed Armitage, excited to a frenzy, was yelling like a Sioux and throwing wildly. The candle-light from one of the jugs, falling on something shining, reflected its gleam, and Wayne recognized the tall silk hat under which was the dark dapper face of Cady Bedson.

"I never did like that hat of yours, Bedson," Wayne called out cheerfully, and splashed a double yolk on its stovepipe silkiness with the utmost confidence that some hen had gone to extra effort that day in his behalf.

Long before this the loungers around the stove had picked themselves up and joined the hubbub in yelling ecstasy until there was one grand uncooked omelet between the Prairie Rapids delegation and the court records.

The visitors left, oozing wrath and albumen.

To have pelted the Prairie Rapids delegation with eggs when they came to take the records away, was not to have settled the court-house affair. Hearing the low muttered threats of the departing members as they rubbed white shells and yellow yolks from coats, hats, pants, and whiskers, one could have predicted that the sticky mixture would cement together their individual resolutions to win now by other means than physical.

For the time, though, it put Wayne, Phineas and Ed Armitage in fine fettle. They forded the Red Cedar and rode home out the river road in high boyish spirits. To have ousted the Prairie Rapids delegation was to have taken the British at Yorktown.

All the way home they sang at the top of their voices, ribald and silly songs, to give vent to their pleasure, and would have raced the entire way out of sheer jubilance of feeling but for the fact that the trail was half-frozen in deep ruts and might have ruined their horses.

At the Martins' everything was bending toward Sabina's wedding. Even Christmas, usually sharing the big event of the entire year with Fourth of July, was taking a secondary place by the side of the first marriage, which was to be on New Year's Day in 1855.

Phineas brought the goods for the wedding dress from Dubuque, sent there by Aunt Harriet who had picked it from her husband's stock in Chicago. Sabina said it seemed terrible to think of that grand plaid silk, so important and so expensive, but in such a little package, rattling around among the barrels of crackers and brown sugar in the big wagon—it just ought to have had a special conveyance to bring it.

"Maybe a gold coach like Queen Victoria rode in a few years back," Jeremiah teased her.

But it came safely, if slowly, the last of November, so that Emily had ample time to make it. All the girls could sew, but not one with such dainty stitches as Emily, nor could any one get quite such a "good do" on the full skirts and the tight-fitting basques of the day. Aunt Harriet sent some fashion pictures, too, of chubby ladies with flowers in their hair, and with their hands, the fingers of which were apparently all grown together, placed stiffly across plump stomachs. The girls all laughed when Sabina put soggy dead morning-glory vines around her head and stood in the middle of the room with her hands stiffly across her front in foolish imitation of the smirking ladies.

The weather had been bad. Phineas got into the first big snow-storm and had to stay at the Independence tavern for two days. When he started home over the long cold trail it was slow going, shoveling a drift every little while in which the oxen had floundered. Sometimes he thought he would never again drive the stupid things; it angered him unaccountably, the way they would stop with heads hanging down at the slightest provocation, not even looking around as a good intelligent horse might do.

"Like some folks," his father said when Phineas had been railing about them at home, "never tryin' to pull through any bad goin' unless made to. That's what I always want you children to remember. *Pull yourselves on through.* No matter what you get stuck in . . . mud, swamps, gumbo, snow, jobs, difficulties, disappointments, hurts . . . any hard place or thing in life . . . don't stop like an ox and wait for the black-snake to crack. Do your own thinkin' . . . your own decidin' . . . then put your neck to the yoke and do your own pullin'. Nobody in this world is ever goin' to help get your load out but yourself. If you forget everything else I ever said to you: *pull on through.*"

Sarah sniffed. She found a good deal of fault with this man to whom she had been married for nearly thirty years. "Pa's awful good on advice," she sometimes scolded to the older girls. "It would be a big help around here if he took some of it to heart."

"Now, Ma," the girls soothed her, "all the settlers like Pa and he has lots to see to."

"Oh, yes, they all like him all right. He's always got some of *their* business to see to . . . helpin' here and helpin' there . . . writin' east all of the time for more people to come . . . talkin' with the surveyors . . . writin' to the railroad officials . . . ain't goin' to rest *now* 'til he's found out all he can about a railroad from Dubuque . . . and all the time there's a thousand things right on this place that never get done. I could do right well without a railroad out from Dubuque if I had some more shelves put up in my bedroom. He's talkin' now about some sort of County Fair Association . . . goin' to the meetin' to talk things over. I could do without a County Fair just as easy as an old shoe if I had a buttery. And some day, accordin' to hear him tell, there ought to be a Agricultural or Horticultural Society. I could get along as easy as pie without either of 'em if I could have somethin' convenient around here."

"What you want now, Ma?" It was Sabina.

"Stairs." Sarah's lips set in a thin straight line. "Where I come from in York State folks had *stairs* to walk down when they got married. You'll look pretty climbin' backwards down

that loft ladder in your weddin' dress, showin' your ankles
before everybody, maybe even some of your legs.''

They all shouted. ''Ma, you'd think, to hear you talk,
Sabina had a lot of legs like a spider.''

''But I've decided not to come down from the loft, Ma.
I'm coming out of your bedroom. Nobody'll ever *dream* I've
got any legs.''

The weather moderated. Not quite so cold now for Suzanne
and Celia were those shivering mornings of dressing behind
the cook stove in the lean-to or in front of the snapping logs
of the fireplace. Not quite so bitter the trip to the log school-
house, nor so frozen the water-pail, nor so cold the school-
room away from the iron stove while Ambrose Willshire
heard the parsing and the reading.

Now, for the first time, Christmas, as big as it was, seemed
only the first part and lesser of the coming events. But the
girls all hung up their stockings as they had done ever since
they were little, and every one of them put something in
every other's long home-knitted leg covering—a newly hemmed
handkerchief or a pincushion, ginger cookies or caraway
ones. Sarah made maple-sugar hearts in a mold which Jeremiah
had shaped from tin, and Emily made each person a different
animal from dried apples with English currant eyes, so that
every one had a good laugh over it and the funny verse which
accompanied it. Then there was the big dinner—fish which
Henry got over at the river through the ice and prairie-
chickens and venison that Phineas killed. Wayne Lockwood
and Ambrose Willshire were the only ones invited outside the
family, for Tom Bostwick, within one week of belonging
permanently, could scarcely be called an outsider. But Wayne
was far from his New England home, and, for that matter,
Ambrose's home near Iowa City across nearly eighty miles of
mud was for all practical purposes as far away as New
England.

Christmas noon when Tom Bostwick came out from Sturgis Falls for dinner he had a present for Sabina that had come
from Chicago via Dubuque on the merchandise load. When
he opened it before them all, it proved to be a rich Paisley
shawl, the rusty reddish-brown of a robin's breast, with a
black border and a wide fringe, more grand than any Martin
girl had ever hoped to own. Then he walked over to Sabina
and standing behind her placed it around her shoulders where
it fell to the bottom of her skirt in flowing lines. Without

taking his arms away from Sabina he kissed her in her new shawl before the whole family.

Suzanne was embarrassed beyond measure. She liked to *think* of such a thing but to *see* it was more than she wanted. The Martins' kissing was reserved for farewell partings and babies. People in her magic world could do very freely what Tom Bostwick had just done but it was always behind the closed door of her imagination. So when Jeremiah added to the disconcerting moment by saying: "You can hand the shawl on down to your children and your grandchildren, Sabina," Suzanne got up and went into Ma's bedroom and sat down on the edge of the bed in the shivery cold to think what a queer thing it would be if she were Sabina.

The week between Christmas and New Year's was virtually Sabina's own week. Jeremiah took her to Prairie Rapids over the four slushy miles to buy her wedding bonnet. When they went out to the buckboard they found Melinda sitting there and no amount of persuasion on Pa's part that the roads were bad and the load should be light could get her to change her mind since she had Ma's permission.

The millinery shop was in the the lean-to behind the Sherman House and was owned by the proprietor's wife, so they had to go through the tavern kitchen to get to it. When they finally reached there, Sabina was almost beside herself to know which one to choose from the nine bonnets, and even then Mrs. Sherman said if none suited she had plenty of material to make something else. But Sabina, trying them on one by one and surveying herself in the walnut-framed glass hanging on the wall of logs, seeing there the reflection of her rosy cheeks, crow-black hair, and snapping eyes, knew very well that she improved the looks of every one of the nine.

Finally she chose it, a dark green velvet with soft white silk shirred full under the brim and the green and white brought down together in double strings to tie under her chin. But so seldom did she see cash, it almost took away the pleasure to have Pa pay three dollars for it from wood he had cut and hauled to sell to one of the Sturgis Falls taverns. When she protested a little with guilty conscience, Jeremiah said not every one had such a good-looking girl to get a bonnet *for*, and laughed jovially that one of these days he'd maybe be lucky enough to get them *all* married off. So the milliner, Sabina, and the self-invited Melinda were all pleased at his taking the big price so good-naturedly.

Almost before they could realize it, New Year's and Sabina's wedding day had arrived. Unbelievably it was a warm day. Trees in the grove were soggy with moisture. The last snow melted on the south side of the stacks so that the chickens scratched wildly in the wet straw, thinking spring had come. Manure steamed in the barnyard. The outside doors of the house stood open until cake-baking time when not a breath of air must get in. Never had there been so much to do. Sarah was beside herself with anxiety over the work, dictating the girls' various tasks like a field-marshal.

Jeanie was to see about the candles, set out the dishes, and make one of the cakes. Emily, as always her mother's right-hand man, was to help with the bread and cooking of the chickens in the house and the whole pig in the outside oven. Phoebe Lou had much of the scrubbing and cleaning of the house. Melinda was set to wash the pans and pots as fast as the cooks were through with them, a task for which she had no liking and over which she grumbled no end, wanting instead to go on errands. After Sabina had made her own bride's cake, she was free from orders, but still the busiest of all, laying out her clothes, browning flour with which to powder herself after a hot wash in the wooden tub, and sewing into the bosom of her dress the little netting bags containing dried wild-rose petals. Celia and Suzanne were sent up the road, each with a pan containing cake dough which Mrs. Horace Akin was to bake in her oven. There were raisins and dried English currants in them, and because the girls had a heated argument en route over which of the two dried fruits was the most edible, it took various and sundry experimental tastings of the dough-covered confections before they could come to any decision.

The work was all done at last and by dark the teams began arriving. No one could rightly estimate how long it would take to make the trip over the muddy roads, so that the first arrivals came at six o'clock and the last ones at nine-fifteen, long after the ceremony, when Tom and Sabina had to stand up again to show how they looked when married.

Sarah had on her black dress and her breastpin made of the children's hair, which, because of the mixed colors ranging from Emily's bright red to Sabina's crow-wing black, with all the shades between, made a beautiful pin as variegated as a piece of striped marble.

Emily, who had so much to do toward the supper as well as to help Sabina dress in the new plaid silk, looked less neat than the others because of that last mad dash to get into her clothes. She wore her best dress but the bright blue color was not very becoming to her, her freckled face was so red from her hurried labors, and her hair had been combed so hastily that she gave the first arrivals the impression of having run breathlessly across the prairie to get here.

Jeanie, too, was in her best blue with the washed linen lace at the neck and sleeves, but she looked very neat and pretty, for she had slipped up to the loft early before the work was finished and dressed carefully, brushing a little corn-meal into her ashy hair to give it body so that it would stand out in its loops more firmly. Phoebe Lou, arriving in time to catch her doing it, warned her that if her head got moist during the evening, her hair would be full of pancakes.

Phoebe Lou, herself, in her first pair of hoops, had on the dark green dress from THE BOX, made over by Emily and trimmed with half of the silk galloon braid, and with her blue-green eyes and light brown hair she looked very nice in it, too. Tomboyish Melinda, dark and tall, was in the made-over wine-red and the other half of the silk galloon braid, but with an apron over it, complaining that she felt too dressed up, and for fear of spilling something on it or tearing it was not going to have a whole evening of fun spoiled.

But it was Celia who blossomed like the rose, even though her pleasure over the new apparel was somewhat lessened because she had to share honors with Suzanne. Emily, by much contriving and planning, had been able to make two dresses grow where only one had grown before. The volumi-nous light blue dress of the cousin's with the matching cape of plaid had been made to do service for both girls, the plain goods trimmed with the plaid for Celia, the plaid goods trimmed with the plain for Suzanne. So efficiently had Emily laid her plans and her newspaper pattern that not one scrap larger than a maple leaf remained, and even then the inverted pockets and the facing of the skirts were made of flour sacking. Lamenting only that she had no hoops, Celia preened herself like a blue jay with a plaid crest and labored under the illusion that the wedding party was being given for her.

Suzanne felt rather nice herself in the blue plaid with the plain for trimming and had only one regret that, try as she might, she could not think up any reasonable excuse whereby on New Year's Day in her own home she could appropriately carry the green silk parasol that was under Ma's bed.

Teams were tied around the place, at the iron rings in the log stable, to the hitching-post, and to the stake-and-rider fence itself. Because the evening was so mild men stayed out around the wagons talking, principally over the court-house feud, until Sarah motioned to Phineas to call them, when they marched in on creaking boots as solemnly as pall-bearers.

The rooms were filled with Martins and Mansons, Akins and Burrills, Wayne Lockwood, Ambrose Willshire, George Wormsby, Sam Phillips, Ed Armitage, people east on the river road, some from the Big Woods and Tom's friends out from Sturgis Falls, including the tavern-keeper and his wife who were losing one of their best paying boarders, for Tom had a four-room house ready for Sabina near the block where the new court-house would some day stand.

From her place behind the tavern-keeper's wife in the red-covered rocker, Suzanne was so emotionally disturbed that her cheeks were burning and her hard little palms were cold and moist. Involuntarily she put her hand to her throat to still its throbbing. Glancing at Celia beside her, she could see that Celia was excited and anxious for the wedding to go on, biting her lips and looking around at every one. As for herself, she wanted to go away somewhere, to hide while this wonderful thing was taking place, and yet did not want to miss one single bit of it, tried to ponder how those two opposite things could be. For how could this prairie child of 1855 know she was an idealist—that always she was to be half afraid to look at beauty for fear it would not measure up to what a lovely thing should be?

So now, a great stillness was upon the room, for the door to Sarah's bedroom opened, and there was Sabina in her green plaid silk dress, her crow-wing hair parted in the exact center and combed down in smooth loops over her ears, and—a surprise to them all—two cinnamon pinks in it, her cheeks rosier than the flowers and her dark eyes shining. And there was Tom Bostwick in a fine black cloth suit with a black satin vest, a blue satin handkerchief tie, and one of the twelve ruffled shirts that had been made for him in Dubuque. Oh, but they were a nice-looking couple.

The justice of the peace stood in front of them by the fireplace.

"Dearly beloved, we are gathered here together . . ."

And now Suzanne felt like crying, for Sabina was not to live at home with them any more. All at once she thought of Sabina as the favorite sister of them all, so kind and jolly, forgetting those times when she had found fault with her bossy ways.

"Sabina Martin, do you take this man . . ."

How would it seem to take a man? She glanced across at Wayne Lockwood in his fine suit standing there so tall and straight by the loft ladder, his arms folded across his broad chest, and knew if she ever took a man he would have to be as near like Wayne Lockwood as he could possibly be.

"Thomas Bostwick, do you take this woman . . ."

She looked around at all the folks and wondered what each was thinking. Ma was holding the back of one hand across her twitching mouth. Pa stood close to her, his face serious above his big black beard. Emily was looking straight at the bottom of Sabina's dress, probably to see if after all her pinning she finally had it even. Jeanie was rolling her dark eyes up at George Wormsby . . . no, at Sam Phillips now. Celia was biting her lips and acting as though she would rather have people look at her than at Sabina. And now Suzanne was afraid she was going to laugh, for there was Phoebe Lou making Melinda's shoulders shake with laughter by putting her hands with stiffly held fingers across her stomach like the women in the fashion-plates.

The ceremony was ending, a queer mixture of church and civil services, quite original on the part of the justice who had never married any one before and who now was saying, "By the grace of God and the church triumphant and the laws and constitution of the State of Iowa, I pronounce you man and wife."

Man and wife! It didn't seem possible that was all there was to it, after all the fuss and work and borrowing of knives and forks and chairs. Because of those few words Sabina could go away and live in the same room with Tom Bostwick.

The justice shook their hands solemnly and said God and the State of Iowa both blessed them. Ma who never kissed any one but a baby now kissed Sabina, her face working miserably until she bit her lip and said: "Pst! There's no fool like an old fool. I don't know why I should begin bawlin' at my age!"

Every one went up to congratulate them and wish them long life and prosperity—all excepting Mrs. Burrill, embarrassed at this journey into the realm of etiquette, who said politely, although she had known them several years, "Pleased to meet you."

Then the solemnity broke. Everybody laughed and talked as though it were a party instead of a wedding. And all the girls had to scoot right into their assigned tasks for supper, all but Sabina who, for the first time in her life, had nothing to do but to sit still in one of the barrel-chairs and be waited upon.

CHAPTER 12

IT seemed queer to have Sabina gone and to know she was not coming home except to visit. Every one said Sabina had feathered her nest so that Celia and Suzanne bragged a little at school to the two Smith girls from the north prairie, telling about their sister's house being built out of bricks made at the new local kiln and asking pointedly who else had better things? To which the Misses Smith made ready answer: "The Overmans and the George Clarks," an assertion that temporarily stopped the braggadocio of the Misses Martin.

Every one knew the Overmans' status. As for George Clark—he had been employed at the Mullarky store, sleeping on the counter at night, and only recently had gone back to Wisconsin to marry his girl. When they came back to Dubuque they had found the Mississippi too solidly frozen for the ferry to run, but not solid enough for horses and sleigh, so he had pulled his bride across on a hand sled. They had stayed all night in Prairie Rapids at the Sherman House with all the passengers on the stage-coach occupying that one room, so that the little discouraged bride wanted to go back home. Now they lived in Sturgis Falls and had the first piano, brought overland by wagon, and all the children in the settlement would come and stand on tiptoe peeking in the windows to watch the bride play on it. No, the Martin girls could not argue down the presence of the only piano in that part of the valley.

Though there was no Sabina at home, Phoebe Lou was back from helping the Mansons. Ed Armitage must not have been too deeply annoyed at her sly and constant teasing of him, for he tore into the yard every few days with a great upheaval of snow clods or splashing mud, bringing up his horse so suddenly at the lean-to door that Jeanie said he was going to pitch through head first into the woodbox some day.

Phoebe Lou chose to ignore any specific reason for his presence, pretending that he came always to see some one else. She would stick her head out of a loft window and say pertly: "Phineas has gone to Prairie Rapids, Ed," so that Ed would stand, embarrassed and grinning up at her from the tree-trunk stoop, not knowing just what move to make next.

Sabina's wedding was only a three weeks' memory when Jeremiah came home from her house, so filled with news that the moment he arrived he called the women folks all around him. "Ma . . . Emily . . . Jeanie . . . Phoebe Lou . . . Melinda . . . Celia . . . Suzanne!"

He stood in the lean-to, pants tucked into high boots, cap pushed back on his crisp black hair, his big beard moist with melted snow, around his shoulders a gray shawl fastened with a long pin whose head was made from red sealing-wax.

Sarah and some of the girls came in hurriedly from the other rooms. Celia and Jeanie scrambled down one of the loft ladders. Pa always had news.

"Cut . . . cut . . . cut . . . ca . . . *daw* . . . cut!" Emily called out. "Pa's calling the hens." So every one was laughing when they came up.

But Jeremiah told them it was no laughing matter. While he was at Sabina's, Tom Bostwick had come home and said that word had just come by a wagon traveler from Cedar Rapids that some of the Prairie Rapids folks (Cady Bedson, for one), to get even for that egg-pelting, had gone all the way to Iowa City to the capitol (lobbying, you called it) and had succeeded in getting a passage through the General Assembly that the electors of this county were to *vote* on the county-seat staying in Sturgis Falls or being moved to Prairie Rapids. The voting was to be the second of April and if Prairie Rapids won, Sturgis Falls could like it or lump it but they'd have to turn over the records on the Fourth of July.

"There'll be dirty work as sure as you're born," he told them excitedly. "I wouldn't put it past them. They'll call in every Injun down by the river and corner every transient."

"*They'll?*" Sarah sniffed. "You don't think it's just *angels* livin' in Sturgis Falls, do you?"

But Jeremiah would admit of no wrong-doing by those on his side of any fight. They must all, he said, work hard now to help hold onto what was rightfully their own. He wouldn't take the spring Dubuque trip but send Phineas, so many people must he interview before the election. When he went out and got on Jupiter again, riding away up the north prairie, Sarah scolded long and vehemently about Pa seeing to everything but the farm.

Spring now in this year of 1855, with the maples running, and every available pan, bucket, and dish from the Martin cabin commandeered for the sap! Maple trees in the near-by grove were tapped, but because there were so many more up in the Big Woods, Jeremiah decided that some of the family should go there and open up a sugar camp. The discussion over the personnel of the campers was long and wordy, Melinda almost wringing her hands in her anxiety to be one to go. Sarah said she didn't care so much who it was went if Emily stayed, that while Emily was just as big a talker as any of them, she could work and talk at the same time which was more than you could say for some of the others.

It turned out that Henry, Jeanie, Melinda, and Celia were to go, driving Red and Baldy. Phineas was to make the trip to Dubuque when they got back, but in the meantime Jeremiah and Phineas would have one yoke of oxen and the horses at home for spring work. There was wild commotion the morning every one left, Phineas started to Sturgis Falls with a load of wood for the Winslow House about the same time the others started northwest to the sugaring.

Suzanne was disappointed not to go with the campers but Pa would not let all three girls stay out of school when there was as good a teacher as Ambrose Willshire. One or two could go, he agreed, as sap wouldn't wait for scholars to get their learning.

Jeremiah gave his last directions to the campers before the pan-laden wagon left. "Take care of all your things. Keep an eye on any Injuns ridin' through . . . more up that way than around the river here . . . liable to pick up somethin'. They're restless and movin' around now that spring's come. Anything come up, use your gumption, Henry . . . and all of you. That's what the Lord give you gumption and Yankee ingenuity for. Think a thing out and once you come to decidin' what's best to do, stick by it and pull on through."

They were gone, old Red and Baldy plodding along over the prairie to the northwest, their brass-tipped horns shining like little lights in the early sun.

It gave Suzanne a queer sensation of freedom to see them off—neither girl left behind to go to school with her. She felt light-hearted, switching her skirts along through the soggy weeds and jumping over the spring freshets on the way to the school-house as though now for a few weeks, left to her own imagination, she could hobnob undisturbed with more interesting and beautiful people than the tomboyish Melinda and the matter-of-fact Celia.

One rainy afternoon three weeks later Wayne Lockwood, getting a blatting ewe disentangled from some new fencing, saw the Martin oxen coming across the sodden prairie and rode Blackbird across the intervening space to greet the returning sugar-campers.

Henry was hunched on the front seat in the drizzle but the three girls were under a canvas spread over the spoils of the trip, and all more worried about the possibility of water-soaked maple sugar than water-soaked femininity. Riding all the way home by the side of them in order to exchange news, Wayne was set upon by every one at the cabin to stay to supper, told that he'd better help them begin on the estimated three hundred pounds of sugar they had as well as some kegs of syrup.

The wagon was loaded to the hilt with sweetness, two raccoons, and a dressed venison. The first few runs of the sap had made nice light-colored sugar. Even the critical Sarah could find not one bit of fault with the tan-colored contents of those jars. The second week's run had made a darker brown grade. This last week's run of dark sap had been boiled down into the syrup, enough for about a million pancakes or platters of fried corn-meal mush or dishes of samp. They told Wayne he must take a jar of the syrup with him when he went home.

They were filled with news of the long trip, not stopping to think they had been only nine miles away; the sponginess of the prairie after the spring snows, the slowness of the plodding oxen, and the fact that they had received no word from home in all that time gave them the feeling of having been around the world.

One could scarcely hear himself think above the clatter at the table. So anxious were those who had stayed home to eat some of the new syrup, they were having a supper of corn-meal cakes early before candle-lighting time, even before all the chores were done. But the campers had said, no, sir, you couldn't give them maple syrup to-night—they just couldn't look that sweet stuff in the face and what they wanted more than anything was a platter of good fried eggs that they hadn't seen for weeks.

Talk. Talk. Talk. Like grackles in the timber. Wayne's

biggest news was that an eastern family by the name of Emerson had arrived up north of him. They had ferried across the Mississippi at Dubuque between ice cakes. It had taken them ten days to come the hundred miles. Mud holes were bad and sloughs almost impassable. The stage and Mr. Emerson's wagon both mired down at Delhi, so that they used his team in addition to the four stage horses to pull the coach out, then hitched on an extra pair of the stage horses with his team to pull out the wagon. He had told Wayne that, what with several wolves tagging after the stage at one time, a pouring rain, the almost impassable sloughs, fourteen people sleeping in one room at the tavern in Independence, and the landlord there greeting them in a dirty apron with evidences of fresh meat stain on it, and holding a loaf of bread tight under his arm from which he was cutting slices to pass out for them to eat, his wife thought she had forever left behind her the bounds of civilization.

The campers had experiences to tell, also. There had been Injuns not far away but minding their own business. Henry had got the raccoons, the deer, and plenty of prairie-chickens. They had had all the fish they wanted, too, thick as anything, for you could catch one any time you tried. Some campers had been there from the Janesville settlement, part of a family named Brown, the father, two girls called Lucy and Nora, and a brother. They had come over and sat around the campfire several nights, all singing and talking.

"Who did the *talking* . . . you or the Brown women?" Ma wanted to know.

They all laughed and admitted: "Well, maybe, mostly the Martin girls did, but, anyway, Henry was quiet and polite and never opened his head."

Home news was more exciting—it did beat all what could happen in three weeks. First, Prairie Rapids was working, tooth and toe-nail, to get the court-house. Cady Bedson was riding to every cabin in the east end of the county and south. Some said he was even buying votes. But Jeremiah had done a little riding himself, he said, and grinned at that. Sarah, snorting, said some day they'd invent a contraption you could tie on a horse's leg to see how many miles it went.

As enthusiastically as though he had just come from there, Jeremiah told the homecomers that at least one fight had come to a head: after all this time of pulling and hauling, like boys hold of a rope, with Iowa City and the surrounding counties hanging on, and the south of the state doing the pulling, the Fifth General Assembly had passed the removal bill and the capitol was going to be changed from Iowa City to Fort Des Moines soon as they could get one built.

Sarah sniffed and wanted to know what difference it made to Pa, Iowa City or Des Moines, both so far away and likely he'd never lay eyes on either one. But Jeremiah said it was just as important to him and to the most humble resident of the state as it was to the governor, with Phoebe Lou whispering to Celia in imitation of him: " 'I always say the state ain't no stronger than its weakest link.' "

Supper over, the men finished their chores and all had a "sing," with Jeremiah's jews'-harp and Phineas' fiddle for accompaniment, but every one missing Sabina. Then Wayne went home up the new lane road, the sodden grass of the prairie and the spongy ground making squashing sounds under the *clop-clop* of Blackbird's feet.

With the feel of the spring winds in his face, the smell of the newly turned loam in his nostrils, and the friendliness of the Martin family still wrapping him in pleasant warmth, he broke into song, taking up, without thinking, the last one they had sung:

"None knew thee but to love thee,
Thou dear one of my heart;
Oh thy memory is ever fresh and green . . ."

Gosh all hemlock—it was good to be alive, with spring coming on.

And now with no word to any one, excepting a laconic "All right with you, Pa, if I build a cabin of my own over here a bit?" Henry, like some animal of the woods silently making its nest, was putting up a log house a few rods away from the home cabin.

Jeremiah had been dumbfounded but met the issue without blinking.

"Figurin' on marryin'?"

"Maybe . . . one of these days."

"Wouldn't rather build a room onto the other end of the home cabin, would you?"

"No," Henry had grinned. "I'll get a little farther down the yard from the girls."

"Well," Jeremiah had attacked the problem, head on, "I figure the land'll be divided equal between you and Phineas some day. The girls'll all marry and be took care of. Just let

Ma and me live in the old house till we drop off and then half
the land is yours. Anything happens to me, though, see that
Ma don't ever want."

"I'll take care of Ma." It could not have been more
honestly meant if written and signed before a notary. Henry's
word, like his father's, was as good as a legal document.

It was all the information concerning a potential marriage he
had vouchsafed. Jeremiah, repeating it to Sarah and the girls,
saw for practically the first time in his life the entire feminine
aggregation shocked into speechless wonder. Not once had
the taciturn, hardworking, twenty-five-year-old Henry appeared to pay the slightest attention to any girl.

"Who *is* she, Henry?"

"You might, at least, give us a notion of who our sister-in-
law is to be."

The girls kept at him all that first week of the house-
building, to be met only with silence, even if with a half-
humorous drawing down of his bearded lips, so that it was
almost unbelievable that he belonged to this talkative group.
When they could get no satisfaction from him, they decided
that because he had made those long trips to Dubuque by
himself, it must be some one there.

March slipped away as meek as one of Wayne's lambs and
almost before any one realized it the day for the court-house
voting was upon them—that critical first Monday in April.

Phineas was away on the Dubuque trip, sent off with
Jeremiah's admonition to get back before voting day. "More
than once a single vote has made a change in history in this
country," he had told him, "from Supreme Court on down.
Makes it a duty for every man to vote on every occasion.
Majority rules, but that ought to mean everybody has his
say."

What the polls would reveal was the entire topic of conversation that morning, with every Martin girl arguing hot-
headedly that women should be allowed to vote, too.

"Not but what I wish you could on this issue," Jeremiah
said, "but just by nature women wasn't intended to wear
pants or vote."

"How do you know that for sure, Pa?"

"I think maybe it says that some'ers in the Bible. Give me
time, I bet I could find it: 'Thou shalt not vote.' "

"Seems funny we haven't got enough brains to know we
want the court-house left in Sturgis Falls."

"I ain't denyin' you haven't got heads on you and Lord

knows all of you know your own mind, but polls is no place for women folks . . . *dirty* and . . .''

"Oh, your grandmother's eye-tooth!" Emily put in. "We ain't too nice to clean out the dirty log hen-house."

"Or even fork the manure out the horses' stalls . . ." Jeanie's contribution.

"Or . . ."

"Hush!" Sarah slapped her hands together smartly. "Not another word from one of you. Such table talk!"

"And I'll thump you, too," Jeremiah put in lamely, half glad that Ma had come to the rescue.

Riding Queen and Jupiter, Jeremiah and Henry with masculine importance left for town to vote. Henry was to come right back and finish hanging the wooden doors of his cabin but his father would stay all day and help with the counting of the votes. Both were worrying about Phineas not getting back to cast one, although the day was young and perhaps he would pull through.

As the day went by, every eligible voter was looked after, and quite a few not so eligible, if hairs were to be split, but no one was engaged in that meddling occupation. No votes were challenged, for presumably every vote that went into the Sturgis Falls ballot-box was in favor of Sturgis Falls, as inversely every one in Prairie Rapids would be marked for that thriving and ambitious burg. It was rumored that several home-seekers who had just come in by stage were recruited from the three Sturgis Falls taverns and informed they were already prominent citizens; a roving tin peddler was persuaded that Sturgis Falls was temporarily his home; and a few settlers from near the county's border, riding in on horseback, were a bit vague about the location of their lands when they voted, but were not unduly pressed for details.

When the hour was approaching for the voting to close and Jeremiah saw that Phineas had not yet come in from Dubuque with merchandise, he suggested that the polls be held open while Wayne Lockwood on Blackbird was dispatched down the grassy trail to meet the late comer. Wayne encountered Phineas about six miles east of town, turned Blackbird over to him, and took charge of the slow-plodding oxen, while one more vote for Sturgis Falls hurried on horseback to the welcoming committee around the polls.

Prairie Rapids won.

A stunned and angry group of people were the Sturgis Falls claimants when they found that they had lost. The vote stood two hundred and sixty for Sturgis Falls, three hundred and eighty-eight for Prairie Rapids. The county-seat was to be moved down the river to the smaller and newer town.

In the days that followed a great many words were said on the subject, some found in neither polite literature nor the new *American Dictionary of the English Language*. Cries of pain could be heard in Mullarky's general store, in the taverns, and from wagons drawn side by side on grassy trails.

"Where in tunkit they could have raised three hundred and eighty-people without everybody votin' twic't is beyond me." Jeremiah could scarce believe the truth of the figures, talked about it constantly, rode Jupiter to town every day for a week to talk over with Tom Bostwick and others the prospects of bringing fraudulent charges. Oh, the kettle called the skillet black in no weak language.

He said he almost felt a personal responsibility in the catastrophe as though in some way he had failed in his duty, vowed with others of his spleen that if possible the thing would be fought out in the courts. By the bill in the legislature the records could not be moved until the Fourth of July. Maybe they could work out something before that date.

Every person in Sturgis Falls seethed with resentment when they looked at the block of wooded land which the Overmans had given for Court-House Square. Something must be done soon, for already the Prairie Rapids people were planning to build on their west side of the river.

The Martins, the two Akin families, Wayne, Ed Armitage, Ambrose Willshire, the Mansons and the Burrills, out of loyalty to Sturgis Falls, vowed they would never set foot in Prairie Rapids again as long as they lived, kept their vows religiously for a time until tempted by a traveling showman.

When Henry's cabin was finished, on a day of that April, he dressed in his Sunday suit, hitched Lassie and Laddie to the buckboard and disappeared toward Sturgis Falls. What could you do with a man like that?

Sarah was clear out of patience. She was tired and her thick hair sagged down heavily from its pins. "You girls all talk too much but it's better than never sayin' anything."

"You must have marked him before he was born, Ma," Phoebe Lou volunteered pleasantly.

"If I did, it was because I met up with a clam-shell," Sarah snapped. "Who knows if he's comin' back or not to-night? *Who's* he bringin'? Is he bringin' *any* one? Are they havin' a weddin' supper *there,* wherever that is? Will they be back *here?*''

"Let's go ahead and get a good one," Emily suggested. She was tired, too, and her own heavy red hair sagged a little like her mother's. "Then if he does bring somebody, we'll be ready."

"And if he don't . . . ?"

"Then we'll send Suzanne up the lane road to get Wayne Lockwood to come and help us eat it."

Emily killed and cooked chickens. Sarah fixed the last of the turnips that had been buried under a straw stack all winter, although they were strong and withered now. Jeanie baked a three-layer white-flour cake and Melinda made the maple sugar filling. They whisked about in anticipation of some potential happening for which they had no assurance excepting the premonition which Sarah said she felt in her bones. At the last Suzanne was sent up the lane road hurriedly to tell Wayne to come to supper anyway, so that all the work wouldn't go to waste. Phoebe Lou saw to the candles, dusted, and set the table.

"And what's Celia doing?" Melinda was as sweet as the maple sugar she was using. "Oh, yes, now I remember— Celia is going to sit in a chair and look pretty."

Phineas came from the first spring plowing, dirty and tired, to wash in the tin basin outside the door, Jeremiah on Jupiter from town, jubilant that he had helped talk up a restraining order for the removal of the court-house.

Just before sundown, in ample time to do the chores as usual, Henry returned. Phoebe Lou ran to get the spy-glass when she was sure she could see the horses far up the prairie. With so much laughter that they could scarcely scramble up the rounds, all six girls climbed the loft ladder to their rooms where the higher window gave a better view.

"Yes, there's somebody with him," Phoebe Lou announced, while three or four hands were pulling the glass away from her, and genuine awe over the mysterious happening began suppressing the giggles.

When the buckboard came closer to the river road they climbed down again hastily, the last two falling in their excitement, and peered out the lower windows. He had driven into the yard now and they could plainly see the shawled figure with him. When they saw he was going on around to the stable they ran hurriedly out to the lean-to, pushing and scrambling to get to the windows there.

He was helping a young woman to alight. She stood by while he tied the team to the ring in the lob stable and removed a rolled feather-tick from the back of the wagon.

"They're planning to sleep somewhere," Jeanie giggled, and Sarah told her to hush, looking significantly at Celia and Suzanne, which irritated Miss Celia no end.

The young woman turned toward the house with Henry. *Lucy Brown!* One of the girls who had sat by the fire with them in the sugar camp! Jeanie, Melinda, and Celia all whooped with laughter.

"Why, Ma, he never said *one* word to her."

"We was there all the time."

"He must have talked in Injun sign language."

They laughed themselves sick.

Then the two came into the house and Henry said, "Ma, this is my wife. Her name is Lucy."

"Howdydo, Lucy," Sarah said stiffly and shook hands. "You give us quite a surprise."

Jeremiah came out to the lean-to and said jovially: "Well! Well! It's nice to have another girl in the family to take Sabina's place," and put a hospitable whiskery kiss upon the bride's cheek.

Phineas stepped forward and shook the bride's hand and said gallantly. "Henry knows a nice-looking girl when he sees one."

The three girls who had become acquainted with her in the sugar camp all laughed and made a big ado over her and the sly way Henry had got her to marry him.

"Why, we didn't know he even *talked* to you."

"He wasn't alone with you a *minute*."

"We never saw him say *one* word to you."

Lucy laughed happily, too, and her plain gentle face looked almost pretty. "He walked down to the spring with me once," she said shyly.

Emily, Suzanne, and Phoebe Lou all shook hands with the strange girl, and every one talked so that the new Lucy must have thought she had scared up a flock of blackbirds by her coming. Jeanie said if they had known a thing about the marriage they would have had Sabina and Mr. Bostwick come out.

"And got up a good supper," Emily, who had worked all afternoon for it, put in.

Then Wayne Lockwood came and was introduced to the new-comer.

After that Sarah said politely: "Will you step in the other room and lay off your things whilst the girls and I dish up the supper? We're sorry it ain't fancy."

And this is practically all there was to Henry's courtship and wedding—just as easy and simple as that. Queer that it was to last for fifty-four years.

CHAPTER 13

ALL the land between Prairie Rapids and Sturgis Falls was taken now in this spring of 1855. By fall of that same year the last piece of acreage in the whole county was to be preempted

The old trail grew more distinct. No longer did the prairie grasses and the goldenrod, the wild sweet-williams and the blue lupines lean toward each other, closing over the tracks after the lumber wagons had passed along. They stayed obediently apart on each side of the wide indentures as though there were no use attempting to combat the westward surge of iron rims. Between the Martin neighborhood and Sturgis Falls the track was wearing down to a narrow black road-bed.

North of the river road and at right angles to it the lane road was still grass-grown even though four families beside Wayne were now using it. But it took more than the travel of the teams from four families to conquer the tough prairie grass. For years in the great midwest it held its own against the incoming hordes, would not be vanquished by mere animal hoof prints. It gave up only when man's inventions proved too strong to combat. The sharp steel of the plowshare, the pointed teeth of the harrow, the multiple gorging jaws of the tractor—before these it could no longer hold out.

But in 1855 there by trails and roadsides and in all but the new wheat- and corn-fields, it was still king of the prairie, green, thick, lush with moisture, flower-sprinkled, holding down the soil. A pity it came to be conquered!

So there were more new families along the river road and up the lane. Jeremiah Martin was as personally concerned as though he had presented them with the land. As they came in to settle, he rode to each place to welcome them, routed out

Henry, Phineas, and Wayne Lockwood to help with cabins. Some of the families, though, were building of sawed lumber, at least two were employing a Sturgis Falls carpenter, and putting up fairly substantial frame homes. It took no urging for Wayne Lockwood to help with the cabins, remembering the neighborly hands when he had come the year before.

This was Wayne's first spring, so he went into his sod-broken fields with high hopes. He had brought his little bunch of a dozen sheep safely through the winter, his ewes presenting him with seven new-comers. He wrote in rather glowing terms to his parents, stressing the better points of the country, touching lightly on a spell of the shakes he had gone through and the primitive way in which every one lived.

In June, Jeremiah in conjunction with Tom Bostwick and several Sturgis Falls men, obtained a writ of injunction restricting the removal of the court-house. Prairie Rapids citizens were irate. But when the injunction was dissolved by the judge of the district court in Dubuque, because it was "injurious to the interests of the country," bitterness welled up again in every Sturgis Falls heart.

In July, the court, in a desperate effort to put a stop to all these bickerings, ordered the removal of everything pertaining to county records. And Prairie Rapids, as represented by a room on the second floor of a brick store building on the west side of the river, became the county-seat. All this added nothing to the friendliness of the two towns. So bitter was the feeling that when the records were really removed on the Fourth of July, no one from Sturgis Falls or from those families who were on the Sturgis Falls side of the feud would go to the Prairie Rapids celebration. Later that summer when a new-comer to Prairie Rapids came up to the Sturgis Falls sawmills to buy lumber, not even the sight of his cash would induce the owner to sell him any. After the summer harvest, Cady Bedson in his shining buggy, driving into the Martin neighborhood with the object of buying grain, unaccountably found none for sale. Not a bushel of wheat could he purchase west of the creek bed.

When he pulled up the high-stepping bays at Wayne's cabin he met a cool reception from the owner and Ed Armitage, working on Wayne's new well.

"How you getting along, Lockwood?"

"Reasonably well."

"Making a go of it here on this quarter-section?"

"You wouldn't by any chance enjoy hearing me say I wasn't, would you?"

Cady Bedson laughed. "Why, no, can't say I would."

"Well, I'm afraid I wouldn't give you the satisfaction of knowing it if I went plumb broke."

"I didn't know but you'd be wanting to buy land now closer to a *good* town"—he was coolly provocative—"maybe the county-seat."

"No," Wayne said soberly, when he saw that Ed Armitage was enjoying it, "I have very little need of a court-house. I aim to 'tend to my own business, keep my nose out of other folks' affairs, not make moves in illegitimate ways so I'll need never be hauled into court." To Ed this was plainly directed toward Cady Bedson and his various business enterprises, but the latter only said sneeringly: "It takes a big man to be a good loser."

"Yes, and sometimes it takes a *little* man to manipulate the winning."

"What do you mean by that?"

"I'll leave you to guess."

"Why, you . . . !"

Cady Bedson was making movements as though to climb out of the buggy so that Ed Armitage, nearly dancing up and down in his ardor to take part in a fray, dropped his spade and rushed toward him with doubled fists.

"Never mind, Ed," Wayne called pacifyingly. "Just run out to the haystack and get an egg."

And both young men laughed loud and impudently as Cady Bedson drove away in disgust.

If it was all very crude and childish, the whole court-house feud had been so.

The summer passed with a typical Iowa mixture of heat, cool breezes, rain, hail, lightning, wind, calm—a veritable flirt of a summer. But warm or cool, stormy or clear, there was always work for every one. But there was fun, too. A streak of laughter shot through all the hard work like the zigzag meanderings of the new stake-and-rider fences across the prairies.

Most of the Martin land was now outlined with these timber fences as were the two Akin farms and the Mansons'. The Burrills had put off committing themselves to so much extra labor, not sure whether they would stay or seek greener pastures, presumably some bright clime where stake-and-rider fences came all set up by a foresighted Mother Nature.

Jeremiah's constant reiterations of "what Ioway needs is railroads" appeared to be well on the way to fruition when he came home from town one day in late summer, reporting that the Dubuque and Pacific Railroad from the Mississippi on west would be commenced soon, according to rumor. Railroad men and those posted in such matters were reported taking over land in wholesale quantities. Thousands of acres in a body in the western part of the county and in Grundy County along the way of the proposed line were being preempted, every acre between Prairie Rapids and Independence having been gone since spring. Jeremiah was jubilant, referred pridefully all through supper to this rumored expansion.

"If talking up the state got you anywhere, Pa would be governor of it," Sarah said.

"Nothing but the actual laying of rails could make prospects brighter in Ioway than they are now. We won't have long to wait."

Sarah threw her dipper of cold water on his enthusiasm. "*We* wait . . . for what?"

"Why, for the railroad to come through. It will probably run right along in front of us here following the trail."

"I still don't see where much benefit to us comes in but amusin' ourselves lookin' out the window to see it go by . . . with smoke blowin' on the wash in the bargain."

But not every one had Sarah's outlook. Tom Bostwick thought it a good time to buy up land while it was still cheap, maybe some away out in the western part of the state, for when they started to build the road it would mean going straight across from Dubuque clear to the little town of Sioux City on the Missouri. He talked about taking a trip out that way in his buggy, asked Wayne Lockwood if he would like to go with him sometime for company and the experience, brought Wayne a crude map, and traced the route they could take. West of the little village of Ford Dodge as far as Sioux City there were no settlements shown.

It gave the youthful Wayne that thrill of anticipation which the potential traveler feels at the prospect of exploring uncharted countries. Yes, he would go if he could get a neighbor to take care of things for him.

Sabina, coming out home to visit on a fall day, nearly cried when she told the folks what a dangerous thing Tom and Wayne Lockwood had cooked up to do in the spring. It would take weeks to make such a jaunt and Injuns beyond Fort Dodge weren't these half-friendly kind down around the river.

Even while she was telling this in front of Wayne to her sisters in the lean-to, Jeremiah stomped in, coming home from Prairie Rapids. It was his first trip there since the fight, one for which he had been obliged to swallow his pride and go to the court-house in spite of his avowal never to set foot in the town.

As always he had news. The Sturgis Falls sawmill folks had turned a poor trick when they refused to sell lumber to the Prairie Rapids customer, for the town had a sawmill of its own now. A man by the name of Washburn had just brought in mill machinery and a heck of a time he'd had, too. Road between here and Dubuque was in frightful condition. It had taken fourteen yoke of oxen to pull the machinery and some one had met him at that bad slough at Delhi with two more yoke, but the mud was so deep it ran into the flues. They had pulled on through, though.

Wayne, listening, thought to himself that if the settlers here in the Valley had any one phrase of speech that could be called their motto, he was sure it would be that one of Jeremiah's: "Pull on through." It was being used constantly, was back of practically every undertaking. Pull on through.

They pulled through mud. They pulled through snowbanks. They pulled through high water. Spells of ague. Hard winters. Hot summers. Arguments. Feuds. Bad crops. Disappointments. They put on more oxen. Put their shoulders to the wheel. Knuckled down to work. Parceled out their food to last longer. Made over clothes. Replanted washed-out corn. Rebuilt stables torn down by winds. Nothing daunted Jeremiah Martin and his kind. If he, himself, ever had moments of feeling that he had tackled too much out here—"bitten off more than he could swallow"—he had only to converse with any of these breezy Martins and the Akins and the Mansons to realize that he could get through somehow. A year and a half he had been here in the Valley and he was no longer a new-comer. As young as he was, he was one with the settlers, an old-timer now.

Almost before any one could realize it, December had arrived and then Christmas.

Christmas Eve of 1855 in the Martins' big log-and-frame house there at the edge of the grove which swept up from the timberland along Iowa's Red Cedar River!

It was very cold. Several settlers had frozen to death in near-by localities, so said the papers. There was a little newspaper in each town now, the *Iowa State Register* in

Prairie Rapids, the *Banner* in Sturgis Falls. That was progress for you.

The west windows in the lean-to were packed solid with snow, the east ones only less so by a few square inches of peep-holes. The main room was warm as far as the fire from the four-foot logs could throw its heat. Beyond that it was as cold as though one stepped into another clime. In Sarah's bedroom the frost sparkled on the whitewashed logs of the walls. Up the loft ladders the east bedroom was only less cold than the outdoors by the slight advantage given from a roof breaking the sweep of prairie wind. The west loft had one mildly warm spot in it. By standing with one's back flattened against the wall where the fireplace chimney passed through, one could detect a faint response of heat.

But as standing with one's back flattened to a chimney was inconvenient for any protracted period, the inmates of the west chamber were as near to a state of freezing as those of the east. All the girls wore flannel nightgowns, flannel nightcaps, and flannel bedsocks, and rather perilously, with much squealing, carried up the ladders each night pieces of hot soapstone wrapped in fragments of clean worn rugs. Safely up the ladders without having dropped hot stones on whoever came behind, they climbed onto feather-beds, pulled other feather-stuffed ticks and several pieced comforts over them, and if their clattering tongues ceased and their exuberant spirits calmed down sufficiently soon, were not long in going soundly to sleep.

To-night all were around the fireplace except Sabina, who was over in her Sturgis Falls home getting ready her first Christmas dinner for them all on the morrow. Henry and Lucy had come over from the other house so there were still eleven people. Lucy sat in Ma's red-covered rocker out of deference to her delicate condition, a concession that had its humorous side when one stopped to think that all year she had washed, ironed, baked, scrubbed, made soap, hoed in the garden, gone after the cows in the timber, and on occasion helped milk. But this was Christmas Eve and all at once every one was deferential to the Madonna-like potentialities of Lucy.

Christmas Eve was Suzanne's own night. It had been made for her. Sitting on the floor with her back to the edge of the fireplace, arms around her knees while the light played over the room, she had that feeling which always came with this special night. She could not put it into words which satisfied her, but in some vague way knew it was magic—the night for which one lived all year.

In the summer, with the mourning-doves and the bouncing-Bets, the wild grape-vine swings and the long walks in the timber, you forgot entirely the feeling that this night could bring. To think of it gave you no emotion whatever. In the early fall you began to remember it. By November it became a bright light toward which you walked. And now to-night you could not think with one bit of excitement how much you liked the summer things. Yes, it was magic. The snow piled against the window was not like other snows. The wind in the chimney was not like other winds. If you scratched a frosted place out of which to look, you saw that the snow-packed prairie to the north was a white country in which no other person lived, that the snow-packed timberland to the south was a white woods forever silent. It was as though there were no human at all in any direction but your own family. Christmas Eve was a white night that drew a magic circle around the members of your own family to hem them all in and fasten them together.

Every one was laughing and talking there in front of the fire where the long knitted stockings hung. Soon now they would all get up and go after the funny-shaped packages hidden in drawers and under beds and put them in the stockings. Suzanne had something for every one—a little pincushion fitted into a river shell for each girl, a fancy box for Ma, with tiny shells fastened thick on it with glue made from old Rosy's hoofs, handkerchiefs hemmed from an outgrown petticoat for Pa, Phineas, and Henry, a corn-cob doll for—she still felt undecided whether or not it would be quite nice to put a corn-cob doll in Lucy's stocking.

The pale yellow light from the tallow candles on the shelf and the brighter reddish light from the wood logs made all the faces stand out from the darkness behind them.

Something about the magic of this night made the folks seem queer and different, too. You could not tell why, but to-night every poor quality about them fell away and only the good ones remained—Pa's big certainty that his way was always right, Ma's scolding, Henry's stubborn quietness, Phineas' smart-Aleck ways, Emily's freckled homeliness, Jeanie's silly changeableness, Phoebe Lou's teasing, Melinda's rough tomboyishness, Celia's vanity. Her heart warmed to them all.

"I'll never think of those imaginary people again," she told herself. "I'll just stay by my own real folks."

Pa was telling about Christmastime back in England; things his grandfather had told him that had come down in the tales from there—about the piping and dancing, the carols and the maskers and the woodcocks cooked in gin. "My great-grandfather's family was landed gentry back in the mother country. Ma's grandfather hung the light in Old North Church when the British was comin'. Ma says her father told her his pa was to hang one light if they come by land and two if they was comin' by sea. Both sides they bore arms for the country, faithful and loyal. You children don't never need to take a back seat for anybody. Just hold up your head and speak up all your lives. Both sides good landed-gentry blood runs in your veins and . . ."

If you listened above the din of the talking you could hear the wind in the chimney turn into music. Christmas Eve was a night of song that wrapped itself about you like a shawl. But it warmed more than your body. It warmed your heart . . . filled it, too, with melody that would last forever. Even though you grew up and found you could never quite bring back the magic feeling of this night, the melody would stay in your heart always—a song for all the years.

CHAPTER 14

B Y the next forenoon all the fragile magic of the night before had vanished entirely to make way for the hustling activity of getting ready to go to Sabina's "to have Christmas." To-day Suzanne could scarcely remember the enchantment of that night in front of the fire with the wind in the chimney and the song in her heart. Last night had been the magic world. To-day was the real one. Yes, it was true, you could close the door between the two as easily as shutting the lean-to off from the main room.

She thought she had never experienced quite so much fun as to be able "to have Christmas" at one of her own sisters' but who lived in another house. It was almost like playing at going visiting the way she and Celia and Melinda used to do down in the timber.

They would never play that way again, never go there together to sort their river shells and acorn dishes. Melinda was too old and Celia *thought* she was too old. Celia liked boys now and would smile and drop her eyelids and shake her curls whenever anything masculine came in sight. Jeanie and Celia were two of a kind, Phineas said.

The baskets were all packed now—the baked tame goose and prairie-chickens, the fresh pork roast, the wild-plum pies and the big hot dish of dried corn which Emily had wrapped in an old quilt.

They banked the fires, set the eggs, the breadbox, and a thawed-out piece of side meat on chairs in front of the fireplace in the hope that the lingering warmth would keep them from freezing during the day.

The women folks bundled themselves in their shawls, hoods, scarfs, and mittens, while the men folks hitched the teams. Jeremiah and Sarah went in the buckboard, on runners, so that

125

it slipped along easily enough over the hard drifts. Phineas rode Queen, for he wanted to be free to come and go as he pleased on the chance there was some girl he might want to see. Henry and Lucy, Emily, Jeanie, Phoebe Lou, Melinda, Celia, and Suzanne were going in the big wagon-box on a bobsled, from which the board seats had been removed so all might sit down flat among the oat-straw, quilts, and buffalo robes.

When Lucy found she could not sit comfortably flat on the wagon-box, Emily ran back and brought out one of the barrel-chairs for her so that she towered high above the others like a Queen of the May who had chosen winter for her celebration.

The whole sled was quite filled when the six girls, bulky with wraps, arranged themselves, three on a side, with Lucy perched high in their midst and Henry standing up at the front to drive.

The three older girls' hoops all gave them a good deal of trouble springing up across their knees and letting in too much cold air.

"There's no great loss without some small gain," Melinda said. "Thank goodness, I'm more comfortable than elegant."

When all were settling themselves like so many hens in their straw nests, the horses started too suddenly and Lucy's throne tottered so perilously that all scrambled up to catch her, with Jeanie and Phoebe Lou bumping their heads together hard, which caused every one to laugh themselves sick for a good half mile.

For the most part, they kept warm, with a piece of hot soapstone for every two pairs of feet, the buffalo robes, and the tanned hide of old Rosy which Emily, who was under it, now said she could distinctly hear moo.

This made them laugh again so that Melinda swallowed too much cold air and got a buffalo hair in her mouth.

When they were semi-quiet some one smelled scorching straw and Henry had to stop the team while they hunted the source of the conflagration. "Probably set by friction from your jaws working so much," he told them.

Although it was only two miles over to Sturgis Falls, it took an hour for the shaggy-legged plow horses to get there because of the deep crusted ruts, snowbanks, and crossing the Cedar on the ice. Lassie's and Laddie's bells jingled constantly on their fat sides. When they went down the steep river bank and the bob-sled nearly tipped over, there was so much feminine shrieking that Henry told them a little crossly to hush up, folks would think the Calathumpians were coming into town.

Town was getting to be quite a place, too, four hundred inhabitants, even if they were scattered over a wide area.

They drove up the other high river bank, past the taverns and the general store. Henry had to drive very carefully for Main Street was still so thick with stumps that Emily said it was a pity more people didn't get drunk to grub them out. The snow was packed high in the street excepting in the single track worn by sleds. Scattered homes sat in the midst of timber, dense woods bordered several of the platted streets, and the block which so optimistically was to have been the courthouse square, but would never be, was thick with huge native trees, snow-laden and ice-crusted. But to the Martin girls living out on the river road, the sawmill, the three taverns, the general store, the half dozen other buildings near, and the houses scattered up and down the long streets laid out through the trees, looked quite metropolitan.

They turned to the right up a sloping hill, drove past the court-house block which Henry said would now be called "the park," and came to Sabina's low square brick house set there in the trees behind a whitewashed frame fence.

Sabina herself, red-cheeked and hospitable, bustled out to meet them. And they all trooped into the house "to have Christmas."

The winter stayed as cold as Greenland's icy mountains about which Emily sang, off-key. Snows fell often and with no thawing packed to great depths. Sleds were driven over stake-and-rider fence tops. Cabins were buried in the white silence. A man south of the river was reported to have emerged from his house only by working a roof board to one side. Stage travel was practically abandoned for a time. Jeremiah fretted a great deal over not being able to know what a called meeting of those interested in this new Republicanism did in Pittsburgh.

"As though Pa had to know *that*," Sarah scolded.

It was in the middle of one of these twenty-below-zero February nights there in 1856 that Henry called his mother. Suzanne from her bed in the same room sleepily heard him: "Ma! Ma! Come quick, can you?"

Sarah had been sleeping at the front side of the bed these nights to be ready for action, and now she was out on the

floor in the dark, feeling for her quilted flannel petticoats, her
dress, and long knitted stockings. Even while she held them
to her, she padded across the cold floor to the bottom of the
loft ladder. *"Emily!"* she called sharply. "Come! You'll
have to heat water! Get right down."

It came to Suzanne lying there in bed that it was always
Emily that Ma called when she needed quick help. Emily
never gave an excuse like the others.

Suzanne raised herself, reached across Celia to pull aside
the tester, and looked out at her mother's wiry little figure in
the darkness near the sputtering candle and the spidery shadows of waving arms and legs that went up and down the
whitewashed cabin wall. Ma had her hair braided down her
back, and with no long flannel petticoats on, just a short one
to her knees so that her legs showed, she looked young. Why,
she looked like a girl about Celia's age. In fact she looked
like Celia. And Ma was an old lady, forty-nine years old.

Still on her elbow she watched the short-skirted figure with
braided hair and thought about Ma being a girl once. You
couldn't believe it. Pa must have courted a girl who was just
like Celia.

She stayed in that awkward position and listened to the
sleet crackle against the cabin windows until her mother
picked up the candle and left, with the flame trailing behind it
like the fiery tail of a little comet.

The cold came in around Suzanne's back like an icy liquid
being poured down her shivering spine, but with some half-
realized feeling of sympathy for the sister who was always
Ma's helper, until Emily came hurriedly down the loft ladder,
she stood the torture before cuddling back into the feather
quilts. Peter's hat, it was cold! She could hear the whinny of
Henry's horse out there and then its thrashing steps in the
crusted snow. Wouldn't it be awful to be having a baby?
There was more to getting married than romance. You were
courted and got married in the magic world, but you had your
baby in the real one.

Nothing went right in the morning. With Sarah and Emily
over in the other cabin the breakfast seemed to have no head.
Phoebe Lou made the fires and as soon as the ice in the
tea-kettle turned to water so she could use it for coffee, Jeanie
wanted it to thaw the chicken dishes. Phineas and Jeremiah,
having all the chores to do without Henry, were handicapped,
so that Melinda and Suzanne had to put on men's coats and
boots, tie knitted scarfs around their heads, and go out to

help, Suzanne chopping the ice in the watering-trough and taking care of the horses, including the doctor's, Melinda helping milk. When they came in they were nearly frozen, their hands stiff and white at the finger-tips, so that Melinda was cross, wanting to know why Celia had to be the one to keep her hands warm and nice, and the two kept carrying on the fussing into their joint making of beds.

Jeremiah, going back and forth between the cabins, reported that things were about over and the doctor would probably be in to breakfast before long. But the cakes grew cold and the hominy dried down in its pork fat. Things were not going just right. Nature was supposed to take its course, but Nature was falling down a little on her job.

Emily, coming over for an old sheet, looked pale and worried. "Lucy's having a terrible time," she told them, adding gloomily. "So many young mothers never get through their first time."

It took away Melinda's and Celia's peevish faultfinding and stopped the sharply bandied words. They had all taken the gentle little Lucy as a matter of course in the past year, but now she seemed suddenly very dear to them. They moved about quietly and efficiently with no more sharpness. It was noon before Pa and Doc Pierce came in, the laps of the doctor's cap flapping loosely over his ears, his face fiery red from the cold even in the short walk from the cabin.

Lucy had her baby—it was a girl. Suzanne, all ears, heard the doctor and Pa talking about bad lacerations. It sounded pretty awful.

Emily came home to stay, but Sarah went back, her little face pinched and tired-looking, her heavy hair sagging at its pins. Suzanne wondered how she ever could have thought the queer thing in the night, that Ma looked like a girl. Why, Ma was an old woman and a grandmother.

The baby was named Nora for her young aunt up near the Big Woods, although Sarah rather resented dragging the maternal side of the family into the affair at all. Emily made her mother a black netting house-cap with narrow black ribbons to tie under her chin—the official badge of grandmotherhood. When it was finished and put on, Sarah, surveying herself in the glass hung above her walnut bureau, said: "It makes me look as old as Methuselah's first wife, but you have to get along in years so I guess there's no use being mulish about it."

* * *

Wayne, preparing to take the long hazardous trip with Tom Bostwick out to the Missouri River to look for suitable government lands, wondered sometimes just why he was doing it when he was satisfied here. But since all the excitement had come up about the possible building of a railroad across the state from Dubuque to Sioux City, every one was saying that settlers would come in the Valley thick and fast, and that land would go right up. In that event he might be able to sell out for five dollars an acre and buy more dollar-and-a-quarter land farther out, a whole section, but still along the line of the railroad. At any rate it would be a good idea to take the trip with Tom Bostwick and see for himself what it was like out there.

To that end he made preparations, getting Horace Akin to take over his little bunch of stock. As for spring work, he would be back in plenty of time to go into the field.

Several times at the Bostwick home he and Tom pored over the map, picking their route for the drive. A stage line was now offering three trips per week to the Fort Dodge settlement, but beyond that there was no means of transporation at all, hence there was nothing to do but drive.

"But what's beyond?" Sabina asked, in the tone that the wife of Balboa or Magellan must have used.

"Nothing much but prairie, I guess. They say there's a trail, but so poor we'll probably have to get down on our hands and knees to find it."

"No settlers? No cabins?"

"Oh, three or four maybe—there's one stretch of fifty-five miles, though, without a cabin between Fort Dodge and a settlement called Ida's Grove."

Sabina's black eyes, usually merry, looked frightened, and her pink cheeks lost so much color that Tom Bostwick laughed long and loudly and pinched some of their roses back.

They were to start out the last Monday of February, there in 1856, with horses and sleigh. The snow lay hard packed yet but no one knew when the sun might melt it, leaving the sleigh a poor thing with which to travel. So, added to provisions for themselves and horses, they were to carry saddles in case it would be necessary to abandon the sleigh.

Because Tom was taking his team, Wayne was to ride Blackbird over to town and leave her with Sabina in case she should want to get out home.

He stopped at the Martins' as he was leaving. Suzanne, watching him ride into the snowy yard, thought she had never seen him look so big and fine, sitting his horse so easily, his body and the body of the galloping horse in perfect rhythm, for all the world like that queer Centaurus in the almanac.

"I wish I could go." Melinda, as always, envied any one departing for any place whatsoever.

"It'll be a wonder if you don't find Melinda under the seat of your sleigh after you've left," they told Wayne.

"I could stay with Sabina while Tom is gone," she suggested hopefully.

To which they were all saying virtually the same thing: "Yes, but you'd want to ride on back again if you saw a team coming out this way."

Then the most exciting thing happened that Suzanne could have imagined. Sometimes a surprise just came to you that way out of a clear sky when you were looking for nothing at all. Emily said maybe, after all, somebody should go over and stay with Sabina, and Ma seconded it, but thought if any one was to go it better be Suzanne. So there was the wildest scramble to get her ready at once to ride over to town on horseback with Wayne Lockwood.

Emily made up a bundle of things in almost no time at all and Jeanie got out some cookies for her to take. Phoebe Lou put in one of her little aprons. Celia, carried away with the excitement of the moment, loaned the traveler her bead ring, a magnanimous gesture which she later regretted. Only Melinda, pouting a bit because she was not chosen as the riding delegate, made no sacrificial offer.

So quickly had every one worked, Wayne was scarcely delayed at all, for in twenty minutes from the time he had galloped into the yard, he was galloping out of it with Suzanne in front of him and all the others waving their good-bys from the tree-trunk stoop.

"I'm going to call to her it looks like an elopement," Jeanie threatened, with Sarah telling her to hush putting such notions in a young girl's head.

But when they were turning out of the wide gateway, Phoebe Lou, who had run bareheaded down the snowy path toward the little gate where the horseshoes hung, called after them saucily, "Suzanne, I saw him first," so that Suzanne turned red, thankful she was in front of Wayne and that her winter hood covered her burning ears.

Two snow-packed miles are very long if one be old and ill and sad. Two snow-packed miles are very short if one be young and healthy and secretly excited because of the intoxicating nearness of one's ideal.

The horse floundered about at times and threw soft snow in a shower of clods, with Wayne bracing the hard strength of his young body against Suzanne's back to help her keep the precarious perch, so that to Suzanne, Wayne Lockwood behind her there on his galloping horse was a plumed white knight bearing her away into a far country.

But to Wayne Lockwood, Suzanne Martin in front of him there on his galloping horse was a young girl from a neighbor's family whose presence had made him twenty minutes late.

CHAPTER 15

TOM BOSTWICK and Wayne left Sturgis Falls after an early noon dinner for which the bustling Sabina had cooked practically everything she had in the house so they would start out well filled. Every one of the Martin girls could get a palatable meal out of the most common ingredients, and Sabina, having plenty of light brown sugar, butter, and wheat flour, could get an especially good one.

Wayne thought he had never tasted a better dinner and had no need of Tom's urgent: "Fill up, Wayne. It may be your only big one for weeks. Remember those dry crackers and that ham and tea in the sleigh."

And now the two were out on the snowy trail, driving all the long afternoon on that little-traveled road, reaching by night Peck's Tavern, a log building near where the town of New Hartford was to stand later. Here they found a warm, if ordinary, meal and rest in a loft into which snow had seeped. A long second day of driving over a lonely snowy trail, at the close of which a family in a tiny log cabin, where the town of Ackley was to be built, gave them shelter.

On the third day they reached the little county-seat of Hardin County, a village called Marietta, whose expectations were so great that its citizens harbored thoughts of becoming a big metropolis, but whose anticipations were never to come to fruition.

Another seemingly endless day's driving brought them to the little town of Newton, and the night of the fifth day out they reached Des Moines, that straggling village whose loyal founders also harbored great expectations and whose hopes in this instance were to become more than realized.

And then for the hardest and most dangerous part of the trip—the long journey across the barren snow-covered prairies west of Des Moines to Council Bluffs. It took them four full hard-driving days during which time they must forever be inquiring where they could find a log cabin or sod house by night so that they would not be left shelterless in the chill winds and at the mercy of wolves.

One hundred and fifty miles from Des Moines in four days, with the horses mud-splashed when the snow began to lessen and the settlement of Council Bluffs on the Missouri River came in sight.

And now a new element of fear entered into the picture. Before this, all the danger to the two had been that of cold and wolves and the ever present possibility of losing one's way. But here on the rough frontier with a lawless element all about them, Tom Bostwick had a definite fear for the money and land warrants on his belt. Wayne, having very little, was still as loath to lose that little as was Tom Bostwick his greater amount, so when they had arranged for a room there in the tavern, in addition to ordinary precautions they barricaded the door to their sleeping quarters by moving the head of the bed against it, and passed through the night in safety.

The snow had so far disappeared here that the sleigh had to be left and the rest of the journey was made on horseback. It took three days to follow the trail up the Missouri Valley from Council Bluffs to the village of Sioux City. They stopped for a little while near the Sioux City settlement, at the grave of Sergeant Floyd who had been a member of the Lewis and Clark expedition across the continent a half century before and who had died at this point and been buried there on a high bluff overlooking the Missouri.

Dismounting and involuntarily removing their caps, they walked over to the grave marked by the post of red cedar still standing and sound after fifty-one years from the time it had been set in the ground. In the grove near-by they could see the stump of the tree where the post had been cut, the top of the tree still lying where it fell.

They found Sioux City a village of a dozen log houses, all of which were made of native cottonwood with the exception of one—a private land-office which had doors and finishing lumber from the cabin of a steamer wrecked near it in the Missouri a year or two before.

For several days they drove about the vicinity, examining land, frequently running across camping bands of Indians. One large band was camped along the little Sioux River on land which Tom purchased at the local government office—a band of Sioux under Inkpaduta which just a year later was to be heard from with frightful consequences in the Spirit Lake region.

As for Wayne, his mind was made up. No more would he think about pulling up stakes and seeking cheaper land out here. It was too wild. White neighbors were too far away, Indian neighbors too close. It was all right for Tom Bostwick to invest in some land with which to speculate, having the money to do it. But his own investment meant his home and his work. For himself, give him the fertile Valley of the Red Cedar with its friendly people. Something of this he told Tom Bostwick, laughing as he said he wondered what his folks back home, who thought the Cedar Valley was the jumping-off place, would think if they could see *this!*

And now a very pleasant thing happened. After several days, when Tom Bostwick had selected all the land he felt he was justified in taking, the two found that during their stay a road had been broken through from Fort Dodge to Sioux City and they could ride back with the men who had made the long trip. So, instead of retracing their steps, they were to take a newer and shorter trail. This other way found them at the close of the first day in a large double log cabin at a point called Smithland—the half of the cabin used for the family's home, the other for travelers. Thirteen men slept on the cabin's floor with some jovial and fearless references to their unlucky number. With the exception of Wayne they were all after land.

Land Land! Every one wanted his share of Iowa before it gave out. But looking at the vast rolling prairies, broken by rivers and creeks, low hills and groves, as he followed the long trails the next day, when no mortal other than the immediate company was in sight, Wayne thought it a little ridiculous to be rushing so for it. Surely after this long trip, he could see that new land in Iowa would last for more than one generation.

Another day of travel and then the company stayed all night at the only cabin in the county, at Ida's Grove, with a large band of Sioux camped near-by. The following night found them at a cabin near the future site of Sac City. And then came the very hardest day of the trip, for fifty-five miles must be covered by nightfall because not so much as a single cabin, sheep shelter, or cave lay between the Ida's Grove cabin and Fort Dodge.

All day they rode the tiresome miles over a trail so poorly

trodden that at times it was with difficulty they kept to it, so that no more welcome sight could greet them than the cabins which constituted the Fort Dodge settlement. From Fort Dodge back to Sturgis Falls in three travel-filled days, and they were home. Eighteen days only had they been gone, to make the circuit—truly almost a phenomenal accomplishment.

Wayne ate supper with Tom and Sabina, finding that Suzanne had gone home with her father the day before. When he rode out to his own place and arrived at his cold cabin, he had his first sharp sense of wishing that some one were there waiting for him as Sabina had been waiting for Tom.

For the first time he wanted a woman there in the cabin and did not care who she might be—just any girl to cook his food and sweep his floor and lie by his side that night. But the desire had vanished by morning, and he went into his field free of it entirely, content to bide his time until he met the girl without whom he could not live, satisfied with his location, the fertility of his land, and his future. The trip had been instructive and reassuring by settling in his mind once and for all that there was no better place for a young man to get ahead than in the Valley. If he could not make a go of it here, he would not be able to do so anywhere.

Other men went into their fields this spring with high hopes, too. Everywhere up and down the river road black dots moving slowly in the distance would turn out to be a Martin or an Akin, a Burrill, a Manson, or an Emerson breaking new sod, or plowing those older previously broken fields.

By the last of April in that year of 1856 word came to the settlers that a bridge across the Mississippi from Rock Island to Davenport had been completed, connecting Illinois with Iowa. On the twenty-first of the month an engine had puffed its way over to the Iowa side. The next day a train with several locomotives and eight coaches had crossed the Father of Waters bringing passengers. Iron linked Iowa with the east now as definitely as the coupling-pins linked the cars.

Even though all this was far from the river road, Jeremiah, passing the news on to Sarah and the girls, was enthusiastic in the telling. "This is the biggest thing that's ever happened to the state. More'll come now, you see—right along. There'll be a bridge across at Dubuque, too, some day. No more ferryin' or crossin' on the ice then. There'll be a train out here soon, right down the river road. By granny, I wish I

could'a been in Davenport to see that sight of the cars crossin'
the long bridge.''

Sarah sniffed: ''You'd think Pa built it.''

All that spring the Indians were camped down around the
river, an estimated band of seven hundred, among them a
wizened old buck in an ancient three-cornered hat who claimed
he had once shot at George Washington. Sometimes a few
came wandering up as far as the neighboring settlers', fishing, hunting, looking for anything they could pick up, the
squaws begging at the cabins. It had the effect of keeping
Suzanne away from her favorite haunt. Ever since the night of
the big scare she was of no mind to meet any of these
blanketed and moccasined people when alone.

On a quiet afternoon when Henry's wife, Lucy, was behind
her cabin putting out onion sets, and the new baby, little
Nora, lay asleep in the trundle-bed that Sarah had donated,
Suzanne skipped over to see her, fascinated these days by her
two-months-old charms.

Entering the cabin she stopped short to see a fat squaw
bending low over the trundle-bed and pulling the red flannel
blanket off the baby.

No war-whoop emanating from an Indian ever rang out so
wildly as Suzanne, half expecting to see the baby disappear
before her eyes, let out a shriek for Lucy. As a matter of fact,
the blanket was all that the Indian woman wanted, babies
being easily and often acquired but red blankets a luxury.

The frightened Lucy came running, and rushed at the squaw
like a little wren suddenly frantic in the presence of an eagle,
snatching her baby from the cradle, caring nothing for blankets as long as the child was safe.

Suzanne never knew how she manufactured so much courage, but all at once she was furious that the squaw, still
pulling on the blanket, should dare to touch anything of the
baby's and hung onto it until the intruder gave up and left.

Jeremiah's whole conversation that early summer seemed
to center around his interest in the official assembling of the
new political party in Philadelphia. He liked the call that went
out for it and read it aloud to the women folks.

''To all the people of the United States without regard to
past political differences or divisions; who are opposed to the
repeal of the Missouri Compromise . . . that's me . . . to the
policy of the present administration . . . that's me . . . to the
extension of slavery into the territories . . .''

''That's me,'' Jeanie said, mischievously, with him.

"*. . . in favor of Kansas as a free state . . .*"

"That's me," Melinda joined Jeanie, making of it a sort of chant.

"*. . . and of restoring the action of the federal government to the principles of Washington and Jefferson . . .*"

"That's me," all six girls shouted with him.

But it was more than a big joke to Jeremiah and he threatened to thump them.

He read the report of the convention later in both the town papers, even wrote his sister Harriet to send him what her Chicago paper had to say about it.

"This new party don't skip issues," he told the women folks. "It looks facts square in the face. Ag'in the extension of slavery, tooth and toe-nail. In favor of admitting Kansas as a free state without no quibbling. That's as clean-cut as turnin' over prairie sod. By granny, *I'm a Republican.*"

"I can't say you look different than ever," Sarah met this conversion acridly.

"That's because I've always been one and didn't know it," he retorted, grinning. "Sidesteppin' Whigs!" He went off, muttering.

Of all the settlers on the river road Jeremiah was the one most deeply state-conscious. To his sons, Phineas and Henry, Iowa was the Valley and the trail to Dubuque. To his daughters it was the six miles of river road with the settlement at each end. To his wife, Sarah, it was the acreage inclosed within the stake-and-rider fence.

But Jeremiah was conscious of the whole land that lay there between the Mississippi and the muddy Missouri, the Minnesota territory to the north and the older state of Missouri to the south. He expanded his chest with the news of her acquirements. His pulse beat faster to the tales of her accomplishments. His heart ached with her disappointments and setbacks. He longed to build her schools and her churches, lay her railroad ties and break her prairie sod. Every day at his homely tasks, in the field and the barn, or galloping along to town on Queen or Jupiter his mind mulled over the happenings of the season, reviewed the new state's advancement and unconsciously planned for its future. He realized he could do little personally, knew that all growth was slow, but with his whole mind and heart he wished he could live to see "Ioway" forge to the very front ranks of the union.

Bigger men than he were managing the state's affairs, some with more schooling, lawyers and business men, but he knew about them, got the drift of happenings at the General Assembly through the little Sturgis Falls weekly paper, the *Banner*, applauded or disapproved whatever was done at Iowa City at the capitol, some day to be moved to Fort Des Moines. Already a few Des Moines men were planning the erection of the building with private funds as a gift to the commonwealth.

No, he couldn't do very much, he realized, but, after all, he was no small potatoes here in the Valley. The settlers were always asking him what he thought about this or that, hanging a bit on his say-so in regard to politics. Take now this movement toward a new political faith. Most of the community, having come like himself from the Eastern states where the Whigs were strongest, were still of that party. But it was dying, you'd have to admit that. The whole country was upset and in a pretty howdydo. The Whigs were splitting. Democrats were splitting. There were strange bedfellows these days. There were proslavery Whigs and free-soil Democrats, anti-saloon Democrats and license Whigs. Undercurrents of unrest and dislike of conditions were moving faster and faster, coming to the top of the waters in bubbles of violent disapproval. The ripples were spreading to the last little house on the Iowa prairies, to the last log cabin in the Iowa timberland.

Governor Grimes was right with his "No more slave states." He was right, too, about public schools. They should be supported by the taxation of property—this educating rich youngsters in private schools to the exclusion of poor ones was not good. "Property has its duties as well as its rights," Governor Grimes had said. Well, he was for Governor Grimes lock, stock, and barrel, and just about all he stood for. He was for this new lake-district Republicanism, too—this protecting of personal liberties, and freedom to the territories. The movement was making headway along Lake Michigan from Chicago and Milwaukee, in the Quaker and Yankee counties of Indiana, down in the Miami Valleys, and southern Illinois. The whole Cedar Valley ought to join up with them, too.

So it came to be that other men in the Valley were "for Governor Grimes and just about all he stood for," and for something different than the old Whig party which the Governor himself was beginning to repudiate. Some of them were of that opinion on their own account. More than one were of that opinion because Jeremiah Martin stood long and late by their wagons talking to them or, with one foot up on a log of their stake-and-rider fences, harangued them into his way of thinking.

Jeremiah Martin was not only sitting at the bedside of the dying Whig party but he was assisting at the birth of the lusty Republican child.

But that early summer of 1856 was the year of the big quake, too. Or so Jeremiah Martin called it, referring facetiously, as was the Martin way, to any hardship which could not be helped and so must be gallantly borne. No cracking upheavel of the rich new lands was this, but ague, malarial and bilious fevers, which shook those who succumbed as the terror of the earth shakes its victims.

Whole families were in bed, often with not enough able-bodied ones left to care for the sick. There was divergent reasoning concerning the cause of the epidemic. Sarah said she had had a dream that punishment was to be meted out in some form to a lot of people gathered in the south pasture waiting for something to strike, and this must be it. Mr. Burrill down the road said there were poisonous gases from rotting grass roots creeping out of the newly plowed lands.

Jeremiah pooh-poohed both guesses, but, cornered about giving a reason, found himself in a tight place. "Only I know there ain't nothin' to a dream that come from eatin' too much headcheese at night, and there ain't any poisonous gases crawling around in this good old prairie soil."

In the meantime flies were patiently shooed out of the cabins day after day and harmless-looking, if pestiferous, mosquitoes flew up from the swamp lands in endless swarms at night. Every evening some member of the family made up a bonfire, throwing green boughs over it to create a smudge, starting it at the side of the house from which the wind came so the smoke would drift through the cabin.

"I declare, I don't know which is worse," some one was constantly saying, "the smoke or the mosquitoes."

Only three of the family escaped, and by what reason they did not know. Jeremiah, Emily, and Melinda did not take the chills, but waited on the others, forcing them with dire threats of "Do you want to die?" to swallow their quinine. And quite often, in the throes of a shaking which rattled the bed, the victim made a weak, if emphatic, answer in the affirmative.

Over at Wayne's cabin, he, too, was shaking his bed. Each day he crawled out and looked after his stock, milked, brought in water, tried with all his strength to do more, cultivated a little, or worked in his garden. For a time he would fondly imagine that he could get through the day without the illness creeping upon him, then a chill would strike him like some monster playing its daily fiendish trick, and the shaking would begin. When he could no longer stand it, he would creep into bed, there to pull over him all the quilts he possessed and shake until it seemed the very ropes laced across the young tree branches would snap.

Emily, making soup for him or a custard, would ask her father, with an unaccustomed averting of her eyes, to take it up and see how Wayne was, and to tell him maybe he'd better come down where she could take care of him with the others.

But Wayne stuck it out alone. He tried for several days to dig a few early potatoes that rolled out of the sandy patch of soil near the creek bed almost as clean as though they had been washed. He would dig for a time and then the chill would come on. Shivering, teeth chattering, he would stoop for the potatoes until too sick to continue, then give up and go into the cabin to crawl onto the bed, shaking the boughs under him until the chill would stop and a raging fever come on him.

One morning he vowed he would work all day if it killed him. In that crucial event, at least his miseries would be over. The shaking started as usual but, teeth set, he worked about the place until the perspiration came in great drops and his agony was intense. Working and perspiring until the sun went down, he drew well water in his bucket, heated it, removed his dripping clothes, bathed, and got into bed. The next morning he arose feeling fine and saw no more of the shakes all summer.

THE BOX from Aunt Harriet came by stage, sitting up on top behind the driver, as Suzanne said, for all the world like a person who could hardly wait to get here. The contents turned out to be a little less interesting than usual, Suzanne thought, running largely to flannel and gray calico, but when she ventured as much, Jeremiah asked her if she'd ever heard of looking a gift-horse in the mouth. There was a hoop-skirt, though, this time for Melinda, her mother saying it was high time, as maybe now Melinda would calm down her boyish ways and try to be a lady.

"The way she always cavorts around, she'll get her long legs caught through the wires," was Celia's pessimistic forecast, the acidity of it caused by her disappointment in getting no hoops for herself.

The two big events of the year—and quite opposite in character—were Christmas and the Fourth of July.

"What are you going to do for the Fourth?" was the stock question to be perpetrated on the neighbors from the first of the year until the momentous day had arrived.

This year with the shakes so prevalent, recurring attacks coming upon one with practically no warning and all work in arrears because of the sickness, Sarah thought it the height of folly to attempt any celebration at all. But Jeremiah, belonging to the school of patriots who thought one had not done his duty unless he had his ear-drums nearly punctured by some manufactured noise, was quite on the side of the young folks' desire to go either to Sturgis Falls or Prairie Rapids.

The latter was attempting a celebration this year and from all reports it was going to be a very ambitious affair, so that it became the choice of the younger members of the family. That old court-house feud stood in the way of their undiluted pleasure in attending down there, however, for the decision of the votes still rankled.

After much conversation anent the attraction of the pending event offsetting the pride one must swallow in attending the rival town's celebration, the family by some quirk of the conscience decided it would be within the realms of dignity to eat their picnic dinner on the little island in the Cedar known as Lover's Retreat, thus within hearing distance of the celebration but not quite a part of it. So informed and invited to make up the crowd, the Akins, the Burrills, the Mansons, Ed Armitage, Wayne Lockwood, and several others were all planning to go there this morning of the Fourth in 1856. As though this unusual event were not enough, the older girls were going in the evening to the dance over at Overman's big new stone mill.

The invitation to it had been on the mantelshelf for two weeks. "Independence Now and Forever. 1776–1856. Promenade Concert. The company of yourself and ladies is respectfully solicited to attend a promenade concert at the new mill." There was to be a committee in charge, of which Tom Bostwick was a member, a floor manager, cotillion music by the band. The girls wondered whether their Chicago cousins could possibly have more gaiety than this.

Suzanne, in her tester bed, awoke very early with the delightful sensation enveloping her that this day was set apart from all others. She looked over at Celia still sleeping, her yellow hair on the pillow, her face pretty and pale, because she never so much as put her foot out on the tree-trunk stoop without wearing her shaker bonnet.

Two things were marring this lovely day for herself and Celia, otherwise it was to be perfect—driving to the river, going over on the island, a big dinner, games, hearing the noise of the celebration over on the mainland, all the neighbors to be together. The discordant notes were negative ones, but a missing note or two may keep the melody from reaching perfection. Specifically, one was the lack of hoop-skirts and the other that they could not go with the older girls at night. Now that Melinda had joined the rank of the stylish, only Suzanne and Celia were left hoopless, and to-day these elastic frames of fashion seemed the most desired objects in the world. Of no avail that Emily in her sympathy for their wishes had starched their pantalets and petticoats to an almost boardlike stiffness so that Sarah complained about her using so much of the starch which had been made laboriously from potatoes. No balm was their older sister's insistence that it was not necessary for girls of their age to wear them. In Celia's and Suzanne's minds to be hoopless was to be hopeless.

But from Suzanne, now, in this early morning hour of the great day, came an idea in practically the same way Minerva sprang forth from the brow of Jove.

Because she could not wait for Celia to wake up by the natural method, she achieved results by hopping out of bed, obtaining a foxtail grass just outside the cabin door and waving it delicately back and forth under Celia's abbreviated nose. When that young lady responded by vigorously slapping the author of the bright idea, it looked for a time that no good results would come from the plan, but as peace was restored, and Suzanne revealed the solution of the hoops problem, Celia entered into it not only with agreement but downright enthusiasm.

It was a busy morning, for Sarah would never step foot out of the cabin until it was immaculate and the last item in place, in case any one stopped when they were gone. There was never any locking of the door—a latch-string made of a narrow piece of leather hanging out of the lock could be drawn inside at night. So the latch-string was always out.

In addition to the regular work, the cooking for the picnic dinner and the packing of the wash-tub with the results of that cooking made the morning almost too filled for Celia and Suzanne to carry out their pleasant scheme.

But inasmuch as one almost always can find time to do the

thing he wants most to do, they succeeded in stealing a few
moments for themselves, so that when the family assembled
at the door-stoop to get into the wagon and buckboard, and
found Celia and Suzanne not present, there was some conster-
nation as well as amazement that the two who had looked
forward so enthusiastically to the day were missing.

Jeremiah had just finished saying he would thump them for
delaying the start when they appeared around the corner of
the cabin with their skirts floating out in stylish bell-shaped
wideness.

"Oh, my great granny!"

"For goodness sakes, girls, what have you done to
yourselves?"

"Where'd you girls get hoops?"

On all sides curiosity was rampant. But it gave way to loud
laughter when Sarah made them, protesting, lift up their
dresses, and there were revealed wild grapevines hanging
over their pantalets, with particularly large and robust stalks
at the lower extremity running around the bottoms of their
skirts and forming the wide circumference.

"You go back in the house and take them vines right out."
Sarah's command was terse.

"Oh, let 'em, Ma."

"Yes, what harm can it do?"

"For one thing, it's goin' to look nice, ain't it, to maybe
see purple stain come through on their dresses?" Sarah was
cross. She had worked hard and was tired already before
starting. Her black dress and bonnet were too warm for
summer.

"Ma, the grapes haven't begun to turn," the two protested.
"And anyway, we took care to pull off every little green
one."

So the two youngest Martin girls went to the celebration
entwined in grape-vines, quite like two young Bacchæ riding
forth to a revel.

Phineas, Ed Armitage, and Wayne Lookwood all rode
horseback. Suzanne was torn between her desire to ride Jupiter
with them and to go in the wagon with the girls, but obtaining
no encouragement from Phineas to join the horsemen, she
climbed decorously onto a seat of the lumber wagon.

Jeremiah and Sarah went in the buckboard. Henry drove
the team for his sisters and Lucy who carried the five-months-
old Nora, wrapped this warm day in several layers of red
flannel as a small child should be. Ed Armitage, riding at

breakneck speed up to the cabin the previous day, had hinted strongly for Phoebe Lou to go along with him, but she had ignored his roundabout maneuverings, laughing at his discomfiture, and was now with the girls. Three different young men had asked Jeanie to go with them, but since she preferred her freedom so that she might enjoy their little tiffs over her all day, she too was with the family. No one had asked Emily. Lucy's brother from up the Big Woods way had stopped in, intending to do so, but she had been too busy helping Ma to talk to him so he had given up and gone on.

The day was warm and the wagon jolted over the dusty road where the wild morning-glories tangled. The sun shone down directly on them most of the way for the road left the trees behind after the home place. They passed the green silk parasol around so that each took her turn holding it excepting Emily who made Lucy use it on her share of time for the baby.

It took so long to drive the four miles that the young fellows on their horses had been to a Prairie Rapids store and back to the island before the wagon arrived.

The water between the mainland and the island was too deep to ford so it took several trips for the Indian canoes to go back and forth the short distance with all the loads. There was much feminine squealing getting in and out of the tilting things, and once when a stiff breeze came and the parasol which was temporarily in Melinda's possession went with it, the squealing became such a shout that Melinda, always more or less awkward and encumbered now with her new hoops, lost her head and her balance, and followed after. She floundered out, mad and dripping, while Phineas paddled hastily after the floating parasol.

The island was probably six hundred feet long and about one-fourth as wide, a long narrow needle of land out in the stream and covered with some of the grandest elms in the Valley. The contour of its eastern bank followed almost minutely the shoreline so that it did not take a student of topography to decide that it had once been part of the mainland. A strong current once running against its sandy foundation must have succeeded in cutting away a peninsula of land and forcing it in time toward the center of the silvery Cedar. There the lovely island stood, covered with century-old elms under whose lacelike boughs intertwined a dense underbrush of wild crab-apple trees, grape-vines, hawthorn, sumac, woodbine, maidenhair ferns.

"Some day it will all be washed away," Jeremiah said dubiously, as he spread down a quilt for Lucy's baby.

"Oh, no, Pa," the girls chorused.

"Look how big it is."

"About a quarter of a mile long—it won't ever wash away."

"Look at the trees at the edge." He was insistent. "Either uprooted and fallen into the stream or else most ready to be. May stay on during our lifetime but foundation's too sandy to last long."

"Well, we won't worry about future generations, Pa, but enjoy ourselves to-day." Sabina was shaking out a checkered table-cloth. She and Tom Bostwick had driven over in a shiny new buggy. She had on a pale pink print dress with tiny crimson flowers in it and her rosy cheeks and black hair set it off excellently.

"Married a year and a half now," Sarah whispered to Emily, cryptically, "and no sign yet."

Jeremiah was examining the bank's edge. "You can't expect anything to last on such a sandy foundation. That's what I say about the country—can't anything ever happen to our country built on such a sturdy foundation. The Constitution can't ever be changed unless the people say so. Political parties'll always balance each other. One part of the country'll hold the other down. The level-heads'll neutralize the fool doin's of the fly-up-the-creeks. The judicial and the . . ."

"Pa's saving the nation again," the girls told each other.

Because it was so near noon when they arrived, there was nothing to do but go right ahead with dinner. Let the games come afterwards, the women said. They were hot and wanted to get the work over so there would be an hour or so for them to sit under the trees and visit with each other before setting out the late afternoon lunch. The chores had to be done early at home so the young folks could go to the dance at the new stone mill.

Emily pitched right in to help Ma put out the fried chicken and the vinegar-cabbage, the wild crab-apple pickles and hard-boiled eggs colored red in beet juice. Melinda was in a state of chronic dampness but Ma told her she could be slicing cold pork while she dried.

"What's Celia doing?" Melinda wanted to know. "Sitting under a tree with her bonnet still on to save her complexion, I'll be bound. Celia," she called loudly before the boys, "if you sit much longer, that *you-know-what* of yours will take root there and grow, and we'll all have to come back with baskets and pick *you-know-what* off of you."

It was just before the games started that Suzanne, seeing Wayne Lockwood pass not far from the grape-vine swing in which she sat, called to him: "Do you know why this island's called Lover's Retreat?" She could always talk more freely when she was alone with him, knowing that the girls were not laughing at what she said.

"No."

"Haven't you ever heard it?"

"Never."

"I can't believe that you've been here two years and never heard about it."

"Well, I have and I haven't."

"What makes you say that?"

"*Have* been here and *haven't* heard it," he said tersely.

"Well . . ." Suzanne crossed her ruffled ankles and patted her wide skirts into place over their temporary vitaceous arbor.

"Say, Suzanne . . . if you're going to tell me a long story . . ." Wayne cast disturbed eyes toward the picnickers. "They're wanting me to cast horseshoes."

Suzanne was unperturbed. "It won't take long," she assured him, so that he half reluctantly dropped down on a log facing her.

"Well, once upon a time . . ." Her eyes lost their usual look of shining inquiry and became deep and dark and tender. Even the impatient Wayne noticed it—that the candles in her eyes flickered low, brightened, blew out, flamed up anew as she talked. "There was a young man came out here from the East where something had happened . . . something that made him *hate* all *mankind*. I guess . . ." she dropped her voice to a dramatic whisper, "I about *know* it was on account of a girl."

"Oh . . . *that* reason." He laughed lightly.

"Yes. The Indians lived around here more than now . . . like they do up in the Spirit Lake country. Well, this young man from the East, he had *loved* this girl, but now he could no longer love her . . ."

"I thought you didn't know for sure it was about a girl."

Suzanne came to herself abruptly. It was true. She didn't even know there *was* a girl. Dear, dear, there she was again thinking things out to suit herself.

"Well, anyway, the rest of it's true." She went on hurriedly, losing herself in the description of the unfortunate hero of her tale. "He was a handsome young man . . ." Suzanne's lids dropped. "He was tall and broad-shouldered and he had light hair. It was quite wavy." She had almost forgotten her listener in the enjoyment of her thoughts.

Wayne stirred uneasily. "What's his wavy hair got to do with the Indians? Did they snip it off and hang it on their belts?"

"Wait until I tell you. He met with an accident when he was hunting. He shot his foot and would'a died but an Indian girl found him and took him to her father's wigwam and nursed him until he was all right. And then he loved her with all his heart. The Indian father chieftain *forbid* it time and time again. But they didn't pay any attention. He used to come to meet her . . ." Suzanne's voice dropped to its deepest throaty tones and she threw out her arms to take in the log and the grape-vine swing . . . *"right here."*

"Right here?" In spite of himself, he was interested.

"Right here." She barely whispered it.

He looked about him at the intertwining of grape and sumac, haw and crab-apple. The atmosphere of the tale was enveloping him so that he, too, felt a faint glamour of the setting. Then he came to himself with something of a start. "Suzanne, you're sure you're not making that all up?"

"Of course not. Ask the folks. She loved him and met him *right here.*"

"Well . . ." He unlimbered his long legs and stood up. "I guess it's too late to do anything about that."

"Ho . . ." Suzanne stepped out of the swing, as though to dare him to leave with the tale unfinished. "If you think that's all there was to it, you don't know. The father chief would say they couldn't meet . . . and threatened . . . and they had a tribal council and said the young man was to be killed. They named which ones of the tribe was to do it. They knew just when the two were meeting . . . the girl and the man with the *wavy light hair* . . . and the Indians all headed their canoes across the river to this island, right from over *there* by that willow hanging over . . ."

"How do *you* know just where?"

Suzanne came to herself. Yes, how did she know just where? What made imaginary things always seem so real?

"Because I know," she said stiffly, dignity itself. "They paddled over here. And here we were . . . I mean, here *they* were . . . and she saw the Indians were going to start shoot-

ing their arrows and she jumped in front of him with her arms
out . . . like this . . ."

Wayne set her very neatly aside. "Oh, no, Suzanne, I just
couldn't *think* of letting you sacrifice yourself for me."

He started away laughing, so that Suzanne had to raise her
voice to call after him the end of the story. "But her sacrifice
did not save him one bit and together they perished right here
on this island, and that's why it's called Lover's Retreat."

Wayne grinned over his shoulder at the young girl.

"All right, Suzanne," he called back. "Then I'll retreat."

It was after sundown and Suzanne sat with Celia on the
tree-trunk stoop at home, in the early prairie twilight. She
was thinking that the lovely day for which she had lived all
year was over. Why did such a perfect thing have to come to
an end? And it hadn't even come to an end yet for any of the
girls but herself and Celia.

The other four were getting ready to go over to Sturgis
Falls to the dance. Ma had said she and Celia were too young
to go gallivanting around to dances, and Pa, coming by, had
sided with her. You could maybe have stood up against one
of them—well, you could have made the attempt anyway—
but against their united front there was no use trying.

They could hear the other girls laughing up in the heat of
the loft, trying to get Ma's earrings fastened onto Melinda
without holes in her ears. Emily was using thread to tie them
on and they could hear Melinda hollering with laughter and
saying, "Well, if I had ears like a *mule* . . ."

That was the hardest part of all to bear, that Melinda was
going. The three of them had stayed home and watched the
other girls go away more than once. Just yesterday Melinda
had been a long-legged tomboy ready to play ante-over at the
school-house or wade in the creek. To-day she wore real
hoops and was going to a dance.

Ma had made Celia and Suzanne change their dresses after
the picnic to help with the supper work, but for the sake of a
remote chance that she might relent about the dance they had
left on every other best piece of apparel, their white cotton
stockings, good laced shoes, starched petticoats, and even the
clumsy grape-vine underpinning, withered a little now, but
still staunchly rigorous.

Sitting here on the stoop they clung like shipwrecked mari-
ners to that floating hope, knowing that if the rescue word
came, they could change into their best dresses in quicker

time than dresses had ever been changed since the world began.

Wayne Lockwood drove into the yard in his wagon, Ed Armitage, Sam Phillips, and George Wormsby with him, all in their good suits with soft stock collars. Phineas came up from the stable, calling to the girls to hurry with their primping. Emily arrived down from the loft.

"There's still a few minutes," Celia moaned, as one whose life sands are fast running out.

"Ask Emily . . . she'd be willing, maybe," Suzanne suggested optimistically.

"Emily . . . couldn't *we* go too?" Celia's voice dripped pathos.

"We could get ready in a minute." Suzanne's quivered with whispering hope.

"My no," Emily said briskly, "it's a real dance with just grown-ups, not a mixed crowd of all ages like our neighborhood things."

That practically sank the only floating plank in sight. If the softest-hearted one in the family said no, the whole cause was a lost one.

All four girls came out now in their best dresses—Emily, Jeanie, Phoebe Lou, and Melinda *in hoops and Ma's earrings!* They were all laughing, holding up their skirts and picking their way out toward Wayne's wagon.

Down past the tree-trunk stoop a short distance, Melinda stopped and turned around to the two sitting forlornly there, her long earrings swinging out with her vigorous whirling movement. "Be good children," she called back cheerily.

Melinda, who had played house with them, sorting acorn dishes and shells! Life's lowest depths can be plumbed at the oddest moments.

Ed Armitage and Wayne were handing every one up over the wagon wheel with exaggerated courtesy. Emily was waving and calling back her good-bys. Jeanie was squealing not to drop her. Phoebe Lou was saying: "Don't forget Evangeline Burrill." Melinda was laughing fit to kill over nothing. The wagon rattled out of the yard with every one talking at once.

The two sat without words, chins in their hands. The darkness deepened. A night-hawk dipped near them with its *boom boom*. The smell of the prairie grass in the east pasture was strong under the heavy dew. A sheep's bell tinkled back of the house. Lightning-bugs flashed here and there in the dark yard. An old cow bawled in the timber. Faintly and far-away you could hear the repercussion from a cannon's report.

Suzanne put her head down in her arm and cried for all the lovely and exciting things that lay out there beyond the stake-and-rider fence.

But Celia did not cry. She sat with knuckles pressed white against her mouth and kept saying with deadly calm: *"Just you wait . . . just you wait."*

And Suzanne on the tree-trunk stoop waited. There was really nothing else to do.

CHAPTER 16

THAT fall of 1856 saw many changes and improvements in the Valley. There was a noticeable spirit of progress in the air around the two towns lying six miles apart there at the western and southeastern ends of the curving river road. Sturgis Falls had grown from its three or four buildings of four years before to nearly two hundred, some of brick and stone, as the former were now being manufactured in large quantities and the quarries in the bluffs along the river were producing some of the best stone in the new state.

There was a lodge which met "every Monday on or before the full moon." Presbyterians, Methodists, and Episcopalians were rallying around their church standards preparatory to building small edifices. There was Mr. Packard's newspaper, the *Banner*, giving the national news, somewhat belatedly, and the state news even more so, for it was easier to hear what was going on in the east than over the state itself, isolated as were its various communities. The little newspaper dealt largely in jocular vein with local events, with many familiar references to the affairs of the home folks. "Joe Trine is making weekly visits up near the Big Woods. Let us in on the secret, Joe," and "Some one was trying to serenade a certain young lady in the west end of town last Sunday night. Any one obtaining a clue to the intruder whose voice was concealed under a heavy black mustache, please report to this office and receive reward."

It also gave the purported schedule of the four lines of stage-coaches passing through town, but which were flexible affairs, as the hour of arrival was entirely dependent upon the amount of mud or snow encountered, the condition of the horses, and, alas, occasionally of the driver.

The Overmans had finished the big new stone mill. The

first grocery store, as differentiated from a general store, came into being. There were two doctors, a gunsmith, a wagon-maker.

Down the river, Prairie Rapids, too, had a flour mill, one of the most important additions yet made to the little town. Building lots were being sold to buyers from various parts of the country. Churches were organized, the Presbyterians and Catholics beginning the erection of modest buildings. Young John Leavitt, who had worked for the first bank, started one of his own. A two-story frame store was built, a two-story stone one, a brick one, two sawmills, a planing mill. Some one built a double brick house. The thirteen-thousand-dollar court-house was started, a project which brought forth both angry outbursts and no end of chuckling on the part of the losers in the court-house scrap. Because the whole country could cast a vote for the exact location of the building, all Sturgis Falls voted to put it on the east side of the river in Prairie Rapids, the new raw sprawling side of the town, in order to get even with the westsiders who had taken it away from them.

There were other important votes cast that fall. An election was called to confer authority upon the country judge to subscribe for and take over two thousand shares of one hundred dollars each of the capital stock of a new railroad company to be paid for by the county in twenty years at ten per cent.

All the yearning for a railroad which Jeremiah possessed was secondary now to his conservatism. He rode hither and yon to put the fear of this dubious venture into men's souls.

"Everybody wants a railroad . . . that goes without sayin'. But not *that* way. Stop and think what you're votin' . . . giving the judge jurisdiction to sign two hundred thousand dollars' worth of bonds. Signin' it away before a spade's turned a shovelful. Can you figger? Can you multiply? Do you know in twenty years' time this county would pay out pretty nigh a million dollars? We'd be saddlin' our children and our grandchildren with it. The railroad'll come through in time without *that* much gamblin' on the part of a single new county. Indebtedness is the poor man's curse. Just so, it's a county's curse . . . or a state's . . . or a nation's."

Even so the vote was declared to have gone in favor of the bonding.

But before the bonds were signed, a new judge took office—Judge Hubbard, one of Jeremiah's good friends. And when the blank bonds came, lithographed, waxed, and gaily rib-boned, conferring with legal minds and such level-heads as Jeremiah, the new judge refused to sign. The officials coaxed, promised, cajoled, flattered, and threatened, but Judge Hubbard stood firm. Then they tried the well-known thirty pieces of silver, but received only the judge's indignation and scorn for their pains.

"There ought to be a monument to him . . ." Jeremiah said jubilantly. " 'Judge Hubbard, the Solomon of his time—he kept us out of debt.' "

If the previous winter had been severe, that one of '56–'57 was even more so. The snow fell before the corn was all gathered and the unpicked portion was to lie under the white blanket until spring. On December first a fierce storm descended upon the midwest plains, lashed itself into a three-day frenzy before its hysteria wore itself out, and left behind a snow eight feet deep in places. There was not much traveling about, but when one did so, he could drive over the top of field fences. Hard-packed roadways were ridged up two or three feet above the surface of the ground with regular places for passing, and woe to the driver who thought to disregard these, for often he would find himself sinking down into white space from which he could extricate himself only by unloading and scooping out the sleigh and thrashing team.

Icy-winged prairie-chickens, sitting along on protruding rail fences, floundered in the snow when approached and were caught by hand. Dressed and the breasts dried, they made many a later meal for the settlers. Phineas clubbed to death an elk in the near-by timber.

The whole winter was one endless fight to care for the stock, dig away drifts, cut sufficient wood ahead for both houses.

There was not any too much feed. Those long spells of the shakes which every one had endured in the summer had cut short the working days so that the amount of prairie hay stacked was less than usual. The newspaper said hay was ninety dollars a ton in Dubuque, wood thirty dollars a cord.

Jeremiah and the boys were worried about the feed holding out. At every storm's cessation they hoped to turn the stock out to find a little forage, but the storms seldom ceased. All winter the winds blew across the prairie and the snows piled high. The Martin, Burrill, Manson, and Akin houses were but other white mounds in a valley of drifts. Wayne Lockwood's cabin was an isolated island in a sea of crystallized foam.

Whenever possible he split and hauled wood to the Sturgis Falls taverns which took all he could bring, but so often the storms were severe and of such long duration that he was driven indoors for days at a time. He took advantage of these periods to make himself a big fireplace chair, a new table, cupboards.

The Martin women were careful and saving about their supplies, for there was no knowing when they would get to either town again for more, and, what was worse, no telling how the little towns were faring either. Neither the Dubuque trip nor the Cedar Rapids one had been made by any one for weeks. Every night now they ate only samp for supper, a porridge made by boiling cracked corn for a long time and then letting it cool. With this they ate milk and molasses and when the sorghum supply ran low, they ate it without sweetening.

Into the monotony of the wintry weather came news which gave them all conversation for many a mealtime. The only railroad in the whole state was that little strip from Davenport to Muscatine through Wilton. But the residents of Iowa City had offered a big sum of money if the company would build the road on from Wilton to their town by January first. And now in January word got through by sled-driver to the *Banner* that in the early evening of New Year's Eve the track had been still nearly a quarter of a mile away from the depot, but that all the men in town turned out and in the bitter cold weather, with bonfires along the right of way, they had worked by the side of the railroad men laying rails, with the engine creeping along behind them. In sight of the depot with only a few minutes to spare the engine froze, but a great crowd had taken hold and pushed it into the depot just when the bells rang for the New Year.

The excitement and drama of it appealed to Jeremiah as nothing had ever done, so that he talked about it a great deal, living over in fancy that exultant moment of seeing the engine roll up to the platform at the last minute. "By granny, they pulled through by the skin of their teeth!" He would roar and laugh at the joke of it, envious of those who had been there.

When little Nora's first birthday arrived in the midst of the winter's privations, Emily made her a birthday cake from cornmeal with the last bit of maple sugar for filling, and put a single little candle in the center. Suzanne made her another corn-cob doll, the husks braided into two fat pigtails. From a thread box and two spools Sarah concocted a little toy wagon, scolding at her own silliness in doing it, when the child wasn't old enough yet to play with it.

But scarcely had the week of her birthday passed before Henry, white of face above his black beard, came over for his mother in the evening of another hard snow, saying that the baby was sick with croup. So short a distance could one see ahead of him that, stumbling into the lean-to door, Henry still held in his hand the clothes-line which he had tied to a tree near his own cabin door, that he might not waste time finding his way back.

The various members of the family were all around the fireplace—Jeremiah reading his paper by the candle's light, Phoebe Lou, Jeanie, and Sarah sewing carpet rags, Phineas, Suzanne, and Emily shelling corn into a wash-tub. Only Melinda was missing, having slipped out to the lean-to to blacken her face with charred wood, intending to come in saying, "You folks got any room heah for a po' ole trodden-down runaway niggah to stay to-night?" and give them all a laugh.

The girls had been chattering over the big balls of rags and the corn-shelling, laughing at some absurdities of Phoebe Lou in mimicking Ed Armitage, but when Henry stumbled in, worried about his baby, the fun was over.

Sarah and Jeremiah bundled up and went back with him, Sarah carrying her jar of goose-grease, and all three holding the rope.

The girls were a silent lot now, their thoughts only for little Nora with her crisp black curls and her funny way of wrinkling her nose and pointing to whichever one was named. Smart as mustard, that was, to be able to tell them all apart.

Their father came back, his shoulders and beard loaded with snow, the wind tearing in madly with him as he opened the door.

"Ma's afraid it's lung fever."

Lung fever! There was milk-fever, walking fever, slow fever, summer fever. But lung fever was the sickness that got into the chest and burned it until one could no longer breathe, that took its toll of babies in the Valley every winter. And now it was little Nora who laughed and wrinkled her nose and pointed to them all when they were named.

Jeanie and Phoebe Lou sat staring at Pa bringing the bad news. Celia's face puckered. Emily's went so white that the freckles stood out on it like little brown raisins. Suzanne cowered as from a blow and her hands flew to her throat to stop its wild beating. Melinda, crying into the foolish black-ing and blowing her nose, looked more grotesque than she had planned.

"Now . . . now . . . pull yourselves together," Jeremiah said sternly. "Shame on you. There's things to do. Jeanie, go fetch all the onions. Celia, get a comfort off o' somebody's bed. Emily, get all the flannel rags together you can find. Get candles. Phoebe Lou—Ma wants more light. Pack 'em all in a basket. I'll take the onion sack on my back done up in the blanket. Melinda, get the hot drops from the top shelf. Su-zanne, find the baby's doll they left here in case she notices. Phineas, can you make it to town for the doctor the minute daylight comes?"

"I can get there if anybody can," Phineas said, and was in the lean-to getting his wraps together and the freshly oiled bridle as though he were starting at once.

They were all carrying out orders now. The onions were the last of the vegetables. They had been hoarding them, taking good care that they did not freeze. Now they were to be baked to make compresses for the baby's lungs. Jeanie brought them from their place back of the lean-to stove and tied the sack inside the comfort that Celia had taken from her bed. Melinda and Phoebe Lou were packing the medicine and the candles. Suzanne brought the corn-cob doll, hugging it to her breast as though it were little Nora. Emily came hurriedly down the loft ladder. "I can't find enough flannel cloths," she said in despair. Standing in the middle of the floor she suddenly pulled up her dress and yanked off her red petticoat.

For five days and nights Sarah stayed over at the other cabin with Henry and Lucy, holding the child on her lap much of the time near the red hot stove around which Henry had hung horse blankets and buffalo robes to form a shelter so that no wind from crack or crevice could strike her. For all of that time, with little or no rest, Sarah battled Death, holding it at bay with warm goose-grease on the little throat, rubbing the tiny chest and back with hard hands grown gentle, while her sagging red hair loosened from its pins and her eyes were bloodshot from loss of sleep.

She would not give up, not even when the baby's breath came so fast and hoarse that it sounded like a whistle made from the willows down by the slough. Jeremiah helped Henry and Lucy keep the stove red and the hot water going, the flannel cloths wrung out and the onions roasted. Steadily he fought side by side with Sarah, baking and opening the onions to make the hot compresses for those little congested lungs. Constantly he encouraged Henry and the almost prostrate Lucy with "She'll pull through. Ma'll pull her through."

On the morning of the fifth day Suzanne in the lean-to was looking through a place on the window scraped free from ice. She saw her father and mother coming home through the drifts together and, too fearful to tell the other girls, watched their slow, floundering progress. They would not be coming home together unless the baby was better or—

Too frightened to think clearly she could not draw her fascinated gaze from Pa and Ma coming through the deep drifts. Pa had his gray shawl around his shoulders over his coat, and his cap pulled low over his forehead. Against the wind his black beard blew up across his face. Ma's shawl was pinned tight around her, but her hood had slipped, so that you could see her reddish hair half-way back as she held her head down into the face of the wind. It looked queer to see Pa and Ma have hold of hands, coming along that way. They would soon be here and then—

Little Nora was better. No, she was dead. Whichever way it was, she was glad they had had her. Even if she was dead, it was better than if they had never known her at all. You could always see her in your mind as plain as anything, remembering her crisp little curls and her funny little nose. She knew the thoughts in her head were crazy, jumping about that way. She ought to tell the other girls that something had happened. They were all there in the room right behind her, but she could not turn and tell them Ma and Pa were almost here, could not make any word come from her dry throat, could do nothing but stand, fascinated and fearful, looking through the scraped-off place in the window, and wait.

The door opened and they came in. Ma almost fell in, so that Pa caught her with his arm.

"Well, she's pulled through," Jeremiah said cheerfully. "The rattle in her throat's stopped and she's sleepin' natural."

Sarah said nothing. Her little thin face was pinched and gray, her reddish hair stringing down at each side.

"Girls, get Ma to bed," Pa said tersely. "You let her lay all day, too."

Sarah dropped down wearily on a lean-to chair, with Emily and Phoebe Lou unfastening her shawl and pulling off her hood gently, and Celia tugging at the felt boots. Jeanie brought a pan of warm water and washed the pinched gray face and bloodshot eyes.

For ten minutes, perhaps, Sarah sat with her hands in her lap, a drooping little figure. Then suddenly she jumped up, almost scattering her attendants. "Good land!" she said. "I'm all right. Such a fuss! How's the housework come on? Pa's goin' to butcher. We got lots to do. You girls have to hump yourselves. Now scoot!"

Winter lessened its grasp for a few days as a wild animal loosens its hold on its prey, but even then it did not fool the settlers. They knew it would play with them a few weeks longer, releasing them only to hold them tightly again in its cruel paw. The men folks of the neighborhood all took time to get to Sturgis Falls or Prairie Rapids for supplies, while the stores there took advantage of the mildness to send wagons to Dubuque or Cedar Rapids for replenishing their goods. The stages came in with delayed passengers and mail. People came out of their cabins and went on necessary journeys as the wild things of the forest scurry about after hibernation.

On one of those first milder days two young men came across the north prairies in a sled and stopped at Wayne Lockwood's cabin. They were personable young fellows who had driven down from the far-off Spirit Lake region and were en route to Prairie Rapids for supplies. Learning they were hungry as bears after a winter's sleep, Wayne made corn cakes and chopped off large slabs of his frozen side meat, insisted on their eating as much as they could, keeping it to himself that unless he got out and restocked his own larder he would soon be in the same predicament they were.

He enjoyed the young fellows' stay, their talk of the region in which they lived, their light-hearted manner in the face of the hard trip through the snows made because of their constantly diminishing supplies. In fact, he liked them so well that he rode horseback along with them to Prairie Rapids in order to have their company while he purchased his own goods.

When he left them there, they promised to stop to see him again en route back.

Two days later he was in the Martin yard, sitting his horse, just ready to leave for home, but chatting a last minute with Phineas, when he saw the team and sled of his newly found friends coming up the river road. He waved his hand and called to them and they turned at once into the Martin yard. But now there was a third person with them, whom Wayne and Phineas recognized at once as a young fellow who had been working in the grist-mill at Prairie Rapids.

The five men talked there in the snow, Phineas at the well curb, the three young fellows standing in the sleigh, and Wayne on Blackbird who stepped about in the crusted snow as though impatient to stop this foolishness and be off.

The young man from the grist-mill was returning to the Spirit Lake region with the others. There was still plenty of government land up there, he said, but here there was no longer any way for a fellow to get ahead, with the last acreage in the county preempted these eighteen months. Presented with glowing pictures by the two as they were at the mill, he had given up his job at once and was off to the land of the Sioux, somewhere around Spirit Lake or Okoboji. He was enthusiastic about it, looked forward to settling in the lake region, explained that something in him responded to the call of the blue lakes. He said that all at once when the two settlers of that region were describing them, the sparkle on their blue expanse in the summer, the hunting and fishing, and the fertile lands between the big waters, he could not think of staying longer in the Valley with only its Red Cedar River and its little creeks and sloughs. So here he was off to the more attractive place. And what was more, he was all urgent that Wayne join him. All the four miles out of Prairie Rapids, they had been planning that Wayne go, too, right along now with them. It was too early for field work. He was to get some one to care for the stock, go along with them now and choose lands, then come back and sell.

When Wayne told them that he was of no mind to locate away from here since his trip out to the Missouri River, they changed tactics and teased him to go there just for the sightseeing—Phineas too, they said. So much the merrier with five of them. They knew a place near the Big Woods where you could get a jug of "Cedar River Water," laughing loudly at their name for it. But Wayne would not do that either, although the youthful adventure was tempting.

As they were talking, two of the Martin girls came around the corner of the cabin so that the young travelers were all interest.

Jeanie, seeing so much strange masculinity in the yard, had wanted in the worst way to make some excuse to get closer to the source of excitement. All the girls peeping out had been piqued with curiosity, but only Jeanie had dared think up a plan to satisfy it, and only Celia could be prevailed upon to accompany her.

Now, with their best capes on, and their dresses drawn up over their shoes to reveal shapely ankles while they stepped high and gingerly through the crusted snow, they came around the corner of the house, conversing vivaciously and so utterly unconscious of any one within half a mile of their presence that they were frightened into gay squealing when they suddenly saw so many young men before them.

"*Oh . . . my goodness,* Phineas, how you scared us!"

"We didn't *know* any one was *here.*"

In their fright they even forgot to lower their dresses until they caught Phineas' brotherly glare, when they dropped them in complete and blushing confusion.

Now that they were here, they lingered, because the young men in the sleigh were all laughter and wit, talking no longer of government requirements and the Mendota treaty whereby the Sioux had promised never to lay any more claim to the Iowa land, but only paying attention to Jeanie and Celia, quite as Jeanie and Celia wished.

The strangers joked the girls, asked Celia if the bees made her hair which had tumbled (with a bit of aid) out of her cape's hood, and wanted to know which two of the three of them might hope to take the young ladies to a dance in Overman Hall when next they came down this way.

Jeanie rolled her eyes merrily and suggested drawing straws, and Celia, who had so recently been judged by a power above her too young to go to a town dance, tossed her yellow head and said she guessed they'd *all* be too late to ask *her* by the time they next got away down here in this part of the country.

Only Phineas, leaning on the well curb, looked a little disgusted over the give-and-take conversation, and Wayne, sitting his horse so perfectly as she stepped about restlessly in the snow, grinned in complete comprehension of the little scene and winked openly at Suzanne in the window.

"Maybe you've got another sister?" one suggested hopefully.

The girls burst into gay laughter at that. "Sister! We've got enough to dance with you and all your friends," Celia said daringly.

"We're the two *homeliest!*" Jeanie rolled her merry eyes, knowing that they would all deny the possibility of the statement, as they immediately did.

And then one jumped out of the sleigh, saying that he must get closer to Celia's hair in order to see whether they were really little curls there or yellow shavings from a piece of pine board which she had pinned on under her cape's hood. Coming close, he touched a curl lightly, and before Celia could realize what he was up to, he had snipped off an end of one with his concealed jack-knife, so that she squealed this time without pretense, and called to Phineas and Wayne to protect her.

And now the three young men were leaving the daring one holding up the piece of yellow curl over his own ear with pantomime of twisting it like a primping girl. They rode laughingly out of the yard, saying they would be back in a few weeks, calling out saucy things as gay and light-hearted as though they were on the way now to that Overman Hall dance instead of to the snow-locked lake region where the blue waters were still frozen and the warrior chief Inkpaduta and his band of Sioux were creeping in from the southwest to pitch camp on the bank of Lake Okoboji and crouch there in the bitter cold while the drums beat in weird steady rhythm.

CHAPTER 17

THE cold around the lake region was not more bitter than the hatred in old Chief Inkpaduta's heart. The snows had long lain deep on the north prairies and in the timberlands, and Inkpaduta's people were cold and hungry.

Six times had the seasons come and gone since the white man had made them give up their hunting-ground. The white man said the lands were his. The white man had raised food on those lands by the shores of the lake sacred to the Great Spirit. For the length of two moons now Inkpaduta had been taking food away from the palefaces and frightening them.

Camped on the eastern shore of Lake Okoboji with the drums beating their weird steady rhythm, something was getting into the blood of this outlaw band which neither the white man nor red called friend.

All night the drums beat. All that night of March seventh in 1857 the drums beat on the eastern bank of the lake of Okoboji. The drums beat and the shadows crouched low. The drums beat and the shadows took on form and substance, became livid figures that sent forth piercing war-cries.

On the eastern shore of Lake Okoboji the drums beat. Not far from the shore of the lake sacred to the Great Spirit the drums beat.

All night the drums beat.

The drums beat . . .

The drums . . .

The Martin family was assembling for the noon meal. Hearing a horse's hoofs splashing through the mushlike snow, and thinking that only Ed Armitage tore into the yard so fast, they were all expecting to see him. But it was not Ed. It was Wayne Lockwood, his face curiously strained looking, as though he were holding himself steady rather by force of will than natural poise.

So definitely did they all sense something was wrong that Jeremiah's quip about him smelling their pork and beans clear up the lane road died in the making.

"Bad news," Wayne said in the doorway, surveying them all with that strained expression on his face, the muscles under the skin moving jerkily. "I just came from town. The Sioux have been on the war-path up around Okojobi."

Jeremiah began, "Oh, now . . . I've heard that rumor so many . . ." and broke off.

"It's no rumor this time," Wayne said crisply. "Fifty people at least are dead. Those three young fellows who stopped here . . ." he turned involuntarily toward Jeanie and Celia, swallowed as though he could not bring out the words . . . "are dead."

"Dead?" Jeanie said in a whisper.

Celia gave a little cry and put her hand up to her hair as though to feel for the end of a curl.

Then Wayne turned and left for home, his horse splashing through the melting snow of the yard.

Yes, all the white settlers in the Okoboji vicinity were dead but the little fourteen-year-old Gardner girl, whose story every Iowa school child came in time to know—how Inkpaduta and his band crept into her home, demanding food and guns, how the child saw her father shot through the heart, her mother clubbed to death, and the other children's brains dashed out against the walls, how the young prisoner, after a long time of cruel treatment and weary marching on the snow carrying a heavy pack, came near a band of friendly Sioux whose chief purchased the girl for horses, blankets, powder, and guns, and sent her to the white missionary.

All of this and much more the Valley people came to know in time, but just now they knew no details excepting that the lake settlers, about fifty in all, were killed and that three light-hearted young men who had planned to come back and dance with Celia and Jeanie would never come.

Spring came on with the screaming wild winds dying down in the timberland and the honking wild geese settling into the slough, with the grass green and lush on the prairies, and the meadow-larks spilling liquid notes from the stake-and-rider fences.

By May the Dubuque and Pacific Railroad, with no bonded

indebtedness on the part of Judge Hubbard's county, had laid thirty miles of track west of Dubuque to the little town of Dyersville. That began to look like real progress. Everything would build right up now, every one predicted, even though the only other railroad in the state was that little Y-shaped strip between Davenport, Muscatine, and Iowa City.

Summer came on with the corn hurrying to be "knee-high by the Fourth of July" and Aunt Harriet's box arriving.

Celia said there might just as well be no box as far as she was concerned if there proved to be no hoops. You could starch a skirt so stiff it would stand alone, but *what of it?* It didn't look any more like the stylish ones over hoops than the man in the moon.

The opening took place with customary ceremony. Already Sabina, married over two years and having as good things as any one in Sturgis Falls, was more or less disinterested over its advent. Suzanne, thinking how Sabina was once so enthusiastic over its coming, told herself that never as long as she lived could she outgrow the excitement over THE BOX'S arrival.

They all gathered around the table in the lean-to while Pa pried off the top and went through that exasperating ceremony of bending every nail straight and taking out his share of the donation, the newspapers, pressing them carefully for future reading. The Chicago papers would tell a lot about the new Democratic President Buchanan. If they were critical of him, Pa would chuckle and enjoy himself immensely, calling all the women folks to come and hear this. If they were laudatory, he would fume and fuss, maybe walk the floor snapping the paper against his knee and argue into the air that any one who could see good in a Democrat wasn't worth listening to.

There were two full-skirted dresses, one wine-colored with black bands, and the other the most luscious of anything that had ever been sent out here. It was richly golden in hue and too nearly new to have been worn much. Only when Emily was looking it over did she discover the badly scorched panel which was without doubt the cause of its sending.

"It's not sensible." Sarah was disgusted. "What do they think we could do with it out here but color it dark with walnut bark?"

"Oh, it would be a shame to color it," every one said.

"I could make it over without the scorched piece." Emily surveyed it with a practical eye. "Somebody ought to get married now, to wear it."

"Oh, *I* will," Jeanie volunteered, and they all laughed at

her readiness to lay herself on the sacrificial altar in order to be the beneficiary.

There were flannel nightgowns, a dark gray cape, a brown straw bonnet with eight glassy red cherries on it, some black silk mitts, and a pair of stays. There were no hoops.

Celia going up into the loft to hide her disappointment caused Jeremiah with unaccustomed masculine insight and sympathy to go slyly to town and return with a contraption from the new tinsmith's, a series of narrow tin bands soldered together in spiral formation which caused the girls all to have a good laugh and Celia to praise Pa to the skies for his Yankee ingenuity.

The summer was hot and dry. The Indians camped up by the Turkey Foot—where the Red Cedar, West Fork, and Shell Rock come together like a wild turkey's toes—said the beavers had all disappeared, that there would be dry weather until they came back and went to work.

More and more as the summer went by was it apparent that times were getting hard, the boom balloon gradually deflating. Money was scarce, wildcat bank paper as thick as leaves in the timber. Financial troubles in the east by a sort of creeping paralysis came into the new west. Weekly trips for merchandise were dropped by the general stores. Construction upon the railroad which was to have come through from Dubuque with such promptness had been stopped at Dyersville before it even left that country. Phineas, coming through with a team and an unusually small load of purchases, said the ties were piled there beside the grading, a forlorn-looking sight, and that maybe, after all, the line to Muscatine and Iowa City was the only railroad Iowa would ever have.

Jeremiah was intensely disappointed, felt a personal loss in the cessation of work, as though something had gone out of his own life. He had gloated so much over at town about the Dubuque and Pacific finally coming through (without the county's indebtedness) to connect the Valley and the east coast that he grew almost apologetic whenever any one asked him if it were true work had been stopped. He would explain it all with excuses, as though he himself had been derelict in his duty.

One thing in the state though, he usually included optimistically in his conversation, was going along quite as planned. The new capitol was under construction in spite of the panic, even though it had been uphill work for those men to finance it. All the records were to be moved over there to Fort Des

Moines as soon as the building was finished this fall. Hold on
a minute, he'd told that wrong. It wasn't *Fort* Des Moines
any more—the "Fort" was dropped. It would be a big town
some day there at the fork of the Des Moines and Raccoon
rivers. *That* was a forward step for the state, he told every
one, taking the personal attitude he always assumed about
civic questions, as though he must choose sides and pull for
which side he thought right.

There were a few other improvements of local type, even
though times were noticeably hard, wildcat money abroad,
and crops not any too good that summer. A bridge was built
across the river at Sturgis Falls, the posts from native elms
cut in the Big Woods, and hewn by hand. No longer would
one have to ford the Red Cedar in low-water times, ferry over
it when the flow was too deep, or "sled" across it in the
depths of Iowa's cold winters. And a steamboat came up the
river from Cedar Rapids to Prairie Rapids to make twenty-two
trips altogether. *That* looked as though the country was coming on, Jeremiah bragged.

But the country was not "coming on" very well. Times
grew more dull as the summer passed. Very little building
was being done in either town and only the court-house was
under construction in Prairie Rapids. For the first time there
was no growth in population.

Every one was in a sober mood about it. It seemed that
everything one had to buy was "sky-high," anything one
sold "cheap as dirt." Corn and oats were ten and twelve
cents a bushel, wheat twenty and twenty-five. Henry drove to
Dubuque with potatoes which he had to sell for ten cents a
bushel, but the tavern-owners in Sturgis Falls had offered
only five cents, the Sherman House in Prairie Rapids six, so
he took the long trek for the difference.

Sarah's sweet butter, packed in stone jars with a water-lily
pattern indented by her paddle on the top, sold for eight cents
a pound. Most of the women got only six. In the east, artists
signed pictures, authors autographed books, sculptors chiseled
their names in marble. Out in the Valley of the Red Cedar
Sarah Martin stamped the artistry of her nimble fingers with a
symmetrically formed water-lily when she packed her butter
in jars in the summertime, modeled a fat fish with evenly
matched overlapping scales when she worked it into pound
molds in the winter.

No one knew what made prices low, so there was much
speculation as to the cause. Tariff, transportation, this anti-

slavery talk, weather, the national administration, state politics, human sins, predestination, all figured largely in the
discussion up and down the river road.

Mrs. Burrill thought Satan had planned it so.

"I'll swallow anything but that the poor old devil is to
blame," Jeremiah said. "He ain't settin' the price of corn, I
know that."

Ambrose Willshire said they should lean on the Lord and
wait until He sent better times, ask Him for more help.

It caused Jeremiah to explode in one long blast: "Leave it
all to the Lord! Ask Him for more help! Maybe I don't do as
much leanin' on the Lord as some. Maybe I'm wrong. But
this is the way I figger. The Lord equipped me, so to speak.
He give me a brain, two good eyes, speech, sharp hearin',
smellin', hands, feet, health like a ox. Then He turned me
loose in a world where there was fish in the streams, meat in
the woods, bread in the ground, timber for houses, and
springs all up and down the Valley. But, by granny, He
expected me to fish for it and hunt for it and sweat puttin' in
the seeds and harvestin' what come, to cut down the timber
and fetch the water. Now what'd I be doin' always askin' the
Lord for help? Why in tunkit should I always be sayin',
'Lord, help in this and gimme that'? Thank Him, humblelike,
every day. But by granny, I'm agin prayer that's continual
askin'. When He was good enough to give me health and
courage, He ain't required to keep on handin' out other
benefits."

There was more scattering now of the Martin family than
usual. Phoebe Lou was working for Mrs. Mel Manson again,
and Melinda was at the Horace Akins'. Jeanie went over to
Sturgis Falls for a few weeks to help a friend of Sabina's who
was sick and had to have rest and quiet, but when George
Wormsby, Ambrose Willshire, and Sam Phillips all kept
coming to see Jeanie, the lady suddenly grew enough better to
do without help.

No one called them hired girls—they just "helped out a
little," famous for their good food, their neat persons, and
their vitality, so that any one who could get a Martin sister to
help was fortunate.

Jeanie came home laughing and filled with sprightly news
for the girls, that two of the three men wanted to marry her,
but she wouldn't tell which two. Just for fun, she wasn't
going to choose from them until the third one asked her, too.
It would be fun to keep all three guessing.

Jeremiah—as Sarah put it—kept the road warm to town.

"Ma," he would grin, eying her to see how she would be taking it to-day, "I'll have to be going over to the Falls for a little while, I guess."

And when this was met by a mere look of scorn he would add an explanation: "Some opposition to all this buildin' up of the new Republican ticket. It's a big venture, this party. Has to be gone at just right with no fallin' down on choice of good candidates this fall. Have to launch the new capitol out right, you know. Most important general assembly comin' this winter the state's ever had. Wildcat banks, school lands bein' speculated on instead of in the right hands . . . plenty o' things . . ." His voice would trail off into nothing as he got his straw hat or cap.

At the long silence ensuing while Sarah vigorously scrubbed with home-leached lye the very grain off the wood of a corner cupboard, he would ask pleasantly: "Anything you want from town, Ma?"

No, there was usually nothing Sarah wanted from town, telling him shortly that had she wanted anything, she would send for it by some one who would remember to bring it.

If the day was pleasant, he would have on his big straw hat, pants tucked into boot tops, and blue shirt open at the neckband, the aperture covered by his jet-black crinkling beard.

If the day was cool he would have on a cloth cap and his gray shawl fastened by the long pin made from a darning-needle with red sealing-wax for a head. Rain or shine he went to town several times a week to assist at the bornin' of the lusty Republican child. The king was dead. Long live the king.

"Other folks get ahead," Sarah would say to the girls after he had gone. "Tom Bostwick does, for one, and his partner, Cady Bedson, for another. They buy cheap land and sell it for more. Buy grain cheap and sell it again. Tom would charge his grandmother forty per cent interest on a loan. Cady Bedson would pinch a dried herring in two if he sold 'em. But your father, he has to squander his energies all over the county. Wallace Akin don't care the toot of a tin whistle whether the county's governed right or not so's he gets good crops."

The girls sided with her sometimes by mere way of smoothing her ruffled feathers, but on the whole they rather approved of Pa's dipping into the political pot. Everybody liked him, they told her. Maybe he was a real help to the men over at town. And after all, the boys got more work done around the place in an hour than he ever did in half a day with people stopping to talk to him. They had seen Pa leave his team and plow and walk clear across the field to the fence, stand there and talk so long to some man on horseback or in a wagon that after a while Lassie and Laddie would start to amble toward the stable.

There was one thing about Pa—when he got home he told everywhere he had been, named every one he had seen, repeated everything they had said. His "I says" and "he says" lasted for a good hour after he came.

Phineas laughed once at his mother's faultfinding. "Ma, you better be thankful Pa is wrapped up in politics instead of petticoats. I could name some not three miles from here who wouldn't want to tell their wives and girls how they'd put in every minute like Pa does."

Toward the close of the summer Jeanie laughingly told the girls she'd had the third proposal now. It was from Ambrose Willshire. And now that George Wormsby and Sam Phillips were away looking up land in other counties, Ambrose was taking things right into his own hands and settling them.

Suzanne, remembering Jeanie saying he fascinated her like a snake, could not reconcile this new attitude with it.

Ambrose, himself, addressed Jeremiah formally just outside the lean-to door on a Sunday afternoon.

"Mr. Martin, I wish to take this opportunity to ask for the hand of your daughter, Jeanie."

"Well . . . now . . . Ambrose . . . what's Jeanie got to say to that?"

"I am making her gradually see the light about it."

"And what good have you got to say for yourself?" Jeremiah thought to joke him a bit.

But Ambrose's make-up included very little humor. "I can say, sir," he said seriously, "I never drink a drop. I am chaste. I don't smoke. I don't chew. I don't swear. I think no evil thoughts. I . . ."

"My God," Jeremiah burst out, "*you're* just about perfect, Ambrose."

"I try to be, sir," he answered with becoming humility.

So Jeanie, practically letting Ambrose decide the three-sided issue while the other swains were away, was to marry a paragon of virtue in October and live on a farm six miles north on the prairie.

The nearer it got to the time of the county convention of

the new Republican party, the more politics were discussed around the long table in the lean-to. In truth Jeanie's coming marriage and politics took up practically every mealtime.

Jeremiah took the newspapers from both towns, the newly christened *Courier* and the *Gazette*. Sarah had a good deal to say about the extravagance of it this summer with every one hard up.

"What you need *two* for is more than I can see. We can go without refined sugar, but we have to have all the newspapers in the county. I suppose the one says the weather was good last week and the other one says it wasn't. I suppose one tells you the railroad is comin' through and the other says it ain't, so whichever way it goes, you've got the right of it."

"Now, Ma." Jeremiah was reproving. "I live nigh unto half-way between the two towns, and I don't see no pa'ticular call to be partial to one town more'n the other. Besides," he grinned slyly, "the *Courier* took some of your tomatoes in payment for it and the *Gazette* took some of Henry's wood."

But Sarah was suddenly curious. "Another thing, how does it come you've got so sweet on Prairie Rapids this summer?" Her little thin face looked sharp and suspicious. "Fire and brimstone wasn't good enough for 'em when the court-house scrap was on. Nobody else's got over it. None of the neighbors or Sturgis Falls folks is hardly speakin' to Prairie Rapids folks yet. All but *you*. You're maple syrup to 'em. And what you talkin' so long for at the fence to Judge Hubbard from down there?"

"Oh, I just think the whole county ought to begin to pull together now," he answered mildly. "Just let bygones be bygones."

Then he rose and walked out of the cabin and with dignity, his six feet one straight as an Indian, his black beard covering lips half parted in surprise. Outside and alone he slapped his knee in appreciative mirth. Trust Ma. She was nobody's fool. She'd noticed that, had she? Smart as horseradish, Ma was.

It was only a little over a week before Sarah knew the answer. On September third the first Republican county convention was held in the court-house headquarters at Prairie Rapids. All the Sturgis Falls men who had vowed never to set foot in those rooms over the brick store building glanced a little sheepishly toward each other when they first arrived, but soon forgot the embarrassment in the importance of the occasion.

Jeremiah got home at sundown, tied Jupiter to the iron ring

in the stable, and walked hurriedly to the cabin. Sarah was mending one of her black netting caps. Celia was setting the table, Emily frying potatoes. Suzanne came in with the nightly gathering of eggs. Jeanie was bringing in water.

Inside the door Jeremiah paused and surveyed them all, gloating over this moment. It went through his mind that the occasion would be perfect if only Henry, Lucy, little Nora, Phineas, Melinda, Phoebe Lou, Sabina, Tom Bostwick, Wayne Lockwood, Ed Armitage, Ambrose Willshire, the Akins, the Burrills, and the Mansons were here.

"Well, did they have the meetin'?" Sarah looked up, only half conscious of her question. After all, Pa's life was just one succession of meetings after another.

"Yes . . . they had the meetin'."

"Go off satisfactory?"

"Yes."

"Who'd they nominate?"

He went through the list of nominations with assumed lack of interest—County Treasurer, County Judge, Recorder, Surveyor, Coroner, Superintendent of Common Schools.

"I thought the most pa'ticular one was to be a state representative," she said testily.

"It was."

"Didn't they nominate?"

"They did."

"Well, is it a big secret? Did they make you promise not to tell?"

"No."

"What's come over you? We don't usually have to prod *you* into talkin'. Who is he?"

"Madam, you have slept with him for thirty-two years."

The women folks all stopped short in their very tracks. Emily's skillet, Suzanne's egg-basket, Celia's plate, Sarah's needle, Jeanie's water-pail, all were suspended in mid-air, as though the motivation had suddenly ceased to function.

Suzanne was the first to speak and surprisingly she shouted: "I guess *now* you won't poke fun at Pa any more!"

"To go to the new capitol down at Fort Des Moines?" Jeanie looked awe-struck.

"Not *Fort* Des Moines—just Des Moines," Jeremiah primly corrected, as though that were the main point.

"To be gone all winter?" Sarah asked, and her thin little face looked as startled as a frightened child's.

"Oh, this ain't no election," he explained humbly. "This is only a nomination. But," he added with candor, "it's a strong ticket."

Emily's face beamed through the red freckles. "Pa!" She could scarcely comprehend it. "*You* . . . with all those lawyers!"

"Oh, I ain't never seen the lawyer I couldn't hold my own with," he admitted with becoming modesty.

Right away Henry and Lucy must be told, and Phineas. Sabina would know it soon for Tom had been at the convention.

Suzanne was allowed to ride Queen to the Mansons' to tell Phoebe Lou, and to the Horace Akins' to tell Melinda. And then, because she was galloping over the ground so lightly to-night and the moon was coming up to make white magic and the news was so very big and exciting, without permission to do so she ran Queen all the way up the lane road to tell Wayne Lockwood.

"If he's elected . . ." she said, the candles lighted behind her eyes . . . "oh, Wayne, if he's elected, we'll be *landed gentry*."

CHAPTER 18

INDIAN summer came with the sunshine palely yellow filtering through a screen of haze, with the maple leaves spreading red fire through the tops of the timber and the oaks wrapped in a greenish-bronze smoke. Stalks of goldenrod like so many lighted candles burned along the stake-and-rider fences, spread themselves up the lane road.

Emily finished making over the yellow dress and when Jeanie tried it on for the last time she looked like a part of Indian summer, too. With honey-colored hair and dark eyes and a yellow dress standing stiffly over her loops, Jeanie was a stalk of goldenrod, herself.

And now there were all the things to do for Jeanie that had been done for Sabina. Suzanne said she seemed to be living over the very same occasion as though you had looked once at a picture in a book and now turned the leaves back to look at it again. Only the faces of the main characters were changed.

One or two other things were different, however. There was a preacher coming out from Sturgis Falls instead of a justice of the peace, although Sabina bridled when she heard it and said she was just as much married as Jeanie would be. And Ambrose requested that the wedding be more dignified than the other, as he thought the occasion too serious for unseemly levity.

Everything for Sabina's wedding had gone forward without a hitch. She had loved Tom Bostwick and no other, and he had loved her in the same way, so there were no complications. Now, however, with the day set and the neighbors all invited, so many people reported to Jeanie how Sam Phillips was wearing his sensitive heart on his sleeve, and threatening to jump in the river, that she sent for him to come and talk it over.

174

"Well, the river's low," Sarah, tired from all the extra work, said grimly when she heard about it. "He'll land on a sandbar."

Sam, misinterpreting the message for him to come, thought Jeanie had changed her mind and had the whole disappointment to go through again, half tearfully, so that Jeanie for a few brief moments wondered whether she ought not marry him instead of Ambrose.

Sam Phillips' lachrymose farewell was only a week past and the wedding two days off, when George Wormsby, arriving back from Grundy County, rode up on horseback and created a loud and turbulent scene in the vicinity of the tree-trunk stoop, calling Jeanie out and accusing her of coquetry, double-dealing, changeableness, lack of backbone, everything but mayhem and arson, and hinting strongly at a possible shooting of himself. He upset her so that she was almost ready to give in and take him instead of Ambrose, when Sarah came out and told him that if he was going to shoot himself to get off her clean tree-trunk stoop that she had just scrubbed with lye.

But there were no suicides either by fire or water to mar the wedding. Sam Phillips would not attend, however, but sat at home in the log stable all evening and shucked butternuts. George Wormsby came, though, sustained by something from a jug in his buggy and spent most of his time bragging about a pretty girl he had met south of Prairie Rapids.

It was true that the wedding turned out to be more dignified than Sabina's. Something about Ambrose's unbending manner and critical attitude toward anything that verged on hilarity cast its spell over the assembled family and guests, subduing the laughter and practically engulfing the jokes.

When the affair was over and the bride and groom were leaving for their north prairie home six miles away, Jeanie, gay and tearful, half laughing, half crying, clung to them all with such an unusual show of affection that every one spoke about it after the sound of the lumber wagon had died away up the lane road.

Jeremiah, standing at the gate of the stake-and-rider fence, looked after the disappearing speck. Then he turned to Wayne Lockwood who happened to be nearest him. "Wayne," he said meditatively, "if a man's chaste . . . don't drink . . . don't swear . . . don't smoke . . . don't chew . . . by granny, the pent-up old Nick has got to come out in some way, singin' or laughin' or jokin'. And if he don't do any of them either . . . that's too much steam compressed in one human."

It turned out that the very day of Jeanie's marriage had been the day Governor Grimes issued a statement that the newly built capitol at Des Moines was acceptable.

"It better be," Jeremiah said, "thirty-five-thousand-dollar buildings don't grow on bushes."

November turned raw and cold. Great flocks of ducks came down from the northern lake country, rested on the slough waters, winged on to the south. A light snow fell. The small creeks carried thin opaque glass on their surfaces. The river ran, blackly sluggish beyond the timber. The Indians up at the Turkey Foot, pointing out to a settler how the beavers were at work, lifted brown faces to the sky. They meant a wet year was ahead.

Election day came. To the surprise of every one Jeremiah rode back home right after he voted in the morning. He put Jupiter in the stable, chopped wood all day, and sat down quietly in his arm-chair before supper with the newspaper. Such retirement behind the scenes of activity knew no precedent.

When the meal was ready, he took his place, mumblingly asked the Lord to bless this food, but pecked sparingly at the same. The chatter around the board was far less than usual, laughter almost entirely missing.

"Try a little o' this baked squash, Pa," Sarah said, coaxingly, as though he had been ill.

There was a feeling of suspense in the very atmosphere. It was as though they did not know which part to act, laughing jubilation at the supremacy of Pa and the Republicans, or disgusted resignation at the winning of the opponent and the Democrats. Pending the decision, and until such time as they knew their cue, the only—and unusual—thing for them to do was to sit in the audience.

The night was clear and cool, the roads frozen but not too bad, so that a horseman riding as soon as the votes were counted in one community brought the news to the other. The newly platted villages of La Porte and Hudson had a small vote to add.

Wayne Lockwood and Ed Armitage, riding into the yard in the late evening, took every one to the door with their yelling.

"Hey!" Wayne called out jubilantly. "Is the Honorable Jeremiah Martin here?"

Suzanne, shivering in the doorway with the raw November

wind and excitement, had to pinch herself to be sure she was not living only in that world of fancy.

The whole family was laughing and saying that everybody knew those old Democrats would get snowed under by the good new Republican party.

"I always say right triumphs in the end," Jeremiah said pompously, not quite knowing what the "right" was or where "the end."

The Honorable Jeremiah Martin! Yes, that was Pa's title.

Was everything going to be strange and different now? My goodness gracious, how should you act when your family got to be landed gentry?

But after all, even as others less childlike than Suzanne have discovered, life under the bright light of an honor was not going to be so vastly different.

Great snows came on. Jeremiah butchered, with Sarah and Emily making headcheese and sausage and pickling the pigs' feet. Melinda and Phoebe Lou were still away "helping." Celia and Suzanne wallowed through the deep snows to school, Celia threatening to stop the very minute Pa got away to Legislature. Everything centered around that great event now. Even Christmas, sharing the highlight of the year with the Fourth of July, was overshadowed by this fact of Pa leaving soon after New Year's for the capital, down at Fort Des Moines—no, just Des Moines.

"We've got to forget this *fort* idea out here now," he reminded them. "A state that's getting as settled as ours don't need to emphasize *forts* any more, as though we're backwoodsy or afraid of Injuns."

News came that all the state offices and the state money had been moved from the disgruntled Iowa City to the jubilant little Des Moines. If that wasn't the court-house scrap all over again on a bigger scale, every one said.

No one in Iowa City would move the treasurer's safe with the money, so Des Moines men had been obliged to go after it. They had used eight or ten yoke of oxen and even then such a bad snow-storm came up that they had been obliged to abandon it, and for days the state money lay out there on the prairie.

"That just goes to show how useless money is in itself," Jeremiah took occasion to say. "Thousands of dollars layin' out there on the prairie . . . and what good would it be to thieves comin' along in that storm, freezin' and starvin'? Couldn't eat it. Couldn't get warm by it. Always let that be a lesson to you. Never go dependin' on money alone. You girls tell that to your husbands when you get 'em. Tell 'em no matter what business they're in, always own a piece o' land and you can fall back on it for food and fire and shelter. The good land won't go back on you like gold or a piece o' paper that only *says* it's worth so much. Own a little land and you've got shelter and food and warmth and independence. You're a king in your own kingdom. Nobody can ever tell a farmer what he can and can't do.''

The new Governor Lowe was to be inaugurated January eleventh in that year of 1858. How Jeremiah was to get there, the Lord only knew. Sarah prophesied dire things. Roads would be terrible in any event. If it stayed as cold as it was now, ice and sleet and snow would render them impassable for staging. If it turned mild, creeks and rivers would be unfordable. It all made Jeremiah half a mind to go horseback. A horse with no cumbersome vehicle was about as good as a pair of wings.

"What this state needs more than anything is railroads." For the hundredth time he said it and for the first time Sarah agreed. Iowa *did* need railroads, she suddenly decided, which had the effect of making the Honorable Jeremiah grin and say that it all depended on whose ox was gored. Now that a Martin wanted to travel, Ma could see that the country needed steam-cars.

But Ma said she wouldn't rest a minute while a member of her family was in one of the dangerous things. That last summer's *Harper's Weekly* which Aunt Harriet sent had just cured her relish for steam-cars. "Every man who leaves the city by a train," it said, "must cast a lingering look behind, doubting whether chances of a safe arrival are not entirely against him. . . . Boilers are bursting all over the country, railroad bridges breaking, and rails snapping."

"You've no call to worry then, Ma, for I'll carry my track on my back and Queen's boiler ain't goin' to bust."

There was not so much actually to do in preparation for the event as there was conversion concerning it.

"Now you girls will all have to help Henry and Phineas."

That caused a surreptitious rolling of eyes so Pa wouldn't see them. He probably didn't even realize how little he had done around the place since he got this political bee in his bonnet.

Sometimes he talked about where he would live, how much board he would have to pay, two dollars and a half a week, maybe, how long the session would last, and what questions would come up. But more often he discussed how he could get there, pondered whether to try to ride through to Cedar Rapids and over to Des Moines from there, or go to the southwest to Eldora, then to the town of Nevada, and down to the capital. Either way would take many days, and he must plan it so he would be sure to find shelter at night.

"Pa, you're fifty-seven years old," Sarah said dubiously. "It's a big horseback trip at your age."

"Just about old enough to begin to have horse-sense," he retorted. "Don't worry about *me*. I'll pull through."

Pull through! Suzanne, listening, told herself she bet she had heard her father say that a thousand times. Yes, you could count on Pa. When he said he'd be in Des Moines by the eleventh of January, he'd be there, rain or shine. Pa's word was as good as gold—that's what people said about him.

The last night he was to be home was a strange one. Suzanne thought she could scarcely stand it to see him wind the clock for the last time, saying, "There! Day's over. To-morrow you can have a fresh start." Why, it just seemed that the days belonged to Pa and that he was the one who gave you the to-morrows.

And then all at once it was morning and he was getting ready to leave.

*"This is the day I long have sought,
And grieved because I found it not,"*

he sang in a husky tone like Emily's as they were sitting down to breakfast. The great platters of spare-ribs and corn-cakes, baked potatoes and hominy, sat in a row down the center of the table in a long appetizing parade. Pa bowed his head. "Bless this food to Thy glory," he rumbled through his beard. A lump came in Suzanne's throat to think of all the food they must eat unblessed by Pa.

It was bitterly cold to-day. Snow was frozen solid on the small-paned windows in the east wall of the lean-to. The west windows were black as night with gunny-sacking nailed over them. The whole house was banked four feet high with manure and straw which had been packed up from the stable in November. It had frozen solid and kept out a lot of the cold. In the spring it would thaw and steam and smell horsy, and Sarah would scold every day until it was carted off.

Suzanne, picking at her corn cakes and spare-ribs, knew

that if she lived to see the end of the world it could not give her more of a "gone" feeling in the pit of her stomach.

Sarah and Emily had packed Pa's bag, the nap of the flowers on the carpet sides looking more worn than they would have wished for a state legislator to use. There was no telling how long he would be gone into the spring so they had put in calomel, quinine, and sassafras, although how he was ever going to get anybody to steep this last for him was a puzzle which they did not try to solve. He had on his good clothes. Phoebe Lou had come over from Mansons' in time to grease his boots with mutton tallow until they shone. Sarah kept worrying about what he would do without his bootjack but Jeremiah laughed and said maybe he'd just sleep with his boots on. She had cut his hair as he sat in a lean-to chair with a sheet around him, and trimmed his whiskers so close that he claimed he felt sort of undressed and immodest. But Sarah knew he'd forget himself when he was gone and like as not get to looking like a prairie-wolf so she had sheared off as much as she dared.

Soon after breakfast teams began driving into the yard with neighbors coming to see him off. Every little while another sound of screeching sleigh runners on the hard-packed snow brought a new load.

By no means did he dislike this being the center of centripetal force. To all and sundry he had dropped subtle remarks anent the time of his leaving—ten o'clock on Wednesday morning. One would have thought he was taking steam-cars at a scheduled time instead of the back of Queen, he had given out the time of his departure with such accuracy. But there were still no steam-cars to take and if Sarah was right in her prediction there was no likelihood of there ever being any for that long out-of-the-way trip to Des Moines.

"I'll bet you anything the day'll come when you can get right on cars here in Prairie Rapids or Sturgis Falls and shoot straight to Des Moines," he challenged her.

"Well, you and I won't be here to shoot," was her decisive answer.

Both the Wallace and the Horace Akin families came, Mrs. Wallace Akin wearing three layers of capes to keep out the cold, so that, short as she was, she looked as round as a butterball. The Mel Mansons came, the Emersons, and the Burrills, who were moving to Missouri in the summer where according to them everything was better than here.

Wayne rode in on Blackbird. Ed Armitage came tearing up

to the lean-to door and, thinking to frighten Phoebe Lou into an admission of liking him, pretended that he had decided to go to Missouri with the Burrills. But Phoebe Lou only laughed and said Evangeline Burrill was probably the magnet.

When every one else had arrived, Jeanie came driving alone into the yard all the way from her home up on the prairie, her hands half frozen to the lines, her lips blue with cold, and so ill when she came into the warm lean-to that she had to go back outdoors.

"Where's Ambrose?" they all wanted to know.

Jeanie tossed her head and essayed a smile. "Oh, he couldn't leave very well," she said brightly. But every Martin there knew that Jeanie was having to "pull through" something by herself. "But I came on anyway. I couldn't let Pa go without saying good-by and I was just *starved* to see you all and have a good laugh."

"I suppose it ain't *polite* to laugh up there," Sarah muttered to Emily in the confines of the dark new buttery.

Suzanne was almost overwhelmed with the emotion of it all. It was like a funeral and yet not like it, either. The rooms were filled with men and women who had taken off their wraps and put them in Ma's bedroom. Sarah was going to have them stay for dinner after Pa left. The day would be spoiled anyway and they might as well put it in visiting together.

Sabina was the only member of the family not there but Jeremiah was going through Sturgis Falls on his way and would stop to bid her good-by. Grundy County, Steamboat Rock, Eldora, the town of Nevada—that was his itinerary.

Stopping in town a little while would give him a chance to see some of the folks who had helped elect him. There had been some regret on his part that the way he had chosen to go would not take him through Prairie Rapids. In his anxiety not to make any point of partiality about it, he was wishing heartily that he could start from both places in order to save any possibility of ill feeling.

"Hell," he said under the emotion of his magnanimity, "after all, I represent 'em both, as well as all the settlers in other parts of the county."

Henry brought Queen up from the log stable and tied his father's carpet-bag to the saddle. Phineas had curried the mare until she shone, and Suzanne, seeing Queen's glistening coat and thinking of Pa riding her up to the new capitol building, had a swift if confused vision of George Washington with upraised sword astride his white mount.

Jeremiah drew on his big gray felt boots over the greased calfskin ones, then put on the undervest that Sarah had knit, his overcoat, cap, and mittens. Celia tied a thick knitted muffler over the cap, and Suzanne put the gray shawl around his shoulders and fastened it by means of the long pin with its red sealing-wax head.

There were jokes on all sides about loading Queen down, and that maybe the mare ought to have some of the wraps on *her*. And then the jokes died down as though no one had any more heart for them. A silence fell on the room so that the Seth Thomas clock with the great iron weights and the *E Pluribus Unum* eagle sounded loudly insistent in the sudden hush.

Jeremiah looked around on them all, his ice-blue eyes clouding a bit anxiously above the coal-black whiskers so strangely neat and tidy to-day.

"Well," he said, taking in wife, children, and neighbors alike, as though they were all his family, "be good to yourselves. Anything comes up, use your gumption. Pull yourselves on through." He might have been Moses bidding his flock farewell, or Abraham troubled over his people.

Sarah stood off at the side. Her face looked small and pinched under its sagging weight of reddish hair, graying a little at the sides. He singled her out from the others with his eyes. "Take good care of yourself, Sarah—I'll let you know how things are, soon's I can."

Suzanne looked at her mother quickly. How funny to call her *Sarah*. She'd never heard him say anything but "Ma." It was like a love word to say "Sarah" so kindly. He must have called her that all the time before she was Ma. Maybe she wasn't their mother to him just now. Maybe for just a minute she was that girl she used to be.

Suddenly she felt it was terrible that this was happening, that there were times in life when you could scarcely stand things for the queer feeling that tore at your throat and hurt your heart. She looked across at Wayne Lockwood standing there so tall and straight against the loft ladder. Nothing ever moved Wayne. He was always the same, so cool and undisturbed, no matter what happened. Sometime in her life she hoped she could see him deeply moved, caring intensely about something.

Pa was outside the lean-to door now, and Ma and some of

the girls had followed as far as the stoop where they stood shivering. Suzanne got her shawl and galoshes from behind the door, tugging hurriedly to get them on. She could hear: "Well, good-by, everybody."

"Good-by, Pa."

She pulled her wrap around her, ran out the main-room door, and sped on down the yard, plunging through crusted drifts, to the small rail gate, was up on it when her father rode through the larger one. She was bound to be the very last one to see him go. Life would be so queer without him at home. Why, he was just the center of everything.

"Good-by, Pa!"

"Good-by, Suzy. Be a good girl."

"I will."

Her hand was at her throat and she could scarcely see him for the tears in her eyes. Pa had called her by her baby name, too. It was just terrible to see him ride off into the ice-locked country to the southwest all alone.

She clung shiveringly to the gate, leaning over it to watch him go. Far up the snow-packed road he turned and lifted his arms high so that his gray shawl formed wings. Through her tears she was laughing that Pa looked like a big gray moth flying into the cold wintry sky.

When she went back into the house to tell her mother about it, Ma was nowhere in sight. She was in the bedroom by herself with the door shut tight.

CHAPTER 19

LIFE was so queer without Jeremiah all through the winter weeks—a little dull and unexciting without his news from Sturgis Falls and Prairie Rapids, his constant remarks about coming elections or past ones, his loud-voiced political arguments and his hearty laugh. Something was missing, some vital thing for which every one scrubbed and cooked—the time when Pa would come in the house from his trips!

There had been no word from him since the day he had gone up the river road on Queen, his gray shawl wrapped tightly around his shoulders and his flowered carpet-bag whacking the mare's sides. But that was to be expected as there was no direct stage from the new capital. So any letter that Pa had written must of necessity go from Des Moines around to Iowa City, Cedar Rapids, or the town of Nevada, and wait over until another stage could get through to Sturgis Falls.

Every time Phineas came home from the Falls he was met with ''Any word?'' But none came.

When Jeremiah left, Iowa had been in the grip of snow and ice with a twenty-below temperature, but the last part of the month the ice king released his hold as suddenly as one lets go of a rope, and almost overnight an abnormal warm spell enveloped the state, so that creeks were running high and rivers were foaming. If the cold and ice had slowed the stages, now the mud and water laid even more detaining hands upon them. It was as though Pa had disappeared for good and all into some isolated country off there to the southwest. And then suddenly a stage and the letter came. Phineas brought it out to his mother—a large sheet of lined blue paper, every inch filled with Pa's cramped shaded writing, folded over and sealed with the red wax from his shawl pin.

Sarah was as excited as a girl, forgetting to put brown paper over her baking bread, and the top crusts pushing up against the oven scorched and had to be cut off.

Every one at home gathered around while Ma read it out loud—Henry, Lucy, Emily, Phineas, Celia, and Suzanne.

Pa said he took his pen in hand to let them know he had pulled through all right. He had been a long time on the way, staying his first night in a cabin in Grundy County, when a storm came up and he had to lay over. He was ashamed it took so long, but all told he had been seven days on the trip. Just pulled through by the skin of his teeth the night before the inauguration. He had been lucky to decide on riding the horse. Several of the legislators had not got there in time for inauguration on the eleventh.

Suzanne broke into the reading: "What did I tell you?" Pa had said he would be there on the eleventh. And there he was.

The letter said Des Moines was going to be all right some day for the capital—a good choice, center of the state and all that—but so far, it was just about the end of nowhere and worth a man's life to get there. One senator, the one from Council Bluffs out on the Missouri River, had come the hundred and fifty miles by stage in that twenty-below weather and like to froze. What this state needed was railroads.

When Sarah read that part they all laughed out loud—it was just as though Pa sat right there saying it.

Des Moines folks had been cordial. Maybe it would get to be a city some day. Just now it didn't appear to be near as much of a trading town as Prairie Rapids or Sturgis Falls. Board was higher than a kite, three dollars per week.

The letter was much more stiffly written than Jeremiah's easy conversation. When Ma finished and they were passing it all around, Suzanne, reading it to herself, thought of that peculiar thing and wondered why it was that when people wrote letters it didn't sound like their talk. "Respectfully your obedient servant," Pa had written. It made her laugh all by herself in the cold bedroom when she was thumping up the feathers in Ma's bed under the calico tester. Pa wasn't very respectful at times, he never was obedient to any of them, but did about as he saw fit, and you just couldn't think of him being anybody's servant. She had heard him say more than once that he'd rather raise skunks for a living than work for any one else.

When Melinda came down the loft ladder and asked her what she was grinning about like a Chessy cat, she refused to tell. She didn't want any one to think she was making fun of Pa, a big man in the legislature that way. But it made quite a joke just the same when you stopped to think about it: *"Respectfully your obedient servant."*

It grew cold again, snowed, froze the river and streams as "tight as a drum," turned warm suddenly, and started thawing. The top snows and the upper layer of ice melting so quickly under the warm spring sun sent streams of yellow water surging over the ground, seeking their level in every gully and creek bed. Underneath this rushing of water one could see ice which the warmth had not yet penetrated. But soon that too was breaking. Ice in the river cracked and boomed like artillery, its great cakes piling high on each other, grinding and crunching with the river's flow. Every little stream choked, trying to swallow its own ice. Suzanne said Deer Run ought to be called Deer Run-over. With the spy-glass one could see the river backing into the lower timberland. Creek and bayou, slough and river—it was no longer possible to tell where one left off and the others began. Wayne, going to town once for some necessary supplies, had to swim Blackbird through such high water in front of the east-side taverns that he wished he had not tried to come.

Jeremiah was having to stay in Des Moines for some committee work so that it was almost like summer weather when he got home through the high water, his beard grown shaggy since it had been away from Ma and her sharp scissors, his carpet-bag tied on the saddle, and his felt boots, astraddle of mud-soaked Queen, thumping up and down behind him as though an invisible man were riding there, too. Queen had eaten her head off in the winter, he said, but when the snow thawed and the first green showed through he had staked her out to browse near the capitol.

They had a big family dinner for him on that first Sunday after his arrival. While Henry, Lucy, and little Nora, Tom Bostwick and Sabina, Ambrose Willshire and Jeanie were all expected home, with Ed Armitage and Wayne Lockwood thrown in for good measure, no one realized until they began turning into the yard that both families of Akins, the Burrills, and the Mansons were all coming, too. Jeremiah, riding around to greet the neighbors after his arrival, had invited them to add their presence to the occasion but had forgotten to tell Sarah and the girls.

Seeing the first of the loads turn in behind the stake-and-rider fence, Celia and Suzanne, who were setting the long table in the lean-to, threw up their hands and uttered moans of protest. But Emily, coming by, her face red from the hot fire, said, "Oh, don't be snivelers. Get a-hold of your bootstraps and pull yourselves out of it." So the girls called to Phineas to help, and the three hurriedly put boards across sawhorses out in the rain-soaked yard where Sarah's hollyhocks were coming up, and set the table there.

Happily, the two Akin families had brought dried-apple pies and a cooked shoulder of pork, and the Mansons a dried-pumpkin pie and corn cake. Mrs. Burrill brought three dozen gooseberry jam tarts, although they were acid sour, and so tough that Melinda's whispering to the girls about people probably eating the jam off and passing the crusts back for more, thinking they were dishes, had the effect of sending them all into such paroxysms of laughter they could scarcely go on with the dinner.

Henry and Lucy brought over their chairs, little Nora, and a batch of fresh bread. Tom and Sabina drove out from town in their shining buggy and brought one of Sabina's big cakes for which she was noted, but because the filling had not quite set and the ruts in the road were so bad, the jouncing had caused the layers to slip a little, so that it looked like a snowy white leaning tower of Pisa.

When Ambrose and Jeanie came in the lumber wagon, they drove up to the side stoop and Jeanie slipped into the lean-to where she sat all the warm afternoon back of the stove so no one would notice her. Sarah tried to get her to go in the bedroom where she would be cooler, but Jeanie said no, she was so starved to see them all and hear their silly talk and laughter that she didn't want to miss one word or giggle.

"Don't *you* ever laugh any more?" Jeremiah asked so kindly that quick tears came to Jeanie's dark eyes, and she said suddenly: "Oh, Pa, it takes two to make fun and laughing."

Sarah sniffed and muttered something to Emily about being married to a hitching-post.

When all were finally seated, there was a great deal of scattered talk around the long table, but it was Jeremiah who was the important personage of the day, so all deferred to him whenever he started to speak, even the talkative girls ceasing their chatter at frequent intervals as he began telling about something at the capital.

The legislature had done some big things. "We sanctioned the new Constitution," Jeremiah said, and if there was a slight pressure of the vocal chords on that "we," every one pretended not to notice. "We put county governments on a workable basis. We got rid of the 'wildcat money,' made a revenue law, and liquidated the state debt. We got school lands away from speculators and started a property tax. We did just about everything, in fact, but put a bounty on old bachelors' hides," which sent the girls into spasms of laughter. You never knew what daring thing Pa would say.

The men folks were all curious to know just what Jeremiah himself had done, the part he had taken personally in all this. Had *he* introduced any of those bills that really became laws?

"Well," he answered them, his black beard wagging as he wrestled with one of the tough gooseberry tarts, "I believe I can safely say I did more *settin'* on *unwise measures* than anybody there. Sometimes I think I was the official killer of bad bills. One I recollect at this minute was about exemptin' debtors from their just debts. The more I listened to 'em argue about lettin' people get out from under their legitimate obligations, the madder I got. If the day ever comes when you can legislate people out of their honest debts . . . well, I never want to live to see it. The country will be in a bad way, that's all I got to say for it.

"By the time I was madder than a wet hen, I got the floor, and I says something like this: 'Mr. Speaker,' I says, as dry as dust, 'Mr. Speaker, America's based on honesty and fairness. That's what America *is*. Iowa's based on honesty and fairness. That's what Iowa *is*. Our liberties we prize. And our rights we will maintain. They'll never in this world be humans with *equal* brains or *equal ability to get ahead*. Consequently they'll never be equal amounts of property owned. Some things we can't help. Our souls may all be equal in the sight of the Lord, but our gumption and ingenuity ain't. So the results of man's labor will never be equal.

" 'I'm a farmer. I'm goin' to raise as good corn and wheat, hogs and cattle out here in our new state as I can. Mine'll be better than some of my neighbors and not as good as others. That's because some of 'em has more ability, foresight, ingenuity, and gumption than I have, and others not as much. But gettin' out of my just debts because I didn't do as well as some, or seein' my neighbors shuffle off *their* just debts because they didn't do as well as me—*no, sir*. That ain't Iowa and it ain't America. Our rights we will maintain.

That's for them that gets much and for them that gets little. We better stick to that or we'll have a pretty kettle of fish in our midst.

" 'It might be nice and *benevolent* to try and fix over the laws to help out some poor cuss. But even if it looks benevolent on the surface it ain't good horse-sense. It'll work out evil in the end. Mr. Speaker,' I says as dry as gunpowder, 'I hope our *benevolent* friends won't tinker up the law to prevent a honest feller from payin' his debts *if he wants to.*' "

"What did they say to that, Jeremiah?"

"Yes, what did they do, Pa?"

The Honorable Jeremiah Martin worked energetically with a bite of robust gooseberry tart. "The bill," he swallowed, "was killed deader'n a door-nail."

CHAPTER 20

IT rained much of the time that early summer. The Indians up at the Turkey Foot were not surprised. The beavers had forecast it so. The Cedar, which had rolled over its banks angrily, foamed into the timberland, and spread out over low fields, was acting like a steady old friend turned inimical. Familiar sand-bars were no longer in sight. Places which once afforded a good crossing were too deep for safety. Currents and cross currents came together in whirling madness. The new bridge at Sturgis Falls looked from a distance like a long floating raft with railing on the sides. Over in Prairie Rapids boats were used among some of the stores for transportation; the mail sack was thrown out on a platform above the high-water mark.

There was much crop damage. Corn was washed out and had to be replanted. The wheat was a failure, sometimes not as much harvested from one acre of ground as had been sowed. Jeremiah took a few sacks of this to the mill, but the flour made from it was poor, Sarah's usually light loaves of bread being about as hard as cannon-balls and only a little more palatable.

Ducks and geese settled down complacently over the region for a summer's stay, thinking they had reached the lake country. Wall-eyed pike and catfish were seined in erstwhile prairie pastures, and a majestic muskellunge, the only one of its tribe ever known to the river devotees, came into the waters from somewhere, like a lone wanderer seeking its own, was ignominiously caught and served at a tavern.

Roads were impassable, stages delayed so long that all schedules were disrupted. Business was almost at a standstill, farming difficult for the first time. The influx of strangers was materially lessened, of new settlers practically stopped. Every

one felt hard up. Most of the population was in debt. Added
to the local depression over the rains, high water, and crop
failure, the national financial depression had not yet ended.

In the midst of all this, Death came riding down the Red
Cedar.

Heretofore the river had been a sparkling happy-dispositioned
stream, content to carry the settlers on its broad breast, to turn
their mill wheels, and proffer them its fine fish. In its new
attitude this summer it flowed darkly through the timberland,
unrecognizable in its sullenness. Like a human whose mental-
ity is unbalanced it moaned at times with a quickening of its
ripples, quieted down, shrieked anew with an insane madness
of tearing waters, turned pleasant again a short distance away,
spread languidly into quiet coves, rushed out a few yards
farther on in a wild frenzy of foaming cross currents. And by
its very insanity it fascinated.

To go to the river and ride into the currents was a modern
brand of 1858 sportsmanship which took daring and nerves of
steel.

On a Sunday in July, all the neighborhood young people
took their dinner and went to a shady place above Lover's
Retreat—Emily, Phoebe Lou, Melinda, Celia, Suzanne,
Phineas, Ed Armitage, Wayne Lockwood, Evangeline Burrill,
Sam Phillips, and George Wormsby. These last two—Jeanie's
discarded beaus—were now trying to "shine around" Celia
and Suzanne with very little encouragement from Celia and a
downright cold shoulder from Suzanne.

The picnic itself was something in the way of a farewell to
Evangeline Burrill who was about to move with her parents to
Missouri.

All afternoon they had been taking turns in the two boats,
riding from the languid waters of a willow-lined waterlily-
filled cove into the swift current, the girls shrieking with
excitement and fear as the boat swung into its dizzy ride.

Emily, as the oldest, had said it was time to pack up and go
now, and Phineas and Wayne agreed, for they both had chores
to do. But Melinda and Evangeline Burrill, about to get into
the boat with Sam Phillips, set up a tremendous wail, so that
every one said, "Oh, go on, go on once more. We wouldn't
want to take two children bawling all the way home."

They pushed off, swung out into the current. No one knew
just what happened to make this different from all those other
rides of the afternoon. Did Sam not get started right? Were
they farther out on the breast of the river than before? Did a

new rushing current of water come in from some released
brush or beaver dam? For a lifetime they were to wonder
what took place. For with Sam Phillips working desperately,
the boat stayed sidewise in the black current, then whirled
like a little fragile pea pod with which a child plays in a tiny
stream.

Wide-eyed with horror, frozen into fascinated fear or roused
into shrieking terror, the crowd on the bank watched the
whirling boat which was but a maple chip on the treacherous
water.

"They'll be all right when they hit Lover's Retreat,"
George Wormsby said, his lips white.

Already Phineas, Wayne, and Ed Armitage were pushing
off in another boat.

The girls on the bank, crying, praying, moaning, or, as
was Suzanne, bereft of all feeling excepting that of being
locked in the black vise of a nightmare, saw the boat strike
Lover's Retreat, tip, spill its human cargo as the pod spills
the three peas a child places therein for passengers. Running,
stumbling, hoping, and yet half knowing their hopes could
not come true, they worked down nearer a point opposite the
island, crouched together in their moaning, saw the boys
land, strained their eyes to see which girl they brought out of
the water and could not tell, saw two of them working over
her, the other helping Sam out of an overhanging tree, saw
Sam join that boy to run up and down the island looking,
looking, looking—

It was Melinda who was saved, Evangeline Burrill who had
disappeared from the very moment of the boat's tipping.

And then people came from Prairie Rapids—volunteers
with grappling-hooks. Fires were built on the island's edge.
All night long and all the next day and the next, people were
to look for Evangeline Burrill. But the Martin girls must take
their baskets and go home with Melinda, white and wet and
shaken, wrapped in coats and the quilts they had brought for
sitting upon. And Wayne Lockwood and Emily, because they
did not refuse to take the hard task upon themselves, knowing
that some one must shoulder it, had to go to the Burrills'
cabin door and tell Mrs. Burrill that Evangeline was drowned.

In the days that followed, Sarah Martin almost lived at the
Burrills', trying to care for the wild woman who had lost her
only child to the mad waters of the Red Cedar.

It was a week before they found Evangeline in one of the
quiet coves where the river was calm and tranquil, the shal-

low water shimmering gaily between white water-lilies in the late July sunshine. A deceptive, two-faced, lovely thing, that Red Cedar River, sparkling and flowing on to the Mississippi, and taking a hundred lives in these years of its sparkling flow.

There were services then at the school-house over the drowned body of Evangeline, and a long procession going across the prairie up to the north country cemetery so many miles away.

The day was to come when only relatives and close friends would attend funeral services, but that day had not come in 1858. When Death entered a community it came as a mighty Power whose presence was acknowledged by a cessation of activities. Men hearing of a death unhitched their teams and went to the house, thinking it not seemly to appear unaware of the grim rider. So the field work and all the home work ceased, while from far and wide, from farm and town, wagons and buggies came bringing settlers to stand in the school-house yard near the dead body of Evangeline.

Jeremiah and Henry said they would take the coffin in their wagon, but Mr. and Mrs. Burrill said no, they would carry their girl themselves.

Suzanne thought she could not stand it for the aching in her throat and the agony gripping her heart to ride in that slow-moving procession, so long that one could not see the end across the prairie. The wild grass was drying now on the hill-side after the long rains so that it was brown and knee-high, crackling a little when all the people walked through it. Crickets and grasshoppers jumped ahead of the sweeping skirts and the late July sun beat down unbearably.

The great pile of dirt under which Evangeline was to lie was heaped at the side of the long grave, black at the base, yellow clay at the top. The slough at the foot of the graveyard hill was thick with cat-tails, and the grackles came noisily there while the preacher was saying, "Ashes to ashes, dust to dust . . ."

Suzanne and Celia stood on each side of Melinda with an arm around her, and Melinda shook like a leaf, crying and whispering to them that she wished she'd gone, too, and could lie there peacefully by Evangeline, but took it all back when she got home and was glad she was alive.

Jeremiah, looking around that evening at the girls with their swollen eyes and red noses, said only this: "Girls, you'll never forget it as long as you live. But you don't need to let it spoil your young lives. Why our girl was let live and the other took, no human knows. Some say predestination. They don't know that either. She's gone. Nothin' can bring her back. Life closes up over the vacancies and goes on. They'll be deaths, births, marriages, fun, and sorrow for you all. Just meet 'em all fair and square. Face facts no matter how bad. Then, come what will, you'll be ready for everything. Now, pull yourselves together and just go on with your livin' like as always.''

Vaguely it went through Suzanne's mind how much better a sermon Pa had just preached than the real preacher with his talk about angel wings and the resurrection so far away.

They were all partial to Melinda for a little while, thinking how she might not have been here, but as the summer wore on, the tragedy became a bad dream, and soon she was the butt again of many a joke. Mr. and Mrs. Burrill had moved to Missouri, thus making it easier to get back into the old natural ways. Yes, life closes over the vacancies and goes on.

Because the rains had abated and the weather settled down to a normal attitude in late summer, the stage headquarters in Dubuque, as though to make up for past discrepancies, sent one coach through in a day with no stop-over except for a short time at the taverns in Delhi and Independence. It arrived, if the elements were on their good behavior, at ten every night, and left with another driver and fresh horses at four in the morning, arriving back at Dubuque at ten at night—the whole hundred-mile trip in eighteen hours. That was service for you.

Sometimes when the Martin girls heard the pound of the horses' hoofs and that special clank of harness, they all ran laughing in their night-dresses down to the stake-and-rider fence, where the horseshoes hung on the gate, and crouched there in the night watching it go by, trying to make out by the light of a bright moon or perhaps only the pale stars how many figures were silhouetted against its windows. But often they were in bed and asleep when the hoofs pounded past toward Sturgis Falls, although on summer mornings they were usually up in the early dawn ready for work when it started east. For this fall was one of harder work than ever and of hand-to-mouth living. Every potato down to marble size was cooked, every edible thing in the timber utilized for food. Hickory nuts, walnuts, butternuts, crab-apples, grapes, plums, prairie-chickens, quail, wild geese, ducks, raccoons, rabbits, squirrels, maple sugar, honey—these were Dame Nature's gifts to the settlers. But it took long days of labor to get them, other days to prepare them. The lady did not hand out her meals ready prepared on platters.

Surprisingly the corn had come on after the rains abated. Though some of it washed out, too late to be replanted, nevertheless there was enough in the fields for home use. All fall and winter it was to be their mainstay as wheat flour was almost prohibitive in price. No one could make such palatable things out of it, or such a variety of dishes as the Martin women. Cornbread, hasty-pudding, Indian pudding, johnny-cake, white pot, muffins, gruel, griddle-cakes, dodgers, samp, creamed dried corn, hominy, Indian dumplings, apple corn-cake . . .

"I hope there ain't a grain of corn-meal in heaven," was Melinda's grumbling wish until she stopped suddenly to remember that even now she might have been there to find out.

Because of that high water all summer, the steamboat plied back and forth from Cedar Rapids to Prairie Rapids, but it could not go on up to Sturgis Falls. A brush and frame dam had fixed all that. Once it brought nothing but salt so that the whole Valley could turn to making salt-rising bread if it wished. Optimistically steamboats were being built to carry goods between St. Louis and Prairie Rapids, but it was to turn out that nothing much would come of this long-distance venture. But the new railroad, the Chicago, Iowa, and Nebraska, was being constructed to Cedar Rapids and there was much talk that it might send a branch line up the Valley.

On a fine fall day Wayne Lockwood and Ed Armitage drove the girls on an all-day jaunt away up to Turkey Foot Forks to see an Indian council taking place. When Wayne came over to ask them if they wanted to see it, Melinda said at once enthusiastically that she didn't know anything she would rather do. The girls all hooted and reminded her that she would have said the very same thing if the boys had asked them to go over to the creek to see a school of minnows swimming, proving that their recent unusual regard for her was waning.

When they got back in the evening they were full of talk about the powwow with its peace-pipe smoking between the Pottawattomies and the Winnebagoes, and laughing that Suzanne had her first proposal.

A squaw had tried to take the green silk parasol away from her, they told Ma, and Suzanne had held onto it, spunking up and telling the squaw to keep her hands off, so that a young

buck, grinning, had come over and made her understand he
was impressed and wanted her for his own.

Jeremiah came home from town while they were telling it,
so he, too, must hear at once how Suzanne had been almost
of a mind to stay with the good-looking Winnebago. And
right before Wayne Lockwood, Phoebe Lou said: "He looked
for all the world like Wayne would look if he had walnut
juice on him, wild-turkey feathers in his hair, and elk teeth
around his neck."

They all laughed at Suzanne's red face, telling her it was
silly to care what an old Injun said. But Suzanne's face was
not red because of the Indian.

When they were still laughing at her, Jeremiah said he had
a piece of news, too. George Clark over at the Falls had
brought one of the new kerosene lamps with him from Illinois. It had a glass bowl through which you could see the oil
just like the woodcut in the paper. There was a wick that
turned up or down for a high or low flame, and a glass
chimney.

He was enthusiastic in the telling, as he always was with
the new, and wanted to be the next in the community to own
one, but Sarah had something to say about that.

"What does this oil cost?"

Well, he guessed maybe if he heard George Clark rightly,
George had paid a dollar and a half a gallon for it, but he bet
it would get cheaper.

"And how about this glass chimney—what do you do to
take care of that?"

Well, he guessed maybe it got smudged up pretty easy and
you had to wash it every day, but just the same they'd be in
use everywhere in a few years.

Sarah sniffed. "I'll stick to candles."

It was only the next day that Ambrose drove down from the
north prairie to tell them that Jeanie had had her baby, the
tone of his voice implying that Jeanie was the sole parent. It
was a girl, and the sex, too, appeared to be a dereliction of
Jeanie's. Also he was sorry to report confidentially to her
parents that she had lost control of herself during what was
only a natural procedure.

Sarah, with set lips, slapped together some belongings,
gave multitudinous directions to the girls, and left with her
son-in-law, her little wiry figure in its black bonnet as erect
and stiff as a poker on the seat of a lumber wagon jolting
along north over the prairie.

CHAPTER 21

JEREMIAH MARTIN'S entrance into the lean-to, wiping his feet for dust on Sarah's piece of old rag carpet by the door, scraping mud, or stomping snow, was a signal for all to cease their labors to hear what Pa had to say. He was a magnet which drew all community and state news. Nothing escaped his listening ear. From newspaper, neighbor, townsmen, stage-driver, traveler, peddler, drummer, he gathered to himself all the happenings everywhere as a lodestone draws iron.

Suzanne said he shook off news like the dogs shook off water when they came out of the slough. Lately he had been hearing a lot more underground talk about that fellow John Brown, living down in Cedar County among the Quakers and so fanatical about the slavery question. Now he'd actually made a raid over into Missouri, freeing a dozen slaves who were supposed to be right here in our state hiding somewhere. All fall it was a never failing topic of the wrong of owning black people, and whether if John Brown came right to the lean-to door with slaves, the Martins would help hide them, with Pa saying they certainly *would* and Sarah not so sure she was *that* much interested in them.

A Miss Cotton taught the home school all winter, a strong-minded, capable woman in her thirties, who had come from Ohio to see what the new west was like. Of the Martin girls only Suzanne was still in school, one of the two oldest pupils whom Miss Cotton introduced to the mysterious thing called algebra and the diagramming of such intricate sentences that their skeleton-like structure rambled into the far corners of the small blackboard.

Miss Cotton said Suzanne had an excellent mind and that it was too bad to think that her schooling was to be over in this spring of 1859. Furthermore, Miss Cotton said, the two times she had left the children under Suzanne's care proved that she would make a good teacher.

It gave Suzanne a thrill of self-confidence and ambition to take the county teacher's examinations.

And then all at once Jeremiah had a new interest and a new topic of conversation. The Horticultural and Literary Society had been formed by Mr. Peter Melendy, one of Sturgis Falls' most prominent citizens, and as Sarah told the girls, "Pa was in his element to be going to something where there was plenty of opportunity to talk all night."

There were plans for festivities in Overman Hall, oyster suppers and debates, prizes to be given later for good gardens, maybe the beginning of a library. An English family by the name of Bancroft, who had been seven weeks crossing the ocean in a sailing-vessel, had located and started a real greenhouse. Jeremiah, enthusiastic over the improvements, said it looked as though the community would blossom like the rose. Sarah sniffed and said it looked as though all the roses would blossom over at town and the Martins could get along with burdock and pepper grass.

By fall Mr. Melendy, the Overmans, and Jeremiah had laid plans for a lecture course for the winter, local men to talk on their favorite topics. Mr. Melendy's was to be "Horticulture," Jeremiah's "Agriculture," while the press, the bar, and the pulpit were to be vocally represented.

Suzanne's plans for taking a teacher's examinations went into nothing because Phoebe Lou was helping the Horace Akins, Melinda was up on the north prairie at the Emersons', Celia was over at town as an apprentice in the new milliner shop, and so she was needed at home.

It seemed very queer to her to be through school, as though something told her that this must not be all of learning. Sometimes she talked about it to her father, saying that she craved knowing more about those things of which Miss Cotton had given her glimpses. It was as though you could look up a long road and see pleasant experiences all along the way. She believed she would read all the books in the world if she had a chance. So she reread the copies of the *Atlantic* and *Harper's Weekly*, *The Indian Lover*, *A Mother's Recompense*, *The Parlor Annual*, and all those sentimental poems which Emily cut and pasted in the old agricultural reports.

Jeremiah sympathized with her, said that anybody who craved knowledge ought not be kept from it and that, by granny, if there was a school near-by for older pupils he would be of a mind to see that she went.

All this was scarcely understandable to Celia who was more than glad to be rid of the dry lessons and into the silks and velvets of the little shop in Sturgis Falls. In those moments of confidence when the two girls were buried under an avalanche of goose feathers or sprawled out on hot nights slapping at mosquitoes, Celia sometimes told Suzanne just what her plans for the future included. She was ready to marry now any time, was quite clear-headed about it and to Suzanne's way of thinking not in the least romantic. She would marry with her eyes open, she said, and so far there was no one she really wanted. She called the roll of eligibles, including a few in Prairie Rapids whom she did not know, giving their status in her own mind with complete freedom and frankness. She would choose some one with lots of life and, above all, with plenty of land or town prospects. There was Cady Bedson for one—he was getting ahead fast, Pa said. He and Tom Bostwick knew how to buy cheap and sell for plenty. She had thought of Wayne Lockwood some recently, but he was too serious-minded, and Emily showed pretty plain that she liked him.

Suzanne, with her head in the cup of her arm on her pillow, felt her heart pounding foolishly at this and said quickly: "You can't just *pick* out a man."

"Oh, yes, you can." Miss Celia's approach was nothing if not practical. Sometimes Suzanne wished she could be more like her.

And now as though in answer to Suzanne's craving for reading came an unexpected and wonderful book from Aunt Harriet. It was called *Uncle Tom's Cabin* and Jeremiah read it aloud by the fireplace every night that fall while Sarah, Emily, and Suzanne sewed carpet rags. They all grew so excited that often when a big ball of sewed rags rolled off no one would retrieve it until the end of the chapter. Sometimes Jeremiah would lay the book down and tramp around the room to cool off because of the contents. Suzanne, not able to wait for another evening of reading, often went into Ma's room and took the book out from the walnut bureau, climbed the loft ladder with it, and read on ahead, answering "Making beds" to Ma's calling up to know what she was doing.

They talked almost constantly about the book and the evils of slavery. And when Jeremiah read how an assistant editor of the New York *Independent*, who was a relative of Banker

Leavitt in Prairie Rapids, was rotten-egged for conducting an anti-slavery meeting and would not allow the egg-stain cleansed from his coat, averring that it was a mark of honor, he made the man a hero, talking about him to every one he met.

Two other important events occurred that fall. The Honorable Jeremiah Martin was reelected to the legislature and the Dubuque and Pacific Railroad was completed to Independence. Trains came two-thirds of the long distance now so that grain had to be hauled only about thirty miles. That was an improvement over the old hundred-mile trip, but even so, the talk of further building died down and it looked as though that stretch of country between the two points was not to see an engine yet for some time.

Christmas came on with every one at home for Christmas Eve and a family sing around the fireplace, all the beds filled and some pallets on the floor, and a big dinner the next day.

A few days later came news that old John Brown had been hung.

"They think they're crushing antislavery sentiment," Jeremiah told the family, "but they'll find they've made it worse. This may even be the thing that will split the country . . . all this disunion talk can't go on."

And then almost before they could realize it, January had arrived, the year of 1860 was here, beginning a new decade, and it was time for Jeremiah to leave for Des Moines again. This trip was not to be taken on horseback. The newly elected Senator Powers of New Hampton was driving through in a wagon with his young bride, and Jeremiah and representatives from two other counties were to join them at Sturgis Falls and all go together.

There was not so much excitement over the leaving this time. Pa was a man of the world now. He had mingled with senators, state representatives, and the governor. He had held his own on the floor of the house, served on an investigating committee, talked back to a Democrat critic, told a big lawyer to speak Ioway language so they could all understand what he was trying to say, given the legislators more than one good old belly-laugh at the dry wit with which he took the wind out of some orator's full-blowing sails. The wag of the house, they called him. No, the family had less fear now to see Pa disappear into the snow-locked southwest.

There was a farewell dinner for him on New Year's with all the family present but Jeanie and Melinda. It rather spoiled the day for the others to think of Jeanie away up there on the

north prairie, not well enough to come back so soon for the
day, knowing how she would wish to be with them. At
Christmas-time Ambrose had asked one of the girls to go
home with them to help. He explained the situation with cold
austerity, as though Jeanie had overstepped the bounds of
good taste in expecting a second child, so that after he had
gone Sarah said the Lord's biggest mistake was making the
women have all the babies. They had taken Melinda as she was
anxious to go, but every one knew that by now she would be
wanting to come back home.

Sabina and Tom drove out in their new cutter, both to see
Jeremiah before he left and to celebrate their wedding
anniversary.

"Five years and no sign yet. What do you make out of
that?" Sarah whispered to Emily in the dark buttery where
the walls were frost-laden and the shelves held six dried-apple
pies, frozen solid but ready to be thawed out and eaten during
the week.

The two Akin families and the Mansons all drove in at
different times in the afternoon to see Jeremiah before he left,
and still later Ed Armitage and Wayne Lockwood rode over.
Ed had been to Missouri but was now back, full of talk about
going to Colorado and mining. Gold was just thick in the
mountains around the city of Denver. He told Phoebe Lou he
bet she'd look nice in earrings made out of gold ore.

The other girls all laughed at that, saying to imagine Phoebe
Lou walking around lugging chunks of ore that would be
dangling from her ears. But, surprisingly, for the first time,
Phoebe Lou would not laugh with them. She looked frightened instead and said, "Oh, Ed, you don't mean it, do you?"

The Burrills had sent word for the girls to go up to the
cemetery when spring came and put wild flowers on Evangeline's grave and maybe build a little fence around it so the
wolves couldn't dig into it. A family by the name of Beard
had bought the Burrill place and would move there in the
spring. It was queer to think that already a settler had moved
away from the river road where so very few years ago every
one was just moving in.

The morning of the third of January Jeremiah left for
Sturgis Falls to join the other legislators and the newly elected
senator and his bride. It was snowing and twenty below zero.
Henry said if the wind got any harder it would turn into an
old blizzard of a storm. It worried the family considerably.

"Pa, you're two years older than last time," Sarah said

with unaccustomed gentleness. "A big storm on that long trip wouldn't do you no good."

"Ho!" He made light of it. "This won't be the first storm I've bucked. We'll pull through."

They all clustered about the lean-to door to see him off, Sarah, Lucy, little Nora, nearly four now, Emily, and Suzanne. He would say his farewells to Phoebe Lou when he passed the Akins'. Celia and Sabina he would see in town. But Jeanie and Melinda on the north prairie were too far away.

Suzanne fastened the gray shawl with the pin made from a darning-needle. Ma had built up the head with new sealing-wax.

And now there was that old feeling which was half sadness, half fear of something happening—an emotion which Suzanne knew all were experiencing but not allowing to come into the open. The whole family was like that, she thought, never wanting to show out what they felt, always laughing or scolding to cover it. But you knew the feeling was there underneath like timber moss under sodden leaves in the springtime.

Phineas drove up from the stable, the bells on Lassie and Laddie jingling. He had put on the bells not so much for their elegance as that the snow was getting more dense and they would signal the presence of the team on the road. Henry, too, came up from the stable where he had been looking after old Queen who was acting a little under the weather. He had just turned thirty, but with his heavy black beard and sober ways,· one would have taken him to be nearly as old as Jeremiah.

"Well, good-by, all. Take care of yourself, Sarah." Pa hadn't called her that since the day he left two years ago.

"Good-by, Jeremiah."

"Good-by, Pa."

"Good luck to you all. Good-by."

Remembering how sad she felt that other time, with no other emotion, Suzanne knew now that she felt no more sadness than pride in Pa and his big duties. The county just about couldn't get along without him, nor the Valley—maybe the whole state.

Lassie's and Laddie's huge shaggy legs, the hair clotted with snow, pulled out of the drifts and were off. The bells jangled all the way out of the yard with Pa waving his arm and looking back. By the time the sled had started up the river road toward town it was lost to sight in the thickly falling snow, but you could still hear the bells faintly.

The family was anxious to hear from him but there was not that deep worry connected with it which they had known when he went alone. The weather was even worse this time, however. The snows raged all through January, piled over the west windows of the lean-to, formed great drifts everywhere, across the tree-trunk stoop, up to the roofs of the low out-buildings, over parts of the stake-and-rider fence so that in some places it was completely obliterated, in others only the tip of a stake showed through. Snow sifted on the girls' beds in the night, giving the pieced comforts new and varied designs each morning. Every evening Sarah brought her milk and eggs into the main room near the fireplace, for the fire in the wood stove was allowed to go out in the night. In the morning she was always up first to find the lean-to as cold as out-of-doors, its windows opaque with white whiskers of frost, the water-pail frozen solid, and if by chance the smoked ham or side meat had been left out there inadvertently, it had to be cut with an ax.

Through all this Jeremiah and the other two representatives, and Senator Powers and his bride, had driven in a wagon the long way to Des Moines. Small wonder the folks at home were anxious to hear.

When the letter came it was directed to Henry—a large piece of writing-paper folded with the blank side out and sealed with wax from the shawl pin, and inside it opened the discourse to his son with the words: *My trusted friend.*

Yes, Pa had a trusted friend in Henry, Suzanne thought, as she listened—he was always so faithful here at home while Pa went away.

They had pulled through. The cold grew more severe as they crossed the prairie in Grundy County. Senator Powers' bride almost froze to death and the couple stopped in Steamboat Rock, but he and the other two went on to Eldora where they stayed at the tavern. They got to the town of Nevada on the second day and had a very decent bed and deep sleep. The Powers couple joined them here and they proceeded together again toward Des Moines. However, they took the wrong trail, lost their way, and, when night came, were still many miles from Des Moines. They stopped at a cabin and asked for shelter but were told by a bumptious man to move on.

*   *   *

I shall now relate the happenings to you, for I done what my conscience told me to do. I jumped out of the Sleigh and told the party to unload at once, that there was ample room for Man and Beast. We had scarce taken the man by storm, replenished his fire and settled ourselves to warm when another load arrived, which had lost their way. These too I invited in. I took complete Possession of the house, ordered our men to take down the beds and make more room on the floor, turn the Cattle out of the straw barn and housed our Steeds therein. We brought in our robes and blankets and made a bed for the Bride and Groom in the shed. I was loath to oversee a man under his own roof but when one so far forgets the rules of Christianity and Hospitality—which be in many ways the same thing—I shall ever deem it my duty to set him straight.

They all discussed for a time what Pa had done until Henry said to come now, he was going to get on with the letter.

Pa said they found they were but eleven miles from Des Moines so they reached their destination at the hotel at the foot of Capitol Hill before noon the next day.

Governor Kirkwood had made his inaugural speech and it was a humdinger. Kirkwood may have been a plain farmer and miller but he hit the nail square on the head with his common sense. He made it plain he would ignore threats of disunion and insist to the utmost that the union be preserved. The serious outcome now was that the Democrats were fighting against letting the address be published, claiming it was biased in opinion, upholding the John Brown affair, and openly accusing northern Democrats of ignoring real northern sentiment.

The letter closed by saying all good feeling shown at the opening of the Assembly was over and the two parties had gone to their corners like fighters glowering at each other. There was much talk of gold-seeking in Colorado so they could tell Ed Armitage he had company a-plenty in his schemes. The town of Des Moines was coming on now, quite a noticeable improvement between this and the other session. What the state needed was railroads. He hoped they were all in their usual health. He was their obedient servant.

Into the warmth of the spring with the grass green on the prairies, and wild plum and crab-apple blossoms, Dutchman's-breeches and bluebells thick in the timber back of the river road, came more of that strange and serious antislavery talk. It came in constantly by stage and steamboat, by newspaper and letter—seeping into the Valley as the waters of the Cedar seep into the lowlands in the springtime.

The Iowa prairies, newly settled as they were, and isolated from the country's more thickly populated centers, were none-theless shaken with the threats that rumbled underneath them like tremors of an impending quake. All up and down the river road men drew teams up side by side to ask each other what in tunkit the country was coming to.

When he came home from the legislature, Jeremiah Martin was one of the most talkative of these participants. Although he went back into his corn lands with a great show of settling down, yet was he doing less and less of actual field work. There was always a hired man up in the loft with Phineas now. Sometimes he worked for small wages, sometimes helped for mere board and tobacco money.

Henry, Phineas, and the hired man of the moment worked the place, with the girls helping out when necessary, and little wiry Sarah always there to have the last word in a decision. So more and more was Jeremiah speaking his mind by rail fences and beneath roadside elms, in stable doorways and under the wooden awnings of new store buildings.

One foot up on a rail or a tree log, a wagon-wheel hub or high wooden sidewalk, his big knotted hands gesticulating, his crisp black beard straggling over the bosom of the clean blue shirt with which Sarah kept him constantly supplied, he discussed the country's political situation with whoever would listen. Starting to town in the morning with wood or grain for delivery, he might not arrive home until after dark, when the supper things would be put away and only his plate left on one end of the long table surrounded by a little group of covered dishes, with Sarah scolding that Pa had no sense of time when he had any one backed up helpless against a fence.

To help elect a Republican president and all other candi-dates, and thus put an end to slavery in the new states and extravagance and corruption in public office, was his life-work now. Every waking thought was to this end, every hour he spent in anything but furthering the cause was so much wasted time. The new Republican party was to be the coun-try's life-saver. Whatever man might be nominated its standard-bearer must be a Messiah. Providence and the new Republican party would work hand in hand, and if either one failed, all was lost.

Conversation was almost entirely political whenever Pa was in the house. Sarah and the girls entered into it with vehement one-sided partisanship, enjoying thoroughly the opportunity to say malicious things about those old Democrats and the dumb Whigs and Stephen Douglas—Celia alone holding out for his good looks—enjoying each other's sharp jokes about them and laughing hilariously at some unusually tart remark.

If politics kept them all stirred up there was one other equally disturbing factor in the household conversations this spring. Ed Armitage was upsetting Phoebe Lou with that constant talk about going out to Denver City to hunt for gold. No one knew just when Ed's jovial persistency began to make an impression on Phoebe Lou, but somewhere along the line during the years, that good-natured if violent dashing about had done its work, and now whatever Ed planned to do next was of deep interest to Phoebe Lou.

As he was constantly talking some new venture, no one was surprised that gold-hunting in the Rockies came next on the program. Since the family first knew him he had farmed for his brother-in-law, gone to Missouri, returned because of his fascination for Phoebe Lou's teasing ways, clerked in Mullarky's store, bought an eighty on credit, sold it the same way, driven a stage for two trips, purchased some sheep, sold them in three weeks, built a stable for Mel Manson one summer that fell suddenly and noisily over on its side during a spurt of wind in the autumn. But he had a dashing way with him and Phoebe Lou said she couldn't think of any one who was more fun.

"I declare, Phoebe Lou, I'd as soon think of marryin' a Winnebago and takin' my chance of settlin' down," Sarah said with her usual candor. "It'll be like tyin' yourself to a dragon-fly—you'll be always dartin' and skimmin' around with a man never having any plan in his head or lightin' more'n a minute."

But according to Ed if one could only arrive safely in Colorado, it followed that one immediately picked up gold on ledges in the Rocky Mountains. He made it sound so plausible to Phoebe Lou that she began to visualize the ledges as looking rather like Ma's buttery shelves with the gold chunks arranged in as symmetrical order on them as the stone jars.

All this gold talk called for more scolding on the part of Sarah. "A fly-up-the-creek if there ever was one."

Even Jeremiah mildly admitted that Ed was not always practical.

"That's a polite way to say it," Sarah snorted. "I'd say he's rattle-headed if not plain daffy."

Tom Bostwick sided in with Sarah and said a great deal against the Colorado scheme, too. Even though he himself had made a little money from his California trip in '49, had moments in which he wished he had stayed out there to grow up with the country, he was conservative, wanted always to be on the safe side, was satisfied that he had decided to cast his lot with this midland state and its agriculture. He was making money right along in Sturgis Falls. "There's plenty to be made here if you keep your eyes open," he was wont to say. So he put up two store buildings and loaned out cash privately in addition to a partnership with Cady Bedson of Prairie Rapids buying and selling grain and cattle. Sabina often told the folks Tom had his heart set on building one of the nicest houses in town some day.

But because Jeremiah had a streak of adventure in him or because of his interest in everything which lay beyond his stake-and-rider fence, or mayhap just to be a bit contrary because Sarah was so deeply resentful of Ed Armitage's large talk about taking one of her girls far afield, he feigned a deep interest in Ed's plan, really thinking that Ed was but wanting to impress Phoebe Lou.

So he read everything about Colorado he could find, enjoying Sarah's acrid comments. "See here, Ma," he would say, "see what the editor of the New York *Tribune* wrote home from Denver City, Rocky Mountains."

Sarah sniffed. "Who's he?"

"Name's Horace Greeley. Writes, 'I am here in the vicinity of the gold-diggings nearly half-way across the continent, although only one-half of the way through my journey. I have a lame leg caused by an upset of the express wagon, which has bothered me a good deal and will keep me here for the next week. I have been riding almost constantly since my accident and have spent the last three days climbing the Rocky Mountains and looking through the new gold-diggings. There is gold here but it' . . . and so on and so on." Jeremiah had run into an argument on Sarah's side and was surreptitiously attempting to abandon the reading.

Sensing it, Sarah demanded that he finish, so that he read

rather mumblingly: " 'But it is harder to get by digging than in almost any other way. A few will make fortunes here, but many will lose all and go away utterly bankrupt.' "

"So *that's* what you'd let your girl run her head into?"

"Now, Ma, you moved out here with me."

"Yes, and sometimes I think more's the pity we come. At least I had *stairs* back in York State."

"Why, Ma, you and me will be climbin' the golden stairs together some day." He laughed long and heartily at the thought. "Then you'll feel foolish you made such a fuss about any other kind."

But Sarah would not laugh. Stairs were serious matters.

Suzanne could not understand Phoebe Lou's meek submission to her lover's wild scheme. It looked as though all the Martin girls had minds of their own until they fell under the spell of some man. Sabina thought what Tom Bostwick said was the law of the land. "Tom says . . ." "Tom thinks . . ." "Tom believes . . ." Jeanie had been putty in Ambrose Willshire's hands. And now Phoebe Lou . . . !

"You don't *want* to go away out there, do you, Phoebe Lou?"

"Why, of course not. I couldn't bear it."

"Then *say* so to him." Suzanne was beginning to be alarmed at the continued threat of his going, sensing that what had started as a joke might turn out seriously. "Let him know how you feel. Have some backbone."

"Wait till you lo—like a man, Suzanne. You'll be willing to go where he does."

"Oh, your grandmother's eye-tooth! There isn't any man in the world I could ever think *that* much of."

But she said no more. After all, *was* there one man in the world with whom she would go to the wilds of Colorado—or *anywhere*—if she had a chance?

CHAPTER 22

ALL of Ed Armatage's continuous talk about going to the wilds of Colorado to pick gold off the ledges was unimportant now. And all the antislavery and threats of secession talk at the table and on the front stoop, faded into the background by the side of the fact that a big new house was going up on the river road. Being built by new-comers, too.

Their name was Scott and they were from some place down south. Some said Kentucky, some said Virginia, others held out for Tennessee or North Carolina—the roll-call of the southern states was made in the various arguments over it. No two people agreed on the facts of the news, except on the points that a Mr. Scott had bought the Mansons' land lying to the west of the Martins' and was to put up a big house far back from the road, and that the Mansons were moving to another place up the lane past Wayne Lockwood's.

Mr. Scott had appeared out of the sky, even though by way of the stage from Jesup, the railroad having crept a few miles nearer to Prairie Rapids now. The negotiation for the land was made through a real-estate man in Sturgis Falls, the house plan left to a carpenter with instructions to get all the help he could and push the work. And the mysterious Mr. Scott disappeared again over the horizon via the stage.

Lumber and supplies began arriving by team, and the greatest excitement prevailed along the river road since the Indian scares and the court-house scrap. Not even the talk of war loomed as large, for, after all, that was a mere threat which would probably never materialize, while this big new house set so queerly away off the road was a reality. One saw it go up before one's eyes, that is, if one's eyes were keen, for by that most unaccommodating performance on the part of the owner in building it so far back, the mere passer-by could

209

scarcely get the details. And after all, it took a bit of nerve to drive with no excuse whatever down the long trail the supply teams were making at the edge of Mr. Manson's old cornfield, merely to satisfy one's curiosity and return to the river road.

Not a day passed that Phoebe Lou or Suzanne, Emily, Melinda, or Celia, depending on which ones were at home, did not climb the ladder to the loft and train the spy-glass over on the activities down there in the timber at the west end of the slough. It became their favorite indoor sport to see if they could detect anything new from day to day.

In the last of April the Republican county convention went into session at the new brick Prairie Rapids court-house. Jeremiah, making ready to go in clean shirt and freshly greased boots, was twitted considerably by Sarah who reminded him that time was when he wouldn't have set foot in Prairie Rapids itself, let alone the court-house. But Jeremiah was above such small feuds these days. His horizon was enlarged. He felt magnanimous about the decision, large-hearted and forgiving toward Prairie Rapids. Such battles as he carried on now were in a wider sphere, their sole object the complete political annihilation of the dumb and dastardly Democrats.

Those who attended the convention composed almost a roll-call of the settlers who had first broken sod in the Valley. When he came back Jeremiah said quite casually that he had been chosen to go to the state convention in Iowa City. Yes, life for Pa was just one long journeying to far distant points, his days just one unending succession of meetings.

"You might be one sent to the *national* convention, Pa." Suzanne felt there was no limit to Pa's potential activities.

But Jeremiah retained at least a semblance of self-depreciation. "Oh, I wouldn't say *that*."

When he got back from Iowa City via the evening stage, having walked part way out home until overtaken by a neighbor, he had to report that he was not a delegate to Chicago.

"Now you can settle down and get some farm work done, I hope," Sarah said.

Jeremiah agreed cheerfully that he could do so and, as soon as he changed his clothes, went out to the stable to fuss around there, not wanting Sarah or the girls to know how chagrined he was in being overlooked. Every one must have some disappointments, he told himself, in old Queen's stall.

He'd sailed along a little too fast maybe. 'Twasn't good for you to have things come your way too much.

All that month of May in the fields, with the smell of the mellow loam in his nostrils and the prairie larks singing from the rail fence, he held himself to his farm work even while his thoughts were on the country and its problems, on the coming convention and the crucial moment of its choosing the candidate.

By the middle of May the Scotts' house emerged into a skeleton of pine uprights shining white against the green timber. And then on a gray day Mr. Scott reappeared to supervise the finishing. This time a young man, presumably his son, and two Negro men were with him, all driving through from Dubuque in a fine carriage pulled by spanking bays.

And now gossip flew about that the ladies of the family were in Dubuque awaiting word of the house being finished before arriving. The information was followed by the astounding news that they were bringing a woman slave and her children.

"But you can't bring slaves into Iowa."

"Who said you couldn't?"

"The Missouri Compromise bill said you couldn't."

"Oh, I don't believe it had anything to do with *us*."

"What can be done to stop 'em?"

"I'd like to see anybody flaunt a slave under our very noses."

Oh, my goodness—was there any place else in the Union where life was so exciting?

Even Wayne Lockwood, generally oblivious to gossip, attending to his own business with his usual characteristic steadiness, was drawn into much conversation over it with others in the community.

Speculation was rife, guesswork rampant. Some said the Scotts came because they were not in sympathy with this secession talk. Some had heard the niggers they were bringing were free.

"Well, they'd better be."

Not all niggers were slaves. Look at old Bunk over in town at the Overmans'. Free as air! Just lived there and did chores. Some said they came because of this growing talk of war, that they did not want the son to have to fight in case the worst happened.

"That's a pretty excuse," Jeremiah said, "and I don't believe it. If there's to be war, he's got to fight on *some* side. They wouldn't move here now if they was in sympathy with this secession talk. Those ain't *slaves*, mark my word. He wouldn't try *that* on Ioway."

"Oh, Pa, not everybody would have to fight!" The girls were saying it almost simultaneously, each thinking of a different person as she spoke, unless, perchance, Emily's and Suzanne's thoughts turned to the same one.

"I'd hate to be the one that *didn't* shoulder arms."

"Maybe these Scotts don't believe in slaves and just want to live where other people think that way, too."

"I can't reconcile the fact the niggers are with them, though."

Around in a circle, all the talk came back to, "Maybe the niggers wanted to come along."

The whole community was a living question-mark.

On that morning in May, Jeremiah felt that he could scarcely stand the slowness of passing time of this day and the ones to follow until he could hear what was being done in the Chicago national convention. At breakfast when the family gathered about the table where dishes of fried potatoes, sausage, and great platters of fried corn-meal mush waited to be consumed in little ponds of maple syrup, all were surprised and almost embarrassed to hear their father add to that familiar prayer of "Bless this food to Thy glory," a mumbled "and be in the Republican convention to-day."

Immediately thereafter, as though he must justify himself before them for having reminded the Lord to attend the convention he gave them a rambling and long-winded peroration about the vital issues that would be discussed on the floor.

All through the day in the field where he held himself strictly to the first cultivating as though to do penance humbly for expecting too much honor, he ached with the wish to be in the convention in the thick of the fight with the smoke and the stale air and the arguments. What was going on now? Why couldn't there be some way to hear it? There was an instrument called the telegraph. Why in tunkit couldn't there be such an invention as hearing the speeches and the bitter words of the battle? But he put the foolish thought out of his mind, visualizing the leaders walking about the caucus rooms, haggard, sleepless, working hard for their candidates. Who was being nominated? Chase? . . . Seward? . . . Lincoln?

He was for Lincoln, lock, stock, and barrel. Tom Bostwick wasn't. He and Tom had come through many an argument, Tom often saying, "Can you think of him meeting with some of those eastern men . . . breaking out into one of those back-woodsy stories of his . . . with his feet on a desk?"

Well, if meeting eastern men was all there was to it. . . ! They heard results in record-breaking time, the very night following the day of nominations. The papers containing the results came on through Dubuque to Jesup by train and were hurried out by stage, so that night had barely fallen when the news came. Jeremiah, standing with the crowd around the stage-driver at Sturgis Falls, heard it from him before any one had a chance to see a paper. It was Abraham Lincoln.

Tom Bostwick, half angered, half relieved, admitted: "All right . . . I give up. Maybe he'll make up in judgment what he lacks in polish."

"You can put polish on everything from hair to shoes," Jeremiah told him, heatedly, "but you can't give a man horse sense, level-headedness and gumption like Abe Lincoln's been born with."

There was yelling, back-slapping, hand-shaking. Several of the Republicans slipped over to the saloon to celebrate and to drink to the hope of Lincoln's election. Several Democrats slipped along to drink to the doom of it.

Jeremiah did not yell nor back-slap nor drink. He walked quietly over to Queen, mounted her, and rode home over the river road through the deepening prairie twilight. The clammy odor of fresh herbage came from the fields across the stake-and-rider fences. A white mist settled down in the hollows at the roadside. Frogs croaked. There was the feel of green groping things.

Abraham Lincoln! That gangling, honest, smart, tarnation-homely old rail-splitter!

Abe Lincoln, who saw eye to eye with him in everything, whose speeches were just what he would have said if he could talk easy!

Abe Lincoln, who was his kind, whose very blood seemed to flow in his own veins!

Abe Lincoln, who had been a settler, had plowed and planted and husked, split rails and joked and cussed, who had experienced cold and hunger, faced storms and an irate woman!

Abe Lincoln, who would never forget the feel of mellow loam . . . the sound of the cracking black-snake whip . . . the smell of upturned prairie sod. . . !

He pulled his gray shawl around him and spoke sharply to Queen. He must get home to tell Ma and the girls.

CHAPTER 23

So many changes in the Valley as there had been during the six years since the youthful Wayne Lockwood walked into it across the prairies from Dubuque that sunlit afternoon!

The railroad creeping within twenty-four miles of town and met by the stage was one change. Another Concord stage up the Valley rolled into Sturgis Falls behind four horses in a whirlwind of dust or lumbered through splashing mud, having made connections with the new train there in the growing Cedar Rapids. Eight, ten, a dozen passengers sometimes alighted—new-comers, drummers, visiting politicians, an occasional returned resident who had been visiting "back home."

If there were big changes in the Valley, there were changes, too, in Wayne. He was no longer the inexperienced youth of eighteen who, lonely and homesick, had written his mother about the loneliness but never the homesickness. He was twenty-four, a man, his own boss, a respected settler. He had raised as good crops as any one, owned a nice flock of sheep for which he had built a shelter bigger than his cabin, so that people joked him about treating his stock better than himself. A hard worker, yet he was ready at all times to dress up and take part in sociables, mass-meetings, singing school, festivities, church services.

His cabin was neat even though there were no softening touches to the harsh furnishings excepting that Emily had made curtains for it and covered his big chair. More than one young woman in the Valley would have been glad to add that touch. More than one cast demurely pensive or warmly longing eyes toward the young giant whose blond head was set so well on his fine shoulders.

But to all these Wayne was impervious. When the glances were coy he laughed to himself that any girl would let her

214

eyes tell tales out of school until a man had sought her out. When the glances were bold he drew a coat of armor about himself. Sometimes in self-analysis he pondered why this should be. If he had no mind to court one of the modest maidens who yet wore her heart on her sleeve, why not meet one of the audacious-eyed ones on her own terms? But to this he felt a strange repugnance.

Working in the soil and with animals he was a part of Nature herself. He knew the urge of groping, growing things, the force that drove the mating, the mellow feel of Nature at the seeding and the satisfaction of the harvest. But something held him back, some sensitive instinct given him in the blood of restrained New England forebears made him hold himself aloof and wait. For what?

That he did not know, excepting as some predilection to those things which were fine and subtle bade him do, excepting as he sensed that a mating for him would satisfy to the fullest only when he desired a girl too deeply to live without her.

To any masculine friend—to Ed Armitage or Tom Bostwick or Phineas Martin—asking why he did not bring a girl to that cabin up the lane road, he made some slight answer, turning it off jestingly with: "Who'd want to have a flock of sheep for a rival?" or, "Snide is all the company I've needed so far."

For how could he say that marriage meant more to him than that the work in his cabin should be done and a woman lie by his side? How could he tell them that always he carried within himself the thought of a girl whose face was the face of a girl in a cloud? They would have laughed at him and told him no angel was going to drop out of a cloud into a cabin up the lane road, that no unusual girl would seek him out there in the Red Cedar Valley in the year 1860.

And for that he knew they would have been right. But even so, he kept his fancy to himself, attended to his work faithfully both indoors and out, did not shun femininity nor run after it, but bode his time, feeling completely comfortable only with the Martin girls who were always themselves, always jolly—not "girls" at all, just "people."

And sometimes in the evening after the day's work was done, when he went down the lane road, he let his voice out to its fullest, putting into a melody all this that he carried in his heart but would never tell.

Her eyes soft and tender,
The violets outvying,
And a fairer form was never seen,
With her brown silken tresses
And cheeks like the roses,
There was none like my darling Daisy Dean.

Or perhaps another favorite:

Forever shall thy gentle image
In my memory dwell,
And my tears thy lovely grave shall moisten;
Nellie, dear, farewell.

He could not know that his voice, carrying across the north prairie its unconscious longing as the bittern calls for its mate, unaccountably stirred the pulses and brought an unwanted mist of tears to the eyes of a young girl who answered neither to the name of Daisy nor Nellie. For whenever Suzanne heard that voice singing up the lane road she would slip away from the others—to the loft bedroom or into the edge of the grove—drinking in the song alone for fear some one would notice that which she must conceal.

Jeremiah rode home from town on one of those first days in June, tied Queen to a ring in the stable, and hurried to the house.

"Ma . . . Emily . . . Suzanne . . . Phoebe Lou . . . where *be* you all? Here it is. Listen to this."

"*What* is it now?" Sarah's sharp brown eyes peered from under their short sandy lashes.

"His acceptance speech. Listen." He cleared his throat, reading slowly with emphasis on every syllable. " 'I accept the nomination tendered me. . . . Imploring the assistance of Divine Providence and with due regard to the views and feelings of all who were represented in the Convention; to the rights of all the states and territories and peoples of the nation; . . . perpetual union, harmony, and prosperity of all . . . am most happy to coöperate for the practical success of the principles declared by the Convention.' " Without change of expression or monotonous meter he finished: " 'Your-obliging-friend-and-fellow-citizen-Abraham-Lincoln'-Ma-where's-the-shears?"

"What you want of shears?"

"Want to cut this out . . . and keep it. Want to keep it in

my hide trunk for my grandchildren to read.'' Prophetic words, that it was to be found seventy-eight years later.

The Fourth of July celebration was the most elaborate yet attempted by Sturgis Falls. All morning teams came in from the country-side bringing their loads, lumber wagons with three or four boards across for seats, or chairs arranged along the side, single buggies, double-seated carriages, the horses' heads decorated with flags, red, white, and the blue rosettes, or field flowers wilting under the hot sun. Every girl was gowned in her best from the light calico dresses of the north prairie Emerson sisters to the silk dress and drooping white plume worn by an Overman daughter, young Mrs. Joseph Chase, a bride of three months.

There was a parade with girls in white to represent every state, and only brooding Kansas in black because she had been refused admission as a free state.

The Declaration of Independence, new songs and old, a sense of the seriousness of the coming election, and the ascension of a flag-decorated balloon, all stirred together in one long day, brewed a concoction of patriotic fervor that rendered all more or less drunk with the emotion, so that when it was over there was a distinct reaction of fatigue and low spirits.

It was a summer of good crops. Wheat headed out into a golden tapestry ready for the cradles. The green corn stood slim and tall in the fields like so many green-blanketed Indian chiefs with yellow feathers in their hair. There was never ceasing labor to break up more new land so that the green and the gold would spill itself out over more acres another year. More wheat! More corn! More stock! The new Iowa was coming into her own.

Wayne broke up the last of his acreage, hiring Ed Armitage to hold the plow as he drove; at the end of every furrow stopping to file anew the dulling plowshare.

When the new Scott house, there at the edge of the timber, began to be clothed in garments of snowy white paint and green blinds, every feminine heart between Sturgis Falls and Prairie Rapids fairly ached with envy.

To Sarah Martin, remembering her own substantial if plain stone farm-house in York State, scrubbing away on bare planking, running slivers into her hands on occasion, white-washing walls every spring, trying in vain to hide the blackened, weather-beaten logs of the big cabin with morning-glories, the new house flaunted itself with the same result which a red flannel would have had for old Sandy, Pa's bull, in the south pasture. She scolded about it at the slightest provocation.

"We could have a frame or brick house if Pa would 'tend to his business and get ahead. But no . . . there's the school district to see to and the county to be looked after and the state. Now lately here's the whole nation! He's got to manage *that* for a change. 'Twouldn't do to let anybody else look after the union and keep the south petted up."

"Now, Ma, this is a real comfortable home," Jeremiah would soothe her. "The whole family's got a place to sleep and a place at table to eat. We got good feather-beds. Everybody that ever comes along the river road stops. Folks like to put up here. They all know nobody can cook like you and the girls. We ain't codfish aristrocracy like a few beginnin' to come in now over in town. We're just common folks, but substantial, and everybody comes here from preachers to politicians."

"*And* peddlers." It still rankled that Pa had bought a *Life of Lincoln* from a peddler, paying for it by the pound, she told the girls, when it proved to weigh as much as a young hickory log.

It was only the next day after this placating conversation that, grinning cheerfully over the happy surprise of it, he arrived home atop a load of lumber from the Sturgis Falls sawmill, with the announcement that he was going to build on another room for Ma.

This he began at once at odd times with the help of Phineas and Melinda, the latter sawing away as vigorously as any man. Finished later in the fall, the addition made the house look more peculiar than ever. Instead of the appearance of two cabins pushed together by some human with herculean power, three now ranged along in capital-I formation with the lean-to on the back, as though a giant's child in playful mood had built a rambling house of blocks.

They called the latest addition "the company room." It was to contain a stove, lacking completely in the friendliness of the main-room fireplace, a shelf with river shells in a stiff row, cat-tails, bursting milkweed pods, a bed with tester and valance, a rag rug, and such chairs as were moved into it on occasion.

But before it was finished, something happened which made the excitement of a new room, war talk, presidential election, and even gossip over the Scotts moving here with niggers seem idle chatter.

Suzanne knew she would never forget the day as long as she lived. It was a warm morning and they were picking wild blackberries in a swampy place at the edge of the timber—she and Melinda and Phoebe Lou. Celia was helping Emily and Ma, having fussed so about going out to hurt her complexion that Ma had let her stay, so that Melinda had a good deal to say about "the high-toned lady living at the Martins' having her way again."

Suzanne and Melinda squatted or stood by the bushes, but Phoebe Lou lugged a three-legged milk-stool around with her and made a great deal of commotion getting her voluminous skirts fixed on it just *so* each time. No one wore hoops while at work but their full skirts were much in the way. Stiffly starched Shaker bonnets kept the sun's rays from reddening their complexions, but they also kept the breeze off and formed exploratory funnels for multitudinous gnats hovering over the purplish berries, so that sometimes the girls took the bonnets off and whacked viciously at the insects.

All picked at the same clump of bushes and moved together so they could talk easily, talk being the breath of life to the Martin girls. Just now they were discussing their Chicago cousins, wondering how it would seem to be living in that great city of a hundred thousand and to be able to pick out new dress-goods right in their father's own store, when some one on horseback came tearing down the river road and into the yard, drawing up suddenly with tight rein so that even from this distance they could see a cloud of dirt flying in all directions.

"It's Ed Armitage," Suzanne said, and looked hurriedly at Phoebe Lou who was standing there, a little pale, with her berries in one hand and the three-legged stool in the other.

"Come on,". she said huskily. And together the three hurried up to the house.

Suzanne was conscious of something of great import. It was in the air, in the way the horse was pawing and the way the heat shimmered over the prairie, seemingly in the hoarse excited cawing of the crows. Ed came toward them, his dark eyes sparkling and his head thrown back, looking at Phoebe Lou as though neither Celia nor Suzanne existed.

"Phoebe Lou . . . we're going . . . you and me . . . with the Gainses to-morrow. I stopped in Prairie Rapids and got the license. It's right here." He took a paper from his back pocket, so that all eyes concentrated on the white thing as though it had life. "We'll be married right away . . . and on our way to Denver City early to-morrow morning."

"Married . . . right . . ." Phoebe Lou's voice caught and could not finish.

"Yes. Put your bonnet back on and we'll ride up the lane road to Squire Marquis. A justice of the peace can do it just as well as a preacher. His wife can be witness. . . ."

Sarah had come out to the stoop, her graying sandy hair dragging at its pins, her thin face red from the cook stove.

"What's this?" Her voice was sharp.

Ed wheeled to her. "Phoebe Lou and me are goin' up to Justice Marquis to get . . ."

"That'll be about all of *that* from you, Ed Armitage." Sarah's head tossed, and her little pinched face set in authoritative lines. "You'll do nothing of the kind. Phoebe Lou . . . are you still determined to marry Ed, even if you have to go to that jumpin'-off place with him?"

"Why, yes, Ma . . . if Ed thinks . . ."

"Then we'll have a weddin' right here like white folks. You're my girl till you get away. Every girl of mine gets married right here in her own home. There'll be no slippin' around to justices like somethin' was wrong."

"Ma's right, Ed."

"Oh, well . . . anything you say, Phoebe Lou. I just thought . . ."

"If it's *got* to be to-day, we'll pitch in and be ready by night. Emily . . . Celia . . ." Sarah turned to the two behind her. "Go on with your work. Suzanne, go to the field and tell Pa and the boys. Phoebe Lou, you look over what berries you've got and then take the rest of the day to get yourself and your things ready. Come now, all, stir your stumps."

"I'll ride to Jeanie's to tell her, Ma." Melinda brightened at the prospect of going off the place.

"You'll do no such thing. Men folks can do that. You catch four chickens and kill 'em. Scoot, now."

This wedding was so very different from Sabina's and Jeanie's. With only a few hours to prepare, every one turned in to bend all energies toward the event. Emily went into Sarah's bedroom with Phoebe Lou's best dress of wine-colored poplin. There she held communion with herself, a *Godey's Lady's Book*, and a home-made pattern cut from a newspaper, and in the next few hours made over the dress with white collar and cuffs from Aunt Harriet's last package of finery. Phineas rode up to Jeanie's on the north prairie to

tell her the news and see if she was still able to come.
Jeremiah went to town to tell Sabina and ask her to make a
cake, with Sarah calling out after him not to so much as speak
to a Democrat for fear he'd forget to come home from the
arguing. Only Henry stayed in the wheat field and jogged
faithfully along at the binding.

Melinda dressed chickens. Celia pared potatoes. Sarah made
drop-cakes. Her thin little face twitched nervously and sometimes her mouth trembled. Suzanne helped Phoebe Lou finish
the berries and then get together her things, ready to be taken
in the morning. There were very few when arranged on the
bed, but every girl gave something from her own small
supply, Celia her best handkerchief, Emily her good knitted
wool scarf, Melinda an apron. Suzanne, her heart warm and
tender with the sudden experience, made the supreme sacrifice and put *The Indian Lover* in the little trunk which Ma
brought out from under the bed

In the middle of the afternoon Emily called the other three
girls into the bedroom where she was sewing frantically, her
red hair tumbled and stringy, and after a hurried conference
they presented Phoebe Lou with the company-owned green
silk parasol.

It made Phoebe Lou cry a little, so that the girls all laughed
at her, telling her the parasol would think it had dropped in
the Cedar again if she got so much water around. But they all
ran out of the room and turned furiously to their work so that
she could not see their own telltale eyes.

Suzanne thought she could not stand it—that intense emotion under a surface of the commonplace, a torn throbbing
feeling as though you must scream because life was so,
remembering again the green timber moss under the soggy
leaves in the springtime.

Only this morning they had been laughing and talking over
the blackberries as unconcerned as though they had a lifetime
to talk together. All summer they had acted as though the
Scotts' new house was the most important thing in the world,
and as though a new room was something to be excited about,
as though it mattered who the old Republican candidate was
and who would be elected. And now this was the only
important thing after all. Phoebe Lou was going away beyond
the Great American Desert. You could not comprehend it. It
was as though Phoebe Lou was going to die. The only
difference would be that this way you could get a letter from
her sometimes and you never got word at all from the dead.

There would be the long journey first to the Missouri River—it had taken Wayne Lockwood and Tom Bostwick eighteen days to go and return and even so they were driving horses with no load. Ed and Phoebe Lou and the Gainses could scarcely hope to get to Council Bluffs and Nebraska City for over two weeks with their loads. And that would be only a start—seven hundred miles over the Great American Desert after that, seven times from here to Dubuque.

Oh, why did families pull apart this way? All day she thought of Phoebe Lou as the favorite of her sisters, forgetting that she had known moments of thinking the same about all of them. The little fusses they had indulged in over stemming wild gooseberries or the wearing of a ribbon or Phoebe Lou's constant teasing, seemed too trivial now for words.

When Jeremiah returned home, having been of no mind to talk to Democrat or Republican either, because his girl was going so far away, he fussed out around the stables until evening. Suddenly he had lost his appetite for politics. All his life, when agitated, he had made for the stable. The sound of the guzzling horses and the whacking tails of old Red and Baldy were familiar steadying sounds. The smell of the stock and the manure, the oats in the bins and the prairie hay were good substantial earthy odors that kept his thoughts from running riot. To-day one of his girls was going away, out to the Rocky Mountains, a two-months' journey, maybe. He didn't want her to. He wanted his family all together. He wanted Sarah by his side, Henry and Phineas not far away. He wanted Jeanie and Sabina within riding distance, Emily, Suzanne, Melinda, and Celia all near. And he wanted Phoebe Lou. Hell, how he wanted Phoebe Lou.

He curried Queen with unnecessary precision, thinking all the time of Phoebe Lou going away and wondering if maybe he should try to stop it. He kept telling himself that young folks have always done this thing. He had brought Sarah . . . by granny! He stopped and looked out the stable door to the yellow stubbles after the cutting. Was this the way Sarah's folks felt in York State when he brought her out to Illinois? He'd never fully sensed it before. He didn't go to the house until Sarah called him to get chickens shut in a coop for Phoebe Lou to take.

Bewailing that the new company room was not yet finished, Celia and Suzanne fixed up the girls' loft room for the bridal chamber. They put fresh covers on the barrel-stand and the two barrel-chairs, and pressed out the window curtains with the sad-irons hot from the kitchen stove. There was new white mosquito-netting over the windows and Celia laughed about the years when there had been nothing and the flies and moths and an occasional wandering swallow or bat had pestered them so, saying, as she recalled it, that a person doesn't realize how times improve as they go along.

But it was as though something dreadful hung over the house to-day, not at all like the times of Sabina's and Jeanie's weddings. But because Phoebe Lou must not be allowed to go away feeling sad, they put on a great deal of foolishness, even as they hurried at their tasks. They joked her that Ed was so rattle-headed he might forget her and start off with the Gainses alone, told her that they wouldn't miss her very much because they'd be so busy watching the Scotts' uprisings and downsittings. And all the time of the joking no one could look another in the eye.

Toward evening Ed Armitage, all dressed up, drove into the yard, but now there was no pulling of his horse up so smartly that the dirt and gravel flew about, for he had stolid old oxen and a covered wagon, with his saddle horse hitched to the back and a coop of geese on one side. Emily made them all laugh by saying she couldn't imagine Ed Armitage going as slow as those oxen—she could just see him getting on the saddle horse and riding around them in circles.

Jeanie and Ambrose Willshire and their little girl came, with Jeanie expecting again so soon that Ambrose said apologetically he was almost ashamed to have her come, and Jeremiah saying, by granny, he'd have gone up for her, himself, if he'd thought Ambrose was so delicate-minded. Wayne Lockwood arrived and the two Akin families and the Mansons. Sabina and Tom Bostwick came in their nice buggy, Sabina in a new delaine dress so fashionably big and round that her father said she looked like a walking pincushion. She had held the cake on her lap all the way out from town she said, swinging it upward whenever the wheels hit a rut in the road, which made Phoebe Lou ask if they remembered the leaning tower of Pisa, so that they all laughed over the memory, their laughter catching and breaking because Phoebe Lou would not be joking with them any more.

Sabina wondered if Ed and Phoebe Lou wouldn't rather go over to Sturgis Falls and stay at her house to-night in her company room and the Gainses could meet them there in the morning.

Phoebe Lou looked up the loft ladder which she had laughingly mounted so many years with the girls and said: "Yes, Sabina . . . oh, yes, I would."

The minister and his wife came, a little man with black side-whiskers who walked as though his shoes pinched, and a tall thin lady with teeth that slanted outward and would not allow her mouth to close.

Suzanne ran into the south pasture which Pa was letting grow high for winter hay and hurriedly picked long spikes of wild sweet-william, rose-pink and pale pink and the deep magenta shade, bringing them in for the mantel and pulling out the long prairie grasses hastily as she ran. Over in the timberland she could hear the prolonged plaintive wail of a mourning-dove, thinking again as she ran how you never noticed their call unless you were sad and then you heard it and your heart answered back.

"Dearly beloved, we are gathered here together in the sight of God and these witnesses . . ."

Suzanne thought she could not stand it. There would be Christmas dinners and Phoebe Lou not here, Sunday reunions without her—Jeanie would have a new baby that Phoebe Lou might never see. Why, maybe they would *never* all be together again after to-night. You couldn't tell what would happen. *Never!* Her hand was at her throat which was throbbing as though it were trying to answer the mourning-dove's call.

But now it was over and Phoebe Lou was smiling up at Ed Armitage because he was her husband, not remembering at all the time she rode away making fun of him behind his back.

There was laughter and talk and the hastily cooked wedding supper, and then Ed and Phoebe Lou were ready to leave in the clumsy wagon after Tom and Sabina had gone in their nice buggy.

The whole crowd stood there by the stake-and-rider fence to see them off. It was moonlight and warm, but with a mugginess in the air that betokened thunder-showers to come.

There had been so very few times for kissing in the Martin family. But this was one. Phoebe Lou kissed every one of them from Pa down to Jeanie's little girl. And then Mr. Horace Akin swung his arm out, pulled Phoebe Lou up to him, and kissed her, too, so that every one laughed, especially when he said he was going to admit before his wife that Phoebe Lou had always been his favorite.

"Good-by, everybody."

"Good-by."

Suzanne, struggling with her tears, felt that if she said anything she would burst into such wild crying that nothing could stop her.

"Good luck. You'll pull through all right."

"Don't drive those fiery oxen too fast."

"Write to us from Nebraska Territory."

Phoebe Lou called back a last word, her voice catching: "Ma . . . makes me wish I'd helped you better."

Sarah's thin little face twitched and her mouth worked. "Pst! You was always a good girl," she said and hurried up the path into the house.

"Oh!" One of Suzanne's hands was on her throat again, the other clutching the fence top. Why did such things have to be? The tears were starting now and she was not going to be able to stop them. Suddenly she looked up and there was Wayne Lockwood standing beside her, so tall and stalwart, so cool and undisturbed as he grinned down at her. She wanted to shake him, to hurt him, to wake him up and make her feel emotion, too. Something made her say it with hot tears: "Oh, what do *you* know about feelings?"

He put his hand over Suzanne's hard little hand clutching the top rail of the fence there as though she would clutch life and hold it to her.

"Maybe, Suzanne," he said quietly, "I know more than you think."

CHAPTER 24

PHOEBE LOU was gone beyond the horizon where the prairie sun set so gorgeously these summer nights. So there were only four girls to go laughing up the ladder now, each scrambling to escape the pinching of her ankles by the one behind her.

Celia and Suzanne had moved up there at the south end, Emily and Melinda occupying the north end of the room whose sloping sides made one bump her head if she were not careful.

All the hot days at this tag end of the summer, Suzanne did her allotted tasks as energetically as ever, but on her pillow at night beside Celia she took out that little memory of the evening Phoebe Lou was married, turning it over in her mind to revel in its beauty there in the dark as one might take a jewel from its case and turn it in the sunlight to get the gleam of its facets. The hand that he had touched—the left—seemed favored above the other. Sometimes there in the dusk she slipped the right hand over it trying to recall the feeling of that firm supple one that had the strength of one of the new steel traps and yet had lain so tenderly on it. Over and over she had repeated the brief conversation to herself, trying to interpret it in various ways.

"Oh, what do *you* know about feelings?"

"Maybe, Suzanne, I know more than you think."

She knew the words with their every voice inflection as well as she knew all the copy-book maxims she had learned at school. They seemed to belong with those other important sayings of wise people. *Honesty is the best policy. Look before you leap. A rolling stone gathers no moss. Maybe, Suzanne, I know more than you think.*

It hadn't even been a game where you are obliged to touch

226

hands. It was all of his own accord. She looked over at Celia lying there so peacefully asleep in her bleached muslin night-gown, milkweed cream on her face and her oldest mitts over her creamed hands, and envied her that complacent way of thinking she was good enough to have any one she wanted.

As always Suzanne went back to that possible distressing interpretation for Wayne's tender gesture. He was merely sorry for her because she was crying at Phoebe Lou's leaving. "Oh, I don't *want* any pity," she thought, and groaned out loud at the idea of a mere bone of compassion being thrown at her, so that Celia roused and said sleepily: "I bet you ate too many ground-cherries."

"Oh, hush up!" Suzanne snapped. Romance and ground-cherries!

All the wheat was cut and tied, shocked and threshed, four long tedious steps in the harvesting, so that Suzanne and Melinda had been obliged to go into the field twice with the boys at a special rushed period.

There were so many topics of conversation which could take form at the table these days and around the door-stoop at night that one never lacked for a good talking subject. There was the constant wondering about Phoebe Lou, where she was right now, and how soon the first letter would come. There was the new Female Seminary being built in Prairie Rapids, a big two-story brick, with eastern ladies coming out to run it and Pa saying Celia and Suzanne both ought to go. Neither one was of a mind to do so, Celia complacent that a Female Seminary could do very little for a female who was doing right well for herself, and Suzanne torn between the desire for the better schooling she had once wanted and the secret joy of living where she could hear a horseman come singing down the lane.

There was no end to the subject of Abraham Lincoln's chance to be elected. And if he should be, would it really mean secession? And if there was secession, would the north *let* them go through with it? There was the County Fair to be held at Sturgis Falls, with horse-races and stock-showing. Pa had been riding back and forth a lot lately to help get it going. Ma was planning to enter her butter with the water-lily stamped on top and Pa was entering old Sandy, the red bull that acted hateful toward everybody but him and Henry.

There was the ever wordy topic of the Scotts' new house and speculation about them, when were they coming, why were they moving here at all, and the rehashing of the recent sight of the two wagons loaded with household furnishings arriving. There was the prospect of hearing about Jeanie any time, with Ambrose saying he wanted no more girls and Ma telling him to his face he'd take what he got and like it or lump it.

There was Sabina telling pridefully that Tom Bostwick was never going to rest easy until he could put up one of the nicest houses in town. Such bragging. There was the bride, Mrs. Joseph Chase, coming all the way out here to see if Emily would make her a dress because Sabina's delaine was so pretty. There was Celia saying boldly right out to the whole family that she was ready to get married now any time as soon as she saw somebody who answered specifications. And then there was the new company room with tomboy Melinda sawing away on the lumber for it, climbing up on the roof with her full skirts tied into pant-legs until Ma said she was ashamed to look up there.

Oh, life was exciting, with Pa winding the old clock weights behind the American eagle every night and saying: "Day's over . . . fresh start to-morrow," and no telling what all was going to happen to-morrow. My goodness, just imagine Aunt Harriet writing and wanting to know how they put in their time and what they had to amuse themselves with away out there on the prairie in Iowa. Amuse themselves! "Tell her we play 'Button, button,' " Pa had said. When all other topics failed, that silly thing Aunt Harriet had written once could always be trusted to bring a good laugh. No matter *where* you lived, the girls agreed, York State or Chicago or near Sturgis Falls or up by the Big Woods or away out in the wilds of Colorado, you could just bet Martin girls could *make* themselves a good time.

And then, on a late August afternoon with a peculiarly cool tinge in the air vaguely reminiscent of past falls, with the goldenrod and little purple asters beginning to blossom along the river road and cicadas chirping down in Pa's new apple orchard, Jeremiah ordered Suzanne and Celia to go over to the school-house to scrub it and wash the four glass windows set into logs, two on a side. School would take up after a bit now and he wasn't going to have the new teacher think the director who had a school-house right under his nose couldn't get it ready.

So Celia and Suzanne, growling a little because of the splintered floor to scrub, went out with their pails and rags, carrying water from their well and saying they hoped the day would come when the men would get around to dig one for the school itself.

They were almost through, with the benches piled neatly and the windows clean of their summer cobwebs, when Wayne Lockwood rode up on horseback. Without dismounting, he came past an east window opened on its leather hinges and leaning from his horse said: "Hist! If you want to see something, the stage is coming down the road and black Hi is driving fast up the Scotts' new field road in the big carriage. If I'm not mistaken you'll soon have your curiosity satisfied."

Celia squealed and ran first to one window and then another. Suzanne, flustered at the sudden excitement and the fact that Wayne was dismounting and coming in, knocked over a pail of water, so that both girls were breathless with laughter, stepping gingerly through the dirty suds, as he opened the door to join them. He was apparently unconcerned, but laughed a little sheepishly when Celia said, "Wayne Lockwood, you're just as anxious to see them as we are."

The three stayed away from the window but where they could get a view of the open carriage stopping at the corner close to the school, black Hi holding the reins taut over the backs of the stepping blacks. Suzanne did not know which was more exciting, the arriving Scotts or the nearness of that masculine presence of which she was always so keenly aware lately. They could hear the sound of the stage, the harness jangling, and the horses' hoofs pelting along on the road back of them. And then it was in sight, past the school, and stopping.

The young man swung down, in tall beaver hat, with white ruffled shirt front and light gray suit. Mr. Scott got out. The two turned together to assist a lady with a closed parasol and voluminous skirts held carefully away from the dusty weed tops.

And then one other was alighting—a young girl in summer blue, her skirts fashionably full, and on her head a little white straw bonnet from which a blue plume and a long white veil dropped. She stepped down, and in doing so, turned her head toward the school-house so that they could see her pale delicate features. As she stood there looking toward the east and yet not seeing them, a breeze picked up the long white veil and whipped it high about her head.

Involuntarily Suzanne glanced up at Wayne. He was staring at the new girl with a queer expression on his face, so that

Suzanne's pounding pulses stopped in sudden questioning of the strange look.

And Suzanne, you had reason to question. For, peculiarly, at just that moment, the girl's face in the flowing white veil looked like the face of a girl in a cloud.

CHAPTER 25

AUTHENTIC information and wild speculation about the Scotts drifted up and down the river road in such mixed proportions that no one knew for sure where one left off and the other began. The few items that gave indication of being true were that the family consisted of Mr. and Mrs. Scott, the son George, and the daughter whose name was Carlie. The Negroes with them were Hi, his wife Maria, their two children, Plunk and Mamie, and another farm worker called Mose.

Why the Scotts had come north and how they happened to choose the Valley were questions which could be answered only by guesswork because of the reticence of all concerned. This secretive characteristic was scarcely understandable to a community whose families knew each other's every activity, and particularly so to Jeremiah whose "I says" and "he says" were the result of so much frank conversation by roadside and field.

In the days after their arrival, every one in the vicinity kept talking about going down to the Scotts' to make a neighborly call, and nobody went. One wondered why. Certainly no Martin had ever shown any hesitancy before about riding in to see new neighbors, welcoming them, inviting them over. Even Jeremiah, whose prize joke was that *hos*pitality began with a *hoss*, showed an unusual reluctance to ride down to the new home set so far back from the road, its very location telling the neighborhood there was to be a certain sort of privacy about it which no other home proclaimed.

"Somebody ought to invite them to the County Fair," Jeremiah said.

Sarah sniffed. "*You* better. You own it."

Jeremiah grinned. After all was said and done, he liked

231

Ma's spunk. You never knew what she was going to say and sometimes it was as smart as a black-snake whip. That last was a pretty sharp come-back when he had spent so much time helping get up the Fair.

To the Martin girls the new Carlie Scott living there behind the walls of the white painted farm-house with the green blinds was a medieval princess in her tower or the Grecian Exile in the pages of the *Parlor Annual* come to life. Whenever they trained the spy-glass in the general direction of the dormer-windowed castle they could almost always catch some picture of activity about the place, the black farm men, the little black children or their mother, even a glimpse sometimes of Mr. Scott or the son. Once they saw Mrs. Scott on the porch, her skirt flaring over hoops, even in the morning, but never did they see so much as a wave of the blue plume or a flutter of the white veil of Carlie.

And now all this curiosity was dulled a bit by Phoebe Lou's first letter. Suzanne got it from the Post Office at Sturgis Falls where she had gone on horseback to spend the afternoon with Sabina in order to tell her more about the Scotts.

The Post Office was in a substantial wooden building. One could scarcely believe that Demsey Overman had once carried the mail in his hat, for there were sixteen hundred souls in Sturgis Falls now (even twelve hundred in little Prairie Rapids), to say nothing of the farm people up and down both sides of the river and those who were beginning to locate on the prairie to the west and south of town, all of whom came there for their letters from back home.

Suzanne took the epistle up to Sabina's and the two spent the greater portion of the afternoon wondering whether or not to open it, since it was directed to their mother. Sometimes they were of a mind to do so, knowing that the contents would be written to them all, but just as they were about to break the seal each time, they hesitated, remembering Ma's sharp tongue. It ended in deciding that discretion was the better part of valor, and Sabina said she would get Tom to drive her out soon to read it, that just getting a letter addressed in Phoebe Lou's nice shaded hand showed that she was all right.

So Suzanne left on Queen, with the letter inside the stays of her basque and the wide skirt of her best blue poplin ballooning up at the side because she had forgotten to pin the little sack of shot inside the hem to hold it down.

When she rode at a breakneck gallop into the yard and gave the letter to Sarah who was helping Emily take down the clothes, that unpredictable person said, "Land o' the living, you don't mean to say you didn't have the gumption to let Sabina read it while you was there?"

No, you just never could guess how Ma would look at anything.

Sarah sent little Nora over for Lucy and to the stables to get the men folks in to hear the letter. It was not until they all came, Nora's brown bare legs flying ahead of the others, that Sarah broke the seal and read it to the assembled group.

It had been written at Nebraska City, that far-off place on the other side of the Missouri, a river which no one in the community but Tom Bostwick and Wayne Lockwood had ever seen. Phoebe Lou was writing it on her lap, she said, at the side of the Overland Trail.

They had made the trip in two weeks and two days—better than two hundred miles—and wasn't that something to brag about, what with the Gainses' cattle wandering off the trail constantly and their having to ford several streams. When they crossed the Nishnabotna, one of the wagons had tipped over and an old hen of Ma's—the one with the frozen-off toes—had drowned. She had squawked and spread out her wings like a scared old lady grabbing at her skirts and gone down. It had made Phoebe Lou feel badly as though something had happened to a real person from home. They had ferried across the Missouri, finding Nebraska City a queer, noisy, rough place full of covered wagons, mules, dust, oxen, prospectors, saloons. Somebody told Ed there were ten black slaves right in the town, and more than that, although she was half afraid to put it down on paper, there was an underground railroad and that John Brown Pa was always talking about had come more than once through here with slaves from Missouri.

They were camping now not far from the home of J. Sterling Morton. It was the Mortons, folks said, who had negotiated with the Injuns to turn over their land to the government. They said Mrs. Morton had been the only woman at the ceremony when the Injuns assembled to do it.

The country had seemed awful wild coming—just rolling plains and prairie grass. She was always thinking of them all and when she shut her eyes she could almost see them. She'd give anything for a drink of cold water from the well or the old spring.

"If it was not for Ed I would be very homesick. But I love

him . . .'' Plainly Ma was embarrassed at this bold paragraph, probably thinking how people were foolish to write things they wouldn't say, but she read on with fortitude: ''and as long as I have him and he has me, I guess nothing else matters.'' They were ready to start now over the long seven-hundred-mile trail. Ed sent his regards. She was their obedient daughter, Phoebe Lou.

Suzanne wanted to read the letter again to herself as she always did, and when Sarah handed it over, she slipped outdoors, down the garden patch, and through the side gate, thinking to go down to her old haunt by the slough, but stopped at the stake-and-rider fence where the corners of it met the timber-line, deciding it was too near supper time to go on. There was no one in sight and because she still had on hoops from visiting in town, she pulled them and her skirts high and climbed to the top of the fence, releasing them then so that they sprang out into their round fullness, giving her the appearance of a blue mushroom growing like a parasite on the bark of the rail fence.

She re-read the letter, put it in her bosom, and then, chin in hand, sat thinking. ''But I love him and as long as I have him and he has me, I guess nothing else matters.'' She visualized Phoebe Lou leaving the folks and going off that night with Ed Armitage because she loved him.

Other things had happened that night. *Maybe, Suzanne, I know more than you think.* Suppose, just *suppose*, that Wayne Lockwood should come through the woods now, while she was sitting elegantly here in her best dress, along the path through that underbrush, and say right out of a clear sky: ''Suzanne, I've known you for a long time. I love you. I've loved you ever since I saw you the first day I came to the Valley. I'm going to Denver, far away, to seek gold. It will be a long hard trip and you won't see your folks again for years. But I love you so much I can't go without you.''

She was living the part now. Emotion swept her body like a warm sweet wave, so that her breath came quickly with the deep feeling. ''We'll go together, Suzanne.'' His voice would be low and tender. ''Just you and I. It will be hard for you to leave, but I'll have you and you'll have me, and nothing else matters.'' He would be standing by that wild grape-vine over there—no, probably here by this old hickory with the fallen tree-trunk near it—and he would have one foot up on the log. She stopped to consider how handsome he would look standing that way with his head turned toward her. ''We'll be married to-morrow. No . . . I can't delay. To-morrow night we'll sleep under the stars . . . and even though we hear wolves . . . and Indians will be near . . . and wild things . . . nothing will hurt you for I'll be by your side. Will you, Suzanne, *dear one?*"

So far, the scene involving the ardent proposal had been confined to that vague locality known to Suzanne's past childhood as her magic world, always a place of silence, far from human voice. But now in the warmth of the loved one's fervor and her own reaction to his imagined emotions, it broke bounds and she said aloud: "*Yes . . .* oh, *yes,* I will."

"*Will what?*"

Twigs were snapping. A branch was crackling. And Wayne Lockwood came through the underbrush.

No longer was Suzanne sitting elegantly, for in wide-eyed and open-mouthed terror, she promptly and completely fell off the fence. Not gracefully, but in an awkward, sidewise tumble, with her hoops catching on one of the stakes and her best ruffled pantalets a prominent part of the picture. In truth, the lady dangled in mid-air.

Wayne threw back his head and sent out to the skies hearty male laughter. Even so he was hurrying to disengage the wire-and-elastic skeleton structure and its disconcerted owner from their perilous position.

"You don't need to *laugh.*" Suzanne was fiery red, the combined effect of embarrassment and the rushing of blood to a head which normally should have been the other way up.

"I'm sorry, Suzanne. Really I am." He lifted her down and helped settle her skirts, "And I honestly didn't mean to scare you."

"You didn't *scare* me." She was almost tearful.

"Well . . . just frightened you then. I was looking for a couple of stray sheep and heard some one talking . . ." And he broke into uncontrollable merriment again.

When the robust laughter died away, he said, "Anyway, I'm glad I ran across you here alone."

He had put a foot up on the log of the fallen hickory tree trunk and was facing her.

"Suzanne . . ." He was all seriousness now. "I've known you a long time . . . ever since the first day I came to the Valley . . ."

Suzanne's eyes were fixed on his with fascinated fright. It went through her mind with half-delirious terror that she had done something magic. Some uncanny thing was taking place because of the thoughts she had harbored.

". . . and I want to ask you something."

An unseen force was performing a miracle for her. From out the world of imagination by some unknown means she had called an exquisite reality. Her pulses were pounding so loudly that she was afraid he must be hearing them. The familiar trees and undergrowth were swimming in a warm liquid mist.

"I wonder," Wanye's deep resonant voice went on, "would you go down to the Scotts' on some excuse when you have a chance and find out more about the daughter?"

Like the shocked silence after crashing thunder on the prairie, Suzanne's beating pulses were numbed.

"You want me . . ?"

"I hate to ask you. It seems cowardly and underhanded, but I want to get acquainted with her and they seem so stiff and unfriendly, I thought maybe if you could go first and find out a little more about her and tell me. . . . You're the only one I felt I could trust to do it . . . and keep it confidential."

Suzanne moistened her dry lips. "And you . . . trust me?"

"Yes. I don't know just why, Suzanne, but of all you girls . . . you're the one who seems the most . . ." His voice trailed away in half-abashed silence.

Suzanne said quietly: "All right, Wayne, I will."

They walked on up to the house together, the deepening prairie twilight thrown over them like a gray veil.

Even if he had been attracted by Carlie Scott, that sudden news could not keep her heart from beating fast because he was beside her. Even if she was only a neighbor girl that he trusted, the knowledge of that ordinary and uninteresting place she held in his mind could not keep her from feeling his nearness.

The main thing was never to let him know. Keep your head up and don't let him see how you feel, she told herself sternly, summoning to her aid all those things her father was always saying. Life has to be met squarely. You can't always have things the way you want. Pull yourself on through.

Once for a few moments he took her hand to jump across the old hardened furrows of the garden so that her pulses, with no apparent intention of obeying, quickened violently to the touch. At once she turned on that traitorous throbbing with scorn. Stop that. Face facts. She had always said not one of the Martin girls was good enough for him, hadn't she?

That included herself, didn't it? She had *imagined* some lovely girl for him, hadn't she? Well, here she was—Carlie Scott, a pretty girl in a blue plume and white veil. . . .

Oh, that *darned* mourning-dove in the timber!

Supper was a long and irritating meal, including noisy talk about Phoebe Lou and the Scotts, Abraham Lincoln's chances and the County Fair, with the food sticking miserably in Suzanne's throat, and Ambrose Willshire riding in afterward to tell them with cold disapproval that Jeanie had another girl, so that Ma, her lips set in a straight line, hurried to get ready to go back across the prairie with him.

It was nearly bedtime when they heard Wayne singing in the lane road, his voice melodiously rich coming over the ripening corn so that all went outside to hear:

> *"It was here with the bright blue sky above*
> *I told her the tale of my heart's true love,*
> *And long 'ere the blossoms of summer had died*
> *She whispered the promise to be my bride.*

> *"Oh cruel and false were the tales they told*
> *That my vows were false and my old love cold.*
> *That my truant heart held another dear,*
> *Forgetting the vows that were whispered here.*

> *"Then her cheeks grew pale and . . ."*

The words died away but the faint melody came back from the north prairie.

Suzanne said suddenly: "Pa, I want to go to this new Female Seminary in Prairie Rapids when it opens. Do you think I could?"

Jeremiah appraised his youngest with a critical if furtive eye. "Well, those are legitimate desires, I'd say. But just why are you anxious to go this week and was lukewarm last?"

"I've been thinking . . . and I've made up my mind to be a teacher. If I go there this winter I guess I could pass the teacher's examinations and get a school instead of just helping Ma or the neighbors."

"Or gettin' married and settlin' down?"

"Oh, *don't* say that. I wouldn't marry anybody if . . . if every man in the county wanted me."

"Well . . . there's not such a great lot o' danger o' that, but just to save you the possible embarrassment o' giving 'em all the mitten, I guess maybe if Ma's willin', you better go. Celia goin' into the milliner shop again . . . Emily sewin' for folks . . . that'll leave Melinda to hold the fort helpin' Ma. It's fifty cents a week tuition. That comes pretty often for a half a dollar. I'd want you to make the most of your time.''

"Oh, I will, Pa. I want to spend my *whole life* studying!"

CHAPTER 26

THE day before the County Fair, making an invitation to attend it the excuse for her going and thus keep her promise to Wayne, Suzanne dressed in her blue poplin and rode Jupiter down the field road to the Scotts'.

No ambassador to a foreign court ever went in such a mixed mental state including, as did Suzanne's mind, timidity, curiosity, envy, and disrelish.

Although she had often been to the west end of the slough in pre-Scott days, it seemed now a strangely unfamiliar place with the new white house and its green blinds sitting there where once only the maple and butternut trees stood and the hazel brush tangled with the sumac.

There was no one in sight as she dismounted, but almost immediately the two little black children came from around the corner of the house. They were probably only seven and nine years old but they scampered to Jupiter's head at once to hold the bridle. Suzanne felt peculiarly uncertain about her attitude toward these first black children upon whom she had ever laid eyes. A slave race, lots of people thought, just *meant* for slaves and nothing else. "Just as good right to their freedom and live their own lives as you and me," Pa said. You didn't know *what* to think.

She went up to the long front porch, her blue poplin swaying so stylishly that she felt very elegant and at ease. But when she was admitted by the fat black woman to a room with a stairway right in front of her and beheld Miss Carlie Scott coming down that stairway in a wider skirt with more swing to it, she no longer felt elegant, and only the thought of Pa's being the Honorable Jeremiah Martin bolstered her courage.

"My name's Suzanne Martin," she said and knew her voice sounded pinched and squeaky. "I thought I'd come over and tell you about the County Fair to-morrow, and urge you to go.''

Miss Carlie Scott said that was nice for her to come, and to sit down here where it was cool—only she said it so very differently from the way the river-road people talked, "heah" and "fo'."

Carlie Scott was pretty and so pale that Celia would certainly take a back seat, Suzanne thought. Her little mouth was a pouting pink which gave her the appearance of a spoiled child, and even now she looked as though she might have been crying.

With a quick sweep of her eyes Suzanne saw a carpeted room, chairs shining with horsehair upholstering, lace curtains at the windows, a spread peacock tail, wax flowers under glass—for all that, it would be Sabina's turn to envy.

Mrs. Scott came in then, tall and genteel. The black woman whom they called Maria brought in cookies and glasses of something that tasted to Suzanne partly like wild grapes and partly like apple cider.

But even the eating together did not make the call a complete success as Pa said breaking bread always did. Something between them seemed never to be overcome. It was as though they could not reach across a space and meet in a common subject, as though the Scotts stood on one side of the creek bed and Suzanne on the other with high water between.

"How do you like it here?"

"It's very pleasant here near the trees."

"We like the Valley."

"You are the family in the whitewashed cabin?"

"Yes." Suddenly to Suzanne, a whitewashed cabin was a most distasteful thing. "My father's the Honorable Jeremiah Martin. He's in the legislature."

"Oh, a politician!"

Oh, dear, how could she get them to know that everybody looked up so to Pa?

"He's been elected *twice,*" she said sturdily. "And to all the Republican conventions." No one could belittle Pa's honors.

"I suppose there *are* quite a few Republicans in the locality."

Quickly Suzanne had a presentiment that maybe the Scotts were not Republicans. Oh, goodness!

"There are some nice young people around here." Suzanne tried Carlie again. "And they would be pleased to have you join them in singing school and spell-downs, picnics and boat-rides.'' She would do all she could for Wayne. ''Sometimes''—she had a sudden feeling that she was talking like Pa, always putting the best on everything—''there's a nice dance in Sturgis Falls at Overman Hall.''

Reporting all about it at home, she said, ''I can't tell you *what* it was, but I don't believe I'd *ever* feel acquainted with them. I don't believe they ever have fun and I bet they don't know what a *joke* is.''

The Scotts went to the County Fair. The girls, each with an eye in that direction as they dressed, saw the carriage come up the new field road, black Hi driving, Mr. Scott beside him, and the two ladies in the back. They held little parasols over themselves which made Celia say frankly she certainly wished they hadn't slopped over with generosity all at once and given the green silk one to Phoebe Lou.

Sarah was not going. Never sick, she ''took a pain'' that day under her shoulder-blade so that at the last minute Emily stayed home with her.

Henry took Lucy and little Nora in the buckboard. Jeremiah drove with the other three girls in the wagon, Melinda on the front seat by him. As they rattled out of the yard he was thinking they were a pretty comely-looking bunch of girls.

Celia had on her apple-green challis, and her little white bonnet lined with green inclosed a very fair skin because she had not once gone into the field, or ever, under the most trying circumstances, neglected her milkweed cream at night. Melinda, as sunburned as a Musquakie, had on her brown dress with red plaid trimming, and red and brown ribbons pleated across the front of her straw bonnet. Because she had taken some pains with herself she looked neat and proper to start with, although the chances were by night she would be in a state of complete disintegration. As for Suzanne, she was in the blue poplin which once she had so deeply admired, and her blue bonnet of Etruscan straw to match, but now neither one pleased her, the dress being less full than Carlie Scott's, and as for the bonnet—how could *any* bonnet without a plume be worthy of the name? There was a ten-dollar gray-blue plume in the shop where Celia sometimes helped and if it only remained unsold until she could go to school, get her certificate, and teach, she would buy it with her very first money. With a plume the exact color of her eyes, maybe Wayne . . . she dreamed all the way to town.

Dust from the teams ahead hung heavily in the warm

September air so that Celia and Suzanne covered their faces with their handkerchiefs at times to keep clean, but Melinda did not bother to, swallowing dust cheerfully and coughing over it as she talked a blue streak to Pa.

They crossed the new bridge, Laddie's and Lassie's shaggy legs pounding along with clumping hollow sound and the wagon rattling, passed along Main Street between the stores and taverns toward the fair-ground several blocks away. Jeremiah had to pick his way around the stumps still clinging to Mother Earth as though she would not let man forget that he had desecrated her forests to build him a town.

The fair-ground was a forty-acre tract of prairie land with a grassy quarter-mile race-track for its main attraction. Already people were walking about looking at the live stock on exhibition, the pumpkins, apples, and plums, the fanning mills, stirring plows, and a cider press. The town band was there tuning up for the parade around the track. It was all too exciting for words.

They got out of the wagon and Jeremiah, tying the horses, told the girls to watch their manners and he would meet them right here in this very spot at five o'clock. He must get over where Phineas was to see how Sandy was taking all this excitement. They could see Phineas leading old Sandy out of an open stall right then, ready for the parade, a ring in his nose and a wary look in his eye. Near-by Queen was pawing the ground restlessly where she was tied to the side of the rude open shelter.

It was not five minutes before several young men sauntered their way—a clerk in one of the stores whom Celia knew, his cousin visiting him, and two stalwart strangers who were introduced to the girls as Rand and Alf Banninger, sons of a new settler south of town. The one called Rand, with eyes for Suzanne, pestered her continually to walk around with him alone, but she put him off laughingly and stayed by the girls. Celia, too, was refusing Alf Banninger to leave the group, her pale pretty face turned away at times, searching the grounds for the new Scott son. Melinda said loudly and cheerfully that *she* would go, but the young men, with warm looks for Suzanne and Celia, pretended not to hear.

They all stood there together until the passing of the stock parade, headed by the brass band which made all the horses cavort about skittishly but affected the dumb old oxen not at all. A young fellow by the name of Sol Humbert from the west prairies, driving six oxen hitched to a long pieced-out wagon made from new lumber and containing twenty or thirty persons, won the prize for bringing the greatest number in one equipage, although the fair management would not let him go onto the race-track with the heavy load. It was hard to tell which attracted the most attention, Sol Humbert's long wagon or the Scotts' open carriage with black Hi driving and the two ladies with their parasols seated therein.

Jeremiah's friend, Mr. Peter Melendy, mounted the judges' stand and demonstrated the fact that a shrill whistle could be made out of a pig's tail. There was a running race with a man by the name of Brownell winning, even though he ran in heavy cowhide boots.

There were other races with prizes and then a man on a high wooden stand called out between cupped hands? "A race now not scheduled heretofore, ex-*clu*-sive-ly for the ladies. A ladies' race open to each and all of the femi*nine* persuasion. No stipulations or rules *any* age lady and *any* age animal—in fact any *kind* of animal. Whoever starts at the gun going off and gets around the quarter-mile first, by carriage *or* beast *or* foot. Prize . . . ten dollars. Prize . . . ten dollars!''

Ten dollars! Two parts of Suzanne's brain snapped together, connecting ten dollars so speedily and so definitely with a drooping blue plume that not thirty seconds had passed when she said very low to Celia, "I'm going on Queen," and was off before Celia's protestations had been put into words.

She went behind the open stable where Queen was tied, removed her bonnet and placed it on the low back of the sloping roof. With a quick glance around the side of the building to be sure that she was not seen, she pulled up the skirt of her blue poplin and with some fumbling untied the stout strings which bound her hoops, letting them down around her feet, so that, suddenly and rather ridiculously, she had collapsed from a plump semisphere into a very slim perpendicular piece of femininity.

There were only four other contestants, two town girls in real riding habits, leading one to think they might have had some pre-knowledge of the impromptu race, a buxom middle-aged woman from the Big Woods, and a young girl from the west prairies. And then there was Suzanne on Queen, with her best poplin blowing into a big blue mushroom and her hair tumbling over her neck, and Queen, thinking she was tearing madly over the prairies, winning the race for Suzanne amid much cheering, from which Celia's contribution was entirely missing.

But when Suzanne had recieved her prize from the hands of the announcer and was returning with Queen to the shelter of the shed and the collapsed hoops, she saw that which made the winning as ashes in her mouth. Wayne Lockwood, in a fine new gray suit with vest, white ruffled shirt, and gray beaver hat held at his breast, was standing, tall and straight and handsome, by the open carriage and talking so intently to Carlie Scott that he did not even see her pass by.

Ten dollars in her hand—more money than she had ever possessed! Almost more than she had ever *seen!* Virtually the drooping blue plume on her bonnet at that very moment! Suddenly, it came over her in bitter knowledge—you cannot purchase some things in this world at all. You can never, never buy a man's love, nor even his passing interest.

Sarah talked about it off and on all the rest of the month, thinking that Suzanne had disgraced herself by the impulsive and public act. Jeremiah said that what with the sinking of the *Lady Elgin,* a cable for messages being laid between Ireland and Newfoundland, the coming election, antislavery debates, possible secession, and even war talk over the whole country, it did seem that a little thing like a girl dashing around a quarter-mile track on a respectable old mare wasn't such an important topic.

"But when I think of her *hoops* hanging there on the side of that building . . . for any one to come along and see . . ."

"Oh, come now, Ma! Most everybody sometime or another has caught sight of hoops. You don't think a glimpse of those wire birdcages is going to pollute the morals of the whole Cedar Valley, do you?"

But in time there came an end to Sarah's faultfinding with the misplaced hoops for when corn-husking was over Suzanne went to the Prairie Home Female Seminary there in Prairie Rapids, riding along on the high seat of a lumber wagon filled with corn whose sideboards rattled noisily all the way up the street to the big brick building where she was to live and presumably to learn.

Jeremiah, taking her there, was combining, as always, a load of something to sell along with "toting the women folks." Tied high on the corn so that it would not lose off was a bundle containing bedding, her blue poplin dress, two loaves of bread, a roll of Sarah's sweet butter, some tea, a pot of wild blackberry jam (which Suzanne was to be scarcely able to eat for remembering that Phoebe Lou had picked the berries), and bacon so thoroughly smoked that when Suzanne put on her poplin that first evening she smelled like nothing so much as a bonfire in which a piece of meat had been dropped.

Miss Anna Field had graduated recently under Mary Lyon at Mount Holyoke, and her sister, Miss Libbie, also had received some training in teaching.

The two met and welcomed Suzanne, stood for a time and talked politics with Jeremiah, offering such intelligent Republicanized statements concerning the antislavery trend of the times and the importance of the coming election, that he left his daughter happily convinced she was in capable hands.

In the following days his every waking moment was spent in preparation for the biggest political mass-meeting the Valley had ever seen. The old leading political question, the tariff, was overshadowed completely this time by the threatened secession. Something about this particular election was pulling at the very fibers of every one's being.

Sturgis Falls Democrats were practically tickling themselves to death this fall with a song that had drifted here from no one knew where:

> Say he's capable and honest,
> Loves his country's good alone;
> Never drank a drop of whisky,
> Wouldn't know it from a stone!
> Any lie you tell, we'll swallow,
> Swallow any kind of mixture;
> But, oh, don't—we pray and beg you—
> Don't, for God's sake, show his picture!

Well, maybe Lincoln *was* homely, but just wait and see what the crowd would do when the parade went by.

It turned out to be all that the committee could have desired—a great night, and the longest procession the county had ever known, with three bands, flaring torch-lights, and new campaign songs. And now—what was that coming down the street next to the last band? A wagon being hauled down the crooked stump-filled Main Street by a half-dozen men. Abe, himself? No, but gosh a'mighty, it was his spit'n image. A tall angular settler, representing Lincoln, was splitting logs. Sleeves rolled up, a pile of tree-trunks there before him, at work with ax, wedge, and mawl, he was almost the living replica of old Abe. The crowd was roaring itself hoarse. Hats were being thrown in the air. The wagon could scarcely move for men and boys crowding around it. "We're *for* you, Abe."

Jeremiah Martin went home well satisfied with his night's work.

Suzanne shared a room in the big brick seminary with two students from south of town.

There was so much to do for themselves in a physical way the first week that sometimes it seemed there was not any time left to devote to the mental. They washed out their own stockings and aprons and built fires in their room stove there on the second floor, carrying multitudinous chunks up the long stairs, sweeping after themselves each time on account of the constant dropping of pieces of maple or elm bark en route. They cooked all their meals, feasting the first part of the week and fasting at the close, for not one had any money to spend at the stores and all had brought supplies from home for a week's eating.

When Suzanne went home with Phineas at the end of that first five days there was another letter by pony express from Phoebe Lou waiting to be read. It had been written in a huge camp of gold-seekers just this side of Denver with mountains looking as though you could walk over to them in ten minutes and they a good twelve miles away.

There was so much to tell she didn't know where to begin. Just before they left Nebraska City there had been a revolt among the ox-drivers and muleteers with much excitement because they wanted twenty-five dollars for the round trip to Salt Lake City. The long dusty trail had been packed with teams. Seemed as though the whole country had decided to come west. For hours at a time she could keep her mind on nothing but the thought of the cold spring down there at the creek behind the house on the river road. Did they all remember how the old trail out from Illinois had been thick with grass and mud holes and sloughs? This one was all dense gray-white dust. Oh, so many sights—seeing the military company at Fort Kearney, the low sluggish Platte River with sandy islands covered with mud hens, an Indian village too filthy for anything, a place called Gilman's Ranch where they had good spring water and an adobe house—that meant mud walls. There were lots of Indians so that wagons traveled in long trains. Sometimes the stories you heard just scared you out of a year's growth but of course Ed was right there by her.

Sarah's snort, the listeners all knew, meant what was a little matter of hostile Indians if that flibbertigibbet was near-by?

Ed said they would have a fine home in Denver City some day and Pa and Ma could come and live with them. At that Sarah was almost too overcome to sniff, remarking: "They'll visit us, I warrant, long before we'll ever visit them," as she put the letter away for the other girls to read.

When, at the close of the letter-reading, Melinda, excited to a point of giggling breathlessness, told Suzanne that she had another big piece of news: Wayne Lockwood, all dressed up, had gone riding down the field road to Scotts', Suzanne knew at once that she was through forever with the thought of buying a plume. To save Pa the expense she would now hoard her ten dollars for tuition. It would pay for twenty weeks. Twenty weeks of education instead of a blue plume! "Better fifty years of Europe than a cycle of Cathay," was all right for Mr. Alfred Tennyson to say, but what if you had no choice in the matter? What if you *had* to live through a cycle of Cathay instead of wearing a blue plume for some one?

Miss Anna Field had read some of Mr. Tennyson's works in one of her classes. Miss Anna taught English, all mathematics, and even Latin to two aspiring town girls who enjoyed a superior if fragmentary conversation with each other that first month by means of such mysterious sounding words as "mensa" and "agricola." Miss Libbie taught bookkeeping, spelling, and a species of penmanship which involved many shaded tails and curlicues on the letters.

Suzanne was just finishing a chalky version of these capitals in Miss Libbie's room one Friday later in the fall when Miss Anna came to the door and said, "Suzanne, there's a young man here who wishes to speak to you."

Her heart started up foolishly at the sight of Wayne Lockwood waiting for her there in the big hall, explaining in a matter-of-fact way that because he had been obliged to come to Prairie Rapids she was supposed to ride out home with him.

So Suzanne, knowing that keeping men folks waiting was one of the cardinal sins, packed her bundle hurriedly and in a very short time was heading for home on the wagon seat by the side of Wayne.

The hard maples and oaks were a riot of color. The air was crystal clear after several days of rain, all the dust of the summer washed from the Valley. As much as she was liking school it was nice to be going home, so she was gaiety itself, hugging to her this hour of riding out the river road with Wayne. She laughed and chattered, sipping at the fountain of her joy as though, if this moment were never to come again, it must be quaffed deeply.

Wayne, too, fell in with this pleasant mood as they rattled along the road where the scarlet and bronze timber flamed at the south.

"Isn't it nice?" With a sweep of her arm Suzanne took in all of the world that was visible. The gesture included the grading for the new railroad over there to the north—it was nearly finished to Sturgis Falls—that long line of embankment across the farms like a huge runway thrown up by some gigantic mole.

"Yes. You can't think that there's all this unrest and excitement everywhere about the slavery and secession and all, can you?"

"Oh, Wayne, it's so silly. It'll all blow over."

"I'm not so sure about that. I used to think that, too. But you ought to see the papers. They say if Lincoln is elected, the south will rise right up."

"Oh, I still don't believe that part. We've had presidents before some of the folks didn't like. Pa didn't like . . ."

"But this is different . . . and much more serious. Anyway . . . five more days to election. . . ."

But Suzanne was not too interested in the election just now, choosing rather to speak of the important things of school, of the interesting books Miss Field had on a shelf behind the stove, of the Prairie Rapids girls who had enrolled at the Seminary, knowing all the time that not an item was so important as this one of Wayne being here by her side.

Once he broke into singing:

Her eyes soft and tender,
The violets outvying,
And a fairer form was never seen . . .

so that Suzanne, out of the sheer exuberance of her feelings, sang, too:

With her brown silken tresses
And cheeks like the roses
There was none like my darling Daisy Dean.

Oh, you felt as though you were floating on those puffy white clouds to be out here on the river road singing *Daisy Dean* with Wayne Lockwood.

When they were almost home, by the east corn-field, the queer built-on whitewashed house of logs and timber visible through the trees, he said suddenly:

"I never thanked you for going down to the Scotts' for me that time. I meant to . . . but I didn't get to. So thanks for doing it. I wouldn't have needed to ask you, but I appreciated it. I got acquainted with her anyway. Suzanne, she's . . ." his voice wrapped itself about the words, folding them in tenderly . . . "she's like a flower."

"A flower?" Suzanne repeated stupidly. One does not fall from cloud distances without some shock.

"Yes. . . . I guess one of these . . . little wind-flowers . . . you know, dainty and delicate." He laughed suddenly. "Funny I could say that out loud to any one. Sounds pretty foolish, doesn't it?"

They had driven into the yard, were by the lean-to door now, and Pa, Ma, Melinda, Emily, and Celia had all come out to greet her. They were so glad to see her that for a moment it hurt her to think how little she cared for them all to-night.

She went into the house where there awaited her a hot supper of mashed potatoes, baked chicken, creamed dried sweet corn, and even fresh apple pie from the first year of the new orchard's bearing. Also there was much noisy conversation anent the election, antislavery, threats of secession, and split parties. But what did it all amount to? What was an old election? And what did secession matter if Carlie Scott was like a little wind-flower?

And then it turned out that Suzanne did not go back to school Sunday night. No one knew just how it happened unless it was the weather turning cold suddenly and a drizzle starting when she was down in the timber for butternuts Saturday afternoon, and getting soaked that way, but she came down from the loft Sunday morning with a stiff neck and a throat so sore that Sarah made her get into her old downstairs bed to be doctored.

For two days Suzanne lay twisting and tossing in the bed behind the tester there in her mother's room. She could scarcely swallow and her head was hot and throbbing. Sarah worked over her, binding slabs of fresh pork on her neck with flannel cloths, bringing bowls of hot catnip tea to the bedside, dosing her with onion-and-molasses syrup. There was no one like Ma to doctor you. Queer, too, how gentle she was. No matter what she said or scolded about when you were well, always if you got sick, she was all tenderness and patience, her hands seeking unerringly the trouble and sometimes rubbing it away. No matter what she would say spunky to the well ones, Ma never was cross to the sick.

In the evening of the third day Pa and Phineas were in Prairie Rapids waiting to hear the election news. When they heard it in Dubuque, the railroad company was going to send a trainman on an engine out to the end of the line to tell folks.

Sarah, Emily, Melinda, and Celia all sat up to wait for them, but finally the girls grew sleepy and Celia said she'd already put her cream on and what difference after all did it make *who* won? So Suzanne knew they were tiptoeing past her bed and mounting the ladder to the loft, their candles making flickering lights through the tester. She heard suppressed laughing and knew that whoever went first was scurrying fast to keep her ankles from being pinched. The noise of the girls passing to and fro overhead ceased about the time she heard the sound of horses' hoofs thudding down to the stable.

She must have dozed off a minute for just as she thought she was trying to make a good chain of capitals for Miss Libbie Field she heard Ma's voice near her at the foot of the loft ladder.

"Girls . . . girls . . . !" Ma was trying to speak quietly, probably thinking she was asleep. "Are you still awake?"

There was a thumping and rushing sound overhead and the girls' voices were answering, "Yes. What is it, Ma?"

"I just thought," Ma was calling up to them, "you'd like to know your Pa's elected Abraham Lincoln president."

CHAPTER 27

ALL the rest of the year Suzanne went back and forth to the Seminary—home Friday nights, back to Prairie Rapids Sunday night, or so early Monday morning that the pale December sun was not yet up. The winter winds whipped about her as she rode down in the bottom of a straw-filled sleigh, one of Ma's Indian baskets by her filled with the week's supplies: bread, a pie, twisted fried cakes, some side meat or fresh sausage, maybe a cooked chicken, all of these to be shared with the two girls who lived with her, just as she in turn shared their side meat, corn-bread and dried-apple sauce.

With parsing, spelling, diagramming, making those long picturesque tails of shaded ink on penmanship papers, even tackling more algebra than Miss Cotton had given her, the short days were passed. And when it grew dusk in the late afternoon, she wrapped up and went with the other girls to the well and woodpile to bring her own supply of water and chunks, and to fill the school's pail and woodbox.

Christmas was over, the year slipped away, and the cold descended in earnest. For next to the winter of '56-'57, weather in 1861 was the most severe that any settler remembered. A succession of snow-storms blocked roads and entirely shut the Valley off from communication with the outer world. There was no letter mail from east of the Mississippi River for ten days, no papers for over a week. Suzanne, stranded at the Seminary, pieced out her scanty provisions with a sack of corn-meal she bought at the store on promise to pay when she came back from home, almost worrying herself sick that Pa who never went into debt would be disgraced by her asking for credit.

When she finally got home she found Pa so wrought up

over the news which had just come through that he didn't act as though her going in debt was anything very bad. Secessionists, making threats, were shipping arms out of New York and hurrying home to avoid arrest for treason. Pa said that some of them were talking about dissolving the union and then soliciting Louis Napoleon to assume protection of the South. At the supper table he explained jubilantly, gesticulating with his knife and fork and forgetting to eat, that if you counted out the six seceding states, there were fifty-eight members of congress and that the Republicans would have exactly half besides the vice-president; in the house there would be one hundred and fourteen Republicans, seventy Democrats, and twenty-one Americans, a good Republican majority, so that Lincoln would be well abetted if the seceders refused to come back in. She breathed a sigh of relief to think how many Republicans would be there in Washington to make things come out all right.

Life now to Suzanne was divided, like that Gaul Miss Anna Field told about, into three parts: I. School. II. War talk. III. Wayne Lockwood.

She had too much pride to ask any one about Wayne and Carlie Scott when she was home, but, even so, there was no need, for Celia and Melinda volunteered glibly as soon as she arrived that sometimes Wayne went horseback over the snow-packed field road and that the night the storms abated enough to hold singing school he sat by Carlie Scott's side and sang, "Thou only hast my heart," like to raise the dead. Only Emily remained silent on the subject, never mentioning either one. There was lots of gossip about the son. He was a hard drinker and a hard rider, and Pa said if any one ever saw him come tearing down the road to get away off at the side, for half the time he didn't know what he was about.

But even George Scott could not tear wildly about this month, for February's weather did not moderate to the bitter end. A mail was brought out from Dubuque by a mule team which made the round trip in two weeks. When the long string of mules floundered through the last cut into Sturgis Falls the two drivers told the assembled group of citizens that it was authentically reported the rebels would try to take the capital on inauguration day. At that dark news a group of men immediately formed themselves into a potential miltiary company, Phineas among them.

The Prairie Rapids town girls attending school brought such frightening tales that week—how Lincoln was on his way to Washington, how he had stopped in Philadelphia and said he'd rather be assassinated than surrender the principle of liberty on which the union was formed, how their fathers said the whole country was just sitting on a volcano until after the inauguration—that Suzanne could scarcely stand it until she got home to hear what Pa had to say about it.

Even so, nothing big happened on inauguration day. If the country sat on a volcano there was no eruption. Maybe it would all go into nothing after Lincoln saying he was of no mind to interfere with slavery in those states where it already existed. That was the way things turned out lots of times.

Every one had been talking about the inauguration as though it were right there in the Valley. It seemed almost like an anti-climax when Jeremiah got home, rode Queen to the stable, and came in quietly.

"How did it go?" Emily asked at once.

"Did he get there without being shot?" Sarah wanted to know.

"Safe in Washington." Jeremiah spoke with satisfaction as though he had been personally responsible for the journey.

"Safe so far," Sarah said laconically.

But Lincoln's speech of assurance was so much water under a bridge.

Suzanne felt such a childish desire to see Pa after she had heard the town girls' wild talk for a full week that never would she miss catching a ride home these spring Friday nights even if no one came for her. Mud, rains, thunderstorms—nothing kept her from going to the Prairie Rapids stores and watching for any one from the river road. She went home on creaking wagon seats, in springless two-wheeled carts, up on a load of grain sacks, or in front of a penned-in cow bawling lustily in her ear for its calf. Once she rode with Cady Bedson behind his spanking team. He was going to consult with Tom Bostwick about contracting for all the grain in this part of the county in case there was war. And once, when no one came for her and no neighbor appeared in the stores, she pulled her skirts up over her galoshes and started out on the long trek.

All of that March the great crew of workmen hustled to complete the Dubuque and Sioux City track into Sturgis Falls. It was as though they were working against time, trying desperately to reach their objective before some threatening storm should descend. Dark clouds filled with spring moisture gathering there on the prairie and breaking into heavy rains were not the only clouds hanging over the Valley. Others were there, low, black, and ugly, whose damaging disruption was to stop the railroad's progression farther west for four long years.

But now it was finished into Sturgis Falls. On Monday, April first, a train was to come over those shining tracks laid out there on that giant mole-run through the farms of the first settlers, across the lane road, and on into town. It did not seem possible that the thing had really come to pass, that a train was to chug down the long grassy trail from Dubuque which old Baldy and Star, Red and Whitey, had traveled so many times.

For the first time Suzanne stayed away from the Seminary for another reason than sickness or being snow-bound.

Sarah scolded that with her tuition paid and only one more week on her twenty to go it was wasteful, but Jeremiah told her to stay home and see the first train cross the prairie, that a world-shaking event didn't happen often and she would never miss a day's lessons.

He, himself, hitched up to go over to town so that he might be there at the depot when it came. To Sarah's sniffed comment that she knew no reason why he had to be at the depot when you could watch it come across the country as far as eye could see, he said he wanted to be with the crowd and see how she slowed up to stop—calling the train ''she,'' as in truth, he did for the rest of his life. ''She's a little late to-day,'' apologizing for her mistakes, or ''Well, she's on time all right,'' proudly commending her as though now she were reforming. Melinda hurried to get ready and out to the wagon the minute she heard he was going.

Even after the two had gone, Sarah was skeptical over the actual arrival. ''It's April Fool's Day and probably it won't come at all.''

But it came. A little black speck in the distance at first, the smoke of its fires streaming with the spring wind, chugging and blowing across the plowed fields and the pasture land, it came in the late afternoon like a huge black animal snorting its way out from Dubuque, fouling the green prairie.

When they heard the far-off whistle like the long-drawn-out wail of a mourning-dove, Suzanne, Emily, and their mother all stared at each other for a moment as though this thing that was happening had come from some mighty force too prodigious to comprehend, and then clutching each other's hands in most unusual fashion, hurried down to the stake-and-rider fence to watch it go by.

When the others came home they brought Celia along, all three saying the crowd had gone mad, cheering and throwing caps in the air. Furthermore, in the Post Office they had found an invitation to the Honorable Jeremiah Martin and lady to attend the grand celebration banquet next week for which a special train carrying all the officials would come out from Dubuque.

"And Pa's to give a toast," Celia informed them.

"Yes, sir," Pa bridled a bit. "Toasts by them that's done the most to help it get here."

"Toast can get overdone," Sarah said dryly. "Now the train's looked after, girls, get your supper work going. Scoot now!"

So Sturgis Falls and Prairie Rapids were connected with the outside world. No longer would the great oxen pull the loads of merchandise over the green trail out from Dubuque or the lone traveler spend a week on the way. Only a day was needed to come the long hundred miles. It did not seem possible.

Suzanne's twenty weeks of schooling were over and she felt quite confident about her teacher's examinations. Ten dollars had been spent for higher education. But it was surprising how much knowledge could be crowded into the brain of an alert young country girl there in 1861 between her tasks of building fires, cooking, dish-washing and carrying in water and wood. Part of the satisfactory result was due to the naturally keen mind of the scholar, and part to the able teachings of Miss Anna Field only recently away from the influence of Mary Lyon at Mount Holyoke.

So Suzanne was home now in the midst of all the talk about secession and what was to happen next, seeing Phineas ride to town every evening after the spring plowing, tired as he was, to drill with the Pioneer Grays getting ready for any emergency, and seeing Wayne Lockwood ride sometimes down the field toward the Scotts'.

Back to the neighborhood at this time came Mrs. Burrill, all alone, from Missouri. She had no home now, for Mr. Burrill had been shot on his own door-stoop, called to the door by a group of men on horseback and killed. Oh, poor Mrs. Burrill! She hadn't seen it but she had heard the shot. They called them "bushwhackers" and they would stoop to anything. As she told them all this on her first day's visit her eyes grew wild and the Adam's apple pumped up and down her scrawny neck.

Scarcely could Sarah or the girls cook the dinner and get the house cleaned that day for stopping and listening to the tales.

The bushwhackers down there wore home-made linsey-woolseys colored yellow, an ugly yellow like a green pumpkin rotted just when it was turning. They used butternut bark for it, and called the men "butternuts." They all wore badges to show they were on the slavery side—a cross-section of a butternut. It made a handsome pin, you couldn't think how ornamental it looked if you didn't stop to think what was behind it. Some of the people on our side of the state line, right in Iowa itself, wore them.

"I suppose they've been more fights over them pins than you could shake a stick at. One wa'nt five miles from us. A big copperhead fellow with a drink of likker in him just swaggered around daring any one to touch his butternut pin. A Scotch farmer. . . . disremember his name at this minute . . . come into the crowd, saw the pin, heard them brags bein' said, reached and got the pin off o: him and his whole shirt with it."

Jeremiah did not go outdoors even for a semblance of overseeing the boys. He sat and plied Mrs. Burrill with questions, to which she had ready and frightening answers.

Melinda, Emily, and Suzanne all lingered and listened and started up again furiously at their work with Sarah's "Come, come, girls, your Pa has to eat and we have to keep clean around here, if bushwhackers and copperheads should be settin' on the door-step, which they ain't."

"Yes." Mrs. Burrill jumped up then, her eyes wild and her forefinger on her lip.

"Yes," she whispered. "Ssh! There be, too. There be, too, bushwhackers on the door-step. All get back. Don't let Burrill go out. Make him stay in the lean-to. There's bush-whackers comin' down the Cedar in a boat. My God . . . they've got Evangeline."

Rooted to the spot, the girls stared at their visitors, their faces blanched and their eyes dark with fright.

"Bushwhackers have got my girl in a boat that's whirlin' in the high water . . . turnin' and whirlin' and carryin' her down . . ." She was screaming. "Get her! Get Evangeline . . ."

Only wiry little Sarah could do anything about it. She had her arm around the distracted creature. "Now, now, Mis'

Burrill . . . this is Sarah Martin come to help you get 'em. You remember Sarah Martin . . . your friend that always helps you out . . . in sickness and harvestin'? . . . I'll help you this time, too. I'll help take care of Burrill and Evangeline.''

Ma's voice was kind. "Come, now. You and me are goin' in the other room and you're goin' to lay down." Already walking slowly with her into the company room Ma was still talking gently.

The girls stood unmoving, shaken to the depths, hearing Ma's soothing voice through the woman's wild one. "See . . . I'll rub your neck and head a little. . . . Don't that feel better? And a cup of tea will make us both feel good. We'll drink some together in here . . . just you and me . . .''

All day Ma sat with her, combing her hair, rubbing her head, speaking gently to her, until the wild talk stopped and only low moans and the sound of crying, sad and sane, came from the company room.

The blacks over at the Scotts' were a constant source of talk. Men cornering Hi or Mose could never resist pestering them with questions.

"Don't you want to be free, Mose?"

"Ah *is* free."

"But you can leave the Scotts if you want to, then."

"Yassir. Ah knows it."

"Then why don't you strike out for yourself?"

"Yassir. But ah don' know where ah'd go, sir."

Uncle Tom's Cabin, between covers, had been passed up and down the river road until it was in a state of disintegration and merely held together by virtue of Sarah Martin's energy and white of egg. *Uncle Tom's Cabin*, as a play, had been given in a tent with coal-oil lamps for lighting, hard boards for the spectators, and Eliza crossing unbleached-muslin ice. So every one tried to think the Scotts' blacks were ill-treated, and felt rather put out that no one could prove it. There was something amiss when Mr. Scott did not act at all like Simon Legree.

Church services in the log school-house took on a fervid political trend. No longer were sprigs of caraway necessary to keep the youngsters' eyes propped open. The patriotic shouting did that. Brother Osgood had gone on to newer frontiers but a Reverend Josper came every other Sunday afternoon, making the Martins' Sabbaths very full, as Jeremiah and Sarah had just become charter members of Sturgis Falls' newly organized Congregational Church, to which services they went in the morning. The Reverend Josper, seemingly commissioned by the Lord to pronounce judgment on all rebels, preached his heated denunciations with wild abandon. Even his appearance, the fiery red of his face, the snowy whiteness of his hair and whiskers, and the piercing blue of his eyes, took a colorful patriotic trend.

On April eleventh the grand celebration over the coming of the railroad held the boards. Every activity in the Martin household that day turned toward the event. Jeremiah was on the committee to be at the depot when the Dubuque moguls arrived. Alf and Rand Banninger, the two young men from south of town, were coming to get Celia and Suzanne for the evening dance in Overman Hall, and Pa who had just heard the Banningers were Democrats was not so keen for trusting his girls with them. When no one said anything to Melinda about going, she asked the current hired man if he wouldn't like to go with her. It hurt her pride a little but not enough to counterbalance being left behind.

Emily worked so hard all day to help every one off that she was too tired by late afternoon to get herself ready to ride to town with the folks, so she just went over to Henry's, neither one of whom was going as Lucy was expecting a child and Henry said it looked as though some one had to stay and do a little farm work.

All those roads which led to Rome could never have been so muddy as these to Sturgis Falls. Jeremiah and Sarah were over an hour getting the two miles in the buckboard, with the wheels sometimes sinking down to the hubs.

Rand and Alf Banninger took Suzanne and Celia in separate buggies and each young man's prime object in life apparently was to get to town first. Every little way one would get stuck and the other would pass him with a great upheaval of mud, saying, "I won't take anything off of a brother of mine," so that the girls clutched their full skirts in constant fear of getting them splashed.

The brass band in a wagon with four-horse team, the great crowd, the cheers, the train coming in to be decorated with a wreath of evergreens by Sabina's committee as though the iron horse were one of flesh and blood—oh, it was a stirring sight! From the wreath dangled a dozen cards bearing felicitations: from Dubuque to Sturgis Falls—from Sturgis Falls to Dubuque—with much reference to "the iron chain that now unites us."

The events were rather progressive in nature—a program at

the depot, the procession moving on to the Horticultural
Rooms for a second welcoming, the banquet at the American
House, including Jeremiah's toast, and one of the Dubuque
moguls, Mr. Platt Smith, predicting a telegraph some day,
and the dance at Overman Hall for which a band had come all
the hundred miles.

It was so late when the girls got settled in the loft room
after the great event that night was beginning to clear in the
east. Celia said sleepily she wasn't going to bother with
cream, that those Banninger boys were perfect cards, and she
never had such a good time in her life. Suzanne agreed. It
was the easier way, even though the memory of the evening
must include Wayne Lockwood's yellow head bent over the
dark one of Carlie Scott in the dance. She would just have to
get used to that sight.

In the days that followed, sometimes Jeremiah read aloud
and talked of other things than secession—the new steam
passenger-car in the east with the two stovepipes sticking
through the top and carrying fuel enough for a fifty-mile run,
the "parlor skates" that girls in Boston were starting to use,
having little brass wheels covered with leather on runners
(and saying that Ma and the girls ought to have them to get
around to their work faster), a man on Pike's Peak really
getting twenty-five dollars of gold from a pan of iron pyrites
(whatever that was, and wouldn't Ma feel cheap if Ed Armitage
got rich?), a new machine on sale that would reap and mow,
cutting a swath six feet wide (that was too easy, we'd all get
lazy), a man opening an ambrotype gallery in Prairie Rapids
for taking "the immortal type on iron, glass, or leather" (and
which of those foundations did the girls think would hold up
best under the strain of their countenances?).

But more often he read and talked of the one subject that
lay nearest to the heart and mind of all. Would the secession
really lead to war? If it led to war, how many would have to
go . . . and *who?*

Sometimes the talk grew so exciting as to be sickening, as
the day Jeremiah at the table was saying: "It might mean all
of fighting age . . . sending every man that could hold a gun
. . . Phineas, me, and Henry . . . Ambrose Willshire, Tom
Bostwick, those two rampageous Democrat Banninger boys
. . . Wayne Lockwood . . ."

"Oh!" Suzanne burst out, "why *should* we? Why *should*
we fight for a lot of niggers? What's it to *us?* They're maybe
even happier the way it is. Let them *stay* slaves. Look at

black Maria. She's free but she don't even care. Look at that black Mose saying he wouldn't even know where to go or what to do if he didn't live with the Scotts. Who *cares* anything about them anyway? What do we stick our noses in their business for? They've just as much a right to their way as we have to ours. It's their own states. What's secession so bad for anyway? Let them have part of the country for their own if they want to. Then we'd *both* be happy . . ."

"*Suzanne!*" Jeremiah's voice had the sound of the voice of God speaking from the burning bush. "That will do for you." This was no joking "I'll thump you." He had not spoken to her so fiercely since she was small and tied the calf's tail to the fence where it froze in the night.

A horse's hoofs came splashing into the yard, stopping at the side stoop, so that the embarrassing thing of Pa's intensity was averted.

Even as knives and forks were suspended and the customary "Who's that?" was being asked, Wayne Lockwood stood there. With his lithe body in the April sunshine of the doorway, his head thrown back, arm outstretched across the opening, he might have been cast in bronze as the avenging angel with outstretched sword.

"The Secesh have fired on the flag," he said, with deadly calm, "and taken Fort Sumter."

Jeremiah jumped up, his knife and fork clattering noisily to the floor, the plate catching on his pants' band and overturning: "Why, the goddam . . ."

"*Pa . . . that word!*" Sarah said.

He turned on her fiercely, as he had on Suzanne. "As though *words* made any difference now . . ."

CHAPTER 28

NO, words made very little difference now.

Jeremiah came home with Wednesday's newspaper. At the top of the right-hand column in quite ordinary print it said: *Exciting News the War Begun Fort Sumter Attacked and Burned* The detailed article had it that efforts to concentrate a formidable military force around Washington were being made, all roads to Washington were closely watched, that Senator Douglas had called on Lincoln to bury the bitter political hatchet of the past which pleased the president, that the Confederate Congress would at once declare war on the United States. And then, because life goes on its small and unimportant way in the face of great events, immediately underneath all this, in the same size type, the public was informed that Mrs. Capler was opening a magnificent stock of the latest eastern bonnets with trimming and that some God-forsaken wretch stole a cow from Mr. Flower on the east side of the river.

President Lincoln called for seventy-five thousand men. Governor Kirkwood called for Iowa's quota, a single regiment, wondering (so it was afterward learned) where he could find them, surprised beyond words when so many responded that it was going to be impossible to use them all. Or so it seemed then in 1861.

The Pioneer Grays said they were ready. Phineas was a Pioneer Gray. Though the plow stood in the furrow and the fiddle hung on the side of the cupboard, Phineas was ready. So were noisy Alf and Rand Banninger, tearing madly back and forth from drill, trying to beat each other home or to town.

Over at the fair-ground the Pioneer Grays drilled every few days. In the abandoned court-house square, politely called "The Park" now, little boys marched interminably with sticks over their shoulders and tin cans for drums. Tom Bostwick and Cady Bedson advertised they would pay for wheat with gold, hoping by this inducement to get a great deal purchased ahead as farmers were getting sick of losses through bobtail currency, worthless Illinois and Wisconsin shinplasters.

In all this excitement some one found out that the Scotts' son was no longer at home, gone, it was rumored, after a hot-headed quarrel, back to the south where his sympathies were. It was hard to tell anything about the senior Scott's sympathies. He was not for seceding but neither out-and-out loyal to the union. Jeremiah said he was like that muskellunge they caught in the river that time, away from his native haunts and not rightly belonging anywhere.

Meetings! Meetings, every day now, with Pa called back to Des Moines by Governor Kirkwood to attend a special legislative assembly.

And in May, the printed order: "Attention, Grays—all those who have enrolled themselves with the Pioneer Grays are hereby notified that they must report themselves to the commanding officer, as the company should drill daily until the time of departure. The citizens of the town are furnishing a uniform for each member. The company will positively leave on the steam-cars at nine o'clock Tuesday morning, June 4."

Phineas was going to war at nine o'clock on Tuesday morning, June fourth. It had the sound of a time set for funeral services.

And now Suzanne thought of Phineas as her favorite member of the family. No matter which one was leaving the old river road home, that one seemed at the time the best liked. Everything that Phineas did was noticed, everything he said was cradled lovingly in her mind. To see him hustling around in the old familiar way, whistling while he helped Henry with those last chores before joining the company, brought tears to her eyes and an indissoluble lump to her throat. Pa's first leaving for legislature, Sabina's and Jeanie's marriages, even Phoebe Lou's crossing the Great American Desert, sank into insignificance beside this.

Emily made Phineas a red flannel belt to wear over his stomach so he wouldn't get dysentery, and even though he laughed at it, he tried it on under his new uniform. Suzanne made him a fat red heart-shaped pincushion, sewing a little ruffle of linen lace around it, knowing the foolishness of it, but feeling all the time that it was her own heart through which she was pushing the needle.

Jeremiah was gone only two weeks, saying when he got home that never had an assembly been in such accord, pledging the credit and resources of the state, authorizing the purchase of arms and help for volunteers' families, just packing the two weeks with unanimously voted decisions.

One heard bugle sounds all times of day or night. Stores did practically no business except that which had a direct bearing on the coming departure. Every one hung on the news of the daily paper coming in on the train, wishing that the words of Mr. Platt Smith predicting the clicking of a telegraph instrument in the little frame depot would come true.

"We certainly live in a modern age," Jeremiah said, coming home, tired, excited, talkative. "And we're never satisfied. But dissatisfaction makes progress. You can remember the time, can't you, just back a bit when we had to wait for the stage to bring in the papers? That's what enterprise will do."

Sarah sniffed. "We could use a little enterprise around the place here that wasn't all got up by women folks."

But when Sabina and pretty Mrs. Joseph Chase drove in for contributions the next day, she rolled up her gray print sleeves and "whacked out" six dried-apple pies for a hospital supply supper and then sat down to help the girls make undergarments for some of the Pioneer Grays' families.

Henry worked silently about the place in his slow methodical fashion, getting more done than ever Phineas had with his hustling but less systematic ways. Once when Suzanne said, "Henry, *you* couldn't go—we couldn't ever get along without *you*," he looked at her queerly and said: "Some people always have to stay behind and saw wood, I guess."

Celia was in more of a flutter about her new beau, Alf Banninger, leaving, than about Phineas, blaming herself sometimes for not having given him much thought before that dance at the hall. She confided to Suzanne that he was just what she had been looking for ever since she was sixteen, good-looking, lively as a cricket, and with plenty of prospects, one of only two sons whose father already owned a thousand acres of land. It had taken some thought, she said, to decide on Alf instead of Rand as they were so much alike; but all in all, there was something about Alf that took her fancy a little more than Rand, although if she had never met Alf she would have been satisfied with his brother. If she had only started on him sooner! Marrying Alf Banninger, she could show Melinda a thing or two. And now he was leaving with the Pioneer Grays, all full of war talk and plans to give the rebels the biggest scare of their lives, and with no thoughts of marrying at all. She had certainly bungled matters.

Suzanne, listening to Celia's confidences, wondered that she could be her sister. What a queer way to think about love. But Celia had always been like that, cool and self-possessed, making her plans and carrying them out, too. If Celia had her heart set on Alf Banninger, no doubt she would get him. Looking at her, so confident and calculating, Suzanne almost admired her gumption even while she knew that she herself could never so much as raise her finger to do anything toward getting a man. "As long as he *doesn't* . . . I mean if a man *didn't* care for me with every bit of his mind and heart and body and do all the courting, I wouldn't *want* him," she told herself.

The war was a monster that lay in wait over there to the south beyond the horizon. Here they were safe, for it could never come to the Valley. Lying in bed these nights next to Celia and her eternal slippery coating of cream, Suzanne would try to think what it meant. Valley Forge . . . Bunker Hill . . . Yorktown . . . they were paragraphs in the history and dates to recite to Miss Libbie Field. But war was something more than paragraphs and dates. It was Phineas and Alf and Rand Banninger and all the Pioneer Grays. There was even talk that maybe Lincoln might call for more than these first boys. If he did . . . She would lie quietly, staring into the blackness of the logs. "Don't let Wayne Lockwood go," she would petition some unseen force which was composed strangely of both Lincoln and God. "Even if he belongs to Carlie Scott, keep him safe here."

On Saturday they all went over to town to see the soldiers drill, excepting Lucy who was too close to her time to dare venture forth, and Emily, who knew some one must be with her. Sarah offered to stay but Emily said, "No, you go ahead, Ma. It's your own son going."

Yes, it was her own son going. She and Jeremiah went in the buckboard, silent as two wooden posts, thinking of Phineas and his fun-loving disposition and hustling ways. Henry drove the spring wagon with Celia, Suzanne, and Melinda dressed in their best—Suzanne in her blue poplin with a white mull fichu and new ribbons on her butter-bowl hat; Celia in a new dress with a pink vine rambling over its white background and a white hat with pink buds as though the flowers from her dress had rambled up on to it; Melinda who never cared what she wore, in brown with the family red cherries rattling glassily together on her dark straw bonnet.

They crossed the bridge, Lassie's and Laddie's heavy hoofs clumping noisily over it, drove past the stores through Main Street with the stumps still a part of the picture, and out to the drill-grounds where last fall the cows and the horses had paraded at the Fair. Now it was men parading. It was Phineas and the Banninger boys, John Philpot, George Tuthill, and Charlie Boehmler, and all the Pioneer Grays in their new uniforms.

It was like a great gala day—a Fourth of July and County Fair rolled into one—and yet unlike them. Sadness and excitement! Grief and pride! Women biting lips to keep them from quivering. Men swearing lustily to hide unwanted emotion. Young girls in tears. The band playing. Flags on horses' heads and on carriage tops and in the sideboards of lumber wagons.

When the drill was over and ranks were broken, all the brave new uniforms began mingling with the crowd. Here and there a uniformed young man and a white-skirted girl strolled into the timber paths near-by.

Celia, in her pink and white dress, and Alf Banninger were two of the strollers. It went through Suzanne's mind that Celia must have manœuvered it well. Suzanne, in her blue dress and butter-bowl hat, and Melinda, in her dark brown and rattling cherries, were standing there together when Rand Banninger, Phineas, and Celia's clerk friend all came up to them. Rand, with warm eyes for Suzanne, pulled her away from the others so that she must walk with him or create a scene, which she was of no mind to do.

"Suzanne," he said hurriedly when they were a few yards away, "marry me, will you? Marry me before I go." He was bending to her, his dark face close.

Suzanne went a little white with the suddenness of it and his nearness, not really knowing that Rand liked her that well, wrought up, too, with the band's playing and the flags and the excitement. Strangely enough her first lucid thought was that marrying Rand would ease the hurt about Carlie Scott. Just for a moment—for one tempting moment—Rand Banninger and his father with a thousand acres of land held out ointment for stricken pride and solution for groping questioning. And then she was herself, "Oh, no, Rand. I couldn't."

"Why not?"

"I just don't . . . don't think enough of . . ."

"Well, I like *you* enough . . . come on. We'll be all through with the Secesh in a few weeks. Come on, *please*." He was coaxing as light-heartedly as though asking her to take a boat-ride. "We'll build a house on the north half-section. I'm dead anxious to beat Alf getting settled . . ."

"*No!*" She was crimson-faced now, recoiling from his close contact. "Don't speak of it again."

Alf and Celia coming back from their stroll found them standing so. Alf was excited, jubilant, could scarcely wait to get close before calling out: "Celia and I are going to get married . . . right away this afternoon. We don't have to report at the barracks until to-morrow night, Rand. We're going to hunt up a preacher."

Celia was cool, unperturbed, smiling at Alf's excitement. Suzanne looked at her in amazement so that Celia gazed back with knowing half-closed eyes.

"Oh, Celia . . . so soon. You don't think . . ."

"Of course it's all right." Celia tossed her head, frowned warningly.

Rand turned to Suzanne, saying low: "Is that the last word you've got to say?"

"Yes, it is, Rand."

His face flushed and his dark brows drew together. "By gad," he muttered, "no brother of mine can get ahead of me like that—" and started across the parade-ground.

It was all very confusing, with Celia insisting they must hunt up Henry and start right home, Alf saying he would find his folks and then set out on horseback to get a preacher to come.

Suzanne started to look for the folks and break the world-shaking news to them, but just as she turned, they came up with Henry. Celia at once told them the plans.

"Where's Melinda?" Sarah asked. "We've got to get right home if this is really so and you ain't jokin' us."

And then Melinda came up, her wide brown skirts scraping the prairie grass, her bonnet on one ear and the red cherries clicking together because of the haste she was in. Rand Banninger was with her. She looked a little frightened and wholly excited, giggling nervously.

"Rand and I are going to get married to-night, Ma," she said. "Along with Celia and Alf. I hope you don't care."

Sarah's thin little mouth set in a straight line. "I don't know's I could do anything about it, if I did."

"Well . . . well . . ." Jeremiah said. "I ain't been so surprised since I got my first nomination." It was all right with Jeremiah. Old man Banninger owned most a township, seemed like. Time was, he couldn't have stomached these two brash young Democrats. But things were different now. Looked like the war was making him crawl into bed with the northern Democrats.

Suzanne felt a little ill. Her head whirled, and she had a sensation of being blown about in some strange world whose storms she had never before encountered. She wanted to cry out and tell Melinda this was not what love was like. Love was wanting some one person more than any one else in the whole world. It wasn't—oh, it wasn't taking it as lightly as *this*.

With some wild idea of calling Melinda aside, she caught Rand Banninger's eyes upon her, dark and flashing. They held an expression of threat and triumph and something else that was almost little-boy pleading. There stood Melinda— good, funny Melinda—so tomboyish and noisy, so anxious always to be going somewhere. Yes, Melinda was wanting to do something different, to be "going somewhere." What could you do about it?

They were all on the way out home now, Henry pushing heavy old Lassie and Laddie at the top of their clumsy-footed speed. There were chores to do and two weddings to be performed. Alf had found his folks. Rand was ahead, long out of sight, riding his horse at breakneck speed to Prairie Rapids for licenses and a preacher.

Celia was as cool as a cucumber, as though these events were nothing to get excited over. Melinda was all animation, talking a blue streak all the way home, laughing incessantly and trying to get a dab of mud out of her eye.

"What was Rand saying to you, Suzanne? I saw him cornering you. Was he talking to you about me?"

Something caught in Suzanne's throat—the reaction to the memory of three girls playing together with acorn dishes down by the slough, Celia, Suzanne, and happy-go-lucky Melinda—the memory, too, of a dark day when a boat whirled and turned and tipped.

"Yes, he was," Suzanne said. "He was asking me if I thought you would."

These were the strangest of all the weddings that had taken place in the log-and-lumber house. Even Phoebe Lou's had been leisurely in comparison to this double ceremony which was to be performed as soon as Rand came back with the licenses and preacher, and Alf with his folks.

For the first time in her life Suzanne saw her mother falter in her managerial capacity, saw her stand for a few minutes in the middle of the lean-to, the back of her hand across her twitching mouth, then go uncertainly to the door and call: "Emily . . . can you come? I need you, Emily." No, Ma couldn't get along without Emily.

But by the time Emily had arrived from Henry's, panting and a little disheveled, to report that Lucy was all right so far, Sarah had hold of herself, was telling the news of the marriages about to take place as though they were all in the day's business.

"The Banningers will be here most any time . . . and the preacher. We've got to whack up a decent supper. Melinda, cut the heads off some of those young fries. And keep your own head level while you're cutting theirs. Emily, make up a good fire and pare potatoes. Celia, you put the good cloth on and set the table . . ."

"Oh, Ma, I've got to get all fixed . . ."

"That'll do for you. Scoot, now." Bride or no bride, the table had to be set.

And when Suzanne said, "You left me out, Ma," Sarah said, "You ride to Wayne Lockwood's and tell him to come. He's been to every girl's wed—"

"No, Ma . . . I won't," Suzanne said quietly. "I'll do anything else, but I *won't* do that."

So Phineas, riding in then, was sent for Wayne and in the excitement the unusual stubbornness went unnoticed.

The Banningers came in their heavy covered carriage—little Mrs. Banninger crying nervously whenever any one spoke to her, Mr. Banninger, bluff and hearty, saying that if the boys were bound to do this unexpected thing, he couldn't have found better girls for them if they'd sent him out to hunt up a couple. Tom and Sabina drove in, and Henry and little Nora arrived without Lucy who wouldn't come out of her cabin. But there was no time to get word to Jeanie, six miles away, and it was not until Monday on Soldiers' Day that she learned her sisters had been married. Wayne came in his fine gray suit, and Phineas, Rand, and Alf were in their new blue uniforms.

The Reverend Eberhardt who was sending two boys with the troops on Tuesday came out from Prairie Rapids with

Rand. So after the potatoes were mashed and while the fries were still popping and sputtering in the iron spiders, Celia and Alf stood up at one side of the fireplace with the old clock and the wild-turkey feathers above it, and Melinda and Rand stood on the other side, and were married, the young men in their blue uniforms and the girls in the dresses they had worn all afternoon, taking off their kitchen aprons for the ceremony but putting them right on afterward to help Ma.

Suzanne, looking on, felt strangely callous. She did not know why. All those other weddings at which she had been so moved seemed now to have been observed by some other girl than herself, an emotional creature to whom a wedding was the culmination of a romance. Celia and Melinda, the two closest to her in age, with whom she had always played, were marrying these two strange noisy men, scarcely knowing them, living with them to-night, seeing them go off to war on Monday. Surprise—sorrow—repugnance—knowledge of Rand's wanting to marry her instead of Melinda, tore so at her emotions that the sum total of their torture was this cold callousness. Even the sight of Wayne Lockwood across the room looking particularly handsome in his gray suit with fine white ruffled shirt moved her not at all.

"Alf and Celia, I pronounce you man and wife."

"And now, Rand and Melinda, I pronounce *you* man and wife."

And Ma was saying something about hoping the chickens hadn't crusted down in the butter. Then they all sat down to the table, but though there was much attempt at gay talk and noisy laughter, neither the talk nor the laughter could keep them from seeing the shadows of three blue uniforms cast by the light of the candles flickering in grotesque uncertain shapes high on the whitewashed walls.

After supper, Phineas rode away to see some one, Henry and Nora hurried home to Lucy, Wayne Lockwood left, and the elder Banningers. Then Sabina gave the key to her house to the newly married couples, telling them that she and Tom would just stay here to-night in the company room and drive over in the morning. And Alf and Rand Banninger, laughing long and boisterously at the joke that neither one had outwitted the other in marrying first, went away with Celia and Melinda.

Pa wound the big iron weights of the clock, saying "Day's over . . ." And even though his voice caught on the words like a coat sleeve on a bayonet, he finished bravely: "Fresh start to-morrow."

So only Emily and Suzanne were left to mount the loft ladder, each having a wide bed of her own.

"You're going to be a teacher like Miss Anna Field," Suzanne said to herself as though she were speaking to another person.

With her face turned into the crook of an arm deep in her pillow, she drew away from the thoughts of marriage like a little white nun slipping into her cloister. Henry and Lucy! Sabina and Tom! Jeanie and Ambrose! Phoebe Lou and Ed! Melinda and Rand! Celia and Alf! Wayne Lockwood and Carlie Scott . . .

"Oh . . . *yes* . . . a teacher all your life."

CHAPTER 29

SUNDAY, that second of June, was the queerest day Suzanne thought she had ever experienced—a still one, as though the wind in the maples and cottonwoods was hushed for the strangeness of it, because Celia and Melinda had been married so suddenly and gone away with Alf and Rand Banninger, because Phineas was helping Henry around the stables for the last time before going off to war, because there had been nine children around the table in the yesterdays and now there would be only two on all the to-morrows. A queer day and an emotional one, with Ma, her mouth twitching, asking Phineas what he wanted most for his last dinner, and Phineas saying, like a little boy: "Hot saleratus biscuits, Ma, with chicken gravy."

In the afternoon all but Phineas got in the spring wagon and went to Overman Hall to hear the farewell sermon, a solemn meeting which wrapped every one in a mantle of gloom. Phineas rode Queen over, but now that he was staying at the barracks Suzanne rode her home. At the lane corner in the dusk she almost ran into Wayne driving across the river road toward the Scotts' field in a shiny new high-top buggy.

"Well . . . hello, Suzanne." He waved a tassled whip, calling out jokingly, "A dark man with sinister design is crossing your path."

Evidently Wayne was not unduly disturbed that the boys were leaving without him, she thought wryly.

Monday was given over entirely to the soldiers. After the morning's work, pushed through at top speed by the three women folks, they all went to town again except Henry who stayed with Lucy. The town was a moving mass of humanity. Citizens milled up and down the sidewalks in front of the little stories with children darting in and out of the crowd, not more excited than their elders. Horses with flags in their harness stomped bluebottle flies at the long lines of hitching-posts. The band played. The atmosphere was tense, every one's nerves ready to snap.

The whole countryside was there—the Scotts in their open carriage, Wayne Lockwood on horseback, Ambrose and Jeanie with the babies in a lumber wagon, Sabina in and out of the crowd comforting some one here, telling some one there how soon the whole thing would be over, the two Akin families in good covered carriages now, Melinda and Celia with Mr. and Mrs. Banninger, Celia in the back with her new mother-in-law, Melinda in the front seat with Mr. Banninger, so that Emily and Suzanne laughed together, wondering whether he found her sitting in it when he went out to hitch up.

The two brides were enjoying the stir they created with people coming up to shake hands and tell them how surprised they were. Celia looked cool and composed as though being a surprise bride was nothing new; Melinda was excited and red-faced, her cherry bonnet on crooked and her neck ribbon awry.

At noon the recruits from Waverly, a settlement farther up the river, arrived. In mid-afternoon, the Union Guards from Butler County came. Each contingent brought several hundred cheering settlers, so that Sarah said if mere noise could win the war, the Valley already had the Secesh licked.

As though all this were not enough excitement for one day a letter from Ed Armitage arrived by stage saying he and Phoebe Lou had a ten-pound son and that Phoebe Lou said to tell the folks she bet she'd played the biggest joke of her life on them, never once letting on what was up.

At the evening meeting in Overman Hall, two ministers, two attorneys, and the Honorable Jeremiah Martin spoke. When her father was talking, Suzanne stole a glance at her mother's thin face with its gray-red hair sagging a little under the black bonnet, caught in the swiftness of it a distinct expression of pride, so that she whispered: "Pa's real good."

"Beard needs trimmin'," Sarah hissed back.

There was no joking from Jeremiah Martin now. With simple directness, if in homely speech, he was promising the wives and children left behind that the community would not forget them, giving his word of honor to the departing Pioneer Grays that their families would be looked after.

It brought quick moisture to Suzanne's eyes to hear her

father give his pledge to look after these dependents. If Pa gave his word, he would carry it out to the best of his ability.

On Tuesday, the fourth, with the Grays leaving, Henry's wife, Lucy, being nothing if not patriotic, went to bed and had a boy. This procedure had its drawbacks because it was going to keep Sarah home to care for her. But Emily would not hear to that.

"You've got to see Phineas leave," she told her mother. "You take Ma with you, Pa, and I'll help the doctor with Lucy."

Henry, too, was expecting to stay from some vague sense of paternal duty, but Lucy herself settled that. "For goodness sakes, go on," she said with a sudden show of spunk. "It's all over, and it ain't *you* been having it, anyway."

And now this was it. This was going off to war. Five thousand people packed around the little depot. The band playing. The flags waving. Horses skittish and whinnying with fright. The train getting up steam like a black monster about to carry the boys into the Unknown, with two passenger cars and a string of flats trailing behind the snorting thing.

The Pioneer Grays, the recruits from Waverly, the Union Guards—seventy-eight men, with thirty more to get on at Prairie Rapids, all in blue, all saying farewells to mothers, sisters, neighbors, sweethearts.

Phineas, who had kissed half a dozen girls, was saying good-by now to his father, shaking his hand, with Pa not letting go for several minutes, was giving his mother a kiss who had not been kissed by him since he was a little boy, her face working grotesquely. Another kiss for Suzanne, for Jeanie and Sabina, Celia and Melinda, and saying, "Tell Emily good-by again," then shouldering his way down through the crowds.

Melinda and Celia clinging to Rand and Alf, crying for the men they had known as husbands for so few hours. The engine giving an ear-splitting blast. Tears. Moans. Handclasps. Last kisses. Women clinging to men. One woman fainting. Men tearing hands from their necks. Phineas turning to wave from the steps of one of the cars.

"Oh, Phineas!"

Alf and Rand waving, trying to laugh.

"Come back safe!" Women calling out, sobbing.

A few members of the band playing jerkily, tunelessly, as though the instruments, too, were sobbing. "Come back safe." The train pulling out. Hands waving. Caps in the air. Tears. The train a tiny speck across the east farm lands.

*　　*　　*

It was a strange summer with the girls all gone but Emily and Suzanne. Phineas was in camp at Koekuk—the Pioneer Grays now called Company K of the Third Regiment. Jeremiah at sixty was putting his big shoulder to the wheel of the farm work again, but so busy with meetings, war committees, and journeyings here and there that Henry, as hard-working as he was, must have another hired hand. Willie was his name, but Emily and Suzanne, surreptitiously changing the "W" to an "S," had to watch themselves all summer for fear they would do so to his face.

All talk was war talk—how reinforcements were arriving every day at Cairo and Memphis, the federal and rebel strongholds, how the northern troops were planning to march right through to Richmond, how the president was asking in special session for two hundred million dollars (no one could begin to comprehend the vast sum) and a half million additional troops.

Sometimes Jeremiah heard these things from Mr. Scott before he could get to town for his own paper. It galled him secretly that the trainmen threw Mr. Scott's Democratic Dubuque paper off at the lane road where it was retrieved from the weeds by little black Plunk, the men carrying it past the lane a long way sometimes to tease the boy and to see him scurry after the train so fast.

This accommodating of Mr. Scott irked Sarah openly. "Just who does he think he is?" she asked often and sneeringly. If there was to be any "taking-down" of Pa, she preferred to do it herself; most certainly it was not to be done by the uppish Scotts.

Every one went to Prairie Rapids to the celebration on the Fourth. So infrequently had the family seen each other in the past month that it was quite a treat for Suzanne, Emily, Jeanie, Melinda, and Celia to be together again.

Melinda and Celia could hardly wait to see Ma and tell her something confidentially. Whatever it was, Celia evidently was provoked about it but Melinda could hardly whisper it to Ma for losing her breath with laughter.

The day was one long séance of national salutes, martial music, military display, the reading of the Declaration of Independence, orations, a public dinner, toasts, fireworks, ending in the flourish of a firemen's ball to which Suzanne went with Sam Phillips. Wayne Lockwood was there with Carlie Scott, scarcely able to take his eyes from the pretty flowerlike features of her childish face. Once he danced with

Suzanne, whispering with tender inflection, "She's like a doll, isn't she . . . a little china doll?" And once Cady Bedson danced with her, saying heartily and loudly: "Well, Suzanne, *I* didn't know you'd all at once grown up into such a pretty young lady," so that it lay over her bruised heart like the healing leaves of the balsam tree.

So flushed with patriotism and assurance of success was every one in the Valley that the news of the rout at Bull Run was as unbelievable as devastating. It threw the community into deepest dejection and the rest of the summer was filled with gloom.

One variation only from the high tide of war talk came to the neighborhood—a traveling showman holding forth at the school-house.

He was a queer little pock-marked man but the feats he performed were so wonderful that adults were nearly as enthralled as the children. He borrowed Jeremiah's hat and pulled from it a lady's garters, and when the sight convulsed the audience, he added to the hilarity by gingerly removing some baby clothes also. He ate a newspaper outright. He pulled yards and yards of red, white, and blue ribbons from his ears and mouth. He threw his voice into the far corners of the room where it seemed to come from staid Henry Martin in childish voice saying, "Humpty Dumpty had a dweat fall," so that every one roared.

But the climax of the entertainment was all impromptu. Little black Plunk came to the open door and, with eyes rolling, wanted to know of the showman if his mammy was there.

No, his mammy was not there.

"What you want her for?" the showman asked.

It seemed that Plunk was late getting the newspaper up the lane and was afraid to go up the long road in the dark.

"Oh, you trot along," the showman advised, and winked at those nearest him. "You'll be all right."

He stood at the door watching Plunk until the blackness of his little body became one with the blackness of the night. Then there rose from the lane road horrible cat-fighting sounds, and when they died away, a weird low voice saying, "I want a nigger," and in a moment, "I've *got* a nigger."

It was told with a great deal of merriment all up and down the river road, how scared little Plunk was, and how he always scurried for the paper now while it was still light, the episode seeming the one cause for laughter in the seriousness of the summer.

Crops were excellent. The Martins thrashed three thousand bushels of wheat (the neighbors all turning in to help, even as the Martins went in turn to the neighbors, there to help in field and house) and put up countless tons of hay, while the corn stood tall and ripening in the summer sun.

Soon after thrashing, a series of great summer storms swept the Valley—lightning that tore the skies and struck tall trees in the timber like fire from a rebel battery, thunder that crashed and rolled over the prairies like the reverberations of artillery from Bull Run, wind that bent and twisted the tall corn as though so many armies of green uniformed soldiers were mowed down.

And then as Henry and his father were hauling the first two loads of wheat to town ready for the Dubuque train, grain took a great tumble in price. Currency was scarce. There was a heavy advance in freight rates. General Frémont had taken possession of the Illinois Central Railroad, removing five hundred freight-cars, which removed also the prospect of getting any grain to Chicago. They hauled the wheat back and stored it in the long granary, blue over the outlook.

Excepting for that one time on the Fourth the family did not get together all summer—a strange situation for the Martins with their clannish instinct as strong as the birds whose names they so appropriately bore. Phineas at camp, Jeanie up on the north prairie expecting her third child, Sabina so busy with her war work in town, Phoebe Lou out in Colorado writing that the whole of Denver City was in commotion because so many southern sympathizers were mixed with loyal settlers, Melinda and Celia living over across the river with their new in-laws, "finding out," Sarah said, "even if you have a thousand acres of land you can't live on but a few square feet at a time," Emily and Suzanne at home, working hard, once or twice going into the field to help for a few hours on a pinch, or running over to Henry's cabin to assist Lucy in the care of the new baby boy, Suzanne taking her teacher's examinations and passing with flying colors.

By September she was getting the home school ready for her first teaching. Seeing Wayne Lockwood ride down the field road toward the Scotts' she would put him out of her mind for days as completely as long ago she had shut the door to her childish magic world. Now she not only shut but locked it. Then he would ride up, as she was leaving perhaps, stop a few minutes to chat, maybe swing off the horse and stand near her, so big and stalwart and likeable, and the door of that magic world would fly open as easily as though some impish creature, inserting the key with invisible hands, had pushed it ajar in wicked glee.

When the second call came for troops, she was almost sure that Wayne would volunteer. No family, no responsibilities excepting those he made for himself, he was just the kind of young man to go.

But Wayne did not go. He thrashed his wheat, put up tons of hay in his new frame barn, so much larger than his cabin, brought in more sheep, built another new shelter for them, said casually to Suzanne one day as though his thoughts, long-harbored, were involuntarily forming speech: "When I build my new house, Suzanne, it shall be something like my grandfather's old home near the sea . . . wide clapboards painted white   and green blinds . . . and a built in seat on both sides of the stoop."

Hearing it, Suzanne locked the door of her fancy once more and threw the key away—threw it blindly and far this time as one would toss a little unwanted thing into the green sea of the pasture grass.

Now for school to begin into which to put all her energy, all the theories that Miss Anna Field had taught her, and all of her heart and mind! No more philandering.

Nora, five and a half, was starting, the Manson children were coming, the Horace Akin boys and the Wallace Akin children, the Emersons from the lane road, black Plunk and Mamie from the Scotts', and several others. They were full of war talk. All the songs were patriotic, all the lessons ended in chatter about the last news from the south. Suzanne, not wise enough to understand that events unfolding in that year would some day make hard history lessons for other children, tried to keep all such talk out of the school-room, but failed signally. For how could that be done when fathers and brothers and neighbors were moving off to Shiloh?

Even in the first week, school was dismissed because every one wanted to go to town to see the new recruits entrain. All that same sadness of a company leaving was to be gone over again.

It was late that afternoon when the Martin family, just home from the day's excitement, heard a lumber wagon rattling down the road and looked out to see Jeanie driving into the yard, her face pale, her ashy hair stringing untidily from under her bonnet, and her eyes looking wild. Three-year-old Gracie sat at her feet with the second little girl braced against her small body.

Seeing Jeanie come in so unexpectedly, every one went out at once, with Jeremiah saying, "Anything wrong, my girl?"

"Oh, Pa." Jeanie was alighting cumbersomely over the high wheel. She bit her lips, fighting hard to keep the tears back. "Ambrose has gone."

"Gone?"

"To war . . . without telling . . . from Prairie Rapids . . . I didn't even know . . ." She was fumbling for her handkerchief, bringing it out with a crumpled paper which fell by the well curb so that Sarah picked it up at once and with no hesitancy read it aloud:

"Jeanie: I am taking this occasion to notify you of my enlisting. By the time you get this from whatever neighbor I find to send it by, I will be gone to Camp Union at Dubuque. I take this means because I know how opposed to it you would be and how you would have deterred me from doing my patriotic duty which no true wife has any right to do. But feeling as I do toward my country, only a noble desire to help save it, I cannot listen to what would have been your cowardly pleas for me to stay. Adieu and may you have the heavenly blessing of our Father.

Ambrose"

"Well, of all the smug, pious, *godly* . . ."

"Oh, don't, Ma. He means all right." The tears welled now and Jeanie was against her father's old stable coat, sobbing: "Pa . . . you know I wouldn't have held him back if he'd just said . . ." with Jeremiah patting her arm awkwardly and saying, "There now . . . there now."

Suzanne was cuddling the smaller girl, Emily petting little Gracie. They all said she was to stay and live at home with them, but Jeanie straightened her shoulders at that, wiped her wet face, and laughed a little. No, she wouldn't do that. She had a home, such as it was, and she must be getting toward it, too, with the sun slanting already and two cows to milk. Just give the children a bite to eat and they'd start back.

Nothing they could say would make her change her mind, so they loaded a basket with smoked meat and bread, wild-grape jelly and half a sour-cream cake, and made her promise she would rig up some signal for her nearest neighbor if she got to feeling bad.

When she drove out of the yard, the lumber wagon rattling drearily over the hard-packed ruts, she turned and waved, tried to laugh a little, calling back, "Oh, don't look so glum . . . I'm all right."

And Suzanne went up to the loft and cried all the tears that Jeanie was too brave to shed.

CHAPTER 30

WORD came back that the new recruits with Ambrose among them were housed in a big wooden building at Dubuque which had been turned into barracks, that on their first night there southern sympathizers shot into the upper windows just as the boys were bunking on the floor, and that if the officers had not interfered there would have been a struggle at once entitled "The Battle of Dubuque."

The four remaining members of the Martin family sat around the tree-trunk steps talking about this and other news that had come. It was warm and muggy so that every one fanned and whacked at mosquitoes. Queer formations of black clouds slipped slowly across the sky at different heights blown by vagrant winds.

"Look," said Sarah suddenly. "What do you make of that?"

Two long rows of tiny black cloud figures moved slowly toward each other, met, intermingled and fell back, drifted together again, were blown apart, those at the south gradually getting dimmer, the north formation holding their shape longer until they, too, disintegrated.

"Did you see that? It's a sign. Battles . . . as sure as shootin'. And the North winnin'."

The next day word came back of a skirmish by the Third Iowa in Blue Mills, Missouri, in which two of the boys who had gone in June were killed and another wounded.

"What did I tell you?" Sarah reminded them, so that for the first time in her life Suzanne looked with respect on Ma's premonitions.

It brought the whole terrible thing home to every one, as though they had not fully realized before that this could happen to the Valley boys. War had come out of the shadows and struck. It was no longer a menacing generality off there to the south and east. It had assumed shape and form and struck down James Brownell, Peter Dorlan and Lorraine Washburn. Only by chance were those names not Phineas, Rand, and Alf. It cast more gloom over both towns and called for much local criticism of the administration in neglecting Missouri and taking Iowa men east to defend Washington. Peter Dorlan, the wounded boy, was brought home on a cot and his arrival was the signal for a holiday in Prairie Rapids, the whole community turning out to line the streets through which he was taken to his home.

A letter from Phoebe Lou said troops were being organized out there, too, that Ed had volunteered, been made a second lieutenant, and was just here, there, and everywhere. No one was surprised when Sarah read the news to them out loud, Emily breaking into the reading to say it was just what she would expect of him. But when Ma read: "Ed has bought a new dress-parade suit with the very last of our money and he looks so handsome in it with sword and hat and sash," she could scarcely get the words out for a contemptuous snort and remark about that whipper-snapper. Phoebe Lou said there was bustle and confusion on all sides, that a band was parading right now, and that you could hear the sound of fife and drum from morning until night. She had attended a regimental ball given for the officers and it seemed terrible to dance when you thought of what might be in store for all. She had been at the barracks when a recruit affected with snow-blindness came in from a mine up in the hills and she hoped the girls wouldn't care but she had torn up the old family parasol and made him an eyeshade.

The first of October Jeremiah took Sarah across the north prairie, leaving her there to care for Jeanie and the new baby, a third girl, of whose sex Ambrose at the Dubuque barracks would no doubt heartily disapprove when he heard.

In the middle of the month Suzanne went to Teachers' Institute in Prairie Rapids where one of the questions discussed was how to teach geography when the old lines of the country might be dissolving right before your eyes, and another was, why talk as though the only history to teach was away back in the Revolution when you could look at it that what was happening right now was history. One teacher was brave enough to say she wasn't worried about those two subjects half so much as how to keep the children warm on both sides at the same time this winter, and the drinking water from freezing.

When the last session was over and Jeremiah was unhitching the team to take Suzanne home, a noise attracted them both. Men and boys were moving rapidly down the street, some running, others loitering along as though only half decided to join the group. Whatever was happening, its culmination was at the Central House and Jeremiah, never one to stay on the side-lines, hitched the team again and told Suzanne to wait until he investigated.

"What's the trouble?" he asked a man who was walking by.

"Franson, the lawyer, has been talking again. Old Barney, the tobacco man, too. He just came in on his tobacco wagon, pockets bulging with southern papers. The two have been hob-nobbing together over the news. Folks have kind of had enough now and the crowd's getting out of hand."

Suzanne, of no mind to be left out, kept at her father's side as he walked toward the seat of trouble.

The manager of the hotel was evidently pleading with the crowd not to do anything rash. But the temper of the group was unmistakable.

"Boys," some one was yelling "we've enlisted to fight rebels and we might's well begin at home as anywhere."

The crowd gave noisy assent. Some one came from a store neary-by with a rope. Men and boys surged into the hotel.

"They're at the supper table."

"No, they've run upstairs."

"Hang the Secesh!"

"Hangin's too good."

Several men were affixing ropes to the top of the building. And now others appeared at the entrance with the lawyer and the little swarthy tobacco man, their coats torn and hair disheveled.

"Go back to the wagon, Suzanne," Jeremiah said sternly.

But Suzanne, even though sick at the sight, stayed rooted to the spot with fear and interest.

"Make 'em talk."

"Yah! You give us the first speech, Franson."

Two big dry-goods boxes were rolled to the door of the hotel and in no gentle way the men were yanked onto them.

"Give us a *Union* speech, now, Franson."

But the man was plucky, a semblance of dignity still about him. "I've only said . . . and I still say . . ."

"Yah . . . I guess you have," and "We've heard what you said," rose with cries and cat-calls on all sides.

"Is President Lincoln a fool?" called a loud voice.

"Well . . ."

"He ain't quick enough with that answer, boys."

There was a surging toward the unhappy man.

"No. He's no . . . no fool."

"Who ain't?"

"Lincoln."

"Say it again. Say 'President Lincoln' with a little reverence in your voice, damn you."

"President Lincoln," he said acridly enough but in the noise and cheers on all sides it passed for reverence.

"Let him go, boys. He'll keep his mouth shut or next time there'll be one less Secesh. Now, Barney . . ."

The crowd turned toward the little tobacco man who had been shaking visibly. In contrast to the lawyer he began a gibbering pleading: "Boys . . . don't do nothin'. Let me get to my wagon and get you some cigars to pass around . . . honest, boys, I'll pass the cigars . . . I'll . . ."

"It ain't tobacco . . . it's a speech we want, Barney."

"Yes . . . a good patriotic speech."

Shaking, the little man said: "Why, I love the flag, boys . . . all I ask of you if you kill me is to wrap the Stars and Stripes around me for a windin'-sheet . . . and . . ."

"That's better . . ."

Suzanne rode home by the side of her father, silently, almost ill from the nervous shock of the episode. How could human beings treat a refined-acting man like Mr. Franson so . . . and even old Barney? Both must have been honest in their belief. She looked up at Pa, thinking to say so, but his face, set straight ahead, looked as grim as those faces of the men in the crowd. She said nothing, for she did not want to hear what Pa would answer.

School took most of Suzanne's time now and practically all of her thought and energy. Through a dusty path to the log building she hurried all those first weeks, then along a leafy rain-soaked one, and later one so snow-filled that it was all but obliterated.

The day usually opened with an unmusical rendition of:

We have come to our school-room; we have come to our
  school-room;
We have come to our school-room in the State of I-O-WAY.

And in search of knowledge, and in search of knowledge,
And in search of knowledge we will pass the time away.

It passed on to McGuffey Readers and spelling, arithmetic, preparation for spelling school, the transmission of Suzanne's recently acquired knowledge of capitals with shaded tails, and ended in a perfect orgy of musical debauch:

Now three cheers all together, shout for common schools
* forever,*
Shout for blessings on the giver 'til we make the air resound;
And to those who labor for us and whose guardian care is
* o'er us*
We will swell the grateful chorus 'til the echoes back resound.

By working hard at her task of teaching these neighbor children Suzanne filled her time with something which resembled the work of a missionary whose zeal amounts to fanaticism. If one put the whole mind on one's work as did Miss Anna Field, she reasoned, anything could be taking place and one need not notice or heed—relatives and neighbors leaving for war, a young man riding up and down the lane road to Scotts', anything. In truth, Miss Anna Field became a symbol to her that fall, a sort of saint whom she set up in a niche in her mind, the calm orderly portion of her mind undisturbed by fancy or emotion.

Suddenly in December wheat went up in price and cars were available so that Jeremiah and Henry, glad now they had so much stored, hauled their grain to the Prairie Rapids depot ready for shipment. One afternoon they reported that four hundred team-and-wagon outfits loaded with wheat and pork, and packed in too tight for any horses to run away, were lined up in the streets. "Enough to feed the union armies," Jeremiah said, "but one thing's sure, the rebels can't eat their cotton. You can't tell, maybe it'll be food that will win it for us instead of generalship."

He wanted to know, too, if they had heard about the cannon firing, telling about the jubilation he had witnessed over at Prairie Rapids because Franson, the Secesh lawyer, had betaken himself to parts unknown. "Prairie Rapids has gone to lots of pains to get folks to come there to settle," he chuckled, "but first time a jubilee was ever held over one departin'."

The new year of 1862 opened with varying reports so that

one could scarcely tell just what was taking place. So far the south had most of the major decisions. But victory or defeat made very little difference in one respect, either was tinctured always with fear for the safety of near and dear ones. The report might be favorable, but what about individual soldiers? A battle might be won but what about Phineas? What about Alf and Rand Banninger? Or Ambrose Willshire? Or Ed Armitage, dashing around so daringly out there in Colorado in his dress uniform with clanking sword and flapping sash?

Ambrose wrote Jeanie that they were encamped on a beautiful hill on the banks of the Cumberland near Smithland, Kentucky, and had not yet seen active service, but that they had commenced work on entrenchments under General Wallace and staff. It began "My honored wife" and ended "Your obedient husband" so that Jeanie cried for sheer joy that out of the awfulness of war had come this pleasant letter from her man, and then drove all the way across the snow-laden prairie with the three babies, so the folks could read it, handing it about proudly that all might see how devoted to her Ambrose was.

Jeremiah went to Des Moines again but this time he was sergeant-at-arms.

Phoebe Lou wrote that little Theodore was thriving, as husky as could be, all unaware of their constant fears over hostile Indians and that his father's company had been ordered to New Mexico where they might meet up with the Texas Rangers.

And in the Red Cedar Valley, the weather was fine and favorable for sheep. Wayne Lockwood was more ambitious to get ahead than he had ever been, must make the most of the good prices, he told himself. He was to be one of the big land-owners here some day. He must have good stock and fine crops, carriages and a great house, white with green blinds! He must be—

At a sudden thought he stopped and grinned to himself, remembering Suzanne Martin once riding bareback madly to his cabin to tell him they were going to be landed gentry. Yes, he must be landed gentry. No one could think of such queer things to say or make you laugh more than Suzanne. For downright everyday company he could think of no one he would rather have around than Suzanne, happy and full of fun and intensely interested in everything about her. But not delicate and dependent! Not fragile as a little china doll, nor dainty as a wind-flower! No, one wouldn't call Suzanne a wind-flower. She was a . . . he couldn't think just what, but grinned again imagining how readily Suzanne could have answered him with some funny comparison.

Yes, this winter Wayne Lockwood felt almost money-mad, angered that the war was intruding itself just when his prospects were so good. A fragile dainty girl must have everything nice . . . all the fine things that money could buy. Letters from his mother asked constantly about plans, worried that he would be going, cautioned him against volunteering, saying that soon it would be over. Little she knew that he was of no mind to go now. His deepest hope at every dawn's rising was that the next battle would be the last, so he might settle down to work without prick of conscience or goading thought of obligation to his country. "If war ends in the summer there will be piles of money made on produce," he wrote home. But the war was not to end in the summer.

Never had he felt completely at ease with himself since that first voluntary contingent of soldiers, the Pioneer Grays, had pulled out from the new depot the June before. Since that time another company had gone from Prairie Rapids and acquaintances had joined others. These were the men anxious to jump in, he told himself, the restless ones who would rather be at the front in the excitement than the cooler, more level-headed ones, like Henry Martin and himself, who stayed to raise the wheat and the sheep.

"I'll wait a while and see," he salved his conscience. "I'll be neither the one nor the other, throwing myself into it hastily nor hanging back too long. It will soon be over. But if the call comes again and I see I'm needed I'll go, and if there is talk of draft I'll volunteer before it comes." He wrote his mother then to quiet her fears: "I shall probably not be needed, so cease your worry. In the meantime, because of the fine open winter my sheep have done well."

But seldom did he sing. For some reason, even though the flowerlike face of Carlie Scott was often in his thoughts, he was not letting out his melodious voice there in the Valley as of old. For how could one sing of war with thoughts of love stealing through the martial strains? And how could one sing of love with the guns of war drowning out the melody?

CHAPTER 31

WINTER set in more earnestly in February. Snow fell with almost constant regularity. News of the battle at Fort Donelson came. The Twelfth had acquitted itself well. To Jeanie up on the north prairie with her three babies, Ambrose was the whole Twelfth Regiment. There had been only two casualties from Comapny E reported and neither one was Ambrose.

Jeremiah wrote home from Des Moines that nothing like it had ever happened when the message came containing the victory at Fort Donelson. Members of the house embraced each other, laughing and crying. As sergeant-at-arms he guessed he might as well have been an Egyptian mummy, for he made no pretense to keep order. Since the celebration you couldn't tell a Democrat now from a Republican, a statement which the folks at home knew to be the test supreme of Pa's magnanimity. Watch this man Grant, Pa said, too—that unconditional surrender message just beat the Dutch.

Phoebe Lou wrote again. Life was so hard and worrisome. Sometimes she thought if she could just be back in the shelter of the old house she would feel better even though Ed was off with his company as he was now in New Mexico. There was lots of sickness here at the barracks. Often, she shut her eyes to the sight of the soldiers and her ears to their moans and imagined herself at home with them all, around the old fireplace. She could just *see* Pa winding the old clock by the wild-turkey feathers on the mantle and *smell* spare-ribs cooking and *hear* the girls joking each other.

"I guess she don't know we haven't anything much to joke about," Emily said.

It was true. There was not much to joke about. Sarah, Emily, and Suzanne living alone—Suzanne hurrying home from school through the snow to help Emily with the chores. No one had the heart for singing school so there was very little going on in a social way excepting those occasional festivities over at town whereby money was raised for the soldiers.

Wayne Lockwood had a new cutter and sometimes they saw him drive down the field road and come back with Carlie Scott tucked under his buffalo robes, her fur-trimmed pelisse on and a little muff held under her chin for all the world like the Grecian Exile in the *Parlor Annual*. And seeing her dressed so, Emily made Suzanne a new pelisse, too, and trimmed it with the minks Phineas once caught and skinned for Emily for a muff, saying Suzanne needed the fur much more than she did. But even though Suzanne had the new mink-trimmed wrap, almost as pretty and fashionable as Carlie Scott's, it never rode in the new cutter.

Once Wayne came to get Emily to line a fine deerskin he had cured two winters before but never used. When Emily asked him how soon he wanted it, he said he must have it by Friday night for sure.

Friday night, they knew, there was to be a festivity to raise money for the new library, an oyster supper, tableaux, dancing.

The same day on which Henry brought the letter from Phoebe Lou he had one for Suzanne—a strange circumstance which no one could explain. As plain as day it was directed to Suzanne, but inside the envelope the letter itself was to Carlie Scott, only asking Suzanne kindly to hand it to her. Every one questioned why this was sent so, but could make out no answer.

Wayne Lockwood riding in then to get his deerskin robe, Suzanne painstakingly snuffed out the candles in her eyes so that he could not possibly see any interest for him in them, and asked cheerfully, almost laughingly, so good was her acting, if he would take the letter to Carlie Scott.

Wayne laughed, too, saying, "How did you know *I* would be seeing her?"

The family seldom saw Sabina. She was busy from morning until night with her war work, and when not at the headquarters of the bandage workers, could be found going up one street and down another into the homes of the soldiers, a basket on her arm or some little youngster by the hand. "As like Pa as a twin calf," Sarah said. "The responsibility of the whole world on her shoulders."

Jeanie was getting through the winter somehow, and would

still not hear of coming home. "I made my bed . . ." she said the one time she drove down. "I'm not coming back to have you help. I'll pull through." So she cared for her babies, putting the tiny one high up on the feather-bed, tying the second one in the home-made high chair and trusting the three-and-a-half-year-old Gracie to be a little mother while she went out to shovel paths, split wood, and milk the cows. Jeanie, who had been a stalk of goldenrod in her yellow silk! But sometimes when George Wormsby or some other old beau of hers would ride by and stop to do the hardest of her chores, Jeanie would forget her harsh reddened skin, her frost-bitten fingers, and unbrushed corn-silk hair, and roll her eyes merrily and break into girlish laughter.

Emily and Suzanne had long known what it was that Celia and Melinda had whispered so excitedly to Ma at the Fourth of July celebration, and now the last day of February the brides came home to await their time. Rand's and Alf's mother had been just as good as gold, they said, but she was a china-dish kind of woman, worried, and scared to be left alone with them, fearful something wrong would happen, so the girls had Father Banninger bring them home through the snow to Ma who wasn't afraid of sickness. They got stuck once and Melinda scrambled out and helped shovel, but Celia stayed covered and warm under the robes. Sarah scolded a little behind their backs to Emily and Suzanne about the extra work and responsibility, but they saw right through her—she was as proud as a peacock that the girls preferred her to their mother-in-law.

School to Suzanne was like the weather, uninteresting, gray monotonous. The children clumped into the one-roomed building, great clods of snow falling from their thick shoes as from horses' hoofs, their faces red under woolen hoods, their hands too stiff to hold the pencils for a time. The iron of the stove in the center of the room glowed red with heat so that any one within a radius of six feet of it roasted, all others froze. Little Nora told her Aunt Suzanne that she wished she could feel alike all over and not have part of her too cold and the other part too hot. Sometimes Suzanne held the child on her lap near the heat while she heard her lessons.

March came in neither like a lamb nor a lion, rather like an ox, stolid, still, patient, with its monotonous snow-storms. The railroad blocked. "Four feet on the level" was what Henry reported to the folks. Down the river road toward

Prairie Rapids just where the river timber ended and the open prairie began, a pile of snow had drifted as high as a haystack.

On the third of March Dr. Pierce floundered out through the drifts on horseback and helped deliver a ten-pound boy to Melinda, and when Celia showed no signs whatever of following suit but sat, cool and complacent, sewing by a lean-to window, Sarah sputtered no end about the doctor having to wallow back through all this snow and maybe turn right around and come out again, as though Celia were being stubborn.

At that, Sarah's prophecy was quite correct, for on the next day Celia gave birth to a boy, laughing weakly but triumphantly when told that he weighed half a pound more than Melinda's.

In the middle of the month a young man from north of Prairie Rapids who had been wounded at Fort Donelson came home on furlough. He was wanted everywhere for dinner, for supper, to spend the evening, and stay all night. When he first came he said he had killed a confederate in battle there. As his course of entertainment at various farm homes carried him up the river road from Prairie Rapids toward Sturgis Falls, it was noticeable that the number of Johnnie rebels who had fallen before his trusty weapon increased, until by the time he arrived at the Martins' practically a whole company had fled at his attack.

There was a cessation then of snowing around the last of the month but the days remained cold, drear. Sometimes there was no one moving in the whole landscape, no animal stirring or human in sight, as though the prairie lay locked in an eternal ice age. School was depleted because of drifts, only the river road being broken and passable, and part of the lane. The Akin children came and little Nora and the two big Manson boys. The Scotts' Negro man Hi shoveled through the field-road drifts to bring his two children every morning. They were as clean as whistles, Mamie's pigtails tightly braided around little dark blue ribbons, Plunk's neat waists made from the fine material of Mr. Scott's shirts.

Because life was so filled with war, practically every day at school was a patriotic day. On Friday afternoons this was particularly true, the whole program being given to lusty shouts of "My Country *Tizzof* Thee" and "Say, Darkie, Have You Seen Old Massa?" and similar bursts of semi-musical loyalty.

On this last Friday in March with the weather moderating

for the first time, as though April would soon take command, one of these Friday speakings had just been brought to a noisily patriotic close by the hanging of Jeff Davis to a sour-apple tree, so that school was out again until Monday morning.

Suzanne herself was to have something that looked like a real break in the monotony for she was to ride over to town with Mel Manson and spend Saturday and Sunday with Sabina. Emily had suggested it, pretending to put the blame for Suzanne's lassitude on loss of sleep because of the new babies. So now Suzanne's bundle containing her night-dress and comb was lying on her desk until Mel would come by.

There was the customary bundling process by the children and the warning on teacher's part to hurry home. Black Hi came for Mamie and Plunk. Nora left in the care of the Akin boys. Suzanne put on her bonnet and wrap and was getting on her galoshes ready for the jingling of Mel Manson's bells, bending low to fasten them, when she heard the door. She looked up quickly to see Carlie Scott standing in the half-partitioned entry.

Carlie had on her fur-trimmed pelisse with its matching muff and a little velvet bonnet tied under her chin. It was true that she looked like a flower, a pale little snowdrop, perhaps, underneath its winter covering.

Suzanne stood up, startled that any one was there at all, deeply so that it was Carlie Scott who was now saying: "Oh, I thought you'd be gone."

There was something queer about it. Carlie Scott here alone for no purpose—the program over, school out, the day dark and gray, and thinking Suzanne would be gone.

Plainly, too, she was disturbed. Something was not turning out as she had planned, and Suzanne felt intuitively that the something was her presence. Well, she had a right to be in her own school-room.

The two young women stood facing each other in their fur-trimmed wraps so strangely alike, and because there was something of awkwardness about it for both, Suzanne said, rather inanely: "I'm waiting for Mel Manson to come by to take me to town."

"Then you'll be here until he comes?"

"Yes."

"In that case"—Carlie Scott put down her muff as though she, too, were staying until some one came by—"I guess I'll just have to throw myself on your mercy and ask you not to tell. Will you promise me that? Promise not to tell anything about seeing me here?''

Suzanne's heart stood still with fright and the pain of what Carlie was to say.

"If it's . . . necessary."

"It most certainly *is*." The girl's eyes flashed and Suzanne saw that she was not a little snowdrop just now, but a bit of a pepperplant. "Do you promise?"

"Yes, I promise."

"Your word of honor?"

Something of Jeremiah stiffened Suzanne. "When I promise anything," she said quietly, "it *is* my word of honor."

Without answering, Carlie Scott walked over to the wood-box, removed all the top chunks gingerly, and from under others extracted a satchel. It went through Suzanne's mind for a moment how queer it was that the fancy flowered bag had been under there all afternoon, like something alive, and no one had known it.

"Some one is coming for me," Carlie said. "By the time it's found out . . . I'll be gone."

The room spun a little crazily to Suzanne, so that there was a queer blurring of homely wooden benches, small windows on which the snow still clung in half-moons, the tall iron stove, and the white face of Carlie Scott in a brown velvet bonnet. Standing so, she knew that she must say something, give evidence of having heard aright, make pretense of being able to listen to this astonishing confession.

"Wayne Lockwood . . . is coming?"

Carlie gave a short laugh that held irritation in it as well as faint amusement."

"Oh, no . . . how stupid! The man I love . . . that they didn't want me to see any more . . . that they thought they were separating me from for always. Well, they'll find they couldn't do *that*. He's over in town . . . and coming for me . . . and . . ."

Like a tree branch pulled to the limit of its tautness and then snapping back came Suzanne's emotion of fear to such an intense relief that she wanted to cry out from the sudden sharp change. Until she remembered! What would this do to Wayne? Oh, poor Wayne!

For a time they stood in awkward silence and then there was the sound of floundering horse hoofs and squeaking runners, and Carlie Scott was at the door opening it only a crack at first, then flinging it wide.

In the doorway she turned back and laughed nervously, her pale cheeks flushed. "Now, you can have your big solemn farmer. Maybe you think I haven't guessed. I wasn't blind. Well, that's all I wanted of him . . . to throw them off the scent . . . keep them from knowing my *real* feelings and what was going to happen. Good-by."

For long moments Suzanne stood unmoving, eyes to the door beyond which Carlie Scott had disappeared, listening to the receding sounds of floundering hoofs and squeaking runners.

Still in a daze she finished fastening her galoshes and put on her mittens.

At the sound of sleigh-bells she went to the door, calling out, "I've changed my mind, Mell," shaking her head when he failed to understand. "Not *go* . . . ing."

She was of no mind to go to Sabina's now. Sabina was so everlastingly good—all her talk would be about her war work and her committees. No, she wanted to get home to Emily, to crawl into bed to-night by the side of the one sister who knew when to be silent.

Poor Wayne! How shocked he would be! He must have been caring deeply for Carlie. It would be his nature to care intensely when once he did. She felt compassionate toward him for the great hurt, looked up the lane road as though she might see the answer to her question there and send some of that sympathy to him on the sharp spring winds.

The cold was less brittle than in recent days, but with that peculiar instinct of the prairie child, she sensed more snow in the offing, looked askance at the low-flung clouds hanging over the horizon. They were rolling up into the semblance of a giant face, two for cheeks and a third for the nose, great inflated features that no doubt would blow their icy breath on the countryside again in the night-time.

Mind in a turmoil at the knowledge of this devastating thing that had happened to Wayne, clutching her bundle, she lowered her head and walked into the cold wind across the schoolyard. Scarcely had she come to the deep snows at the road's edge until she heard lunging horses and creaking runners and looked back to see Mr. Scott and black Hi turning from the field road toward town so sharply that the sleigh tipped, tottering perilously for a moment before righting itself and going up on the snowy highway.

She shivered with the cold and the nervousness of this thing that had just happened and the added knowledge of Mr. Scott and black Hi giving chase as their mad driving appeared to be. Holding her long skirts above the high ridges of snow where a few sleighs had lumbered back and forth, she started east toward home.

From the sight of the low rolling grayish-white clouds, high above the horizon now, her eyes suddenly caught a glimpse of that which caused her to stop short in her tracks. Other grayish-white clouds were rolling along on the ground, turning, twisting with a peculiar up-and-down bobbing motion so similar to the clouds above them that they seemed but a continuation of those in the sky.

They were Wayne's sheep, crowding together in a tight pack, following the bell-wether, drifting foolishly ahead of the storm as sheep will, heading straight for Deer Run. Sheep would follow a leader into any fool place. She looked around frantically for help, hallooed once or twice for Henry, but her voice returned to her eerily on the silence, so she knew there was no use wasting time in vain calling. Instead, she picked up her skirts and plunging across the width of the river road, turned back and north into the lane.

If the river road had been bad, cut as it was with the ruts of many sleighs and the deep declivities of horses' hoofs, the lane road was infinitely worse. Only a few families came down from that direction, so that the snow was less cut and walking that much harder. But to get to Wayne's cabin and tell him about his sheep was the least she could do for him. Otherwise they were heading straight for broken ice, which meant the utter destruction of all his work. He must not have this loss on top of his loss of Carlie.

To the north she could see his cabin standing at the edge of the grove with no smoke from the chimney, no movement about the place, no pawing horse or leaping dog. It looked silent and desolate. There was no use wasting time, then, in going on up the lane. Cutting across the field, herself, to head off the bell-wether was clearly the only thing to do.

As soon as she had passed the end of the Beards' rail fence, she turned toward the creek to make a diagonal crossing in order to reach its bank before the flock did.

Plunging ahead, sometimes she could gain speed on hard-packed drifts. Sometimes she sank through snow still soft and light from the last falling. Sometimes she broke through hard crusts so that their knifelike edges scraped her legs cruelly, once feeling a warm trickle of blood on her ankle. But always she kept her eyes on those dirty-white backs, like grayish clouds that bobbed and rolled along the ground as though the sky and the prairie were one.

Her long skirts hindered her and made her recall Pa's reading from the *Courier* one night before he left about a young lady from the East who had been arrested for promenading in male attire, but who claimed the right to wear pantaloons, defending herself manfully. She and Emily and Pa had stood up for the girl, but Ma had said it was too unladylike to be condoned.

Unladylike! When would girls ever get to be sensible instead of ladylike? If she had pantaloons on now she could scoot across this stretch of hard-packed crust. At the thought of herself in pantaloons running like a sandhill crane over the tops of the snowbanks she laughed aloud. But it was the last time she was to laugh that night.

It was growing darker, with an uncanny, too early blackness. The low scudding clouds were now coming in from the north-west more rapidly. They rolled low over the prairie, boiling, hissing their wrath at the land. The giant was no longer merely inflating huge cheeks and pursing angry lips in threatening mood. He was snarling his rage, blowing ice-cold winds, spitting sleet. He bent low over the form of Suzanne Martin, laughed at having her slight body in his grasp, tossed it down as though to have his will of her, covered the daylight with darkness so that no one might see his evil.

Suzanne cowered against the frightful venom. The grayish-white sheep were not far away—she could hear their bleating and the tinkling bell of the leader—but suddenly they were no longer visible. The darkness and the storm had leagued together to obliterate them. Only by sense of ear could she tell there was anything near but raging wind and sleet and snow. She could hear the animals crash through the underbrush and down the creek bed, the sound of their cries and the bell lost in the roaring gale. There was nothing she could do now but turn and go home.

Go home! "I'll go in just a minute," she kept thinking. But the sleet was such a stinging blinding thing that she had to cover her face from its lashing and crouch in a thicket of bare rattling bushes which gave not the slightest protection.

As she cowered, a frightened sheep blatted and bumped into her so that she caught at it thinking to hold it to her, but it cried the louder and slipped away.

And now she lived in a world of ice and snow in which no other thing existed. Never had she known such penetrating cold. Snow whirled into her nostrils, needles of sleet cut her face. She wanted to cry out with the hurt of it but her breath would not come. The fur of her collar was a sodden mass against her neck.

"But I'm not far from home," she told herself crazily. "I ought to be able to get there. I know every foot of this prairie. It belongs to me. Right here along this creek bed I've picked wild grapes and haws. I've waded here in Deer Run and ridden Queen across this very spot. The prairie can't go back on me like this. The creek can't treat me so. When you love Nature as I always have, she can't turn against you."

She stood up but there came another blinding blast of snow-filled wind so that she crouched and clung to the rattling bush not wanting to leave its familiar shelter. "I'm in real danger," she thought more calmly. "I've got to keep my head. Now think this all out. Try to plan the way Pa would. Think how to pull through. It's getting even worse and I've got to get home. The best way to go about . . ."

A great blast threw her into the branches of the bush, scratching her face, and with a dull dismay she knew her face was too numb with cold to feel it keenly. That was a far more dangerous condition than to feel the sharpened glass of sleet cutting into her soft flesh. Her hands, too, were numb—the one holding her bundle had no feeling at all.

She could still hear the far-off bleating of sheep when the wind blasts died down intermittently, but it was very faint as though they might have gone on in the darkness, or most of them drowned in the open places.

Quite suddenly her mind was clear and she knew what to attempt to do. Follow the creek bed. It might take hours in the darkness of the storm feeling her way along the ice . . . but she would make it unless . . . like the sheep in those open places . . .

There was another sound now, one of breaking snow crust and thrashing creature coming close. Horse odor came to her nostrils, so that she rose frantically to meet the animal's on-coming riderless flounderings, to try to grasp its mane in the sleet and the darkness. But it was not riderless. A man swung off to bend over her.

"*Suzanne* . . . good God! What are you *doing* here?"

Wayne Lockwood, trying to trace the path of his sheep through the storm, had run onto her.

"Oh, Wayne!"

He had her in his arms and up on the horse, had turned and was trying to retrace his path through the crashing sleet and howling of the wind to the lights in his cabin windows.

CHAPTER 32

WAYNE put the half-frozen girl down in a chair far from the fire until he could see whether her face showed white in the light of the candle's flame which he brought. Then he took off her galoshes and shoes, but her feet had suffered less than her hands because of her crouching over them during the time by the creek bed.

With no words he worked over her, brought a pan of snow for the colorless hand that had grasped the bundle, knelt by her, plunging it in and holding it there until the red blood flowed through her fingers. Tears which she tried to control, and could not, slipped from her at the pain and mingled with the moisture on her sleet-covered face so that he got up to bring a towel and wipe it, drying her hands, too.

"Now you can get close to the fire," he said, and picked her up in the chair to carry her to the burning logs.

He took off her bonnet and scarf and helped peel off the sodden wrap. But she was soaked through and shivering from the icy wetness. Here by the fire, water dripped clammily onto the floor from her long skirt.

"You'll have to get out of the rest of your things, too," he said matter-of-factly. "I'll try and get you something . . ." He broke off. "What's in your bundle?"

"It's only my . . . I was going to stay all night at Sabina's."

"I see. Put it on." He brought her the bundle, its outer covering soggy from the snow.

"Oh, I couldn't, Wayne . . . not here."

"Put it on," he said crossly. He was turning down his bed, folding back the flannel-lined deerskin and the pieced comforts from his New England home. "And get in here."

And when she only stood, clutching her bundle, shaking

still from the wet and cold, he said gruffly, "What are you waiting for?"

He turned on his heel and went over to the cookstove, fed its fire with split wood, and with his back to her, fussed over the iron utensils and his supper.

"Tell me when you're in and I'll get your wet things," he said shortly.

"I'm in," Suzanne said later in a thin little voice from over the comforts and the deerskin.

When he came to get her clothes, he asked: "Chilling?"

"A little." But Suzanne did not know in what proportion it was the cold and what the nervousness over this queer thing that was happening.

He hung her soggy garments in front of the fireplace. Then he brought her soup—a great bowl of it with the huge thick crackers like miniature paving blocks which the Sturgis Falls store sold.

"You'll strangle. Sit up higher," he said shortly, and pulled her up, thumping the pillows at her back.

Suzanne ate her soup—mutton broth with bits of potato and onion and dried beans in it—and it was very good. It warmed her chilled body and sent the blood racing through her veins.

When he came to take the bowl he stopped a moment by the bed and looked down at her. "Now tell me why you did that dangerous darn-fool thing?"

"I saw your sheep heading for the creek . . . and I couldn't bear to think of your losing them, too."

It was out before she realized she had said it. That little word "too," so innocent and so guilty, gone into the air with all the things that have been spoken which never should have been said.

But he did not question her, did not ask what it meant, merely stood looking down at her as though he did not see her. Then he turned abruptly and walked back to the fireplace, dropped down in his big calico-covered chair, and as long as she kept awake Suzanne could see him there looking into the logs with the firelight on his face. He knew. He had heard. Perhaps he had met Carlie and the man when he came from town, or Mr. Scott and black Hi stopping to ask if he had seen anything of running-away Carlie. However it had been, there was no mistaking that he knew. She could tell by his attitude and the strange baffled look on his face and by what her own heart said.

For a long while she watched him sitting so. There was no

sound in the room—only the storm out there like prairie-wolves tearing at the cabin. And then, because of the warmth of the fire and the soup and a comforting thing that was nameless but vaguely reassuring, she slept.

Sometime in the night she woke with a start, incredulous and half frightened to find herself here. He was still there in front of the fire but with his head forward in his hands so that she wished with every fiber of her being she might comfort him. Yes, she believed she would have been willing to bring Carlie Scott back to him if that were possible, so deeply did she want him to be happy. It was of Carlie he was thinking and it was for Carlie he was grieving. Of that Suzanne had no doubt.

For how could she know that queer things were running through Wayne's mind, crazy, confused thoughts he had never harbored before, perplexing questions with no answers. "Oh, Suzanne, what shall I do? I've been hurt and disillusioned. I feel sore and bruised. And above all my pride is hurt. I don't know where to turn but to you. More than anything in the world right now I want to go over where you are and tell you all about it. I want your comfort and your sympathy. And I want you. But you wouldn't believe that, would you? You're the one real thing in life, Suzanne. You're the girl carrying a candle for me to see by. You're the north star holding up the only light to guide me home. But you wouldn't understand that. I could never explain. You would have *your* pride, too . . ."

In the gray of the early morning after the storm abated, and the white prairie lay as still as a dead man in his shroud, Wayne explained about the previous night, standing in the lean-to at the Martin home.

Sarah was upset and nervous. "And we thought she was safe at Sabina's all the time. I wish Pa was here. There ain't ever been anything said of one of my girls. Jeanie may have had some talk of her havin' more than one beau at a time . . . a little foolish . . . but not . . . not . . ."

Wayne stood tall and straight and a little disdainful, confronting them all.

"There are a lot of people in the world who think a closed door never hides anything but evil," he said sharply. "Well, *I* wouldn't want anything said about Suzanne that *you* wouldn't. Thank your lucky stars I set out to get my sheep and found her. Maybe you wouldn't have had her alive to-day if I hadn't. I took her to the nearest shelter—my cabin. I couldn't have brought her home here through that storm if *either* her life or her reputation depended on it. I took care of her and brought her safe home here this morning." His voice rose high and harsh. "Do you believe it or don't you?"

"Yes." Little Sarah's eyes snapped and her voice, too, rose high and harsh. "I believe it."

He swept the staring group with half-scornful glance.

"Then say no more about it . . . *any* of you." He turned on his heel and walked out, slamming the lean-to door.

Melinda snickered. "I bet if it had been Carlie Scott . . ."

"Dry up," Emily whirled on her. "Dry up and 'tend to your own affairs."

CHAPTER 33

OF Wayne's sheep, sixty had drowned, and ninety-two were dead from exposure. Eighty-nine survived.

Jeremiah had just arrived home from Des Moines and Sarah was telling him all this at the supper table, not quite bringing herself to explain Suzanne's part in it. Neither Emily nor Suzanne, who knew sheep were all that Wayne had lost that day, volunteered to help her out, so she said nothing.

But Jeremiah had more news to tell them than they could offer him. Best of all was the account of being presented with the fine silver watch from the legislators, engraved "To an honorable gentleman. 1862." He could scarcely tell it without showing out the emotion he did not want them to see. All those lawyers and farmers and business men doing that for him!

They had barely finished supper when they saw Tom Bostwick and Sabina drive into the yard, and all hurried out to greet them.

"Ma, we've got bad news," Sabina said gently, as though speaking so would soften the telling. "Ed Armitage is dead. He was killed at Pigeon Ranch in New Mexico fighting the Texas Rangers. Phoebe Lou's coming home with her little boy."

After the dishes were done Suzanne went down past the garden plot and sat on a maple log to think about Phoebe Lou, the night of her wedding, leaving them all for love of Ed. And now she was coming home without him. For a long time she sat there wondering how that would be. Phoebe Lou would never be happy again, never laugh any more with the dimple showing at the corner of her mouth. There was a new life though, a part of Ed and yet not Ed. How strange it was!

Word from the south followed almost immediately that the

home boys, the Third and part of the Twelfth, had been engaged in deadly combat for two days at Shiloh.

Jeremiah haunted the depot and army headquarters with Mr. Banninger and other fathers, waiting for the list of casualties, read it fearfully when it came—a long, long list—scarcely able to pick out the ones whose names began with *B* or *M* or *W*, knowing Ma and the girls were out home waiting for his returning, that Melinda, Celia, and Jeanie all must wait, too, to know what it said.

> Brown, A. E., wounded, died
> Merrill, George, wounded
> Moury, George, killed
> Wigten, Thomas J., wounded, died

No Martin or Banninger or Willshire, thank God. But what of others? What of the Brown and Moury and Wigten families? He rode home, sick at heart, but relieved that he could face Ma and the girls.

It was June before Phoebe Lou got home with her year-old baby, a hard-bodied little fellow whose cheeks were red and chapped from the hot winds that blew across the Great American Desert.

They did not know just when she was arriving, so Jeremiah was away at Prairie Rapids attending a meeting of citizens determined to see what could be done about getting telegraph connections with Dubuque. "Though whatever good it will do us to hear news any sooner is beyond me," Sarah said, "when most everything we hear is death and catastrophe."

Tom and Sabina brought Phoebe Lou out home in their carriage. Sabina carried the baby in and would not give him up to any one, but sat down in Ma's chair cuddling him, with the rocker squeaking as she swayed back and forth.

When Phoebe Lou followed, throwing back her long widow's veil, Emily and Suzanne kissed her and cried a little. But Phoebe Lou did not cry. She just stood dry-eyed there in the main room in her black dress and said quietly: "Well, it's all over. I've left him out there. He was just *life* to me, so life's over. He had his faults but he was full of energy and fun and gay ways and there was never anybody that I liked to be with so well. I guess that's what a marriage *is*. And now he's gone."

"At least you had some one," Emily said.

"Yes, for your own," Suzanne added.

"And you've got a *baby*," Sabina said and pressed the boy hard against her bosom.

Ma had gone into her bedroom, but now she was back again, her nose red. "Well, I guess you've got to take men the way they are," she said crisply, and it was as near to a concession that she forgave Ed Armitage for living as she ever came. "Some's one way, and some's another."

There was a flood of joyful news that June. Corinth was evacuated, Memphis deserted, Richmond captured, the rebels at Corinth had taken ignominiously to their heels for a point farther south to save themselves an inglorious thrashing by General Halleck—or so the news came back to the Valley— every one picturing to suit his fancy the utter rout and demoralization of the rebel troops, not realizing that what advance was made one week might be lost the next.

Wayne worked doggedly in his fields, so emotionally disturbed this spring that he must tax his body to its physical limit in order to forget the hurt to his pride and the great confusion in his mind. Self-disgust over memories that burned, self-flagellation over his own mental tumult, and the dawning knowledge that only by one path could he find peace again, embodied all his thoughts as he plunged into the work before the sun's rising to the late hour when he washed the day's stains from his strong young body and fell into bed.

It seemed queer to have Phoebe Lou home with her baby. Theodore was far too big a mouthful for a year-old boy, and so as "Todo" he came to one's call, and in truth, came without calling, for he was lively, toddling into everything, "for all the world," Sarah said, "like his fly-up-the-creek father," and so different from the quiet little Harry of the same age over at Henry and Lucy's.

The old Martin way of joking and laughter was something in the past, a way merely to remember this summer, although occasionally there was a spurt of gay spirits which broke through the feeling of anxiety for the times, so that the three girls clung to those moments as one clutches at logs in mid-stream. But Phineas, Rand, Alf, and Ambrose were all in the thick of danger. Ed Armitage was dead. And never this summer did Wayne Lockwood ride singing up the lane road. Small wonder the jokes were forgotten and the laughter stilled.

There was another Fourth of July celebration—salutes, bells ringing, parades in which a few returned soldiers were the prominent object of cheers divided in lustiness only by those given the stalwart Reserves who would be next to go if any

other call came. One of the returned boys who had escaped
from the rebels at Montgomery was there bringing home a sad
account of the union men from the home company captured at
Shiloh. Fifteen months now since that first shot on Fort
Sumter?—Perhaps the war was not to end this summer after
all.

On an evening in August, moonlight was as thick and
yellow over the Valley as Sarah Martin's butter down on a
shelf in the well. The willows on Deer Run had a queer silver
shimmer over them as though one could walk across their
shining tops to some far country. It was so still Suzanne could
hear the soft lapping creek water from the doorway where
she leaned.

Emily had just lighted one of the two glass lamps, still a
little nervous over results, still watched critically by the whole
family while the ceremony was being enacted. Phoebe Lou
rocked Todo. Sarah had settled herself near the lamp for a
good spell of carpet-rag sewing. Jeremiah had been reading
news aloud from the last of the daylight on into the first of the
lamplighting with acrid comments from Sarah.

" 'There is a rumor to the effect that Jeff Davis' life is in
extreme danger. It is even averred that he was prevented from
escaping out of Richmond. Handbills are displayed over the
city denouncing him and applying to him ridiculous and
opprobrious epithets . . .' "

Sarah sniffed. "If they mean calling him names, why don't
they say so and be done with it?"

" 'Farmers, we are yet in need of good, fresh butter. Bring
it immediately. We will pay you ten cents per pound for
it.' "

"Not Sarah Martin's, you won't. Twelve and a half cents
or nothing."

" 'A novel steam engine propelled by four engines of ten
horse-power each has been sent west to use in transportation
of freight from Omaha to Denver City . . .' "

"Flyin' in the face of Providence. What did the Lord make
an *ox* for?"

"Now, Ma. I wouldn't just go so far as to say the Lord
made an ox. Looks like man has sort of tampered there."

"I ain't splittin' hairs."

" 'The correct thing now for the nice young beau is to
bang his hair.' "

"I'd *bang* a boy of mine . . ."

" 'Our state is called on to constitute Ten Thousand men

toward filling the new quota of Three Hundred Thousand men lately called for by the president. Governor Kirkwood has called for Five Thousand loyal Iowans to be furnished immediately before harvest. The remainder will not be called before the month of September or until harvest is well secured.' ''

There was only silence now. Sarah had no acid comment. More men! More home boys to feed to the monster that lay crouching there in the south.

"Hark," Phoebe Lou said, "I thought I heard . . ."

Suzanne, leaning there against the doorway, had been hearing it in the stillness for quite a while, keeping it to herself as one crouches over a treasure jealously. Wayne Lockwood who had not sung for so long a time was singing as he rode home from town.

The four hurried at once outdoors that they might not miss a note, all listening there—Jeremiah and Sarah, Emily and Phoebe Lou. And Suzanne who still stood there motionless.

Phoebe Lou shifted the drowsy Todo to the other arm. "That's the new song . . ." she said. "*The Song of a Thousand Years.* Ed was singing it just before . . ."

> *"Tell the great world these blessed tidings;*
> *Yes, and be sure the bondman hears.*
> *Tell the oppressed of every nation*
> *Jubilee lasts a thousand years."*

Singing, Wayne Lockwood rode in a more light-hearted mood than for many months. He had enlisted and felt cleansed of some former defilement, rid of an undesirable part of himself because of his decision. Many things were clarified. He knew for a certainty where duty lay. And he knew surcease from pain over an unworthy infatuation. He let out his voice to the extent of its melodious power as though in grateful praise that now nothing was to be seen through a glass darkly. Peace followed in the wake of right decisions. Stoutness of character included following one's duty. And just now duty led to war. Doing one's duty made one strong. The song of years was a song of strength.

To the group by the cabin his voice came across the prairie in the stillness, so true and melodious, so vibrant with feeling that it set every nerve to tingling.

In the moonlight, Sarah's wrinkled face under the mop of sagging hair relaxed and took upon itself a queer elfish beauty. All at once something in her broke, responding to the loveliness of the singing, tying in an indescribable way the song of the present with a lost song of the past. There was something so painful about the process of listening to this old song of remembrance, turning her thoughts back to the time when she was young, that she started into the house, scolding that the night air would harm them all.

Jeremiah, hearing the song, felt his heart ache with the pain and pity of war. But his country! She must be preserved at any price. Nothing was too much to sacrifice for her—his life, his boys, his girls, his farm, his crops—anything for her, everything for her. And it would come out all right. It *must* come out all right. The nation would be preserved, wounds would be healed. If one could but look into the future one would see that with Abraham Lincoln there at the helm. . . ! God, Lincoln, and the good sense of the people! All of one great land—both sides of the line! Somehow, some day in the future, the country would pull through and be united again. To old Jeremiah the song of years was a song of faith.

> What if the clouds one little moment
> Hide the blue sky when morn appears,
> When the bright sun that tints them crimson
> Rises to shine a thousand years.

Emily had gone a little white there in the moonlight, her plain freckled face turned to the singer. "Oh, don't let life pass me by," she was thinking. "I'm getting older. I can't give up life and love just for the folks. Why does every one depend on me? I want the things the other girls have. It isn't mean and rebellious . . . it's *natural*. I'll just go on this way *forever* . . . and get old and resigned . . . but I want my share of life. I want something of my own." To Emily the song of years was a song of desire.

Phoebe Lou looked down at the sleeping child relaxed and heavy in her arms, his body warm against hers, the curls damp on his forehead. She hugged him tightly to her. She had this much of Ed. This *was* Ed. Hearing that singing up the lane road filled her with deepest feeling for her baby, so that the ready tears sprang to her eyes. Oh, she would bring him up to be a good man. He would be active and gay like Ed, but more responsible, with schooling over in town. She would do everything possible to make him fine and understanding. To Phoebe Lou the song of years was a song of hope.

*"Haste thee along, thou glorious noonday
 Oh, for the eyes of ancient seers.
 Oh, for the faith of him who reckons
 Each of his days a thousand years."*

The resonant voice died away up the lane road and one by one they all went into the house. All but Suzanne. She walked to the corner of the old log-and-frame building, her hand at her throat to still its throbbing. As though the bittern can still its answering cry!

"I'll not try to evade it any more," she thought. "I'm no longer a child with dreams. I'm a woman. I love him and always shall. No one will know. *He* will never know. That he doesn't care the slightest thing for me doesn't enter into it any more. To give him my love will have to be all there is to it. But I'm willing . . . and reconciled . . . just that and nothing more."

To Suzanne there was never any doubt but that the song of years was a song of love.

CHAPTER 34

DEAR MOTHER:

I thought you would be glad to have a few lines from me at this time, especially as I have taken a very serious step in my life. I have enlisted and expect soon to start for the war. I know this will be a great blow to you, but surely you would prefer to have me go as a volunteer than to be drafted. I have thought long and anxiously in regard to this matter and could come to no other conclusion but that it was my duty to go if we are to have a country and security to our lives and property. I can see no other way but to turn out and defend our country, and I hope that your patriotism will sustain you in the trial. I know not what will be the fate of my country. The future looks dark, but I do know that I had rather lose my life in defense of my country than live to see the downfall and disgrace of that country without my having made an effort to save it. But we will not indulge too much in these gloomy apprehensions; rather let us hope that this one great effort will redeem our country from her foes and bring peace once more to our land. I will and must believe that this will be the result.

We are raising a company in this place and it is now nearly filled. We will start in a few weeks for our place of rendezvous which will be either at Fort Des Moines or Dubuque. When I ascertain which place I will write you.

And now, dear Mother, good-by. Let us all do our duty and may God defend the right.

SO wrote Wayne Lockwood, saying nothing of the emotional turmoil with which his life had been troubled the past year, dwelling only on the decision with no reference to the events leading up to it.

He cut his forty acres of wheat with a cradle, estimating with practised eye the amount of grain which would make a bundle, binding and shocking it. Physically he was in excellent shape.

And now it was the Reserves, one hundred young men, who were drilling on the fair-ground, whose sisters, mothers, and sweethearts were teary-eyed over flannel stomachers and foolish heart-shaped pincushions.

Wayne Lockwood, tall and stalwart, was drilling with ninety-nine others, tall and stalwart, the pick of the town and near-by country, more business men now than in previous enlistments.

Suzanne's second year of teaching had just started over in the log school-house. It was still summer-like, warm, dusty, and early for the fall session as the terms usually began when most convenient for the families. But the neighborhood had a full quota of small children, so Jeremiah, as director, said she might as well open up. So far none of the larger children had entered, but after husking there would be quite a number.

On a morning of that first week Jeremiah came in from the stable, hung his cap carefully on its peg behind the lean-to door, and washed his hands for breakfast before telling them: "Horace Akin rode by just now and says the Reserves are called to leave to-morrow."

Off and on all day, Suzanne, looking out of the log building at the dusty goldenrod and daisies drooping over limpsy stems in the late September heat, at the cattle browsing along the timber's edge shaking their heads over the biting of flies, wondered how life could go on after Wayne had left.

All through the monotonous reciting, the thought of Wayne wove itself in and out of her thoughts as though one were the warp and the other the woof of her mind's weaving.

"Give the table of two's, Nora."

"Two one's two, two two's four, two three's six . . ."

That night in the cabin! Something brought them very close together, but held them apart, too. What brought them together? And what held them apart?

"The table of three's, Lavina."

"Three one's one, three two's two . . ."

"No, no, Lavina."

Some pedagogical sense of duty kept one part of herself in the school-room even while another part was off with Wayne. Though she realized now she could never be anything to him, she also knew that just to look up the lane road and know he was there, to hear him singing in the moonlight, to watch him come riding into the yard behind the stake-and-rider fence—all these were better than to see him go off to war.

The afternoon dragged on. Reading from McGuffey: *This fable teaches us that it is better to bear slight wrong rather than to resort to law for trifles.* Spelling. Writing—trying to break Lavina Manson from using her left hand and wondering why it was necessary to do it when she could form her letters as well as the other pupils who were right-handed.

It was time now to send the children home. Time! Time, which kept bringing to-morrow morning closer. Time, which let down the weights on the old clock like stones on your heart.

"Is there school to-morrow, Miss Martin?"

"Yes."

"Ain't you goin' to the Falls to see the Reserves off?"

"No."

"Why ain't you, Miss Martin?"

Yes, why, Suzanne?

"You went when the Pioneer Grays left, Miss Martin, and others."

"Yes, I know."

"Is it 'cause it would make you feel queer to see 'em go?"

"Yes, it's because it would make me . . . feel queer to see them go."

When Suzanne went home after school her father was just coming from the lane road. He had gone to invite Wayne down to supper. But Wayne sent back word to the folks that he had some things to attend to at the last and would ride over later in the evening to see them.

Supper was a silent meal excepting for the pounding and jabbering of Todo, wanting first a bite of this and then of that, as changeable in his ways, Sarah said, as ever Ed Armitage had been.

Dishes were washed. Pancakes were stirred. Bread was set, ham sliced. Life is made up of such infinitesimal things.

They were all through with these tasks when they heard Wayne's horse come into the yard. All had been listening for that sound. And now there it was.

The two coal-oil lamps had been lighted as well as two candles. Even then the light was not extra good so that Emily puckered her forehead to see the tiny stitches she was putting into the suit for Todo. Jeremiah in his arm-chair was reading the war news aloud. Sarah nervously sewed her endless carpet rags, the ball in its Indian basket as big as a young pumpkin. Phoebe Lou kept tiptoeing into the bedroom to look at Todo sleeping there behind the calico curtain in one end of her mother's room, his legs and arms sprawled out as though in gay and reckless abandon. Suzanne, with the excuse of setting a few things to rights in the lean-to, had the solace of the dark while she listened for the one sound in the night that meant anything to her.

And now there it was. Hoof beats! Her hand slipped up to her throat as it always did in moments of stress. Then she went to the window at the east of the lean-to and looked out. In the dark she could not be seen. But the faint light from the main room caught and held for her Wayne on his horse. *He was in uniform*. She watched him dismount, tie the strap, and disappear around the corner to the front room where there were lights. She walked to the lean-to door leading into the room, but she did not go in, merely stood in the shadows and waited.

Hearing the steps on the tree-trunk stoop, Jeremiah laid down his paper. Sarah's and Emily's needles paused in their in-and-out journeyings. Phoebe Lou came hurriedly from the bedroom. Wayne stood in the front doorway in his soldier uniform.

Oh, but he was big and handsome and gallant-looking. All eyes upon him spoke it as plainly as words could have done.

"Come in . . . come in."

"Sit down, Wayne."

"No, I'll not stay. There are a few things more I have to do. I only came to say good-by."

"Anything we can do for you?"

No, there was nothing they could do. Horace Akin had bought the sheep and Wallace Akin was to have half of the corn for the husking. Mel Manson was taking the team and wagon off his hands. Oh, yes, there was just one thing—he wondered if some one here would look after old Snide.

"Oh, *I* will," Emily said quickly. "I'd like to."

"I'd be grateful, Emily, and like to think of him down here with you folks." And because it sounded sentimental he went on quickly: "The Akins will put in the crop if by any chance the war isn't over in the spring . . . which it probably will be. Now that I'm going," he grinned boyishly, "I'm only afraid I'll meet them all coming back." But it was only 1862 and Wayne was not to meet the soldiers coming back.

"I wanted to tell you if you want to pasture any stock up

there . . . you or the neighbors . . . help yourself. The land will still be here for me when I get back. And if I don't . . .''

It hung in the air like the sound of the deep-throated tower bell over in town whose reverberations were so long in dying away.

He did not try to finish the sentence for Jeremiah at once said cheerfully: "Oh, hell . . . you'll be back by spring. You'll put in your crop yourself, I'm ready to wager.''

They were all standing constrained and tense.

Sarah, her mouth twitching a little, said: "What time do the steam-cars leave?''

And Phoebe Lou said: "Well, you don't have to think about Injuns anyway . . . like we . . .''

Emily looked pale in the lamp light, her freckles spotting her thin face as though they had been painted on with tiger-lily powder.

Suzanne stood back in the shadows, her fingers white knuckled in the folds of her skirt so they would not fly to her throat to betray her.

Jeremiah said: "I'll be at the train, but the women folks here say they can't go any more. It's been too many times now.''

"Suits me just as well." Wayne forced the ghost of a grin. "Atmosphere's always pretty thick around the depot. Well—'' He started over toward Sarah, his hand outstretched.

This was it. This was good-by to Wayne and life and love and dreams and . . .

He was shaking hands with Sarah, who held the back of her other hand across her twitching mouth. With Phoebe Lou, crying unabashedly. Some of the tears were for Wayne and some for all soldier boys everywhere, but more were for a gay young man riding recklessly off to Pigeon Ranch who would never ride again. With Emily, as white as a sheet, dropping her eyes so no one could see the hunger in them. He was turning now toward Suzanne in the shadows. But he did not shake hands with her. He did not touch her. He only stood, straight and tall, and looked down at her.

And Suzanne, her hands behind her, holding each other that neither one would prove untrustworthy, said very quietly: "I'll be up the lane road and wave to you when the train goes by.''

And Wayne turned and went out of the house.

In the morning Suzanne was glad she was not going over to town. She went down the grassy path, through the small gate, and up the road to school. Queer, how unreal the day looked to her. The sun shone and there was no warmth. The birds sang and there was no music. Goldenrod and daisies and little ragged asters were blossoming along the way and there was no beauty. It was Wayne Lockwood who was warmth and music and beauty.

She crossed the diagonal path worn in the prairie grass by the prints of countless feet. This was starting the tenth year for the old log school. Pa said they would soon be building a nice frame one, painted white with green blinds. Yesterday she would have been pleased to think about it. To-day she did not care. A mourning-dove was giving its long-drawn-out incessant cry. It was true that you never noticed them when you were happy. Their calls were a part of the wild life, one with the brown thrasher and the creek's gurgle and the wind in the maples. But when you were sad their cry struck an answering chord in your breast; that long low mournful wail came from your own heart.

She wondered how it would be if Wayne cared for her. Leaving to-day as he must, would it be easier or harder to have him go? Well, there was very little use to waste idle dreaming on that. Face facts, Pa always said. Wayne did not belong to her and she had to face it.

There were only five of the very smallest children in school, including Nora. For that she was thankful. The others had gone to town with their folks to whom the soldiers' entraining was the big event of the fall. Even these five small youngsters were full of talk about the Reserves leaving, so that Suzanne suppressed it, made them study their reading for a time before she would tell them her plan.

Constantly her eyes went to the rails over there to the north of the school-house. High on the graveled embankment the track shone in the morning sun. It still ran only to Sturgis Falls, no farther. The war had stopped so many things.

It was time now.

"We'll go up the lane road," she told the five, "and watch the train go by with the soldiers on it."

They were surprised, excited. A war was nice. A war let you get out of school to walk up the lane road and see the soldiers go away to it.

They hopped and skipped along, ran off the dusty lane road to pick red prairie lilies and white oxeye daisies and purplish-blue asters.

"See, Suzanne, all the flag colors."

Miss Martin, they called her in the school-room. Out here on the lane road she was just *Suzanne.*

"Can we throw them at the soldiers when they go by, Suzanne?"

"Yes."

"Will they like it, Suzanne?"

"Yes. I think they will."

Oh, why were things so complicated in life? When you were little like these children, the whole world was a happy lovely place. And when you were grown it was neither one.

It was coming, the smoke flattening out into white clouds in the distance. The children squealed with nervous excitement, their flowers poised for throwing.

"Stand away back. It goes by so fast that the suction might draw you right under it."

Now they could see the flat gravel cars, blue with uniforms. There were green boughs of trees fastened to the sides. The bell was ringing, the steam-whistle shrieking. Nora had dropped her flowers to clap small hands over her ears.

But what was the matter? It was not coming its mad pace, roaring its way across the prairie. It was slowing down. What was happening?

"Look . . . Suzanne . . . it's *stopping.*" The children were screaming it above the clatter of the grinding brakes and the piercing noise of the whistle. The smoke was blowing down around them.

Wayne Lockwood was swinging off the last of the flat cars, sliding and slipping down the embankment, gravel rolling under his feet. Wayne in his blue uniform was coming toward them. And now he had Suzanne in his arms, was straining her body to his own, his lips to hers for one long moment, while the bell clanged and the smoke from the engine fouled the prairie and the soldiers called out gay saucy prairie things.

"Good-by."

With no word other than that hurried whispered "good-by," he released her and was up the graded bank again. Hands were reaching for him, pulling him onto the flat car. The bell was still clanging, the smoke blowing. Wilted goldenrod and daisies were flying up into the air on short ineffectual journeyings. The train was pulling out. The soldiers, some on benches, some half reclining on the car floors, were waving countless blue caps. Wayne was the only one standing. In the midst of the blue-coated men and the green tree branches he stood erect, smiling, his arm high holding his blue cap, the morning sun bright on his yellow head.

The children were excited. *The train had stopped.* It was the wonder of the year. What were parting and kisses, love and war? *The train had stopped at the lane road.*

They clamored about her.

"Suzanne, did it ever stop before?"

"Suzanne, I know it stopped for Mr. Scott once and Ma said then it wouldn't have stopped ever for anybody but the Scotts. But it did."

"Suzanne, it stopped for Wayne Lockwood."

"Suzanne, do you think he asked 'em to?"

"Suzanne, was it just because he wanted to say good-by to you?"

And then, as a new and pleasant thought struck: "Suzanne, *why* did he want to? Is he your lover?"

"Yes."

Suzanne's hands were at her throat and she was crying—happy tears—sad tears—cupping her eyes, then trying desperately to push those tears aside so that her straining hungry sight might see the last of that upright figure.

"Yes . . . he's my lover."

CHAPTER 35

ALL the neighborhood knew the train had stopped at the lane road. But no one seemed to know just why. Wayne Lockwood had taken advantage of it to jump off and kiss Suzanne according to the little folks. Not that it meant anything. The soldiers had a sort of privilege to kiss all the girls good-by.

Nora, Henry's six-year-old, with no knowledge gleaned from the realm of romance, told it to Emily as an afterthought to the important talk about the train stopping, and connecting the two events not at all.

Emily, who was taking down many starched and voluminous underskirts from the clothes-line when Nora told her, stood still with her mouth full of clothes-pins and three of the huge cartwheels in her arms, staring at the little girl over their white stiffness. Then she suddenly turned and went into the house, dumped the rattling petticoats onto the table and climbed the ladder-stair to the bedroom.

It was there that Suzanne found her when she came from school. Frightened to hear her convulsive sobbing, she tiptoed to the side of the bed.

"Emily. . . !"

With a jerk Emily was sitting up. "Suzanne, you scared me. You're home early."

"What . . . what is it?"

"Nothing." Emily wiped her face hard as though she could at once rub away all freckles and all feeling showing there so traitorously.

"But it's something."

"Silly! Can't I . . . can't I bawl once in a while just to see if I've got tear ducts yet?"

317

Suzanne slipped her arm around her. "Is it . . . ? Emily, is it about Wayne?"

"Of course not, lunatic."

"Can't you tell me?"

"Well, if you want to know, it's because Abraham Lincoln has a wart on his face."

And they turned to each other and laughed, clung together and rocked and laughed through their tears, knowing that when life is most cruel it must be met most gallantly.

In the days that followed, Suzanne moved in a world wholly apart from the others. The door through which she had so often looked was wide open. If she threw away the key now, it was because she had no further use for it. One does not need a key for a door which is never to close. All that she had dreamed and longed for was to come true when Wayne came back.

When Wayne came back.

When he came back heaven would not be off there beyond the clouds floating in the blue above the prairie. It would be here and now. Heaven would be up the lane road.

"And if I don't . . ."

It rang like a deep-throated bell through the silence of her heart. She could hear it all day long back of the children's reciting. Sometimes when she wakened, too, she could hear it faintly and far away, as she had heard the tower bell over at the Falls years before when the settlers rang it all night long.

And if I don't . . .

There were ceaseless war activities now. Sarah and Emily baked an endless array of pumpkin, apple, and mince pies for hospital supply suppers over which Sabina was supervisor more often than not. Jeremiah journeyed constantly between farm and town, turned almost every day from fixing fences to fixing finances for the soldiers' families, from corn-picking to helping arrange for patriotic mass meetings, from husking to talking for new enlistments.

Another company of recruits was ready to go from Sturgis Falls at the call, one from Prairie Rapids, and two from other parts of the county. Sometimes when Jeremiah was talking about these, Suzanne would notice that queer look on Henry's face as though he were going to speak out concerning something on his mind. But it always went into nothing as he turned back to his farm work. He seldom left the place now, doing his fall plowing and his corn-picking, his husking and his stable work more silently than ever, from dawn until after dark.

Because there was so very much to do, the family had its first hired girl that fall for a few weeks to help through corn-picking—a queer mortal whose eyes did not track right and who gave the girls a good laugh by telling them she buttoned the band of her hoop-skirt with a button her lover had cut from his army pants as a parting gift.

And now a letter came to Suzanne from Wayne. When Jeremiah brought it to her and she saw the heading, Helena, Arkansas, and her name in strong and steady writing—even as Wayne was strong and steady—the thought went through her mind foolishly that this was enough, just to have a letter, no matter what it said. She could have put it unopened in the bosom of her dress and left it there, and still have known comfort and satisfaction from its presence.

When it was opened, it was no love-letter. At least it would not have been to any casual reader. But there was no casual reader to see it. Only Suzanne, who could read heart-warming things between the lines telling about the Thirty-first being moved down the Mississippi on transports, and who knew by the test of her throbbing throat what it meant when he said, "There is so much to say to you now, Suzanne, that I shall say nothing at all."

Of course! She knew how that was. There was so very, very much which did not need words for the telling. It was just there between them. The saying of it did not matter.

All the other boys were still coming unscathed through their battles, Phineas, Alf, and Rand getting safely through Metamora, although the regiment had suffered heavily, and Ambrose surviving Corinth when fully a third of his company had been wounded in battle.

The Scotts withdrew completely to themselves. Mrs. Scott did not even go over to town now for her shopping or to the benefit suppers. Black Hi brought Mamie and Plunk to school as regularly as ever. Once Suzanne with natural curiosity questioned them, half ashamed to take advantage of their childishness, "What do you hear from Miss Carlie?"

When they looked frightened and stammered over the answer, she was sorry she had spoken so, and turned it off. For what did she care about Carlie Scott with that letter against her breast?

In the early spring before plowing time no one was deeply surprised to hear that the Scotts were leaving for Dubuque and that Horace Akin had bought the place. Unhappy Mrs. Scott, grieving for her girl, had evidently prevailed on her husband to follow.

Suzanne found herself genuinely sorry to see the two clean little Negro children go from school and gave over a Friday afternoon program to them. Because of the fuss made over them as symbols of the recent Emancipation Proclamation, and as travelers who were about to move to a city, they left with quite a superior air and two of Suzanne's best lead-pencils.

The days went up and down the scale now with joy and sorrow alternating—pleasure over every victory, a deep depression at every loss. Over in the two towns victories called for mass-meetings, speeches and bonfires, and some whisky to celebrate. Defeats called for mass-meetings and some whisky to drown despair. Prisoners of war were exchanged. The sick came home. Some recovered and went back.

Jeremiah set little Nora to reading the war news and though she did not understand all the reports or the political speeches, he said it would give her a certain definite idea of what it was all about. Suzanne could hear him at times explaining patiently to her "flank movement" and "strategy" and telling her of the station of the underground railroad in Illinois near his former farm, operated by a deacon of the church.

Wayne succeeded sometimes in getting a letter to Suzanne or to Jeremiah, saying that the news in it, if interesting, was to all old friends. The Thirty-first had been in Mississippi, back to Helena, Arkansas. They had engaged in a battle at Chickasaw Bayou soon after Christmas, "if Christmas there still be in the country." In January they had started for a point near Arkansas Post, marched through swamps and mire to the rear of the enemy's works, and captured them. They were now (on April first) at Young's Point, Louisiana.

By late spring the Horace Akins were living in the fine Scott house so that the Martins were in and out of it frequently, and never did Sarah come back from there without plain-spoken envy of the open stairway and vehement criticism for their own loft ladders.

"Remember those golden stairs, Ma," Jeremiah tried to joke her. "You'll enjoy 'em all the more for the wait."

But Sarah would not joke about it. And Jeremiah, seeing how deeply she felt it, would meet her solemn manner with like seriousness: "When the war's over, Ma, we'll see. Just wait till that's off our minds."

"When the war is over" ran through the conversation of

the dark days like a scarlet stripe through Sarah's gray rag carpet.

But the war was over in time, and although most of their daughters had fine big homes, Jeremiah and Sarah lived in the old log-and-frame house until they died. For thirty years it was built onto and patched, calked and tar-papered, white-washed and replastered there on the river road like an old boat which is beached every year for repairs but which is still too seaworthy to discard. For thirty years it was a haven for all its children and the families of all the children, friends, neigh-bors, "preachers, politicians, and peddlers," as Sarah had once said, a warm-hearted comfortable old house with its calico curtains and Seth Thomas clock and wild-turkey feath-ers, even if scarred and weatherbeaten. Sturdy and honest it stood, unshaken in the rains and the blizzards and the scream-ing winds that came down from the north prairies, as sturdy and honest as the man who had fashioned its first rooms out of the timber.

But it was still only 1863, with growing crops not doing well just when they were so needed. Everything was dear and scarce—coffee a dollar per pound, so that only Sabina, Me-linda, and Celia could each afford a few long-hoarded pounds. Sarah and the three girls at home tried half a dozen substi-tutes, rye and wheat, bran mixed with molasses, sweet pota-toes chipped and browned in sugar. Jeanie, alone with her three babies up on the north prairie, drank hot water. Calico was seventy-five cents a yard, and Sabina, cautioned by Tom that it would go higher, purchased three bolts, saw it later priced at a dollar.

Gold and silver disappeared from circulation. Paper checks valued at one and two dollars were passed about. The banks issued little cards good for ten, fifteen, twenty-five, fifty cents.

Jeremiah had it on good authority that Cady Bedson in Prairie Rapids was hoarding gold, saying that he was going to wait until it got to three dollars and then he would sell. Telling Tom Bostwick this and how disloyal he thought it ("When it gets to be three dollars, he'll turn patriotic"), he could see that Tom evaded agreeing with him, sensed that his own son-in-law might be doing the same thing.

But although almost every one was hard up, no one was so poor they could not sacrifice to send boxes to the soldiers.

Clothing, bedding, food, canned fruits all followed the blue uniforms weekly.

There were no more boxes from Aunt Harriet. Clothes were no longer important to her and the daughters, and in the stress of war work she scarcely ever wrote. Once in a great while they heard from her—she had gone down near a battlefield to help or had been working in a hospital. So Emily cleaned and pressed, turned and made over all the old dresses. She put the red glassy cherries on a hat for Lucy, curled Suzanne's modest blue plume with steam and a case-knife, made over Phoebe Lou's black widow's dress to fit better, colored Nora's unbleached muslin aprons with butternut water, and when Melinda or Celia, Sabina or Jeanie needed clothes fixed, she did that, too, never thinking that she was out from under any obligations to do so since they had married.

A letter came to Suzanne from Wayne, the last of June, written near Vicksburg. They had left Young's Point, Louisiana, on April second, gone up the river to Greenville, Mississippi, "foraging for cattle, mules, horses, and hogs," returning to Young's Point, moving with Grant toward Grand Gulf, moving again toward Jackson, Mississippi. They were under fire at Raymond on the twelfth of May, helped take Jackson the fourteenth, were again under fire at Black River, reaching the rear of Vicksburg on the eighteenth, engaged in a successful charge on the enemy's works, and were now (the seventh of June) steadily under fire.

"Governor Kirkwood gave us a call yesterday," he wrote, "talked freely with us and in conversation consoled us this much, that he saw more girls in the corn-fields this season than any year. If this be the case I don't think that we will starve. I hope you are not by necessity in the field, Suzanne. But if this be so, and you must wield the hoe and rake, I will wield the gun and bayonet in good spirits until the rebellion is crushed." *Oh, Wayne, I know what you mean even though you are waiting to say it when you get home.*

The letter closed in this fashion: "If Vicksburg does not surrender before the Fourth, we are going to storm it with or without orders."

In his constant conversation with others over at the Falls and at Prairie Rapids or along the river road while Queen browsed among the sweet wild grasses, Jeremiah found that other boys beside Wayne had written the same thing home. It was common talk in the Thirty-first then, for like a refrain it ran through all the letters. "If Vicksburg does not surrender before the Fourth, we are going to storm it with or without orders."

And now this was the Fourth. And the residents of this part of the Valley were trying to have a celebration picnic on the fair-ground, in Sturgis Falls. There were occasional mourning weeds among the women folks, but white dresses predominated, with colored sashes running largely to red and blue.

There had been a program, band music, the Emancipation Proclamation, patriotic songs, a flag drill, and a youthful declaimer reciting vociferously and with so much bodily activity: "As over Barbara Frietchie's grave, Flag of freedom and union wave," that one of her pantalets began to sag noticeably, so while freedom still appeared to be rampant, the unity was somewhat spoiled.

A few adults were still sitting at the table of planks long after dinner, when Cady Bedson rode so rapidly into the fair ground that every one turned to hear what he had to say.

"Vicksburg's fallen," was the thing he had to say. He had ridden hard all the way up from Prairie Rapids to bring the message.

It went quickly to the far end of the fair-ground like a prairie fire springing from tumbleweeds to dried grasses to tumbleweeds. "Vicksburg's fallen."

"On what conditions?"

Cady Bedson did not know.

All the rest of the afternoon they sat around in quiet groups—fathers, mothers, sisters, sweethearts. Victory! But what was the cost of the victory?

Just so nothing has happened to Wayne. Oh, God, don't let anything have happened to Wayne.

CHAPTER 36

NOTHING had happened to Wayne—*Lantz, Jacob, wounded* —*Linderman, Cornelius, killed—Lusch, Charles, wounded* —but not Lockwood. Suzanne told herself God was good, and then she thought: "But how about the Lantzes and the Lindermans and the Lusches? He's their God, too," and shivered that there was no reasoning about it or philosophy to it.

Fourteen men of the Third (the Pioneer Grays regiment) had been wounded by guerrillas on their way to join Grant before Vicksburg—but not Phineas or Rand or Alf. The last of the month, though, word came that they had been in a battle at Johnson, Mississippi, and lost one hundred and fourteen, killed, wounded, or missing.

And now the list said:

Martin, Phineas, wounded

It took so long to find out more; it was such a cruel wait to hear that the wound was only in his hand. The days went into weeks before they heard it was better. Still later they heard he was to be discharged.

It was fall, with a purple haze on the prairies and the air like fresh apple cider, with Suzanne teaching again, and Lookout Mountain and Missionary Ridge words in every Valley resident's mouth when Phineas came home.

Emily and Suzanne in the main room saw him turn into the little gate and come up the path. They called out and ran to the doorway, but Sarah, a hank of yarn across the arms of her chair for straightening, was caught in the mesh trying to get up.

And then the girls saw his sleeve—the right—was empty and pinned to his side.

"Hello, girls," he called cheerfully, beginning at once to whistle and swagger on up to the stoop in his old way. But glimpsing his mother inside, the whistling broke off suddenly and he brushed past the two over to her, dropped down by her chair and, with his head in her lap on top of the tangled yarn, broke into low painful sobbing.

"There, now," Sarah said, patting his shoulder, smoothing his hair, "it ain't so bad that it couldn't a been worse. It could'a been *both* arms, and that would'a been a real trial. You're alive and well and can't go back and that's a blessing. Come, now, don't you want I should make you saleratus biscuits and chicken gravy for supper?"

So Phineas was home trying to putter around with his one arm, and so awkward at it, but no one must feel sorry for him or help him. Jeremiah gave orders for that. Phineas must have no pity to take away his self-regard.

The Christmas celebration was largely an attempt to do something for the small children, Henry's Nora and Harry, Phoebe Lou's Todo, Jeanie's three little girls. You couldn't take your anxiety about war out on the little folks, the girls all said. No matter that every one felt as poor as Job's turkey and that there was no heart in being gay with more Valley boys killed or wounded, the children must have a good time. Celia and Melinda had not expected to come, thinking that Father and Mother Banninger would not want them to take the little boys away, but when Christmas Day dawned they could not stand it, said they felt like children themselves and had to get home to the old place, surprising every one by driving into the yard with the Banningers just before dinner.

Eighteen-sixty-four began with a snow blockade. The Valley lay supine under its own weather like a fish frozen in the four-foot ice of the Red Cedar. Sometimes the mercury reached thirty below. From the last day of December until the middle of January no train trying to cross the prairie from Dubuque reached the river. The company made every effort to get rid of the snow but it piled in the cuts as fast as it was shoveled out.

"A blockade much more effectual than the blockade of Wilmington," Jeremiah described it.

Day after day went by with no letters from the home folks in the east, none from the soldiers, and no newspapers besides the local one. But now there was a new telegraph clicking in the little frame depot. Scarcely a month ago Mr. Platt Smith of Dubuque had sent the first message: "Did I not tell you so?" It kept them in touch with happenings for a few days, but when poles and lines succumbed wearily to the onslaught of the god of storms, there was nothing left to connect them with the outside world.

"We don't rightly know what Lincoln is doing," Henry remarked, "or what's the latest down there."

Down there! Down where Lee was holding the Rapidan near Fredericksburg and Johnston was still strong in Georgia.

In the midst of this snow-bound condition Death came into the neighborhood as though to prove no snow-storm could balk him, no blockade keep him from his grim duty. Mrs. Horace Akin in her new home at the old Scott place sickened and died suddenly from a premature birth and not even the doctor and Sarah Martin's capable nursing could stay the cold hands. It was impossible to get up to the cemetery. They packed the casket in a huge snowbank of the yard to wait for a time of moderation, and Horace Akin and the two young boys took turns sitting at a bedroom window near it in sad and lonely vigil until the day they could shovel through the drifts over the north prairie to the hillside cemetery.

It saddened every one immeasurably, adding to the gloom over not being able to hear from the south.

On the fifteenth, after laborious shoveling by the Paddies, the black engine nosed its way with snorting vexation across the white fields of the Wallace Akin farm and on into Sturgis Falls.

Jeremiah in the bob-sled, driving the heavy-legged Lassie and Laddie, got through the drifts before the train made the two miles.

There were letters and papers for every one, canned oysters, sugar, and hoop-skirts for those who could afford them, the train bringing passengers, mail, and freight. And six thousand pounds of frozen prairie-chickens stood in the freight depot ready to go back on it to the eastern markets.

In the Post Office Jeremiah ran into Mr. Banninger in the crowd waiting for the long delayed mail. Mr. Banninger said he was glad to see him, as Celia, Melinda, and the two little boys were at Sabina's waiting for a ride out to their old home. The little boys had whooping-cough. The girls thought there was no one like their mother for sickness, and were going out there to stay until the children were over it. So Jeremiah took them all out home to Ma's harsh-skinned hands that were so strangely magical in their ministry, the little boys whooping spasmodically under the buffalo robes all the way out.

Letters from Rand and Alf were in the mail, telling Melinda and Celia they would be home soon now from their three-year enlistment, each asking how that little son-of-a-gun boy of his was and saying not to try to fool their Pas by switching the two around.

A letter from Wayne to Suzanne said they were moving by way of Chattanooga and Bridgeport to Woodville, Alabama, where they would go into winter quarters, that he hoped it would all be over in the spring so he could return to see again his farm lands in the Valley and all his "good friends and neighbors and *you*, Suzanne."

Not a love-letter by all the imaginings of what a love-letter should be. Just a line under the "you," a little half-inch line, so unimportant and yet so informative. It meant that to Wayne there were friends and there were neighbors, and then there was Suzanne. All the long winter days back and forth to school she carried it in her white breast where it rustled remindfully at first and then, because of its worn pulpiness, rustled no more, but lay supinely there against her heart.

Henry went north to another township for a week to help a man get out rails with which to fence a quarter-section of unbroken prairie in the spring. There was more than enough for him to do at home, but the settler offered him cash and he could not refuse the opportunity. It made the girls get out in the cold a great deal to help Jeremiah. Phineas was laboriously learning to milk or clean a stall. Melinda and Phoebe Lou were the two mainstays, Celia preferring to look after the little boys indoors. Emily was sewing now for outsiders whenever she could get a dress to make.

April brought a draft.

Jeremiah announcing at the table he was going to the court-house to witness the drawing caused Sarah to remark: "I don't wish harm to a soul but I could almost hope that smart Aleck of a Cady Bedson would get called."

When Jeremiah got back at night and said, "Well, Ma, you got your wish about Cady Bedson," Sarah almost turned pale with the responsibility of what she had done.

"Yes, sir . . . when the wheel turned three times and the little blindfolded draft boy pulled out a paper, the clerk took it and read 'Cady Bedson.' "

"When will Cady have to go?" Suzanne asked.

"He ain't goin'," Jeremiah laughed wryly. "He got ahead

of you there, Ma. Three-quarters of one minute after his name
was read he pulled a sack of gold pieces out of his pocket and
calls out as big as life, 'Which one of you fellows wants
this?' ''

"Who took it?''

"Yes, who's his substitute, Pa?''

"A man on the north prairie with a wife and two young'uns
said he would go, and he guessed now his children would
have shoes this winter and something to eat.''

April too brought Rand and Alf back, discharged honorably
at Davenport from whence they came breezily home, their
gay boyishness and loud voices seemingly untamed and un-
subdued by Metamora and Vicksburg. As though their offspring were huge jokes they laughed uproariously at the
two fat little boys, past two now, running sturdily everywhere, still whooping occasionally, and ever anon knocking each other over with raucous glee. With a great deal
of argument the two men bet each other which was which,
went into shouts of merriment when they picked the wrong
ones.

And then Melinda and Celia, packing up the children's
things, left with Rand and Alf. Looking at the two strange
noisy men, Suzanne wondered how the girls could go away
with them. "They don't even *know* them,'' she said to
Emily.

She thought about that and other queer things. Ambrose,
Phineas, Ed, Rand, Alf, and Wayne, all Americans—all had
gone to fight other brothers, lovers, fathers, and husbands,
also American. Hating them? No, you didn't hate them,
Phineas had said—not individual ones. It was just the damn
rebel uniforms you hated, like gray lice crawling over everything. Once they shared food with some of them and twice
the pickets of both sides sat around a fire and played card
games.

If it could only be over before anything happened to Wayne.
Pictures marched across her mind day and night in one endless procession of imagined horrors. Over there to the south
and east was the unknown, too far away for one to hear the
booming of cannon or see the gaping wounds or smell the
fetid odors. But they did not escape her. To the extent that
her imagination led, she saw and smelled and heard with an
inner sensitiveness that could not evade the sights and smells
and sounds.

Let it be over before something happens to Wayne. Bring him safe home and I'll ask nothing more of life.

Thus did Suzanne daily try to bargain with God, promising blandly to free Him from other obligations if He would grant her this one boon.

CHAPTER 37

BUT God was not to be bargined with, not to be cajoled into favoring Suzanne Martin on the river road above other praying women.

Lockwood, Wayne, wounded, died

It was May. Suzanne told herself dully in those long hours alone down by the slough that this was no surprise. All the time she had known it was to be. All the time she had prayed, she had felt the prayer could not be granted. It was too fine a thing to come to pass, too perfect.

When the news came there was not so much the shock of what it was, as that now it was happening. That sensitive inner sight had made her know this was to come some day, prepared her to meet it, so that when it arrived she could only think: "Here it is. It has caught up with me. Now it has happened."

People cried when near and dear ones died. But she could not cry. And of what avail would tears be? Could they bring back Wayne from the battle-field or open the closed door of her heart?

The family had never known that there was anything between them unless perchance by guessing so. They did not talk about him. For that she was grateful. She could not have borne any discussion of the wound or the death or the coming disposition of his farm land. The cabin stood empty waiting for the father from the east who did not arrive. Mr. Wallace Akin planted late corn there and the Emersons turned their stock into the pastures.

Once in the deepening prairie twilight she rode up to the cabin, pushed open the door, and slipped inside, waiting there in the shadows. So plainly could she see Wayne standing there, tall and stalwart, that she knew God had been a little kind to her after all. In the cruelty of taking Wayne away He had left her something, given an added keenness to an already imaginative mind. Always she would be able to recreate Wayne with a clarity as strong as though he stood before her. Not so clear were the daguerreotypes or the new ambrotypes as this vivid picture she could make for herself. It was as though in taking him away, God had tried to soften the blow, had done all He could to help. For that she was grateful.

For a time she stood there, crushed, submissive to God's will that this had happened. Then suddenly, thinking of what might have been had Wayne lived to come home, she threw off her meekness of spirit, cried aloud that this tragedy was so, railed at a God who permitted wars and destruction and death, filled the empty cabin with her accusations to Him and her angry sobbing, so that a passer-by, had there been one then, might have heard the loud wailing.

But it did no good. She had pounded upon God's breast with her clenched fists, but He had not cared. All your tears and all your lamentations can accomplish not one thing, she told herself dully. There is nothing but silence afterward, a hollow silence from which there returns only the echo of your wild weeping. All the women of all the wars had railed and cried out in their anguish as she railed and cried out, but it had meant nothing. Down the world they had come weeping. And the fighting went on. It was impossible to stop it, futile to shed a single tear.

She slipped down to the floor in apathetic surrender, her anger gone like a great summer storm which passes, sweeping the prairie land clean of dust and dirt and grime, but leaving it beaten, too, and very quiet.

For a time she sat so, huddled against the inside of the cabin door. Then she dried her tear-soaked face, went out, and mounted old Jupiter, walking him all the way down the lane road toward home.

When almost there she heard Phoebe Lou calling: "Su . . . zanne!"

"Here I am."

"We're ready . . . to pick . . . the chickens . . . can . . . you . . . come?"

Some old memory stirred, one of those quick mental contacts by which one connects a moment of the present with a lost moment of the past. Out of the long-gone days she suddenly remembered tearing over the prairie on one of the horses, Phoebe Lou calling her to come to the berry-picking. How queer to recall it to-night. The prairie had been unfenced then. Now it was all fenced up and down the river road and the lane. She and Phoebe Lou had been very young and girlish and full of laughter. Now they were grown women. And both had lost their men. She and Phoebe Lou would live now only in a world of work—and memories.

A few memories!

CHAPTER 38

THE summer of 1864 was long and hot. News from the south was not encouraging. The armies of the north were not gaining as rapidly as had been hoped by all. Sherman in command of the division of the Mississippi, they heard, was laying waste the country, destroying railroads, ordering the rails twisted so they could never be used again, burning corn and cotton and countless bridges, but nothing was coming to a head. Every one thought when Grant had been given chief command that he would wind things up in a hurry, but apparently Grant was not any more able to put an end to it than Halleck had been.

There was a great deal of argument about it. All summer. Jeremiah and Horace Akin fought the war across the stake-and-rider fence that separated their fields, the latter finding fault always with Grant and his slow ways, Jeremiah sticking up for him. "He's got things up his sleeve neither one of us knows," he told the women folks.

"What, not even you, Pa!" Sarah said acridly, having seen him stand so long by the fence while his team cropped prairie grass near-by. And strange as it was, every one felt a relief to hear Ma speak so. It was more natural than the quiet way she had been this summer.

If the weather was hot in the Valley it must have been intolerably so "down there," every one said. Letters home told of a bad drought, of suffocating clouds of dust surrounding the troops always. There was great loss of life. Soldiers were worn out. News after Petersburg the last of July was especially disheartening with all those four thousand killed. Word got back that the old Third Regiment was so reduced in members that the survivors reënlisted and consolidated with the Second Infantry.

Every one immediately connected with the family, except Ambrose, was home now, so the selfish interest in the war news was materially lessened, but no one thought of that when the papers came or the bulletin boards announced new deaths. The Valley's loss was every one's sorrow.

Rand and Alf were back in their great corn-fields on the other side of the river, and two big new houses were going up for them. Melinda's was on the south side of·the road and Celia's on the north where they sat eying each other in brooding silence, as though at the close of each day one gingerbread-trimmed house could not bear that the other had added a porch or a cupola.

Phineas was working for Pa, sometimes swaggering and whistling, and sometimes unable to conceal the bitterness in his heart, his blue shirt-sleeve pinned to his side and the lines draped awkwardly around his shoulder while he handled the team as best he could. Once he took the fiddle down from the wall, and after pulling off the gray calico bag, stood there snapping the strings with his one hand.

But Ambrose was still in the thick of it—in Tupelo, Mississippi, was the last word that came to Jeanie carrying his letters and laughing girlishly when he wrote for her not to speak to any of the men neighbors on aught but business.

Ed Armitage and Wayne Lockwood would never come back.

Phoebe Lou talked about Ed sometimes when they all sat around the stoop in the early evening after the dishes were done and the milk attended to. Once or twice when she got to recalling something funny he had done she laughed hard at the telling, forgetting for the moment that he would never cut any of those high-jinks again.

But Suzanne never mentioned Wayne's name. She was quiet when she was at work, listless in those few moments when she rested, and at both times looked out upon the world with complete apathy. It was as though she were the shell of something from which life had fled. It communicated itself to the others, so that they, too, grew quiet and listless. Only Todo was noisy and excited over trivia—lightning-bugs, the croak of the distant frogs, heat-lightning, a night-hawk swooping low with its malicious *boom boom*—"darting about from one thing to another for all the world like Ed Armitage used to do," Sarah said, as though the boy were doomed for life. Henry and Lucy's boy, Harry, was about the same age, but a quiet little chap, more given to making miniature roads and fences of sticks in the driveway than tearing about noisily like his cousin.

Often when they all sat out there together, talking over the war or river road news or national events, neighbors would drive in, or town friends from Prairie Rapids and Sturgis Falls, seeing them there, stop in passing. They would all jump up hospitably, ready to go for glasses of fresh cider or cold buttermilk drawn from the deep shelf in the well, bring chairs from the house and another brush for whacking mosquitoes. Rarely a warm evening went by without some one's team tied to the outside hitching-post or to the ring in the stable.

Sometimes when company came and the others launched out into their old-time way of talking and laughing, Suzanne would slip away and go down by the gate where the horse-shoes hung on the chain and look up the lane road, as though there she might see a horse and rider, or catch, perhaps, a wild sweet strain of singing in the moonlight.

One September evening Cady Bedson, driving past with his spanking bays, pulled up short when he saw Suzanne at the gateway to tell her Atlanta had fallen. Then suddenly in a show of warm interest he wanted to know if she wouldn't like to drive over to Sturgis Falls with him to her sister's while he transacted some grain business with Tom Bostwick.

When Suzanne thanked him but said for an excuse she wasn't ready, he hitched the team and came in, talking to the others while Emily and Phoebe Lou insisted that she change her dress and go.

It turned out to be rather pleasant riding up the river road behind the high-stepping bays and cooling off in the humid summer night, to surprise Sabina and have a chance to visit with her while the two men talked. Then they all went over to see the skeleton of the new house that was going up for Tom and Sabina. It stood there like a huge thing of white bones stripped of all flesh, the uprights looking ghostly in the moonlight. They walked around through the forest of studding and Cady Bedson took Suzanne's arm protectingly whenever they approached loose flooring or the stairway opening.

Going home Cady put his hand over on Suzanne's, drawing the high-stepping bays down to a walk. She told herself she ought to pull away so he would know she didn't like it, but after all what difference did it make? So far as her feelings were concerned he might as well have laid his hat on her hand.

When they were nearly to the school-house there on the river road Cady said, "You're a very fine woman, Suzanne, pleasant-tempered and pretty, too. I wonder . . ." he laughed a bit sheepishly at the confession, "I wonder I never noticed it much before."

When she made no comment, not caring what he thought one way or the other, he said: "There's something I'd like to ask you, Suzanne. Were you betrothed to Wayne Lockwood?"

The night was bursting into a thousand brittle pieces around her, the stars and the dark trees of the timber-line and the faintly outlined school-house all breaking into infinitesimal bits that one could never put together again.

Betrothed? What could she say to that but the truth which was no truth at all. For how could she separate the facts from the fancy? Or the dream from the real?

"No," she said in a peculiarly thin voice so that Cady, thinking she was provoked at the inference, said he didn't mean anything much by it and hoped she wouldn't believe him just curious.

The family joked her at breakfast. "Well . . . Cady Bedson! That *is* a beau for you, Suzanne." Jeremiah was jovial, glad to see his girl have this attention.

"Thirty-two years old if he's a day, Suzanne." Phoebe Lou was bubbling at the prospect of romance. "A town old bach, too, *and* a money-maker."

Emily looked narrowly at her through the steam from the tea-kettle.

Sarah sniffed. "Been taking awful good care of his own hide, though, I must say."

Jeremiah said nothing to that. The truth was he *would* have been ashamed if he had been Cady Bedson—unmarried, no responsibilities, and yet he had never volunteered, hiring a substitute to go when his name was drawn that time in the draft.

In October Ambrose Willshire came home, too, mustered out, his three years of enlistment over, only a long healed flesh wound on his leg like a red badge of bravery. Every one had to admit that Ambrose had conducted himself well, but even Jeanie dropped her eyes away from those of the family when he said he had been perhaps the best soldier in the company, doing his duty unsparingly, and a guide and model for others. Neither could she look at them for the hurt when he told them he had been disappointed with Jeanie's management while he was gone—

she should not have sold the cow she did, nor let the pig-raising stop, and she ought to have seen that more prairie hay was cut for winter feed.

Jeremiah was full of election talk these days. It did not seem possible that the country would "swap horses in the middle of a stream," but people wanted peace. Would they be led astray by wishful thinking that McClellan could bring it about more quickly? Every one was sick to death of the dragging out of hostilities, the fatalities, the news of the hardships of union prisoners, the drain of feeding the confederate ones. Certain people felt that something could be done to get it over. It made him feel personally responsible to rally all the votes for Lincoln he could.

Cady Bedson stopped often at the Martins' now on his way over to see Tom Bostwick. He always asked Suzanne if she didn't want to go along with him, and Suzanne would get ready and go. What difference did it make whether one went or stayed at home?

In November with the roads frozen into hard ruts and stalks brown and broken in the corn-fields, Cady and Suzanne rode home from Sabina's where Cady had talked grain-buying with Tom, and Suzanne had listened for the most part to Sabina's animated comparison of the virtues of oak, cherry, and walnut wood for the rooms of the new house.

When he drove into the yard and up to the lean-to where a candle burned in the window for Suzanne, Cady said: "Suzanne, I admired you very much in the summer. Then my admiration turned to affection and I am sure now it is something more. Will you do me the honor to be my wife?"

And Suzanne, whose world now was a real one in which nothing stirred her pulses or gave her throat any throbbing for either its sorrows or its joys, said quietly: "Why, yes, Cady, I suppose I could if you want me to."

No one in the family was greatly surprised when Suzanne without excitement told them the news. Phoebe Lou said that the minute Cady Bedson stopped by the gate that night and waited for Suzanne to drive over to Sturgis Falls, she knew how it would turn out. Emily offered to start sewing at once. There would be sheets, pillow-cases, and table-cloths to be hemmed, a wedding dress, petticoats, and chemises to be made. The winter would be more than busy for the soldiers' supplied must not be neglected.

When Cady wanted to be married at once, Suzanne said no, she must complete her year's teaching just as she promised.

"The next promise is for me, then," Cady said. "In the spring . . . you promise?"

"When school is out."

"Your word of honor?"

"When I promise anything"—and the words brought back a queer sensation of a blurring stove and half-moons of snow in the windows and Carlie Scott in a velvet bonnet—"It is my word of honor."

Almost on top of this announcement to the family came another, and no more astonishing thing could have happened. Phoebe Lou had been gone over to Akins' all day to help with the work and Horace Akin drove her home. She came into the lean-to where Emily was washing dishes, Sarah setting bread, and Suzanne slicing ham for the next morning.

She took a drink of water from the pail as though to spar for time and then she faced them. The dimple was showing at the corner of her mouth and in spite of her twenty-six years she looked very young. "Well, folks," she said, "I won't be living with you any more, I guess." And while they stood and stared, she laughed girlishly. "I'm going to marry Mr. Horace Akin. How will you like me for a neighbor, Ma, over in the big Scott house?"

"Good land!" Sarah spilled some hot water. "With that *stairway*?"

"Why, Phoebe Lou"—Suzanne was half aware of the poor taste of what she was to say—"I'm just remembering something . . . the night you . . . you left for Colorado . . . Mr. Akin saying before every one he'd always liked you best."

Phoebe Lou laughed out loud at that. "He remembered that, too."

Suzanne pondered a good deal about it that night. If a girl loves some one deeply, can she love again? Apparently Phoebe Lou could, although Mr. Akin was nearly old enough to be her father. She thought of Phoebe Lou and Ed, their hasty wedding so they could start west with the Gainses, Phoebe Lou's letter, "as long as I have Ed and he has me," how broken up she was at his death, saying life was over. It was all very confusing, perhaps even a little comforting that one could learn in time to have some affection.

And then, as though these two big events in the old log-and-frame house were not enough for that fall, Jeremiah was ordered by Governor Kirkwood to join the army near Atlanta, Georgia, and bring back to Des Moines the ballots of the Iowa contingent of soldiers.

They were all amazed and excited at the news, but frightened, too. That meant going right into the hotbed of the war. Why, Hood's forces, though scattered, were still not far from Atlanta. Jeff Davis had just bragged that Sherman would be driven back by the cavalry and harassed until like Napoleon he'd have to escape with a body-guard.

But there was no room for fear in Jeremiah's mind. He was unaccountably pleased at the honor, and scoffed at the women folks' talk of its dangers. All this time he had wanted deeply to do something more than these home duties of helping to get enlistments, seeing to widows and orphans, shipping hospital supplies. And here it was, an honorable and important appointment from Governor Kirkwood.

"Pa, you're most sixty-four . . ." Sarah began.

And before he could answer, Emily, Phoebe Lou, and Suzanne were saying in chorus: "And old enough to begin to have some horse-sense," going into their first hearty laughter for a long time because they were all simultaneously remembering what Pa always said.

The day he left, Suzanne was recalling that first trip to Des Moines seven years before and how he rode off into the snow, on Queen. This time he was leaving for the east on the steam-cars right from Sturgis Falls.

Some things had certainly changed. But one had not— Pa's dependability. The governor had appointed Pa to get the soldiers' votes. Well, he had chosen the right man. Looking at his square shoulders, undrooping for all their sixty-three years, and his strong face above its crisp, lightly flecked, black beard, Suzanne felt a swift moisture come to her eyes, said to herself as though she had just made a discovery, "Why, I can *feel* things again. I can feel pride in Pa and faith in him, and I always shall."

Mr. Akin and Phoebe Lou lost no time in being married.

"Trust widowers," Sarah said. "None of this 'We'll be married a year from next New Year's Day' for them."

The day of their marriage, Phineas joked at breakfast about Phoebe Lou getting two men before Emily and Suzanne could get one, but stopped when he saw Emily turn a brick color down to the collar of her gray print dress.

Mr. Akin came for Phoebe Lou in his high-wheeled buggy, and she went away with him looking very young and pretty in a little brown butter-bowl hat with a flat bow on it and the brown dress Emily had made over hastily from her own best one.

"But what will *you* do for a best dress?" Phoebe Lou had questioned.

"Never you mind about me," Emily had turned it off. "You're not going to get married in your black widow's dress, I know that; I'll make me one out of oak leaves— the red and brown ones—pin 'em together with twigs like we girls used to do."

So Phoebe Lou kissed her, and the demonstration was so sudden and unusual that Emily hid her emotion with, "Here, get away from me—I ain't your old whiskery widower."

When they came back from the preacher's over at Prairie Rapids, Mr. Akin lifted Todo high on his shoulder and said, "How'd you like to go away with me and be my boy?" And Todo, who in his short three and a half years had always preferred to do something different than the thing he had been doing the previous five minutes, agreed speedily and noisily to the change.

After they had gone and the house was strangely quiet, the little boy's cyclonic-like activities seemed suddenly to have left a void that could never be filled. When Emily came down the loft ladder her nose was red, and Phineas and the three women ate supper as though there had been a funeral.

Emily made herself a dress out of Phoebe Lou's mourning one, and a long time later when she went to buy herself some new goods, she said she supposed folks would think she was trying to be young and gay if she went back to any other color, so she just bought black.

CHAPTER 39

A S Jeremiah had disappeared into the snowy oblivion of the southwest when he went to the first legislature, so now he disappeared into the war-torn southeast.

One short letter came back, and no more. Apparently all communication was stopped. No Prairie Rapids or Sturgis Falls family was receiving word of any kind from its soldier. All the Valley companies were swallowed by some gigantic and devastating animal, and Jeremiah was swallowed with them. No one could surmise just what was happening to them. The suspense was nerve-breaking. Even those days of bad news seemed now to have been more easily borne than this long period of silence so peculiar and disturbing. Suzanne said it was like those days in summer when the prairie storms were brewing and the silence scared you more than the later crashing of the storm.

November dragged by, cold and dark and awesome. December entered, awesome and dark and cold. What was taking place? And where was Pa, nearly sixty-four years old, carrying his canvas bag to get the soldiers' votes?

That honor which had come to him and about which he had been so proud was far less an honor than a horrible nightmare to the family on the river road. Sometimes Sarah scolded about him accepting the duty, said that Pa was always snapping at outside jobs like a catfish taking bait. But sometimes the scolding ceased and she looked as pinched and white-lipped as a frightened child.

Emily bent all her energies toward sewing for Suzanne, sat much of the time by the new Howe double-thread sewing-machine in the main room under a cabin window or puckered her forehead over some fine handiwork by the glass lamp or candle-light.

And Suzanne? Oh, Suzanne was very quiet and matter-of-fact. She looked no more up the lane road where a cabin stood deserted on the prairie or listened for a horseman to ride singing in the moonlight. She lived only in the world of reality, a very commonplace world in which one hemmed sheets and pieced quilts for a strange man who had said he wanted to marry her.

For the three women living there together through that gray November and December there were countless hard tasks. Phineas was their mainstay, attending slowly and grimly to the milk, wood, and water, but he could not shovel hard-packed snow, try as he might. And on those days when Henry was overworked or took the long cold ride back and forth to Prairie Rapids with wood, Suzanne and Emily had to bundle up and help do the chores.

Sometimes Mr. Akin brought Phoebe Lou over through the snow-drifts to spend the afternoon piecing quilts or sewing for the soldiers, and then the girls would send for Lucy, so that the vociferous Todo might have meek little Harry upon which to let off some of the extra steam in his system. But they did not see much of Sabina, bustling and busy with her war work and her cherry wood, oak, and walnut, nor of Melinda and Celia over on the prairie the other side of the river, nor of Jeanie at home with Ambrose and the three little girls.

On those afternoons with the big logs crackling in the main room and the quilt pieces all about, with Emily jumping up to set out a plate of sorghum cookies and make cambric tea because no one could afford the other with its huge tax, drawn together as the women were with anxiety about Pa, Suzanne felt a measure of relaxation from the tenseness of her own nerves, a semblance of resignation to this world of reality which held nothing that the other one had given. And when she heard Phoebe Lou laughing girlishly, the dimple at the corner of her mouth showing, telling about a joke she played on Mr. Akin, or bragging a bit smugly over living in the Scott house, she wondered if it could be possible that she, too, would some day laugh and brag as easily as Phoebe Lou who had once loved Ed Armitage so deeply.

And then suddenly out of the silence came word by the new telegraph that Sherman who had been in Atlanta so many weeks had accomplished what he set out to do. In all those days when no one knew what was going on he had been marching his forces clear through to the sea. He reported that he had a present for Lincoln and the present was Savannah. It was a big victory and a decisive one, the papers said, for it cut the confederate army into several parts. But what about Pa? Was he all right? Had he been in Atlanta all this time? Or with the soldiers in the thick of things? If he had been with them could it be that . . . ? No one would say it. And Pa always pulled through somehow. Did this mean he could get back now? Or what?

And then an answer to all the questioning and all the anxious hours came in a letter from him postmarked New York. New York! Sarah sat down heavily in a barrel chair. Think of Pa getting back to York State after all these years. He'd promised her they'd go back together sometime. And now he was there without her. Even before she read the letter, now that Pa was safe, she began to think just what a good piece of her mind she would give him when he got home.

The letter said he had got caught like a weasel in a barn-yard trap with Sherman's army and had to go along with them to the sea. There was no way left to get north but to fly, and that was one thing, in spite of all the inventions, humans would never get to do until they turned into angels. But he had pulled through and was here in New York ready to take the cars west and deliver the soldiers' votes. Guessed he would get there just under the wire like an old race-horse coming in.

He would go by way of Davenport to Iowa City on the cars and hoped the staging from Iowa City to Des Moines would not be too awful bad. He would have many things to relate upon his return. He was their obedient servant.

Wasn't that just like Pa, the girls said. Dependable! Sent to get the votes and no telling what all had happened, and yet there he was ready to bring them.

And then rather surprisingly, later, a letter from Des Moines.

Here he was in Des Moines, had pulled through again all right, had delivered the soldiers' votes in time for the counting. He would be home soon after the letter—he hoped to eat Sunday dinner with them—and would have enough to talk about for the rest of his life. As usual he would have to go around Robin Hood's barn to get home and it did look as though there ought to be a railroad right up the Red Cedar Valley. The Illinois Central coming out from Dubuque to Sturgis Falls had just about *made* the Valley. But folks wanted to go north and south these days as well as back east. He hoped they would get this letter before he got there himself and he was their obedient servant.

The weather turned mild. Snow began to thaw and the cabin dropped four-foot icicles maliciously on any entering or departing inmates.

Stages had no schedule. They came in when they could get across slushy creeks and up muddy hills. If Jeremiah had not arrived by Saturday night they could not hope to see anything of him in time for the dinner planned by Sarah and the two girls for Sunday, with all the children coming home. But a Saturday stage arriving with tired muddy horses did not bring him. Sarah said with unusual display of emotion that it took the heart right out of the big family dinner.

So every one was there Sunday but the very person whom they had all come to see. The weather was so coy, with roads half mud and half snow, mild thawing temperatures in January, winter seemingly sparring with spring, that all arriving said they had been "put to it" to decide what to ride on, runners or wheels.

Tom Bostwick and Sabina, deciding in favor of spring, came in their nice buggy, so that Nora and Jeanie's little girls played enthusiastically and grandly under its top all afternoon. Phoebe Lou and her new husband came in a two-seated carriage with Todo and Mr. Akin's two boys, thinking that the long road down to the Scott place might be a regular river by night. Although Horace Akin was to reside there for thirty years, it was always to be referred to as the old Scott place.

When they came in Horace Akin said, half apologetically: "I didn't know about bringing my boys . . . told them I wasn't sure whether they could rightfully lay any claim to Martin reunions or not."

And Emily, seeing the boys stand back bashfully by the woodbox, wiped her hot freckled face on her apron, put an arm around each of their shoulders, and said: "Boys, I'll tell you . . . when the Akins have a reunion, you're all Akin, but when the Martins have one, then you're *Martin*."

Jeanie and Ambrose Willshire and their three little girls came in a lumber wagon-box on bobs with the wheels piled in the end of the box. Jeanie had laughed merrily at Ambrose for suggesting such a thing, thinking he could not be meaning it, but because of her laughter he had been obliged to put her in her place by carrying out his idea. When they drove up and every one laughed, too, at the sight of the wheels, Jeanie was embarrassed and tried to cover it and Ambrose's anger by saying gaily: "Oh, we thought there was nothing like taking time by the fetlock."

"I wish you wouldn't talk nonsense." Ambrose frowned. "I suppose you mean forelock."

"Yes." Jeanie flushed again. "That was just a joke, Ambrose."

Alf Banninger and Celia with their little boy came dashing into the yard, splashing mud and slush all over their shining new cutter. A few minutes later Rand and Melinda with *their* little boy came dashing in, splashing slush and mud all over *their* shining new cutter. Rand and Melinda had started in an old buggy, but seeing Alf and Celia ahead of them in the new cutter, had turned around hastily and gone back home to make a feverish change of vehicles, with Rand saying no one in Sturgis Falls was going to see Alf drive through town in a better rig than his.

Cady Bedson came from Prairie Rapids. Henry and Lucy with Nora and little Harry came over, each carrying his own chair.

"It used to be bad enough when we were all home unmarried," Celia said, "but now with husbands and all the stairstep youngsters we look like a regular multitude waiting to be fed."

"Just so there's more than two loaves and five fishes," Jeanie laughed.

"*Five* loaves and *two* fishes," Ambrose corrected her. "I wish you'd get things right once in your life."

But there was an abundance to eat. Trust the Martin girls for that. Emily and Suzanne and their mother had chickens and biscuits, and great mounds of mashed potatoes like white volcanoes down whose sides molten lava trickled in the form of Sarah's yellow butter. There was steamed dried squash, creamed dried corn, wild grape jam and wild plum jelly, and so many mince pies that they covered one of the buttery shelves and from whose presence Suzanne shooed a whole flock of youngsters, giving answer to her query of what they were doing there by saying, "Nothin' . . . just smellin'."

Sarah got out a fresh roll of butter with the scallops made in such regular formation by her wooden paddle that they looked like the symmetrical overlapping scales of a fish. Sabina brought two cakes which were a treat to those who had not used light sugar during most of the war years. Phoebe Lou brought a crock of vinegar cabbage and a boiled smoked ham. Melinda and Celia both brought pickles. Alf had got it out of Rand surreptitiously that Melinda was going to bring some of her first prize green tomato pickles, so Celia brought some of her first prize watermelon ones, each girl ever and anon jockeying her own contribution to better advantage on the long table.

Henry's wife contributed some of her nice white bread and twisted fried cakes. Jeanie was apologetic for her Indian pudding, just steamed corn-meal that way, but she explained she couldn't think of anything else nice and appetizing to bring, so that Emily whispered to her mother in the buttery, "That's Ambrose for you," and Sarah hissed back, "Horned toad!"

Cady Bedson brought the grandest treat of all, a dozen oranges, shipped up from Florida to a Prairie Rapids grocery. Suzanne cut them in two and piled them in the center of the long table, pyramid fashion, so that they were like a summer sun to whose yellow radiance all the children's eyes turned constantly.

The long table was set with Sarah's best linen cloths, worn now so thin in spots that Emily said there was more darn than damask.

At the side there was a smaller table made with boards and sawhorses for eight children ranging from long-legged nine-year-old Nora to Melinda's and Celia's three-year-old boys whose cousinly activities consisted for the most part in attempting to push in each other's stomachs. At Emily's insistence, the two Akin boys were listed as adults and so seated. Emily and Lucy were to wait on the big table, Suzanne on the children. But the family reunion could not be counted complete in any sense of the word without its head.

Dinner was "dished up," called, and with much joking and scraping of chairs the company assembled. Tom Bostwick, an elder now in the new Presbyterian Church, asked the blessing much more fluently than Jeremiah would have done, but every one missed Pa's mumbling into his beard: "Bless this food to Thy glory."

The dishes went around and around. There was an uninterrupted flow of talk, as always, like grackles in the maples. The war. The time it would yet drag out. Criticism of Sherman's destruction and upholding him. Criticism of Grant's slowness and support for his actions. Recipes—whether to let salt-rising bread get as warm as potato-bread. Celia said the best yeast was started with two quarts of hot water on two tablespoons of hops. Melinda stuck it out for the water to be put on the hops only lukewarm, so that Rand and Alf stopped their war talk to take sides.

"Hark! What's that?" Sarah said, spatting her hands together to quiet the crowd so she could hear.

A stomping—pounding—scraping!

The lean-to door swung open and there stood Jeremiah with his flowered carpet-bag in his hand, gray shawl on his arm, cap pushed back, his pants, soaking wet, tucked into boots that were muddy to the tops.

Pa had said he'd be here. Well, here he was.

They shouted in unison:

"For goodness sake, Pa, that you or your ghost?"

"How'd you get here?"

Todo ran and embraced the muddy boots with ruinous effect to his new suit.

Every one wanted to get up at once to make a place for the new-comer. Gone were the surmises and arguments about Sherman and Grant and hop water. Pa had been to the seat of the war and was safely back. He was the center of attraction, the most important member of the reunion—just now of the whole Valley, maybe the state, for all they knew.

"A big shame we didn't wait dinner."

"Did you see Sherman?"

"Get him his bootjack, Emily."

"I bet you haven't had a bite . . ."

"When'll the war be over?"

"Here's clean water, Pa, to wash."

"Want I should get you dry socks, Pa?"

It was so very noisy. But he liked it. By granny, he liked it! Home. Food. Shelter. Warmth. Sarah. The children. The children's children. A welcome. Laughter. Approbation. Joking. News to tell. The center of everything.

Well, it was like this. He got a chance to drive with a Des Moines man to Cedar Rapids, long hard drive, snow, mud, slush, bad creeks, narrow wood roads. Horses about tuckered. Stayed two nights on the way. Thought he could get the stage from Cedar Rapids up the Valley, but no, it had pulled out. Never felt so bad. Didn't know whether to cry or cuss. Decided neither would get you home. Started out to walk. Got a ride part of the way with a man in a lumber wagon. Had to start walking again. Stayed last night with folks on the prairie, then started out. Got to the creek and no way to get over but to plunge through. Put his coat and satchel up on a forked stick held high, and come through icy water to his waist. Was overtook by a man on horseback luckily leading another horse coming to Prairie Rapids. Man told him he could ride the extra one. Strapped his bag on the mare and finished the trip to Prairie Rapids. Inquired for Cady Bedson, thinking he could ride out with him. Found he had already gone. So started out hoofing it again. Preacher Eberhardt come along driving to Sturgis Falls to a meeting. Said not many families give four boys to the war and a chaplain besides.

Old Jeremiah, nearly sixty-four, his crisp black locks and his crisp black whiskers sprinkled lightly now with frost that would never melt, soon sat at the head of the long table, sometimes unable to talk for eating, sometimes unable to eat for talking. And with so much to tell! No, a lifetime would not be long enough.

Yes, he'd found the boys out of Atlanta. Got the votes, like they already knew. The city was burning when they left. No way to get back. First thing he knew he was sucked into a great march to the south.

"The burnin' was awful. Explodin' shells and magazines and the flames all night. It was like you imagine hell."

"Hush, Pa!"

"Why . . . what?"

"That word . . . the children."

"The children better know it. Right now! So they'll grow up knowin' it's just like hell and we'll never have another." He pointed with his knife toward the small table. "Boys as little as them two of Celia's and Melinda's always hearin' it's worse'n hell will grow up level-headed and peaceful."

The two little boys, noting suddenly that they were the center of interest, embarrassed at the turning of many heads, their grandfather's loud voice and pointing knife, began pushing each other's stomachs in vigorously and adding a few gestures of hair-clutching for good measure, so that the effectiveness of Jeremiah's observations on peace was materially lessened by the ensuing laughter.

He could not answer questions fast enough. The whole résumé was disconnected memories of various happenings, every one of which led suddenly to another. Yes, they had gone about three hundred miles from Atlanta. Cut off from supplies . . . from any communication as though they'd been in an African jungle. Just a few supplies at the start that soon give out. Had to feed on the country as they marched.

"Then what about the southerners themselves?"

Jeremiah threw out his big hands expressively. "That's *war* for you."

Worst was out of Savannah when they got down to an ear of corn a day, even though all the time transports with supplies were out there offshore. Some of the boys stole the corn from the mules. You could hear their hungry braying—the mules, he meant, not the boys. He himself rode part of the way . . . bareheaded . . . had lost his hat. Never had anything on his head until he got to New York. Somebody got him a horse some'ers.

All the time, the fifteenth of November to December tenth, they plodded along. He saw foraging, pillaging, burning, some of the boys stealing—that's what war is. Guessed he couldn't tell Phineas and Ambrose, Alf and Rand anything they didn't know a'ready. Henry and Cady though couldn't hardly imagine it. Then on the tenth there was a new sound you hadn't heard before. They'd got clean to the sea. Found out that Admiral Dahlgren was standin' out there with his fleet and supplies. Never knew for sure just what happened or who did it, but word trickled in some way that some of our men paddled down the river at night skulkin' around in the reeds, hid out all day, and the next night signaled a gunboat, and finally got the dispatch to Dahlgren that we'd got through from Atlanta. The boys captured Fort McAllister—that was below Savannah. Then Savannah itself. A transport steamed north with wounded and to get more supplies. By a note from the general it took on old Jeremiah Martin and his carpet-bag of votes and''—he stopped and winked at the old bag hanging on the lean-to wall so that all eyes followed his—''about three thousand dollars of Ioway soldiers' money.''

''Oh, Pa . . . *three thousand dollars*!''

''In the old carpet-bag?''

''You don't say . . . !''

It was as though the Bank of England hung there on the wall.

Yes, all that money was in the old carpet-bag which—he chuckled in the telling—he would throw under a depot bench or a car seat with assumed carelessness, giving an extra kick to it to show how valueless it was, but never taking his eye off it once.

For an hour or more they lingered at the table. And all the time Jeremiah was talking about the great white homes they had passed, the devastated country, the Savannah harbor, and the way Grant had been keeping Lee pestered so he could not send any soldiers south.

And all the time he was talking, something else lay back

there behind the conversation. A voice like the voice of a prairie preacher shouted that these things he was saying were not the important ones to this family. All the afternoon he guarded that secret place in his mind as a man guards a fractious animal that it may not break out and do harm.

Not now. Not here. Sometime later, he reminded himself constantly.

Always in the whole big crowd his eyes under their shaggy black brows sought out Suzanne, noted her sweet patience and tact with the children, the quiet way with the girls and Sarah, wondered if it were true that she was not laughing as easily as she used to, or his imagination, questioned just what to do or say about the thing that lay prisoner behind the bars of his mind. She was the prettiest of all his girls, he believed. Or maybe that was because she was so fresh and young. They had all been good-looking girls. Well, Ma had been a pretty girl, too. Suzanne was light on her feet, moved with grace, and her gray-blue eyes always brightened and darkened at every change of mood. As a little girl you could always tell how she felt by looking in her eyes. They told so plainly whether she was happy or sad, hurt or interested. It had been a long time since he noticed her eyes. Later on in the day, when he could get closer to her, perhaps he could see and read them. But, no, that was a foolish thought. She was no longer a little girl. She had grown up and was going to marry Cady Bedson. Everything was all right. Even so, he would set a watch on himself, feel his way more carefully.

The remainder of the afternoon was one long dish-washing séance for the women, one long talk of war for the men. Jeremiah, holding forth in the main room, told more about his experiences, with one of the girls darting in every few minutes, a dish and towel in her hand, to hear what he was saying. The dishes were scarcely done before it was time to get lunch again, for the men must leave early for chores.

"Must be pretty nice to live in town and have just one cow," they said enviously to Tom Bostwick. And not one of them who said it would have taken a town house and lot as a gift if they had been obliged to move there.

The women set out the left-over food and every one walked around to get what they wanted. There was no blessing. It was as though the Lord excused you from that service because you had to wait on yourself.

As soon as they had finished, all began leaving hurriedly. Phoebe Lou, Horace Akin, and Todo left, and the Akin boys who, feeling quite initiated now into the noisy Martin clan, said daringly, "Good-by, *Aunt* Emily," and ran as fast as they could to the carriage. Sabina and Tom Bostwick left in the buggy after dumping the little girls out unceremoniously from their canopy-topped playhouse. Jeanie and Ambrose Willshire and the children pulled out on the runners again after Ambrose had blamed Jeanie for having him bring the wheels. Henry and Lucy with the two children went over home. Phineas rode away. Alf and Rand each told his wife to get the youngster bundled up so that when he drove by the lean-to door she'd be ready to hop in and not let the other couple get a head start. But as both girls were expecting additions to the family, neither one could hop with any degree of agility.

After they were all gone, Suzanne and Cady Bedson decided to drive to Sturgis Falls to church. Suzanne looked pretty in the new cape Emily had made her. It was very full and came to the bottom of her dress, the collar trimmed with the fur from the otter Phineas had caught at the slough's edge, using his foot to help open the trap.

Jeremiah, Sarah, and Emily! Just these three were left now. Such a little group after so many. How quiet it was after so much commotion! Emily told her mother she was going up to bed, that she was as tired as a dog but liked to see the family all together. Instead of getting into bed, though, she sat at the loft window and looked out at the moonlight. It was chilly but she pulled a thick padded comfort around her and sat there all evening, looking across the prairie.

Sarah set bread. They had just about eaten her out of house and home. She didn't begrudge food to a single one of them, but nothing would have pleased her more than to be able to slip a little ipecac into Ambrose Willshire's.

Jeremiah put on his old cap and went out to the stable. It was moonlight and very still. Mild, too, for middle of winter. Could almost imagine it was April with the smell of loam coming over the prairie. He sniffed at the barn odors—horses, cattle, hay, machine-oil, dogs, manure, harness. He liked it, an honest old smell. Better than gunpowder. He was glad to be back on the prairie with no sight of blood-soaked bandages and sick and hungry boys. But getting back could not lessen his responsibility. Up here away from it, they were still his dying boys, his gaping wounds, his own blood. He hung around the stables until Sarah, worried about him, called from the lean-to door.

"Just looking after the stock, Ma."

For once there was not a soul in sight to say it to, so she muttered to herself: "Stock's got along without him for weeks now." Pa had been home eight hours so he was no longer company.

He stayed out at the stables until the bays turned into the yard and Cady helped Suzanne out. He saw Cady bend to Suzanne a moment, saw him leave, and Suzanne, from the tree-trunk stoop, answer his wave as the horses turned out of the barnyard, bits of metal on their harness flashing in the moonlight.

He would follow her into the house and talk to her now. But Suzanne, standing quietly there on the stoop in her long cape, did not go in. Instead, she stepped down to the ground and, pulling up her skirts from the snow and puddles, picked her way down the front path to the gate.

He watched her until she stopped, and then walked down to where she stood leaning on the rails, looking across the open prairie. Before she had seen him he paused a moment to watch her. There was something disquieting about her attitude as though she were gazing up the lane road for something that was not there.

He moved then and she turned quickly. "Why, Pa! You scared me. How does it happen you're up? I though you'd be pretty tired to-night."

"Oh, not so bad. I'm a tough old piece, you know."

A breeze, more chilly after the mild day, blew her hair back from her forehead and tossed the dark ringlets at her neck so that to Jeremiah, gazing at her from under the curtain of his shaggy eyebrows, she looked strangely as she had when she was little, her neck curved, white, and babyish. Because she was the youngest, he supposed, she would always seem a little girl to him.

"It was a good thing you made it back in time."

"Oh, I figgered I'd pull through." And as though he had just thought of it, he asked. "How you and Cady comin'? When you marryin'?"

"I guess the last of May, Pa. Cady can get a good rented house on the west side by the first of June."

"That'll be fine. Cady'll probably be well-to-do one of these days. Has quite a head for business deals. You're going to be happy, ain't you, Suzanne?"

"Yes. I'll be happy."

It was too acquiescent, too gently agreeable. Jeremiah,

standing there in the chill of the winter moonlight, had a feeling that he must prod her into enthusiasm. She used to be so excited over everything, her eyes so shining.

"You'll have nice things some day, I figure."

"Things." She said it with a little upward inflection as though it were half question, or, perhaps that it had no meaning.

"You will like livin' in Prairie Rapids, I bet. Much as I hate to admit it, looks to me it may catch up with Sturgis Falls one of these days and beat it in the long run." Idle, but prophetic words. It came to be in time that for sheer size a half dozen Sturgis Falls would be needed to make a Prairie Rapids.

But now to Jeremiah there was only thought of the fact that he was sounding out Suzanne, trying in his clumsy way to approach her with delicacy, tact, and understanding.

He put his big hand over her small one lying on the railing of the gate.

"Suzy, I guess I should tell you."

He hadn't called her that baby name for years. Something about the unusualness of it startled her, so that she looked into his face searchingly.

"Maybe it wa'nt necessary to wait for you to be alone. But I had no way of knowin', and comin' in as I did with all the folks there, I didn't aim to blurt it out before every one, if . . . if it meant more to you than just ordinary. The others will all be mighty glad, too. But with you . . . I didn't quite know. . . . Suzanne, Wayne Lockwood is alive."

She gazed up at him so long, the moon picking out the dark of her eyes, that he thought she had not comprehended.

"Wayne didn't die from his wound . . ." he explained patiently, disturbed at her silence and the queer expression on her face. . . . "Even though it was wrongly reported so. How or why it was so done I can't rightly explain. He succeeded in workin' his way back to our forces before the fall of Atlanta. There's been other mistakes, too, you know . . . men dead that was thought prisoners . . . or alive that was thought dead."

When she did not say anything Jeremiah went on as though he must explain the explanation. "As I say, I thought maybe I'd best tell you alone. I didn't know. I felt like a traitor not to be tellin' the others right away . . . but comin' in that way with every one there . . . Cady and all . . . I had no way of knowin' if it might upset you. Not that you've any cause to let it." His voice took on a gruff tone. He felt such unwonted tenderness for her that he must now cover it with bruskness. "No reason you should feel any more upset or any more or less glad than any of them . . . good neighbors that way. But there was a bit of talk after he went away . . . little Nora comin' home with a story . . ."

He turned to her roughly, thinking of having heard about a night in a cabin, but not wanting to speak of it. "Well, let's have it. After all, I'm your father. I've a right to know. How much was there to that cabin story? Before he ever comes back I want you to tell me this: How much was there between you and Wayne Lockwood?"

It was a long moment before she answered.

"One kiss," she said then, staring at her father as though her eyes, clinging to the homely familiarity of his face could help find anchorage there. For how could she put magic into words to a father who was asking only for realities? How could she say that every lovely thing in her life had been between her heart and the manliness of Wayne Lockwood, when they were but fancies as vague as dreams and as fragile?

Jeremiah laughed with relief and good nature, slapped his knee: "*One k* . . . say, I guess if *that's* all there was to it, I needn't have soft-footed it around so this afternoon . . . waitin' for you to be alone. Makes me feel kind of foolish. But how could I tell? You can't read folks' . . ."

And when she remained silent, only gazing at him with that queer uncomprehending look on her face, he grew confused, realized he was floundering in something deep and beyond him.

It bothered him, threw him out of the realm of everyday practical happenings into one of mystery and challenge and defeat, made him find refuge again in the commonplace. "But if you had any little-girl notions about him, ever, don't you get it into your bonnet that you can do anything about it now. You're rightly betrothed. Cady's got your word of honor. You know what I've always said to you children about word of honor! It would be too late now to think about anything else . . . even if you ever did. You see that, of course . . .?" He finished querulously. "It can't make any difference now."

"No," she said, not taking her eyes from old Jeremiah's, her lips moving dryly. "No, it can't make any difference now."

CHAPTER 40

WHEN Suzanne, who had stared into the darkness all through the night, went down the loft ladder, she saw at once that her mother and Emily knew about Wayne.

Jeremiah had said to them, somewhat gruffly, that there were reasons why he wanted to tell Suzanne first, that soon now he was going over to town for the mail, and that on his way back with it he would stop and spread the good news. Neither one had asked any questions about those reasons. Without expressing it in so many words, it was apparent that Pa had no intention of letting the neighborhood know he had come home from the south with the strange big news and delayed its telling. And while they both had realized it was not in the least like him to dissemble, it was evident he was intending that the neighbors draw their own conclusions about the mail bringing the word. Probably an official report, too, would sometime confirm it.

The most natural thing in the world would have been to talk unceasingly about the exciting news that Wayne was alive. Peculiarly, after the first exclamations and wonderment, there was very little said. A feeling of constraint hung over the breakfast table as though all four were leaving vital words unspoken.

Jeremiah dilated for a time on other instances like this one where reports had been erroneous.

Sarah said she'd had a premonition after Wayne was reported dead that he might be alive.

Emily, occasionally casting a surreptitious glance at Suzanne, threw herself, into the day's work with the energy of a steam-engine. As the morning wore on, she slipped into a state of bubbling gay spirits and sang loudly and off-key the new song which the doctor up the Valley a few miles had composed recently:

> There's a church in the Valley by the wildwood
> No lovelier spot in the dale.
> No spot is so dear to my childhood
> As the little brown church in the vale.

At the lusty reiteration of the chorus, Sarah whispered a little petulantly to Suzanne, in the intimacies of the small buttery: "Looks like Emily may be thinkin' more'n she should about Wayne comin' home. I never in the world could spare Emily."

Suzanne slipped out then, got her hooded cape and galoshes, and went down through the wood yard where butternut and walnut shucks lay thick around the diminishing pile of chunks, so huge earlier in the winter.

The soft snow splashed under her feet and she had to hold her full skirts high. She passed along the edge of the orchard, the trunks of the apple trees black with moisture on the south sides, took a cut through the back pasture, and came then to the timberland and the slough. The ice of the pond was mere slush now but it was not to be expected it would stay that way. Soon it would freeze again. Like herself, she thought, and wondered that she had the steadiness of mind to think it. Yes, that was the way she had been after she thought Wayne was killed—merely existing, doing all the little everyday tasks, vaguely seeing and hearing, but always through shadows, not feeling anything, not really alive herself. Frozen, like the slough.

Out here alone, with only the leafless trees and the brackish water, away from Ma's recital of her premonitions and Emily's cheerful singing, perhaps she could think. Maybe the frozen ice of her mind would melt here, too, and she could remember just what had happened.

Dead leaves from the rattling branches above her blew into the water and floated about with slow rocking motion because of the mild breezes.

Now, then, go back over the years. Face facts. Yes, but how can one pick out facts when they are so intertwined with emotions? Where do events leave off and feelings begin? How separate the real from the unreal? She had liked Wayne from the first day she had known him. Almost could she trace the way her love for him had crept stealthily upon her. The first youthful admiration growing into something steadier and deeper, surviving the days of Carlie Scott, until without so much as knowing how it was done, that very unspoken love had called forth an answering love from him. It was as though that magic door opened and she had caught a glimpse of what love could be and the meaning of all life.

Then Death closed the door—or so she had thought—and because there was no longer any shining vision beyond its opening, it did not seem to matter what turn life took.

Wayne was not dead, but living and coming home when the war ended if God yet spared him,—and even though this would be miraculously so, the door was as tightly closed as though he lay fallen there on the battle-field as she had thought.

Face it. What could you do now? Nothing. "When I make a promise it *is* my word of honor," she had said to Cady. After she thought Wayne was dead she had consented to marry Cady. Why? It seemed appalling now, but it didn't then. Why? No one had made her. "Will you do me the honor to be my wife?" Cady had said honorably enough. And she had said, "Why, yes, Cady, if you desire it." But frozen, never at any time anything but feeling as cold as the icy water over there in the slough.

She had not meant to be that way, hypocritical, saying something she did not mean. It was just that because Wayne was not ever to be here, nothing much mattered. If no one had wanted to marry her that would have been all right. She would have gone on with her teaching, like Miss Field, remembering Wayne all her life.

If Cady wanted to marry her, that was all right, too. Every woman had to have a home. She had thought to keep his house and make him a good and sensible wife, remembering Wayne. Nothing could have kept her from carrying Wayne's image in her heart all her life. Now that he was miraculously not dead it would still be the same. Now that he would come home and marry some one else while she kept her promise to Cady, it would still be true. She could tell that to no one, of course. Cady would never know it. No one would ever know. It was wicked, but there it was and you could do nothing about it. A hand can be taken from you—like Phineas'—but not your heart.

It was turning colder. The wind began sweeping down from the north prairie, rattling the dormant branches above her and blowing dead leaves and bits of bark from them. She watched the pieces of floatage settle on the black water with no further movement. Already the slough water was beginning to freeze. The midwinter thaw was over. She pulled her cape around her, turned and went toward the house.

CHAPTER 41

THE weeks following were strange ones to Suzanne. The world was a cardboard stage where puppets like those she had seen once at Overman Hall were manipulated by strings. And she was the central puppet pulled into her place by the strings of war, a false report, the coming of Cady Bedson, and a dazed feeling that nothing she did mattered much after the story of Wayne's death. And winter was wearing on, the puppets all dangling at the end of the strings which were managed by Fate or Destiny or whatever force controlled them.

There were increasing signs of victory. Jeremiah said soon now Grant would show Horace Akin what he had up his sleeve. The two argued so much about Grant, whether or not he was bungling, that Jeremiah said Horace would almost see a few union battles lost to uphold his side.

The weather moderated, snapped back again into a return engagement of cold with true Iowa fervor in never doing anything by halves. Over on the South prairie across the river Celia presented Alf with a daughter. Two days later Melinda presented Rand with a daughter, which temporarily evened all scores.

Suzanne saw Cady every Sunday night with regularity unless roads were impassable. He had spoken for the four-room frame house in Prairie Rapids, taking advantage of the chance to do so when a family was to move from the west to the east side. The court-house on the east side, as well as the railroad passing through, was giving the newer portion of the town its fling. Now the building of the railroad shops was adding to the boom so that a localized civil war was on between the two sides of town. Citizens of the two factions were cool toward each other, and boys of one side lay in wait with fine plans for the annihilation of all junior masculinity from the other side of the river. Let Sturgis Falls, however, so much as peep a new plan, and the two sides of Prairie Rapids flew together to combat it with concerted action. Civil wars were not limited to the current union-confederate engagement.

It was cold and snowy the March day that the girls all came home to help Suzanne tie her comforts. Sarah said it was a foregone conclusion that when you picked a date it would turn out to be the coldest day of the year or the hottest or the windiest. But because the girls were so widely separated, five and six miles apart, it was necessary to pick a time far ahead and stay by the decision.

They set up the quilt frames in the company room. It had not been opened for several weeks and the air in it was blue and frosty, its odor a combination of plaster, dried oak leaves, stove blacking, and long vanished breakfasts of pancakes and sausage whose smoke had seeped under the door.

Jeremiah's contribution to the day's festivities was the building of the fire in the iron stove. He piled so many chunks for future burning by the side of it that Sarah scolded and said the way he dropped dried bark around, it looked like the wood lot.

Emily and Sarah tacked the quilt lining onto the frames and Suzanne spread the washed wool evenly over its vast proportion.

Phoebe Lou was the first to arrive. Horace Akin brought her and Todo in the cutter, depositing them at the lean-to door with their basket, saying he must get right back to mend fences, but he and Jeremiah got into such a discussion over Grant that it was toward noon when he left.

Melinda and Celia came together in a bob-sled, Alf driving them after he and Rand had drawn straws to see which one would come. They stopped in Sturgis Falls to pick up Sabina, too, Alf plaguing her all the way out that he bet she felt too big-headed over her new house and two-seated sleigh to ride in a bob-sled with hay in the bottom. This to Sabina, who would have traded her new sleigh and house and a decade of her life for one of these four children. Celia and Melinda each held her new baby girl in her arms, warmly blanketed, and the two little boys looked like papooses peering out of their various layers of wrappings.

Lucy and Nora came over with Harry. Suzanne got the four little boys all started at playing train in the main room with a huge chunk for an engine and a row of lesser chunks trailing behind it, so that above the noise of visiting there was the ringing of a cow-bell, much choo-choo-chooing, and the shouting of the train's four engineers.

Sarah and Emily cooked dinner but the others were all seated around the frames, tying the little fluffy knots of red yarn in the exact corner and center of every block with comments: "This was Celia's old blue, wasn't it?" "I remember the first day I wore this—Slade Smith asked me to go to the picnic and I gave him the mitten."

Every one was there but Jeanie. Sometimes Emily or Sarah went to a window to look up the lane road or toward town. There was no more diagonal driving now across the prairie for Jeanie, as the land along the river road was all fenced into symmetrical fields.

It was almost noon when she drove into the yard, nearly frozen from the long cold drive. Gracie, who was not yet seven, had taken care of the two smaller girls on each side of her in the sled. When they all came into the lean-to every one helped with their wraps, Suzanne and Sabina giving their attention to the two smaller children, but Emily wiped her warm face and said: "I guess a regular little mother like you, Gracie, has to have something *special*," and took her up to the loft room to get out her own doll with which she had played back east.

No one had such a good time as Jeanie. She laughed and sparkled, talked and hummed while she was tying. "Oh, it's so *good* to be here," she kept saying. "What *fun* you girls all are! Oh,I think it's nice to have something with just *women* to it."

There were chicken pies baked in the big bread pans with saleratus biscuit dough all over the top in little chunks like so many Lover's Retreats in a river of chicken gravy.

Jeremiah, Phineas, Henry, and Alf Banninger all came in to be fed and when they were nearly through eating every one shouted with laughter because Tom Bostwick surprised them by driving into the yard with Cady Bedson, saying they smelled chicken pie all the way over to town where they were making a deal about buying up some of the soldiers' warrants, and decided to follow the scent.

Tom had brought Jeremiah his mail so that almost immediately Pa was saying angrily: "Look here, Ma . . . Henry . . . Phineas. Listen here, Sabina . . . Emily . . . Jeanie . . . Phoebe Lou . . . Melinda . . . Celia . . . Suzanne . . . ." thinking even as he spoke how nice it was to call the roll and

have them all here at home. "It's from that Dubuque paper.
'Grant *says* he has captured five hundred cannon. It would
have cost but a cipher more to have said five thousand and
been just as true. So far as Grant is concerned Lee and his
army are not yet gobbled up. Let Grant, if he wishes to do
anything, stop his braggadocio and go to work.' By granny,
can't they let him alone . . . ?"

It brought on the usual discussion, but even so there was
optimism that the end of the war was in sight. Lee could
scarcely hold out much longer. It gave every one a more
cheerful outlook. They had not been so jolly in years. Suzanne's first comfort was off the frame ready to be bound, the
second to be put on at once. Every one joked Cady about how
it took all the Martin relations to get him ready to be married.

Every knotting of the yarn in the comforts was tying Suzanne securely to her future. Every joke and every laugh and
every plan was a gossamer thread to weave the web tighter.
And then Tom Bostwick, full of chicken pie and feeling
expansive because he had a fine new idea, said before them
all: "Suzanne, the new house is just about done, and the
crates of furniture are stacked in the basement ready to be
unpacked. Why don't we initiate it with the wedding over
there instead of here? That all right with you, Cady?"

"Of course."

"Why . . . why, I hadn't thought . . ." Suzanne began.

But Tom, decisive always, cut it off with: "That's just
what we'll do," later overrode all objections and obstacles,
even Sarah's protest of, "Every one of my girls is always
married at home."

Suzanne suddenly had a feeling of being pulled into the
marriage plans as Evangeline had been sucked into the deep
dark waters of the Cedar, caught in the current of the stream
that was taking her whither it would. What was there to do
but acquiesce?

When Horace Akin drove back for Phoebe Lou before the
pale sun's setting, he asked Jeremiah and the boys if they
didn't think the neighbors should all turn in and get Wayne
Lockwood's place ready for him when the cold snap was
over, in case the war came to an end and he'd be coming
home.

Jeremiah said he had thought of doing that for Wayne,
too—good neighbor that way.

At the sound of that name Suzanne had to be very careful
lest she show any sign of perturbation. "Is it always going to

be like this?'' she thought. ''Surely in time I can hear his name calmly.''

They were off on the subject of Wayne again, that unbelievable news about him being alive after he was reported dead. A regular miracle, they said, not one of them but Suzanne stopping to think that Death still held him in the hollow of its bony hand, for the Thirty-first was with Sherman in the thick of the mêlée. For Wayne to be killed now, she thought, would be to die twice.

Then Alf said loudly, as a bright thought struck: ''Emily, you'll be the only one of the girls left after Suzanne's married. Why don't you set *your* cap for Wayne?''

Emily's face turned red but she answered quickly enough, ''What, me . . . an old maid? You go on.''

By the time the girls were leaving they had all taken it for granted that the wedding would be in May at Sabina's new house. The comforts were tied. Ma was going to start binding them to-morrow. The sheets were nearly finished. Jeanie and Melinda were making pillow-cases, Celia and Phoebe Lou hemming towels. Emily was to cut out the wedding dress next week.

No, you could not honorably do anything about it now. You could only pray for Wayne's safe return and then let the stream take you whither it would.

CHAPTER 42

THIS year of 1865 was to be a prosperous period, every one felt. There was no doubt but that the war was drawing to a close. Word came that Petersburg had fallen on the second of this month of April, Richmond on the third. Lee had fled in the direction of Lynchburg. These were the telling strokes which Grant evidently had planned and which he had not confided to his critics. It gave Jeremiah many an hour's pleasurable topic of conversation to relate how the general had maneuvered this.

"If Pa would just maneuver more things than his mouth . . ." Sarah said to Suzanne over the binding of the quilt. The weather had turned warm and the thick wool blanket across her lap was so uncomfortable it made her tongue sharp.

When the war was really over the whole Valley would pick up in earnest, every one said. Business would take on new life, building go on when no longer the far-off booming of guns echoed here.

Cady Benson was enthusiastic over prospects for Prairie Rapids in the coming year. Work on the new Central House, a large brick structure, was finished. The old brush-and-log dam across the river had been replaced by a big frame one. The roundhouse and machine shops for the Illinois Central were to be the making of the town. The charter for a First National Bank was received. There was to be a new iron bridge across the Cedar connecting the two sides of town. A midwestern city, busy and prosperous, was in the making there on the grassy prairie where only the Hanna family had camped a few years before.

Tom Bostwick was equally enthusiastic about Sturgis Falls. Already the citizens, sympathetic to the wants of the children left by so many brave Iowa men, were talking of a large soldiers' orphans' home. And even though they could not know it then, the home founded for such purpose was eventually to become the nucleus of a great school so that a fine college town was building there in the woods where once only the Sturgis and Adams families had laid the logs for their cabins.

But it was still only 1865 on a Monday noon, the tenth of April, and because the east doors of the lean-to stood open, the smell of spring came in and mingled with the smell of the dinner cooking, so that the combination became one of swelling tree-buds and fried potatoes, prairie loam and boiled beef. The sounds of spring came in and mingled with the kitchen sounds, so that the combination became one of meadow-lark songs and rattling pans, peeping newly hatched chicks and crackling of woodfire.

Emily had been working on Suzanne's wedding dress most of the morning in Sarah's bedroom, the white tarlatan lying in transparent folds on her lap and overflowing onto a sheet spread out on the floor. Sarah was getting the dinner to-day. She was approaching sixty now. Her red hair, dingily gray, sagged under its own weight, and her little puckered face was pinched and thin, but she was as spry as any of her girls.

Suzanne had come home to get a book, cautioning the big children to look after the small ones over their school lunches while she was gone. From the door she could see Henry going toward his house out of the field, Pa and Phineas and the hired man coming up from the stable single file. Some one riding hard and fast tore into the yard so that for one startled moment she thought of Ed Armitage riding in to see Phoebe Lou. Even then, rather strangely, it turned out to be Phoebe Lou's new husband and his appearance at this time of day, riding so hard, startled her so that she rushed to the door. But the news was not bad. He reined in his horse.

"It's all over," he called out. "Lee's surrendered." And in the joy of the moment added, "I'll take back every word I said about Grant."

Jeremiah sat down suddenly on the platform of the well, an old man tired to death with the worry and emotion of it all.

The women went rushing out into the yard where the men were—Sarah, a long-handled fork in her hand with a little piece of beef on it; Emily with her thimble still on her finger and on her flat bosom two needles from which threads trailed like long white tails; Suzanne taking off her apron absentmindedly as though she were about to welcome some one home from a war that was over, tying it back on when she remembered.

Horace Akin had just come from Prairie Rapids, he said, and if it hadn't been for wanting to tell every one along the river road he'd have stayed to help in the goings-on, the like of which you'd never seen. The news was like a fuse setting off a bomb in town. Folks had dropped their work and were rushing downtown to learn all they could. Cannon were being fired, flags run up, whistles and bells were blowing and ringing.

It was such a good feeling to have it all over. Every one laughed and talked about it and planned about going to town in the evening to celebrate. Then Sarah said, "Hark!" They all kept quiet so that they could hear it faintly in the distance— the far-away sound of whistles blowing and bells ringing. And when a rooster crowed from a fence near-by, Sarah scolded: "Did you ever know it to fail? I never tried to hear anything in my life that a rooster didn't split its windpipe right near me. Here, stop up your gullet with that," and threw it the beef from her fork.

All afternoon if there was a lull in the near-by farmyard sounds one could hear the faint far-off ringing of a bell or the tooting of a whistle, so every one was excited and ready to go to town by night. Cady Bedson came all the way out to get Suzanne. When they drove into Prairie Rapids at eight o'clock they found a solid mass of humanity packed in Commercial Street. Bunting festooned the fronts of buildings. Windows of every store and house, every shop and office were ablaze with lighted lamps, so that Cady said he wished he could have sold all the coal-oil for this one night. Only one set of windows remained dark and when Suzanne noticed it, Cady told her that Barney, the old tobacco man, had refused to illuminate, saying he'd have lighted up if the damn president had been shot.

"Didn't they do anything to him?"

"No, I guess every one has been too busy celebrating to pay any attention to it."

Luckily Cady found a hitching-post and, after tying the team, hustled Suzanne through the crowd to the new Central House which boasted lights in all the rooms. Men and women were crowding the verandas and windows, flying rockets or waving flags. Members of the Red Jacket Fire Brigade came from their engine house in full uniform, each man carrying a torch and marching through the packed masses along the sidewalks. As the last of the red-jacketed firemen passed, other citizens fell in behind them where, eight abreast, they marched and counter-marched singing the "Battle Cry of Freedom" and "John Brown." Whistles, bells, horns, fire-crackers, guns, and cannon kept up an incessant bedlam.

Near the veranda some one placed a huge dry-goods box with the bright notion of carrying out a program. One after another the prominent men of the town mounted the make-shift platform with heroic attempts toward speaking, but each time the din drowned him out. The number of times "the glorious banner of our freedom" and "truth crushed to earth" were spoken into the night air of that tenth of April, 1865, only to be lost in the madhouse of noise two feet away from the speaker, could not be counted. Out of the several dozen attempts but two rose into the ether with any degree of success.

"The American Constitution," a prominent citizen said, "like one of those wondrous rocking stones reared by the Druids, which the finger of a child might vibrate to its center, yet the might of an army could not move from its place, the Constitution is so nicely poised that it seems to sway with every breath of passion, yet so firmly based in the hearts and affections of the people that the wildest storms of treason and fanaticism break over it."

A tumultuous burst of enthusiasm followed the speech and the crowd in its exuberance at the patriotic utterance immediately seized the editor of the *Courier*, pulling off his cap and shawl and placing him upon the box.

"Fellow citizens," he began, "the human mind, ever on the alert to develop some new truth, often finds within its range of thought some dreary, blank, and chaotic void, which it is ever prone to fill up with some fanciful creation of its own imagination . . ."

"Bully for the human mind," yelled an urchin in the crowd as some hilarious individual suddenly tipped the dry-goods box, sliding the dignified editor into the mass of humanity below.

It was all exciting, Suzanne thought, sitting there on the hotel veranda rail. At least it was, if you did not stop to think of all that lay behind it—the dead boys and the dying ones, the wounds and the illnesses, the destruction and devastation, and that because of all those things, this was Cady Bedson beside her instead of—

"No, no," she thought, "I must not . . . it's wicked . . . I must stop it . . .'' She looked at Cady there so near her and slightly lower because of his standing by the side of the high railing upon which she perched. His dark face was flushed with eagerness and enthusiasm, his mouth wide with shouting and laughter—Cady, who had not gone into the hot-bed of the Secession but had hired a substitute whose life was lost, could laugh now and shout the victory. That dark face, looking so self-satisfied, would always be close, always close . . .

She shut her eyes, thinking a little crazily, ''Oh, *what* have I done?''

Relief was so thoroughly felt by every one that almost was it a tangible substance that week on the river road. One went at his work more cheerfully. ''Now we can settle down. Now we can plan.''

On Saturday morning there were so many things to do that one did not know which should be done first.

Sarah was frying odds and ends of pork cracklings to extract every bit of their grease, getting ready to make soap next week. Phoebe Lou was going to bring over her accumulated grease and the lye she had leached, and make the soap with her. Sarah was thinking she must not forget to tell Emily when she came down from the loft that Melinda and Celia, although living across the road from each other, were making their soap separately, each one believing she could make better and whiter than the other.

Phineas and Henry were in the south field plowing. No matter what other duty called, the field work must go on when Nature gave the sign. And Nature had given the sign. She had given it by the shooting-stars and Dutchman's-breeches peering through the soggy leaves of the timberland, by the bluebirds swinging down into the wood lot and the prairie lark's song, by the pussy-willows overhanging the slough, by bursting buds and the strong fresh odor of loam and subsoil. She had given it through animal life, the crowing roosters and snorting Jupiter and the uneasy pawing of old Sandy in the stable.

Henry and Phineas were turning the furrows, walking through the moist clods behind their teams. They no longer owned oxen. Jeremiah had sold old Red and Baldy, Whitey and Star, a few years before, saying that he was glad to be rid of them, yet feeling queer and a little disloyal when he saw them driven out of the yard because of the long treks they had made with him so faithfully between Dubuque and Sturgis Falls.

Jeremiah, himself, did not go into the field any more. He was still strong enough—"hell, yes," he would have said. But what with the legislature, war work, and county board of supervisors, it had been several springs since he had followed the plow. But he found enough to do on those days when outside duty failed to call—looking after the stock, fences, his orchard, and particularly those tasks which took him near the right-of-way so that he might hold converse with every passer-by.

To-day he was setting out a tree by the small gate, wondering why he never had done it before. To have lived here nearly thirteen years and not to have done so was past understanding. Even though there were big trees by the house, this little split rail gate stood out here in the shadeless open like a sore thumb.

He brought water for the wide hole, set in the tree, a fine, upstanding young maple, the largest he dared tear from its native ground, filled in the cavity and tamped it down solidly. Standing back to look it over, he had a sudden notion to cut the date in its bark, and started to the house for his jack-knife, wishing as he did so that he had set it out five days before on the date of Lee's surrender. "That would'a meant something," he explained to Suzanne by the doorway, "but to-day can't rightly be termed anything special."

Suzanne, her head swathed in gray calico, was doing the Saturday cleaning, shaking her dust cloth vigorously at the side of the tree-stump steps as he passed. She had been thinking about Wayne coming home, how and where they would meet and what they would say. "There is so much to say, Suzanne, that I shall say nothing," he had written. And now all he could say would be: "How do you do, Suzanne?" And she: "We were all glad to hear you were not killed, Wayne." She would be married by that time for on the mantelshelf above the old fireplace lay the piles of gilt-edged paper and envelops which were to convey the hand-written invitations to the ceremony at the home of Mr. and Mrs. Thomas Bostwick in Sturgis Falls.

"You ought to say, 'so's to show off Tom Bostwick's house to all and sundry,' " had been Sarah's acrid comment.

But Jeremiah had been more lenient concerning Tom's motive. After all, when you had known Governors Lowe, Kirkwood, and Stone, held a few minutes' interview with

General Sherman, talked with Generals Dodge and Crocker and United States Senator Harlan, eaten at the same table with the state legislators, it made you feel broader minded, more tolerant. Big men didn't always faultfind. Maybe he would feel just like Tom if he had a new house like that.

All this made him stop with the jack-knife in his hand and look around his own house as with the eye of a stranger, trying to visualize just how it must appear to an outsider, attempting to comprehend why Sarah and the girls found fault with it. For himself, he thought it the height of comfort. Once it had been the most commodious dwelling in this end of the county, and he was of no mind to go back on it now.

The logs were fitted in strong, true fashion, the two frame parts solid, and the inside plastered. To be sure no two of the floors looked alike—the main room was wide puncheon, the bedroom was another width puncheon, the lean-to was wide sawmill boards, the company room narrow ones. But they held you up, didn't they? By granny, you didn't go breaking through any of the flooring *he* had laid. A lot of folks had no floors at all in their first cabins, just hard-packed dirt.

The great logs in the fireplace of the main room heated it thoroughly—well, that one side of the room anyway—there was an iron stove in the company room and a cook stove in the lean-to. As for the bedrooms, no one needed to have a warm bedroom, not with all those comforts Ma and the girls had made. The beds were the best in the country, too, great high feather-ticks and pillows.

As for food—that long table in the lean-to had the best cooking on it in the state of Iowa. Those great bowls of stewed chicken and biscuits, mountains of mashed potatoes whipped up with yellow cream, baked prairie-chickens piled on a platter, roasted roosters with break-crumb stuffing bursting from their backsides, fish from the sparkling Cedar, the first pork roast after a new butchering, spare-ribs and Ma's sauerkraut, pork chops with fried apples along side (thank heaven for apple trees bearing now in the Valley), sausage and buckwheat cakes, fried corn-meal mush and maple syrup, baked apples with cream, platters of table corn—eat a dozen ears dripping with Ma's sweet butter—the first green onions in the early summer with big slabs of Emily's white bread, Ma's Boston brown bread and baked beans flavored with side meal and molasses made at the sorghum mill up the Janesville road!

All this gastronomic review made him suddenly recall those

recent weeks on the march with the boys, and at Savannah, rations practically gone, starving while waiting for provisions to be transported from the coast, one ear of corn per day to each man, all the hunger and sickness and destitution. Yes, it was food and outnumbered men that had licked the south, not generalship or courage. You had to admit that. Thank God it was over, all but the rehabilitation and the healing of the scars of hate. That was almost too gigantic a task to contemplate, but with Lincoln there at the helm proffering aid to the stricken south, it could be accomplished. He would help the country pull through. With Lincoln's guiding, steading hand and warm kindly heart, feeling malice toward none and charity for all . . .

What was some one calling out to Suzanne from the roadway?

A horseman had been tearing up the river road from the west, riding so hard that it would look to be a runaway if he had not been leaning forward as though to hasten the horse's speed. It was Mel Manson, reining in his horse momentarily at the small gate. Through Suzanne's mind flashed the stinging thought that this was something new about Wayne Lockwood, and another one equally as sharp followed that she must stop thinking of him now.

"Suzanne!" Mel was calling.

But there was no need to call her, for she was starting toward the gate, noting as she hurried that Mel was breathing heavily like the horse. "Tell your father Lincoln's shot."

Suzanne's hands flew to her throat.

"Oh . . . no."

"Yes—last night in a the-*ater*. An actor shot him. He's dead." He was calling it back over his shoulder as he rode on, an Iowa Paul Revere carrying the news to every river-road farm.

Suzanne turned and ran up the path but she did not need to tell her father. He had heard. Standing in the cabin doorway he had heard, and the blood had dropped away from the high cheek-bones so that the only part of his face visible above the beard was chalk-white.

Sarah had come in from the lean-to, her face flushed from the stove, her grayish-red hair sagging from its pins.

"What is't?" She looked quickly from one to the other.

"He's dead. Shot." Old Jeremiah leaned weakly against the door jamb. It was the end of everything. Now the country couldn't . . . couldn't pull through.

"Lincoln?" Sarah said of her own accord. Afterward she asked them all to tell her how she happened to know who it was Pa meant. "See! I knew it was him without bein' told. What did I tell you about premonitions?"

She hurried into her bedroom. "Emily," she called up the loft ladder and again. *"Emily,"* to drown out the loud singing of "No spot is so dear to my chi-i-ldhood . . ."

"Emily, the president's been shot. He's dead."

Emily's face, white and frightened, peered down from above the crosspieces of saplings. "Dead . . . ?" she whispered it. "Oh, *poor* Mrs. Lincoln!" A queer thing for an old maid, thirty-one to say.

Suzanne grabbed her shaker bonnet and putting it on grotesquely over her dust protector, sped out toward the field where the boys were.

She could see Nora swinging under a big cottonwood tree not far from Henry's cabin, her thin bare legs working herself high up into the branches. "Nora," she called, her throat dry, "Lincoln's been shot. He's dead," saw Nora catapult herself from the swing while it was high above the ground, sprawl in the dirt, pick herself up, and scurry into the cabin.

As Suzanne ran, moisture from the early spring growth dampened her ankles and the young sand-burs caught in her white stockings, clinging there when she went through the wood lot to find the boys.

It was Phineas who was the closer. He was plowing not far away, the lines around his shoulders, as he tried to guide the plow with his one hand. Henry was on the other side of the field.

"Phineas," she called. "Lincoln's been shot. He's dead."

Phineas stared for a moment, wide-eyed, but remembering his brother, shouted, "Henry, Lincoln's been shot. He's dead." Then he leaned weakly against the plow handle and dropped his head into his hand. "Oh, my gosh," he said, his face puckering like his mother's, "what'll we do now?"

Henry left his team standing, stomping the first bluebottle fly, and came across the half-plowed ground. He was only thirty-six, but bearded as he was, and having worked hard out-of-doors for twenty-five years, he looked as old as his father.

"Mel said it was last night in a theater. Shot by an actor. That's every bit I know."

The three drew together there at the edge of the field, Suzanne looking frightened and uncertain, Phineas with his head in his one hand, Henry standing and poking at a clod of moist earth with the toe of his boot.

Just so they stood silently until Henry began talking. He so seldom said much. It went through Suzanne's mind suddenly that she had never in her whole life heard him say more than three or four sentences at a time. But now he was speaking without pause. "There was never anybody like him. He was different from all other men, I tell you. Somethin' set him apart. I don't know what. I doubt if anybody knows . . . or ever will."

Poking at a moist bit of earth he did not take his eyes from it, as though only the earth understood what he was saying, "I never saw him in my life and yet I know him well. Like a close friend. Time's when I've been plowin' or plantin' or harvestin' it almost seems he's been walkin' along side of me in that loose-legged way, jokin', talkin', tellin' yarns, and unfoldin' his plans. Hard to explain, so's I never tried to, but it was like he understood me 'n' I understood him. Take those times everybody else was goin' to war. 'When you goin', Henry?' people would say. I wanted to go the worst way. Phineas and Ed Armitage, Rand and Alf, Ambrose Willshire, Wayne Lockwood . . . everybody goin'. I felt pretty mean and cheap to stay and hide behind a plow. 'Are you a man or a mouse?' seemed folks must be sayin'. One day—that was '62 when the call come for the Reserves—I felt pretty bad about knowin' just what to do, walk off 'n' leave things go here, or stay by it. Pa in legislature 'n' everbody goin' off. Corn was in the ear, grain cut. . . . I come off down here in the south field by myself to thrash out the thoughts in my mind. You won't believe it . . . so not much use tellin' it . . . but it was like I talked to him and asked his mind on it. As clear as day a'most he said what he thought.

"Oh, I ain't plumb crazy. 'Twas only my fancy, I know, but it might just about as well been really him. 'Twas like he laughed and joked me about bein' so cut up, and then said soberlike that he thought my place lay right here, that some was called to one duty and some another. And that the place he had been called to was the hardest of all but 'twas his bounden duty to see the war through. Seems like he said if I felt torn to know what to do, to remember I couldn't never feel as torn as him, that sometimes he didn't know where to turn for the responsibility of it . . . and the decisions . . . and when he didn't know . . . he wanted to get like me close to the earth . . . that's why he come along with me so often, to think out where his duty lay. And that whatever you finally felt inside you was your duty, that must you do, or you would have no peace with yourself.

" 'Twas just idle thinkin' on my part down here all by myself in the corn . . . workin' alone so much outdoors gives people queer thoughts . . . but that don't make no difference . . . it was comfortin' to me and I abided by it and grew to feel all right. So it seems I've seen him and talked with him and know him well."

He looked up and off to the horizon, across the prairie toward the east as though to where his fallen comrade lay. "And now they've shot him," he said slowly. "But they ain't killed him. You'll see. They tried to kill Christ, didn't they? But they couldn't. Well, the president'll live on, too, as sure as you're born—and be real to folks . . . like he was to me here in the corn. It won't make no difference about him bein' dead in the body. They's somethin' about him sets him apart. Next year won't make no difference . . . ten years . . . fifty . . . a hundred maybe . . . don't make no difference *how* many . . . Abraham Lincoln . . ."

He broke off as though the saying of the name was more then he could bear, turned, and went back to his waiting team.

Phineas drew his hand across his eyes, picked up the lines, clucked to his team, and started to the stables.

Henry having plodded across the field unhitched too. It was as though the men had been called in from their work by a death in the family. There *had* been a death in the family. Lincoln was dead.

Suzanne turned and went quietly toward the house. How unusual for Henry to have talked so long the way he did. Something about it had calmed and strengthened her, too, that about doing one's duty. But how queer life was, and what a topsy-turvy world! She had thought Wayne Lockwood was dead and Abraham Lincoln alive. But now Abraham Lincoln was dead and Wayne Lockwood was alive.

CHAPTER 43

THE date that Jeremiah carved on the young tree was an important one after all. He cut large uneven letters because he could not see to guide the knife straight, letting the tears fall without shame, his great shoulders shaking. For a half century the rude initials remained there on the huge towering maple—A L—the rough bark growing in and filling the scars long before those other scars made by the fighting were healed.

Every one on the river road drove into one of the two towns. The shock and sorrow of the news called for a drawing together of the citizens. One could not comfortably stay at home, but must seek out other humans with whom to talk and mourn.

All the Martins drove to Sturgis Falls excepting Suzanne who went with Cady to Prairie Rapids.

It was unbelievable that this was only the Saturday following that early week-day of wild jubilation in which they had participated. The setting was the very same—the crowds, the stores closed, the street decorations, but with what a difference. The milling shouting crowds were silent ones, the decorations were black, a draped picture of Lincoln hung high in the center of the street, others on buildings were black-framed. People talked in whispers, weeping as they talked.

"What will the country do now?"

As Cady and Suzanne stood on the veranda of the Central House, almost at the place from which they had watched the celebration, they saw a little man with a pack on his back in the grasp of two of Prairie Rapids' leading citizens. It was the tobacco man who had wished for the assassination of Lincoln, and he was being escorted to the town's limits.

The weeks following were strange ones. That pall of sadness

375

hung over everything which should have been pleasant for a coming wedding time, over every one who should have been gay for a marriage.

The gilt-edged stationery meant for the invitations lay on the old fireplace mantel all through the rest of April with no writing on its leaves. Suzanne, questioning the good taste of their sending now when every one was mournful, kept putting off the writing of them. But Tom Bostwick told her it was foolish, that people had to go on living no matter what happened. And even Jeremiah said, "Well, Suzanne, we've lost our best friend, but birth won't stop for that fact this next month, and death won't stop for it either, so since that's the way of it, I guess a marriage that's all planned and waiting don't need to stop either."

Suzanne's wedding dress was finished, every little white embroidery stitch and every little white silk binding for the tarlatan skirts, over which Emily had nearly "put her eyes out." In contrast she had sewed bands of crêpe on the coat sleeves of her father and the boys. She had made flat bows of the material for her mother's and Lucy's bonnets, stitched an edging of it on the little face veils which she and Suzanne wore on the brims of their platter-shaped hats, and made Nora a black calico apron. And when Phoebe Lou admitted she was feeling too miserable to get her new family of Akins into mourning, Emily fixed them all up, too.

Yes, it was a strange state of affairs in which were mingled a wedding gown and crêpe, congratulations and condolences, tears and smiles, wishes for happiness and fears for the country.

All eyes were to the east these days. All thoughts followed the funeral train. Every day, they all knew where he was, all these people of the river road so far away from him but who loved him deeply—Jeremiah, Phineas, Sarah and the girls, the Akins, the Mansons and the Emersons, and Henry who had talked with him in the corn-field.

Every night when Jeremiah wound up the weights of the old Seth Thomas clock with the iron key there behind the American eagle, he spoke quietly to the members of the family sitting by the fireplace.

"To-day, there were services in the White House."

"To-day, he lay in state there under the Capitol dome with people passin' by to see him."

"I wish *I* could have passed by to see him."

"To-day, he was in Philadelphia, right there in the room

where he said, 'I would sooner be assassinated than to give up the principles of the Declaration of Independence.' ''

''But he didn't give 'em up, did he, Pa?''

''No . . . he didn't.''

''To-day, he was in New York.''

''To-day he was in Albany.''

''. . . in Cleveland.''

''. . . Columbus.''

''. . . Chicago.''

''To-day, he got home to Springfield.''

''To-day, they laid him away. Day's over. Fresh start,'' Jeremiah's voice broke. ''Fresh start for the country—and all of us to-morrow.''

And on that ''to-morrow'' Suzanne began to write the first of her wedding invitations.

CHAPTER 44

NO ONE but Tom Bostwick could have weathered the years so well, made money, built a residence like this before the war was over.

There was a parlor, sitting-room, dining-room, kitchen, library, and a hall with stairway that turned on a landing connecting mysteriously with a back stairway. It was almost too much for Sarah that while her own house should still possess no real stairs, Sabina was about to revel in two sets of them.

There was a write-up in the paper about the city's new structure. "The wall decoration is of a style pertaining to the Middle Ages. The sitting-room is Oriental. The parlor is of arabesque and the library Egyptian. Each of the rooms has a different finish, such as oak, walnut, cherry. It is not too much to say no more elegant edifice graces any town west of the Mississippi."

" 'West of the Mississippi' takes in a good deal of territory," old Jeremiah said. "I bet I could find a good house or two if I went prowlin' up and down the west bank of the Mississippi."

If the house graced the town, Sabina equally graced the house. Her round pleasant face, jet black hair, and hard pink cheeks made her a very good-looking woman and if her once girlishly rounded body was now frankly heavy, in its tight-fitting stays it looked matronly and stylish. Having no children, she mothered others' children. Indeed, an interest in every one with whom she came in contact shone in her eyes, hospitality oozed from her, and any villager in trouble, whether of a mental, moral, or physical type, was prone to seek an interview with Mrs. Tom Bostwick.

To-day she was all bustling business, getting ready for

Suzanne's wedding in the evening, directing the two girls who were helping her, but trusting only herself with the wedding cake. Even so, she had taken time to send a basket of food to a soldier's family whose head had not yet returned from the war.

In the afternoon everything was in readiness. The new house was elegance personified. Looking it all over for defects with critical eye while she was waiting for Suzanne and the folks to come, she could find none. The heavy gilt wall paper, the flowered carpet stretching as far as eye could see through the parlor and sitting-room, the heavily upholstered couches and chairs, the marble-topped stands and whatnot, the sparkling chandeliers, all combined to make a picture of "ornamental refinement" as the paper had put it. With pride she looked at the elegant scene before her and drew a momentary picture of comparison between it and the old log-and-frame house out on the river road with its rag rugs and wild-turkey feathers, and then loyally, for the good times she had known out there, put aside the thought. And anyway, there were the folks, with Suzanne and Emily, coming into the driveway in their new covered carriage.

"I want the very first people who break bread in my house to be my own folks," Sabina had insisted with clannish devotion. "You can do your chores early and get here by five. The train will be in by that time with Uncle Joe and Aunt Harriet. We'll eat in the kitchen, so's to keep the rest of the house all straight, and it won't be a big meal, just easy to get, and every one but Suzanne can turn in and help afterward."

So Jeremiah, Sarah, and Emily were here. And Suzanne, the bride-to-be, was here too, sometimes thinking she was in a dream of being carried down the river in a whirling boat, seeing all the familiar faces on the bank and calling out to them for help but with no sound coming from her throat.

Soon Phoebe Lou and Mr. Akin came in their carriage with Todo and the two Akin boys, still a little uncertain whether or not they belonged, but so warmly welcomed by Sabina that they forgot their bashfulness. Henry and Lucy came with Nora and Harry in the old buckboard.

Melinda and Rand with the two babies drove in next in a new high and shining buggy, tickled to the point of wild laughter that they had beaten Alf and Celia. In a few minutes Celia and Alf with their two babies came in another new high and shining buggy. Alf had passed Rand once on the road out on the south prairie, and kept in the lead until Rand, whip-

ping up his horses, swept around him just before they struck
town, knowing that because of the dried roughness of the
road there through the timber Rand could not pass again.

Jeremiah drove to the depot to meet Uncle Joe and Aunt
Harriet, but came back without them, saying the train was
late. Phineas rode in on old Queen. They were eating before
Jeanie and Ambrose Willshire came with the little girls in a
spring wagon. Ambrose excused their lateness politely, saying
Jeanie would perhaps some day learn to manage her work
right, so that she was embarrassed but tried to laugh and turn
it into a joke.

There was a queer solemn air over the supper in Sabina's
new kitchen with its built-in pump so that one got rain-water
for washing right there in a sink. (But even that was not so
grand as the tub fastened to the floor in a room by itself into
which you could pour water from a pail, but when it came to
emptying it, you merely pulled out a plug in the bottom.
Between the pumping at the sink and watching the water
gurgle out of the bathtub into some mysterious vastness of
space, the children were kept very busy.)

This unusual solemnity of the Martin clan at a wedding was
because of Lincoln's death gripping every one. It was in the
air—the unforgettable shock, the sadness, the worry over
what this would mean to the country. Added to this was a
half-remorseful sense of carrying on wedding festivities in the
midst of mourning. It did not seem right and yet life must go
on. Suzanne, herself, was taking the president's death very
hard, some of them noticed. She was so quiet and sad for a
happy bride. When Melinda said so to the girls in the kitchen,
Emily snapped back, "Oh, let her alone, can't you?"

Supper was over, with Sarah the first one up from the table
saying, "Now, girls, stir your stumps. Scoot." Married and
mothers, they were still her girls to be bossed and scolded.

Jeremiah, taking out his seargent-at-arms watch at intervals, drove back to the station. Suzanne went upstairs to
dress, with Emily to oversee her.

The fine new bedroom assigned to her smelled of fresh
plaster and the doors stuck. There was a four-poster bed with
a candle-wick cover but no tester, for Sabina said Aunt Harriet had written they were not so fashionable now. The curtains had a fringe of little wool balls. There was a worked
wool antimacassar on a big easy chair by the window which
was the height of something or other to Sarah who could not
imagine any one ever sitting down in a bedroom.

Emily was fastening Suzanne's wedding dress, fitting the last hook into what she had fondly expected to be the last eyelet, but which proved unfortunately to be next to the last one, so that the whole length of the basque would have to be unhooked in order to find the missing one.

"We'll have to go all through it again," Emily was apologetic, knowing what a job it was for Suzanne to hold in her breath so long.

But Suzanne held her breath again patiently, a little disinterestedly, as though it did not make much difference what one did. She was costumed now to the last detail excepting the tarletan overskirt which lay across Sabina's bed like a little white bride who had thrown herself face downward on it.

Emily brought the sheer overskirt then, fitting and fastening it into place. Now that the whole gown was assembled she knelt for a moment to pull at the skirt, sat back on the floor to get a view of it, the dressmaker part of her uppermost.

Suzanne stood with her arms out a bit over the flaring gown so that she might not crush the white silk trimming on its folds. The long sleeves dropped downward displaying undersleeves to the elbows embroidered with Emily's finest work.

From her seat on the floor Emily, looking up at Suzanne, suddenly was no longer the dressmaker, only the sister. "Oh, Suzanne, *smile*! Smile like a bride," she burst out, as though something long pent was hurrying past her lips. "I can't stand it any longer. Are you happy? Is it the way you wanted?"

She was crying now, shaking with violent sobs, clutching at the white frothiness of the skirt.

Suzanne thought she could not bear it, put her hand on the smooth red hair of this sister who always did so much for every one.

"Emily . . . you mustn't. Don't cry." And when Emily could not look up, Suzanne said quietly with some unlooked-for inward strength: "No, it isn't the way I wanted it, but no one shall ever know it, except you, as long as I live. Don't worry, I'll be all right. When we are little we think life is simple but we find that isn't true. There are all sorts of things happen like the cross currents over in the river that cut into the stream. They come and go and change your course, but no matter what happens, you've got to do the right thing. Sometimes it's hard to tell what the *right* thing is. Henry thinks even Lincoln couldn't tell at times what that was. But

if we just go ahead with what seems our duty, no matter . . .
no matter . . .'' Her voice broke, so that she did not finish.

Some one was coming up the stairs through the hall,
rattling the knob of the closed bedroom door.

Emily jumped up from the floor, ''Oh, my good granny . . .''
She was wiping her eyes with the flat of her hands.
''Ain't I a fool? Martins don't cry. They *laugh*.''

CHAPTER 45

WAYNE LOCKWOOD was crossing the Iowa prairies between Dubuque and the Cedar Valley. The steam-cars were filled with humanity, every set of both coaches occupied. Some of the boys in their old blue uniforms were ahead in the baggage-car to relieve congestion. Wayne had ridden with them for a while, but at Independence had changed back to the coach, finding a seat not far from the open water-container that at every jerk of the train slopped some of its contents on the shelf. He had not felt like entering into the spirit of the group's entertainment of itself, a combination of reminiscences of war experiences, ribald stories, and plans for the future. Feeling himself a death's-head at the feast, he had sought solitude in the more or less dubious seclusion of the crowded coach. At least here with an old man dozing into his beard for a seat-mate he would not have to relive sickening episodes of the past, listen to the yarns, or reveal any of his private plans for the future.

How could you do that last, anyway, if you had none—if your mind held no clear perspective on your future, was confused about its procedure, had become a tangled underbrush sort of mind like those places in the timber where wild grapevine and woodbine and sumac all twined together?

Yes, that was it, he told himself analytically, the past, the present, and the future tangled together just now in a confused undergrowth so that he could not feel clear-minded about anything. It was wholly unlike him, too. It used to be that he saw objectives plainly, made decisions in clean-cut fashion. Between that time and this hung a dark curtain that separated the one period from the other.

Back again in memory his still weary mind thrashed over the previous years.

For the most part, they had been compounded of fatigue, crowded box-cars, flies, ugly sores, disemboweled horses, sickness, evil odors, hunger, fears that became dulled in the shadow of larger fears, then a fatalistic acceptance of fear itself, so that one grew to be foolhardy, which was no doubt a low type of courage. A bad business, war! He was sick of the thought of it. These fellows who were talking about forming a sort of lodge or brotherhood of the various regiments, meeting every week, wearing badges . . . for his part, he doubted that he wanted to do anything toward keeping up the memory of it. Perhaps this feeling he harbored now would wear off some day so that he, too, would be glad to meet and swap yarns.

There were naturally some bright spots in these years, even humorous ones. Maybe the day would come when he could enjoy talking them over. For the first time he grinned to himself as for no reason at all he recalled Major Stimming calling out to the boys carelessly running the full length of the trenches near Atlanta: "Boys, if you get wounded or killed outside the works it won't count." And General Osterhaus, riding close to the company, so angered when the fragment of a shell had killed his horse under him that he yelled: "Boyce, make 'em hell schmell."

He was almost grateful for this sudden memory of lighter moments, pleased to find himself grinning. Life recently had taken on itself such an upheaval, he was coming home with less interest in it than he could ever have imagined. Other fellows were apparently as always—glad that the whole sickening episode was over, planning enthusiastically for the future. Those chaps in the box-car—one was talking about going out to Nebraska territory, using his land warrants for obtaining government holdings, one was looking forward to taking up his work in a dry-goods store there in Prairie Rapids, another saying he could scarcely wait to get into his fields, that tomorrow morning before sun-up he would be out with horses and plow. For himself, he was not as these. No enthusiasm. No big plans. No eagerness to get into his fields or emotion over his homecoming as he should have felt. Two years and a half in which he had not seen his farm lands he liked so well, and yet no amount of self-prodding could give him the natural enthusiasm to see them he would have expected.

It was courage that he lacked, he told himself, and wondered why that could be. And just what was courage?

Surely he had not been without it the last two and a half

years. At that thought, his mind slipped suddenly to an early spring episode near Columbia, recalling how Wade Hampton and Beauregard had been driven across the Congaree and their bridges burned, and that stealthy detoured march around to the rear of the city to a point on the French Broad River, the dark of the night and the rapid step march, the fatigue after the hurried journey. Remembered the detail of the newly arrived corps which was sent out to cross the river in a skiff with a coil of rope to be attached to a tree on the opposite bank, how they returned to say the crossing could not be made as the current was too rapid. Remembered how he volunteered to do the job because of his old skill in the Red Cedar currents and succeeded almost miraculously in accomplishing it, so that the others in a detached pontoon boat, by a hand-over-hand process, made the crossing. It had saved the day. Everything which followed had been accomplished almost silently, for the smoldering embers of the Johnnies' picket fires could be seen a short distance from the river bank. Even though the process of crossing by the line was so slow and it was daylight before the attack could be made, there had followed the brisk short engagement and Major Goodwin of the enemy forces approaching with a flag of truce. He, himself, had heard the negotiations for the surrender almost at his very side.

Officers had taken a moment from that night of swift activity to commend him for "the courageous deed" whereby the pontoon crossing could be made. He was not glorifying himself. Any one would have done it. There were a thousand acts as courageous. As a matter of fact, that supposedly "courageous" deed was born of his own physical hardihood and the knowledge that had just come to him of Suzanne's marriage. Of what then was courage composed? Recklessness or fortitude? If one could be courageous in a crucial moment of intense activity, did it follow that one could be courageous in the face of disappointment and loss?

Chin in hand, he stared out at the Iowa prairies, green in the lushness which always came after spring rains.

Here he was going over the same trail from Dubuque to the Valley which he had taken ten years before. There was something dramatic in the comparison of the two trips a decade apart.

He recalled that day when, a mere boy of eighteen, he had swung along the grassy trail, his head full of dreams about riches and lands and freedom. Now he was riding on the steam-cars over the same grassy trail. And where were his riches and lands? And what was freedom?

At eighteen he had sworn that nothing would ever make him bungle one single episode in his life. Just handle every experience wisely, make every move with native good sense, and the years would always do well with you. You could make of life what you willed, do with it as you saw fit. That had been his philosophy. And now he was nearly twenty-nine and where were his much-prized rules of wisdom?

He himself had bungled some things. And war had stepped in and bungled others.

Those two trips a decade apart—coming over this same road—were like boundary lines setting aside these ten years of his life. His first long tramp across the prairie trail and this present one, riding over the same route on the steam-cars, by their very likeness—and dissimilarity—met and surrounded the happenings of the intervening time like a frame around a picture. While one could not cut off any decade from any other because of the sly blending of the years, still, these past ten in his young life were set aside as definitely as any canvas was cut, painted upon, and framed. The picture was a period of his life that would never come again and a period of the settlement of the Valley that was just as definitely ended; the frame surrounding it was distinctly the two trips. Whatever happened from now on must be painted on a new canvas.

He toyed with that thought for a time, looking out at the familiar landscape while the smoke from the engine blew into the north, sent there by a spring south wind. Little cabins sat here and there on the prairie where ten years before only uninhabited lands lay. All of the acreage was taken between the Mississippi and the Cedar Valley. For new claims now one would have to look to the western half of the state beyond Fort Dodge. This was to be the turning-point of the settling of far western land. Of that he was sure. From now on thousands of restless soldiers would pour into the west.

Probably he would be one of them. It was not that he wanted to go so much as that he did not want to stay.

The zest had gone out of living in the old neighborhood. Like a fanatic who inflicts his own punishment he returned to the thoughts of Suzanne. Sometimes he dwelt on memories of her as he had stopped to tell her good-by at the lane road, the loveliness of her face upturned to his, the lighted candles in her eyes; felt again the pressure of her supple body in his arms and the sweetness of her lips. Sometimes he dwelt on other memories, her interest in every person, bird, and flower, her excitement over trivialities, her joy in living. But more often he tried to analyze the stupidity with which he had been enveloped in those days when he had not realized how dear to him she was. In self-flagellation he went over it all, chin in palm, looking out at the prairie so peaceful appearing to the returned soldiery, so uninteresting to one who had nothing but bitterness and disappointment in his heart.

Some one there in the Valley had won her—the girl who had been meant for him but whom he had lost forever.

He pictured now just what his homecoming would have been under other circumstances—Suzanne waiting for him, meeting him perhaps in two hours' time there at the depot. If that could have been, no need for dreaming about lands farther west. He was no rover by nature, no pioneer forever pushing on ahead of the horde. He liked his land there in the Valley as well as any of the other settlers did, would be glad to stay by its woods and creek and its good productive soil. But now the heart was gone out of the Valley. It seemed alien, a thing to be put behind him in the days to come. Maybe when he arrived, the sight of his rolling pasture land and the familiar fields would bring back his zest for them. If that did not come to pass perhaps he could still feel a new joy in the anticipation of pressing farther on to the west. Surely he could recapture some of that adventuresome spirit he had felt ten years ago. No girl could take that away from you. He was not the only man to experience a loss like that. Lincoln had once lost the girl he loved. But death had taken her, not his own crass dullness.

And now he had lost Lincoln, too. Suzanne and Lincoln! It was queer to associate the two, so far apart in their lives, but so close to his heart.

Back, now, over the last few weeks he went; his arrival in Washington from the south to take part in the grand review, obtaining a pass from the colonel and hastening at once to the Capitol to see Lincoln's body.

He closed his eyes that he might shut out the sight of the smoke-wreathed car window and the rolling prairies beyond and look again upon the quiet face of the man lying there.

Filled with sadness and bitterness at the tragic passing, he had taken his place in the unending procession, cautioning his own nerves to hold steady through the ordeal, controlling his facial muscles with set jaw as he approached the catafalque.

And then a strange thing had happened. Gazing for his allotted short moment on those peaceful rugged features, surprisingly, instead of grief, he had felt a sense of exaltation. Something outside himself and greater than his own small personality had filled him, a sense of kinship with all humanity, a relationship to some great whole. In that brief moment he had not once remembered the terrible crime which had caused the death, or the recent bitter disappointment of his own. It had been a period detached from living, as though for that instant he were poised outside and above the world of reality, seeing this thing we call life, each act fitted together with every other one, making some semblance of a pattern to the puzzle.

Leaving the rotunda, he had taken himself outside, walked the streets wrapped in an atmosphere of questioning wonder. The queer experience had given him strength, made it possible to promise himself that he was ready to accept whatever life had in store for him. He had been a part of that vast company of soldiers—and others—who followed their chief to the train on his last journey, had watched him start on the round-about trip which would end in the home town from whence he had been called to serve the nation.

The exaltation—a realization of his own strength of soul—had persisted. It was to have gone with him through life. He had told himself he possessed stoutness of heart and firmness of spirit to carry him all the days he would live. No disappointment could defeat him in the future nor failure discourage him. Once before he had felt something of the same uplift of spirit when he rode home after his enlistment—as though the song he sang would be with him all the years of his life, and the song of those years would be a song of strength.

This same feeling had returned as he looked upon the calm dead face of Lincoln but a few weeks previous. Already it was ending in a sense of frustration. Already the high resolve which had sustained him was breaking. He was no superman to overlook the petty cares of life, no Lincoln to carry burdens uncomplainingly.

He wanted Suzanne. She meant "home" to him. So that all the pondering on the strange and intense moral strength which had been his for a time came back again in a weary circle to the memories of a girl with eyes that darkened and glowed as though lighted from within, and whom he must remember no more.

For a long time he looked across the prairie, thinking of

her, of the dead Lincoln, of the grand review in which he had
taken part, the long lines of blue-clad figures, the Army of
the Potomac and those who had served under Sherman, with
their torn and dirty flags, all marching throught the crowd-
lined streets—and one who had waited and prayed for that
day to come, not there to see.

The cinders crackled on the glass and the smoke seeped
through the car. They were running late, probably two hours
behind time. He could hear some of the passengers complaining about it and the conductor jokingly recalling to their
minds that a little over four years ago they would have been
coming by stage.

The old man next to him roused. "That's right," he said
suddenly to Wayne, in a down-East twang. "Never satisfied.
Fifty years from now they'll want somethin' else, somethin'
that'll go still faster."

Prairie Rapids, now! They were slowing down, with a
ringing of bell and much lurching of the cars. Wayne almost
started with surprise at the appearance of the town. Why,
across there it appeared to be as large as Sturgis Falls, new
brick buildings—more homes, the railroad's roundhouse and
machine shops which Sturgis Falls had lost to Prairie Rapids
by a bungling piece of business. What human force was this
whereby the new town was passing the older?

His seat-mate had left. He could see him with his carpet-
bag standing on the platform looking around in bewilderment,
a Vermont old man silhouetted against the raw western town.
Unaccountably Wayne, suddenly remembered the gaunt form
of a gray wolf he had once seen silhouetted against the night
sky, felt a swift surge of sympathy for him and hoped there
were friends or relatives to meet him.

The train was pulling out. Only six miles to Sturgis Falls
and he would be home. Home to what? Peace, for one thing.
No more shot and shell. No more Johnnies in ambush. No
more hardtack and body-lice. Peace! And a lonely cabin!

All the remaining passengers were for Sturgis Falls, for it
was still the end of the road into Iowa although soon it was to
cross the state as had been the plan before war interrupted.

Four miles across the prairie farms and they passed the lane
road where a thousand years before the friendly conductor, at
his asking, had stopped the train, saying he couldn't refuse
such an urgent request from a volunteer.

A woman came to the water-pail, drank daintily from the
dipper, returned as far as his own seat and paused, met there

by a well-dressed man who was saying, "Sit here, Harriet. We can get out that much quicker near the front."

Wayne took a swift glance at her, noting the plump placid face under a fashionable spring bonnet but with its bow of crêpe, and moved closer to the window, for her full skirts needed two-thirds of the seat.

She turned pleasant blue eyes on him. "One of our boys, I see. What regiment?"

"Thirty-first, Iowa. Company B."

"I've been near the battle line some of the time, too," she said simply.

"Every one is more than grateful." Wayne knew the statement could not convey enough to one of those motherly volunteer nurses.

In a moment she said anxiously: "We're so late, aren't we? I'm nervous about it. My niece is to be married to-night and we expected to get there in ample time for the wedding."

And when Wayne made a polite gesture of sympathy, she added. "You might know them . . . the Martins. Suzanne Martin?"

Wayne stared at the pleasant face. "Yes. Yes . . . I know her. She isn't married yet?"

"Oh . . . I hope not," she said, thinking he meant only the closeness of the hour to-night. "Not unless it's later than I think it is. And the young man . . . ?" she questioned. "Do you know him, too—this Mr. Cady Bedson?"

CHAPTER 46

JEREMIAH put his sister's two satchels between the seats of Tom Bostwick's carriage, and only then found out that the visitors had a trunk, too, which must be set up on the town dray. It took a whole valise for one dress. Harriet said. So it was some time before they could get started from the depot to cross the long river bridge, its wooden planking rattling importantly under the horses' hoofs.

"Seven years ago," Jeremiah said to the Chicagoans with satisfying announcement, "we was drivin' down this embankment and crossin' on the ice or ferryin' over." He flourished his whip toward the Red Cedar, high after the spring freshet, as though like Cæsar he had ordered a bridge thrown across it.

The long row of wooden stores on Main Street lay before them, with a few brick buildings to give it more of a citified air. The sidewalks were wooden, built at different heights, so that one stepped up or down several times when passing the distance of a block. Sometimes the sidewalk formed a miniature bridge over a cavity in Mother Earth through which water flowed briskly. Farther up the street one of the sidewalks ended abruptly, merging into a sawdust path. A few of the stores had wooden awnings, also of different height, so that a short man could have touched some, a tall man standing on a chair could not have reached others.

There were trees from the virgin woods here and there at the edge of the street, although there were no longer stumps in front of the stores, a good deal of hard liquor having been consumed in those early years. To the right and left on the side streets the trees were thick, whole blocks in their primeval state of heavy timber—oaks and maples, walnut and hickory, and a matted undergrowth of hazelnut, wild plum, burdock,

391

grape-vines, sumac and woodbine. Cow-bells tinkled in their dark interiors and boys emerged blinking their eyes as from Africa's deepest jungles. Every modest home had its fence, stable, and pigpen.

Jeremiah showed off the town as always with that pleased air of owning it. After all, there is a sense of proprietorship about something one has seen grow from its beginning. And it had been such a very short time since only Gervais Paul Somaneux had lived here in a cabin in the forest by the Red Cedar into whose sparkling waters no pollution had yet washed and whose adjoining rich sod had never been turned by man.

Just before they reached Cat-tail Pond he turned the horses to the west.

"Here's the court-house block," he pointed out with the buggy whip. It was thick with virgin timber and the vivid new green of grass. "The Overmans give it for the court-house site."

"But where's the court-house?" Uncle Joe asked curiously.

"Hell!" the Honorable Jeremiah Martin made answer, whipping up the horses.

"Isn't that a long way to go to transact business?"

Jeremiah roared with laughter at the sally. "Well, the story itself is about that long. I got to have plenty o' time to tell it. I'll relate it all to you to-morrow after the weddin'," He looked forward to the pleasure with childlike anticipation. It would take a half day to tell all the ins and outs of it, all the "he says" and "I says" with gesticulations.

And here they were. Jeremiah drove into the Bostwick yard with a bit of a flourish. After all it was not such a bad sensation to show off his son-in-law's new home to the Chicago relations.

And it *was* a fine house, no mistake—a white frame two-story with a wide porch running around three sides, and a cupola room high up on one corner which gave the whole house a jaunty look as though it wore a high cockade in its hat. There was fancy ironwork on the top of the porch and on each gable, which Jeremiah thought was a good deal of fencing gone to waste. The huge windows with their wide green blinds came down to the porch floor. The doors were fluted and carved. There were wide steps down the front connecting with a walk and another set of them down the side to the carriage step. Even Aunt Harriet from Chicago was not unimpressed.

There was a great deal of commotion when they drove up,

with the trunk right behind them in the dray. Sarah and Sabina came bustling outside to the carriage. Sarah had on her crackling new black silk and black netting cap with narrow ribbons tied under her chin, and the brooch made from the children's hair. Sabina, buxom and gorgeous in her plum-colored satin, was all hospitality. High-busted and laced tightly into her stays, she looked quite like the ladies in the *Godey's*. Two dozen buttons wandered over the hillocks and valleys of her curves—the buttons of metal, large and heavy as young doorknobs, each bearing in bas-relief what might have been the head of a Roman soldier or the reproduction of a coal-scuttle. Tom Bostwick, very proud of his wife's accoutrements, had told Jeremiah previously that Sabina was carrying about eighty bushels of wheat around on her person. A new town dressmaker had made the gown, hurting Emily's feelings immeasurably, so that it was all she could do to keep the folks from knowing it.

Inside, the hall was overflowing with the adult relatives, while children peered from behind the big flaring skirts of the women, or, finding themselves clutching the wrong dress, darted across the room to the familiar one like so many little Indians scuttling from wigwam to wigwam.

Every one was named to Uncle Joe and Aunt Harriet with much laughter and explanation.

"This is Melinda. And this is Alf. No . . . Alf is Celia's. Here's Rand—*he's* Minda's. These two are Henry's children . . . Nora and Harry. Shake hands with your Great-aunt Harriet, Nora."

Celia and Melinda had on voluminous silk dresses—Celia's was green but Melinda's was greener. "By gad, no wife of Alf's is going to have a brighter dress than *my* wife's," Rank had explained.

Phoebe Lou had a new dress, too, which she deserved, Emily said, for on neither occasion when she was married had there been time for a new one. It was gray bombazine trimmed with festoons of navy blue silk fringe and made with specific allowance for Phoebe Lou's immediate future; when Mr. Akin wanted to pay her for the work, Emily had colored up and said, "I guess your wife's still my sister, Mr. Akin."

Henry's wife, Lucy, had on the same brown alpaca she had worn for best all the war years, but Emily had turned and made it over, sewing the family red glassy cherries down the front as though they were buttons so that the little brown wren had eight red feathers in her breast.

Jeanie wore her wedding dress from 1857, the yellow silk in which she had looked like a stalk of lovely goldenrod, but now with her reddened chapped skin, her once honey-colored hair burned from outdoor work during the war years, and no sparkle in her dark eyes—at times nothing but humiliation and defeat—there was no semblance of the flower about her, unless one remembered how the drooping brown blossom looks when the frosts have blighted it.

So Aunt Harriet and Uncle Joe met all the girls excepting Suzanne and Emily who were not visible, and all the men folks: Henry, Phineas, Mr. Horace Akin, Tom Bostwick, Alf and Rand Banninger, and Ambrose Willshire, thinking Ambrose with his pleasing polite ways made the best impression of all.

"I'll go get Emily to come down," Jeremiah said to his sister. "But I ain't makin' promises about Suzanne. Brides are skittish until they're safe in the paddock."

He started up the long new stairway, his best boots sinking into the thick carpeting, his gnarled hand slipping up the shining mahogany hand-rail. He walked slowly, uncertain just what he was going to do. Questions that were direct and simple were not hard to decide. Always do what seemed honest and right and the outcome would take care of itself. But there were other decisions to be made sometimes. These were not always direct and simple. This was one. To save him, he didn't know which was the best thing to do.

Suzanne was happy. Why, all afternoon she'd gone up and down these same stairs helping Sabina fix for to-night. No girl could flax around the way she had and be sorry about anything. And yet—why was there any need to question it? Why was he wondering at all one way or the other what was best to do? You didn't need to keep it from Suzanne that Sol Humbert had come home from the war to-night, or Charlie Boehmler, or John Parkinson. You had no worry that some of the wedding company would tell those three pieces of news before her.

He was at the landing now with its elegant long colored window. Sabina had a clock here, a tall one with a round plump face. He remembered Suzanne whispering to him that it looked for all the world like Sabina herself. Time was hopping along. Cady would be coming in just a little while, driving over from Prairie Rapids, and then the minister and his wife and the company. And some one would arrive and say excitedly: "Wayne Lockwood got back to-night."

Well, what of it?

He might as well face the truth. He was afraid for Suzanne, that was the "what of it." Up to this evening he had not thought much about how she would take it when Wayne came home. She would be married to Cady Bedson, and married women attended to their own affairs and didn't let their minds go straying around where they shouldn't. But here Wayne was home, and some one naturally would say so, and if Suzanne looked at the bearer of the news the way she had looked at him that night . . . Cady's eyes on her too, like as not . . . Cady and every one would know. Know *what*? Hanged if he could answer that one. There was nothing much between Wayne and her. She had told him so herself. One kiss, she said. Nothing to that. Every one was kissing every one else good-by. Emotional. . . with bands playing and women crying. That train stopping was probably a coincidence. Train had stopped a couple of times at the lane road since. She'd have sent Cady about his business in a hurry if she hadn't thought plenty of him.

He was at the bedroom door. Was that some one laughing or crying? Sounded like crying . . . no, laughing.

He rattled the knob. "Girls, can I come in?"

It was their father, opening the door cautiously, his big beard preceding him a little into the room.

It went through Suzanne's mind that it was rather odd for him to come up here. Dresses, hats, "women's fussiness" were always of so little importance to him. "That a new bonnet?" they had heard him say more than once. "Looks to me just like your other one."

"Uncle Joe and Aunt Harriet are here," he was telling them. "Emily, you'd best run down and welcome them a minute along with the others, before the company begins to come. Harriet's wantin' to get into her finery soon, too."

"All right, Pa."

Emily placed a hasty and unusual kiss on Suzanne's fresh smooth cheek. At the door she turned. "Don't dare touch her, Pa. She's all dressed up in clouds and milkweed fuzz and the slightest breath'll blow her right out the window."

"You look pretty fine, Suzanne." The sight of her in her white dress ready to marry Cady cleared his mind. Why had he made such a mountain of it, fussing like an old woman? Tempest in a tea-pot. Out with it now, just as natural as talking about the weather.

"Suzy, I thought maybe . . ." Already he felt himself floundering under the keenness of those gray-blue eyes. ". . . you'd like to know . . ."

"He's come," she said so suddenly and definitely that it startled him immeasurably.

"Well, if you're meanin' Wayne Lockwood . . . yes, tonight when the folks did."

She went as white as her wedding dress, and her eyes . . . ! It went through his mind that they were like those places in the Cedar where the water was deep and dark under the willows. He wondered for a minute if she would faint. But the Martin girls had never fainted in their lives. He'd seen every one of them take blows without flinching. That this thing which had happened to Suzanne was a blow seemed a certainty now.

But Suzanne only moistened her dry lips and said: "You saw him?"

"Yes. He got off the train with some more of the boys, Sol Humbert and Charlie Boehmler and John Parkinson. They'd all been to Washington. Some of 'em got to see the president. I talked to John for just a minute. He got to walk past and see him—said he looked calm and peaceful and . . ."

"Did you tell Wayne? Is he coming here?"

"No, I couldn't get to him. By the time I got through shakin' hands with Uncle Joe and Aunt Harriet and talkin' that minute to John he was gone."

"Gone? Where?" A hand had crept to her throat, one of those traitorous hands that always rushed to conceal the throbbing there but which only succeeded in telling more.

"Walking out the river road toward home."

". . . the river road?" She repeated it stupidly as though wondering where that way led.

Oh ye'll tak' the high road an' I'll tak' the low road,

*   *   *   *

But I and my true love will never meet again . . .

When she did not move or say more, he went on spiritedly: "Some one could get out there on horseback to ask him. There's still time. Good neighbor like he was . . . used to be at our house so much . . . been at every girl's weddin' . . .

seems too bad for him not to be here." He took out the
heavy silver watch the legislators had given him when he was
the sergeant-at-arms.

To an honorable gentleman
1862

"Yes . . . there's time. Friend of the family's like that.
Too bad to have him find nobody in the neighborhood . . .
been away so long." He was rambling, looking at his watch
steadily because he did not want to look into the troubled
waters of those darkening eyes. "I'll go . . . if you say so.
Hell," he said cheerfully, "I could ride old Queen and get
back . . . or take Tom's carriage. Roads are nearly dry . . .
not very bad."

"No . . . oh, no!"

Old Jeremiah stopped talking against time now, stood there
distressed, wondering if after all he should not have evaded
the responsibility and left the whole thing to Fate. Emotions
were hard things with which to cope. He had felled great trees
and built cabins, broken prairie sod and wrested food from it,
turned streams from their courses, fought through blizzards,
high water, and prairie fires, argued with tricky Indians, killed
rattlers, helped to make the new state's laws, and gone along
with Sherman to the sea. But they were material things about
which he knew. Human feelings—sorrow, disappointments,
mental agonies, heart hurts—to face them took more courage
and understanding. All these he had tried to tell his children
to meet as best they could with joking laughter, knowing that
though the laughter may not heal, it helps to hide from the
world that which the world should not see.

And now he knew for a certainty. Suzanne, his youngest,
had sorrow and disappointment, a mental agony and a hurt
heart. And she could not cover it with laughter. He had tried
to tell her to be a woman of honor. And this was her hour of
honor.

He felt helpless, stricken. Neither one moved. Jeremiah
with his watch in his hand and Suzanne in her wedding dress
stood and stared at each other as though they could not break
the spell, as though they would keep on standing there while
the watch for an honorable gentlemen ticked the time away
through eternity.

And then the spell broke. The door opened and Emily

stood on the threshold, her face as white as Suzanne's, its freckles standing out like brown painted spots.

"I heard," she said. Her hand on the doorknob shook a little and her voice was not quite steady. "Suzanne, *go yourself*. I'll get your cape. Come down the back way."

CHAPTER 47

IN the soft dusk Wayne Lockwood walked out the river road—no longer in the light-footed rhythmic way of the prairie-wolf, but heavily, doggedly, like a man who had marched through mud and dust, swamp, clay and mire, tramped into Tennessee and the Carolinas, Virginia, Arkansas and Alabama, Mississippi, Louisiana and Georgia. To have been with Sherman was to have played a bloody game of tag all over the south, shuttled about through every southern state but Texas and Florida.

He passed a lumber yard, the two taverns and a few houses, buildings that still clung to the north side of the river in a town whose growth was to be all to the south. They were not many, so it did not take long for him to be swinging into the country where only the farm lands lay. Night was beginning to settle down with concealing comfort before he had gone half a mile. There was a spring hush on the shadowy fields. The countryside looked entirely peaceful, but no one knew better than Wayne Lockwood that peace is not a matter of location.

The way was so familiar that it did not seem possible two and a half years had passed since he had been over the same road. Thirty-two months to encompass so much. Nothing there in the deepening dusk appeared to be different. Building had been more or less at a standstill during these war years. Nature, though, had not stood still. Nature taking no cognizance of hard times, had added height to the trees along the rail-fence borders. The road itself, too, looked older as though a thousand teams in passing over it had spread its width.

A few of those teams were coming toward town now, the *clop-clop* of horses' hoofs following each other rather often. No doubt taking the invited guests over to . . . he wanted not to think of what the end of that journey meant, but it came back constantly to tantalize him. He had no wish for any of these people to recognize him. Time enough to-morrow to meet the old neighbors when he would have himself better in hand.

At each approaching carriage or wagon, he slipped into the shadows of any tree-trunks that bordered the way, or if by an open field, walked close to the fence without a glance at the passers-by, for he had no desire to talk with any one.

A team or two passed, going out into the country, but he pressed close to the fence line unnoticing and unnoticed. He wanted no lift from friend or stranger to-night. Quite suddenly that steady forward plodding and looking behind reminded him of the time he walked back to Dubuque casting glances over his shoulder for Cady Bedson and his buggy.

Cady Bedson had won after all.

A galloping horse went by and was lost ahead in the dim light, the sound of its pounding hoofs growing fainter.

He wanted nothing to-night but his old cabin up the lane road, darkness and the bed and comforting sleep. To-morrow he would meet old friends, look over his land, lay his future plans.

It was a relief to be out on the open country road without sound of cannon or bark of gun, with no watchfulness of snipers, cloud of approaching attack, or fear of Johnnies in ambush. His body sensed the peace of it even though his mind could not accept it. Springtime and Maytime in the midlands! There had been no rain that day, for the heavy black dirt of the river road was too easily passable. But rains had been not far in the past as the corn-fields were moist-looking and the fresh smell of the loam was strong in his nostrils. There was the faint aroma of bursting buds and blossoms as he passed the homes set so far apart on their quarter-sections or eighties. And unless his nostrils, too long accustomed to the stench of the battle-fields, were playing him false, there was a faint far-off odor from the timberland at his right, a blending of damp ferns and wet tree bark and waxy Mayflowers. There was a special northern smell, he told himself, as far from the warm heady magnolia-laden air of the south as the poles—that faint light perfume combined of wild crab-apple, wild plum, sprouting corn, prairie grass, wet timber, and the loam—always the good damp earth and its healing odors.

He came to the Wallace Akin place. There was the Horace

Akin one over there to the right where the Scotts had lived.
What was that, a new white school-house? He could see it
faintly in the lifting shadows which were foretelling the rising
of the moon. Beyond was the Martin place over at the grove's
edge, dark to-night because of the wedding in the new house
in town. He wondered what Old Jeremiah, so independent, so
satisfied with his big sturdy cabin, thought of that idea.
Probably a plan of Tom Bostwick's making. And you couldn't
blame Suzanne for having the marriage in a fine house. You
couldn't rightfully blame Suzanne for anything.

Far off in the timber a mourning-dove gave its long lonely
call. *You never pay any attention to them unless you are sad
and then you hear them.* He wondered if he would always be
recalling little things she had said.

He turned up the lane road, and even at the turning, the
moon swung up over the horizon. It was a great silver cart-
wheel of a moon, flung off from some god's shining chariot,
so that it scattered white magic over the fields and timberland, the cabins and the old straw-stacks of winter. Time
was when he would have burst into song at the picture. *Try it
now.* Perhaps it would bring back a lost feeling of aliveness,
make sluggish blood warm in his veins.

> *"Beautiful dreamer, wake unto me,*
> *Starlight and dewdrops are waiting for thee;*
> *Sounds of the rude world heard in the day,*
> *Lulled by . . ."*

The resonance had gone from his voice. He broke off, in
no mood for singing anything, and especially for this last
song from one who had so recently died.

The moon made the trees in the Akins' yard look like silver
towers, but a lone one at the side of the lane on his right cast
a ridiculously long black finger of shadow across the road so
that he thought moodily one could not escape black shadows
in his path.

To his right Deer Run Creek's low fringe of trees looked
familiar in the white light. Frogs were croaking along its
banks and a clammy dampness was hanging above it like a
tangible thing.

And now in the north his own farm land and cabin with its
sheltering darkness until the time when to-night and its marriage would be a thing of the past!

A gleam of light flickered in that direction. The northern

star? *Somebody else is holding up a light for you to see by.*
No, decidedly it was as low as the cabin. A lightning-bug
close at hand and seeming only to be far away? Too early for
those. Queer—it looked a little spooky, like some ghostly
will-o'-the-wisp.

If it proved to be a light in the cottage . . . .

It was, and resentment rose within him like the quills of a
porcupine. After all, it was still his property. He hadn't just
walked out of the community and relinquished all ownership
of it. Then for the first time he grinned. It would be a bit of a
joke to walk quietly in on some one and give him a scare.

But his momentary boyishness dropped away when the
light flickered, passed from one window, appeared across
the other. It angered him again, not so much that any one had
preëmpted it for living quarters as that they should be in it
now, this night, when he wanted darkness and seclusion and
sleep. He had pictured himself walking up the path, opening
the door into a haven where he could throw himself face
down on a waiting bed and lie there until some of the hurt and
disappointment and anger with himself should wear off. Instead he was walking up the path with the prospect of facing
candle-light and people, conversation and explanations.

Now he saw that a horse was tied to a tree at the side,
heard sounds of its teeth nibbling the bark.

He put his hand quietly on the wooden latch with its leather
thong, hesitated a moment, and then flung back the door.

Across the room a girl in a long dark cape was placing a
candle on the fireplace mantel. At the swinging of the door
she whirled toward him so suddenly that the unfastened wrap
slipped to the floor.

In that one long moment Time stopped. For when hearts
cease to beat, does not Time cease, too?

Wayne Lockwood in his suit of union blue stood in the
cabin's doorway and looked at the girl. Suzanne Martin in her
wedding dress of white stood in front of the fireplace and
looked at the man.

There was so sound anywhere. No cock crowed and no
horse neighed. There was no moan of prairie wind or song of
timber bird. Nothing but silence about them, deep and
immeasurable, pregnant with unspoken things.

And then Time, having waited only for the two to understand
the full meaning of that long pause, picked up the broken
moment it had dropped and sped on.

The girl's hands fluttered from her throat and the man's white-knuckled fists relaxed.

"Suzanne."

"Wayne."

They were moving slowly together under the same compulsion by which the prairie compass-plant holds to the north star, the prairie lark flies into the sunlight.

"Why . . . are you here?"

"I came for you . . . but . . ."

It does not take long to cross the floor of a log cabin, sixteen by twenty-four feet, even though in the doing one crosses the width of the whole world of troubled reality into a magic one of peace.

"But *what* . . . Suzanne?"

Wayne's arms were around her now, his lips to hers, with no laughing soldiers to see nor whistling engine calling him to war.

"I love you so, Suzanne."

"And I . . . love you." Then, remembering only now what night this was and why she had come so recklessly, "But now it's too late."

"There's been a ceremony?"

"No . . . oh, no."

"Then it *isn't* too late." He threw back his head and laughed boyishly. It was so simple. "Of *course* it isn't too late."

His purpose was clear, his spirit unfettered by any foolish obstacle, his courage boundless. He was the young Wayne Lockwood who had tramped light-footedly the hundred miles to Dubuque to claim that which was so rightfully his own.

"We'll go back now and tell them."

"Oh, Wayne . . . it's a terrible thing . . . Cady . . . I'm frightened about facing them."

"I'll take all responsibility."

He got her cape from where it had fallen on the floor, put it around her, held her a moment. "There isn't any such thing as a marriage unless it's you and I."

"No . . . just *you*."

"Nothing can ever come between us any more."

"Nothing . . . any more."

"Then you're not afraid to face them now with me?"

"Not now . . . *with you*."

*   *   *

It was all so long ago that the two, arriving at the big new Bostwick house with the first of the guests, said they were very sorry to upset everything but that love was bigger than the conventions, that Wayne had come home to the girl he loved, and nothing was going to come between them any more. As though it were all as simple as that.

Some people felt sorry for Cady Bedson. (More were highly pleased at the turn of events), one widow with four hundred acres of land consoling him so thoroughly that he took her and the land both under his name in a short time.

There are changes incredible in the Valley of the Red Cedar. The slough is dried up and a paved highway (with gasoline station and hot-dog stand) runs through it. Much of the wild life is gone—a prairie-chicken as rare as a sandhill crane. Lover's Retreat has not been in existence for over fifty years, the last vestige of it swept away in the flood of '84.

Prairie Rapids is a fine city with industrial leanings, much larger than its older neighbor. Where Suzanne, her hair flying to the prairie winds, rode Queen over the County Fair race-track in Sturgis Falls, there are solid blocks of substantial homes, paved streets, apartment-houses, schools, and churches. And a mile or so from the place once called Cat-tail Pond where the first tower bell west of the Mississippi clanged all night long when Lee surrendered, a paved road leads to a college campus on which the chimes of a great campanile play melodies in commemoration of the lives lost in two later wars. Jubilee did not last a thousand years.

It is as though the Valley were another world with a different civilization, its people speaking to each other casually over wire instead of carrying messages through wind and storm; touching buttons for light, heat, and water instead of wresting these from tallow, wood, and stream. News of the moment comes over the prairie air itself. Where only the ducks and the blue heron flew, intricate man-made wings sail high. A voice singing in the moonlight up a lane road now would take no one to the door away from a program of orchestral symphonies or the current crooner.

They have been gone for many and many a year—old Jeremiah who wanted to live on in the prairie grass or the wind in the timber or the wild geese riding out the storm, Sarah, his wife, and all the others.

Queer that human emotions can be as strong as a prairie fire and then die down to smoldering embers, turn to white ashes, scatter to the four winds of the past. For there is no one to remember that the state capital fight was sharp, that the courthouse was fought over so angrily as to make lifelong enemies, that the sites of the railroad shops, the stations and the mills, the schools and the churches were argued so intensely that more than one pioneer went to his grave in bitterness. It is now but a tale that is told.

All arguments and bickerings over, all laughter stilled and all tears forgot, the early settlers lie there together in friendly silence on a hillside in the Valley. The graveled walks between the tall tombstones cross each other primly at right angles quite as the miles of midwestern sections now cross the old prairie, the main one long and curving a little at the end like the old river road.

Sabina Beloved Wife, Jennie Beloved Wife, Phoebe Lou Beloved Wife, Celia Beloved Wife, Melinda Beloved Wife (her stone is larger than Celia's), *Suzanne Beloved Wife Of*, and under the old vines the name that meant so much to her, Wayne Lockwood. Only Emily who stayed at home to help the folks was no one's beloved.

Besides the tall old tombstones there are a few keepsakes by which to remember them all. Things last so much longer than people. There is a fine Paisley shawl, its color the rusty red of a robin's breast. There are letters from the little village of Des Moines when the capitol was first moved there and one could picket a horse out to grass near its door. There is a clock with iron weights behind a spread eagle which ticks the hours away as faithfully as it did when brought to Iowa in 1852, although a half century had gone by since any one, windling it, said, "Day's over . . . fresh start to-morrow."

There is an old shawlpin with a red sealing-wax head, and a sturdy walnut rocker, rather gay now in flowered needlepoint but which still creaks dismally when urged to action. And there are daguerrotypes of all "the girls" which must be turned exactly right into the light before one can catch a glimpse of their laughing eyes and tinted cheeks and the cinnamon pinks in their hair.

One other gift remains, one other thing handed down from those early settlers. You cannot sit in it as you can in the old rocker, nor pick it up as you can the shawlpin, nor even point to it as you can to the old farm lands if you are in the Valley. It is immaterial, but nevertheless existent. It is something typically and sturdily American which has not yet been entirely extinguished—a bit of the old pioneers' independence, practical philosophy, ingenuity, and propensity to *pull on through*.

Great Reading from SIGNET VISTA

**Buy them at your local
bookstore or use coupon
on last page for ordering.**

Stories of Courage from SIGNET and SIGNET VISTA

Buy them at your local

bookstore or use coupon

on next page for ordering.

Bestsellers from SIGNET VISTA

(0451)

☐ **YOU WANT TO BE WHAT?** by Anne Snyder and Louis Pelletier.
(132203—$2.25)*

☐ **THE BEST THAT MONEY CAN BUY** by Anne Snyder and Louis Pelletier.
(135938—$2.50)*

☐ **NOBODY'S BROTHER** by Anne Synder and Louis Pelletier.
(117565—$2.25)

☐ **TWO POINT ZERO** by Anne Snyder and Louis Pelletier.
(114760—$1.75)*

☐ **GOODBYE, PAPER DOLL** by Anne Snyder.   (124332—$2.25)

☐ **COUNTER PLAY** by Anne Snyder.   (118987—$2.25)

☐ **FIRST STEP** by Anne Snyder.   (117573—$1.75)*

☐ **MY NAME IS DAVY—I'M AN ALCOHOLIC** by Anne Snyder.
(123360—$1.95)

☐ **TWO BLOCKS DOWN** by Jina Delton.   (114779—$1.50)*

☐ **THE CLIFFS OF CAIRO** by Elsa Marston.   (115309—$1.75)*

☐ **OVER THE HILL AT FOURTEEN** by Jamie Callan.   (130901—$1.95)*

☐ **PLEASE DON'T KISS ME NOW** by Merrill Joan Gerber.(115759—$1.95)*

☐ **ANDREA** by Jo Stewart.   (116542—$1.75)*

☐ **ALICE WITH GOLDEN HAIR** by Eleanor Hull.   (117956—$2.25)*

☐ **A SHADOW LIKE A LEOPARD** by Myron Levoy.   (136985—$2.50)*

*Prices slightly higher in Canada

Buy them at your local bookstore or use this convenient coupon for ordering.

NEW AMERICAN LIBRARY,
P.O. Box 999, Bergenfield, New Jersey 07621

Please send me the books I have checked above. I am enclosing $_____
(please add $1.00 to this order to cover postage and handling). Send check
or money order—no cash or C.O.D.'s. Prices and numbers are subject to change
without notice.

Name _____

Address_____

City_____State_____Zip Code_____

Allow 4-6 weeks for delivery.
This offer is subject to withdrawal without notice.